CATHERINE SNOW

CATHERINE SNOW

a novel

NELLIE P. STROWBRIDGE

FLANKER PRESS LIMITED
ST. JOHN'S
2009

Library and Archives Canada Cataloguing in Publication

Strowbridge, Nellie P., 1947-
  Catherine Snow : a novel / Nellie P. Strowbridge.

ISBN 978-1-77457-065-4

  1. Snow, Catherine, ca. 1793-1834--Fiction.
I. Title.

PS8587.T7297C38 2009   C813'.54   C2009-904675-X

© 2009 by Nellie P. Strowbridge

ALL RIGHTS RESERVED. No part of the work covered by the copyright hereon may be reproduced or used in any form or by any means—graphic, electronic or mechanical—without the written permission of the publisher. Any request for photocopying, recording, taping, or information storage and retrieval systems of any part of this book shall be directed to Access Copyright, The Canadian Copyright Licensing Agency, 1 Yonge Street, Suite 800, Toronto, ON M5E 1E5. This applies to classroom use as well.

PRINTED IN CANADA

Cover Design: Graham Blair

FLANKER PRESS LTD.
PO BOX 2522, STATION C
ST. JOHN'S, NL
CANADA

WWW.FLANKERPRESS.COM

5 6 7 8 9 10 11 12

The publisher acknowledges the financial support of the Government of Canada through the Canada Book Fund (CBF) and the Government of Newfoundland and Labrador, Department of Tourism, Culture, Industry and Innovation for our publishing activities. We acknowledge the support of the Canada Council for the Arts, which last year invested $157 million to bring the arts to Canadians throughout the country. Nous remercions le Conseil des arts du Canada de son soutien. L'an dernier, le Conseil a investi 157 millions de dollars pour mettre de l'art dans la vie des Canadiennes et des Canadiens de tout le pays.

To the memory of
Catherine Mandeville Snow
the last woman hanged in Newfoundland

1793–1834

"... some satisfactory proof should be required that the persons supposed to have been murdered are actually dead; for although we may entertain the strongest personal impressions that these unfortunate people have been made away with, yet we can only arrive at a safe conclusion by adhering strictly to clear rules of evidence, and fixed principles of law, and we must not allow our indignation to get the better of our reason, and indict even the most strongly suspected upon mere conjecture. . . ."

Chief Justice Henry John Boulton
Newfoundland Patriot, January seventh, 1834

Prologue

—ROSE—

Rose gazed out an upstairs window of a large, wooden house facing the St. John's courthouse, her small elbows leaning on the wide sill. Sarah, an elderly servant, rubbed wet, gnarled hands down a white pinafore and came from behind the young girl. She took notice of a white bird chirping on the outside ledge. "Dear, oh dear, oh dear me," she sighed. "A white bird this July evening! Oh 'tis trouble we'll be having before this year of 1846 spends itself. Come away from the window before it happens soon and quick."

Rose stared at the courthouse. She let out a deep breath and spoke in a faint voice. "The strangest feelings come when I look that way." Her voice rose. "I feel as if I'll choke on my own gizzard. At night I wake from my dreams startled. There's someone in them crying in anguish, but she's only a shadow." The young girl looked down at the rosary of garnets scattered along the ledge. "I pray every day on those beads that my mind will settle peacefully. Once when I wore them around my neck I felt strangled."

Sarah knew that, each morning, Rose held the rosary of garnets with its Celtic cross in her hand for prayers. Afterward, she kept them in her little cloth bag. Now the servant righted a white scolly on her head and turned with a scolding eye. "Don't be tormenting yourself. Sure you're only a child."

Rose turned swiftly, her stormy, grey eyes blazing. "An orphan I am – someone who doesn't know from what tree her forebears sprang, having the name Rose given to me by strangers, a name that doesn't seem to be mine."

Sarah answered, "Where did you get the notion that you should know everything? Sure I've no more knowledge of me mudder than if I never had one. 'Tis praising God I am that someone raised me."

"In my dreams I've been troubled by strange voices," Rose cried. Her voice dropped to a whisper. "I'd like to put faces to the voices."

Sarah's eyes held a clouded look, her voice soft. "Sure 'tis staring you bees, girl, and facing Signal Hill. 'Tis it, you're looking at. Tell me it is, and then thinking too much and feeling the tragedy of people shot, and all the bellies and throats slit between French and English soldiers on that hill."

"'Tis not," she answered. "My room window fixes right over the courthouse's blackened window, meets it like one eye gazing into the other. This eye here is harmless; the other one holds evil. Sometimes I've fancied a woman in that square eye, that's now been put out by fire, and only its socket left. But for that, I'd have a mind to – " She stopped and shook her head. "Oh never mind."

Sarah's voice was sharp. "And end up in the gaol – then you would – if you commit an act against the law. Er, but it's too much for you. You can't be telling me all this from some dark place inside your mind." She lowered her voice and widened her eyes. "The mistress'll have you taken to that lunatic hole. You've heard rumours of it. I'm sure 'tis a true place – below ground and no windows, a place that'll keep any one of us from ever espying you ag'in."

Rose looked at her, puzzled. "Why would that be done to anyone?"

Sarah leaned close and said quietly, "I've been told on a good word that the law wakes women believed to be witches – wakes them while they're living. A woman accused of being a witch is stood still. A bridle bit is wedged inside her mouth and fastened with chains to a wall. Then there's women convicted of murder by tainted laws. . . . So silence yourself and bide alive. The past can't be unwritten, and if the present is not bearable, sure you could ask the mistress for another room. Your future can bear your own mark."

Rose turned as her mistress hurried into the room asking, "Who is handling my name in clutter and chatter?"

"'Tis me, ma'am," Sarah answered meekly. "I'm trying to beat sense into the girl you brought into this place as your own helper. She hankers for her forked relatives. I'm sure you'd be telling her if 'twas fit for her to know."

The mistress lifted her chin and tossed her words at the servant. "You'll be going now – and darken the room behind your back."

"Don't mind if I do, ma'am," Sarah replied. She added, aside to the mistress, "She stares so long, cocks her ear and seems to listen. You could swear she knows something, and 'tis the same day too, July twenty-first." The servant hurried out.

The mistress turned back to the girl. "Now what's this nonsense?"

Rose stood up, as if trying to pull herself together. "I'm unsettled, that's it, ma'am. I don't know why."

"Well then," the mistress said, shaking her head, "there's some cause. What is it? The servants have been complaining about you long enough. 'Tis time to do something about it."

"It all started with the sight of a man." Rose, her cheeks flushed and her eyes bright, rushed on. "One day down by a fish stage at the harbour's edge when I went to buy you seal flippers, ma'am, I sensed a presence that made my heart skitter under my bodice. I heard the name Judge Boulton, and the sound was like a strike against my ears. A man spoke to someone standing beside him and his voice slithered up and down my spine. I turned to see his face. Stone-cold eyes, hooded like a monk's head, glanced my way and I saw that the man's eyebrows were like a nest of spiders that the hair on his head was creeping away from."

The mistress said, "It seems to be old Judge Boulton you're talking about, but he's long gone from this colony."

Rose ignored her words. "My strange feelings began then and got worse after I was moved to this room. I fancied I saw a brown-garbed, hooded lady in the window of the courthouse."

The mistress poked a long, thin finger in Rose's face. "Now girl, no more talk of this, not to the servants or anyone in the roads. There are things better left to lie."

"Yes, ma'am," Rose answered in a defeated voice.

A FEW DAYS later, Sarah, who was up early to do dusting in the guest room for an expected visitor, stopped at the sounds of cries coming from Rose's room. She hurried in. "Wake up!" she chided her. "Sure you're going to be the death of this house with your screams, the death of yourself with your words of late. We must call the mistress and she'll settle this."

Rose lay in bed, her eyes wide open above the counterpane she had pulled to her chin and clutched tight, her knuckles white nubs. She whispered hoarsely, "No! No! I'm trying."

Sarah, ignoring her protests, hurried to the doorway and beckoned to the mistress passing by. The mistress's heavy footsteps were quick as she followed Sarah back into the room. She closed the door, stuck her hands on her hips and asked Sarah, in a firm, no-nonsense voice, "Whatever are you blathering about now?"

"'Tis the child ag'in, ma'am," Sarah answered. "She's fair terrified out of her sleep. Something in her dreams shocks her. You can tell it in her face."

The mistress went to the girl's bed and said in a grave voice, "The gentlewoman who raised you and brought you to me was not apprised of your background when Bishop Fleming sent you to her. Nor am I any the wiser, though there have been rumours which I have not seen fit to repeat. Now you're old enough to be in service. I've been trying to ignore your condition, but there's too much talk of your screams and I've asked Bishop Fleming for the name of a forked relative or an acquaintance who knows your beginnings. The bishop is not willing to discuss your situation, but he's given me the name Anastasia Mandeville. 'Tis her right to tell or withhold whatever truth there is."

Rose butted in. "Truth?" Her eyebrows lifted and her mouth dropped open. There came a timid knock on the door.

The mistress turned her head quickly, her voice sharp. "Open it, Sarah."

Sarah rushed to open the door. She curtsied to a tall woman standing there. Then she stepped back quickly as the woman entered the room, her sweeping dark dress jostling a statue of the Virgin Mary on a low nightstand.

"Hello to you, Miss." Sarah curtsied again. She looked into Irish blue eyes in a strong, fresh face.

The woman nodded. "Not a Miss or a widow. I am Anastasia, the wife of Richard Mandeville, Esquire, of Brigus, cousin to the poor orphan." She looked toward the mistress. "Your maid let me in through the main entrance and sent me upstairs saying you were in the room on the right of the stairs. I hope I'm not being intrusive, but 'tis a short day for a long way when 'tis any kind of bad weath – "

The mistress interrupted her. "It's good you came, ma'am, for there is no holding back whatever secrets there be." She nodded at Rose. "The girl must learn and rest from a mystery that plagues her. Tell her all, so that she can place herself in the events as they were and rest from the uncertainty that shadows her innocent mind."

Anastasia pulled a handkerchief from a pocket in her sleeve, fanned herself and asked, "What if I am at your door with unspeakable secrets?"

"Then make them speakable for this child's sake. Unless they be told, she will die for 'tis a white bird that's been hanging around the square and all but pitched inside the window – and would have, had the window been open."

Rose's eyes were bright and fearful, her voice trembling. "I'll take the truth so that I can bear it through my days. Now 'tis unsettled I am in dreams and daytime."

Anastasia Mandeville looked toward Rose and spoke rapidly. "I'll give the truth, child, as I believe it. Your mother was my aunt Kit through marriage. She was a Catholic immigrant taken into the bed of John Snow, a temperamental Protestant landowner who got on the pig's back – prosperous, that is. From 1816 on, they were hand-fasted in the one house. Though Aunt Kit gave him a litter of youngsters, he wouldn't make her his wife. Then, to everyone's surprise, he married her. Sure 'tis in the church records to decipher. 'Catherine Mandeville, an Irish Catholic, and the Protestant John Snow came together and were married in 1828 by Reverend N. Devereaux, the Catholic priest of Harbour Grace.'"

Rose's eyes widened. She let the words linking her to the past roll off her tongue. "Catherine is my mother's Christian name and Mandeville her maiden surname, and John Snow is my father."

"A cup of tea for the company," the mistress said, nodding toward Sarah whose face clouded in disappointment at having to leave before the story was finished.

"Yes, ma'am," Sarah complied with a sigh, dragging herself toward the door. She looked back; then she hurried her step.

Anastasia stopped to look after her. Then she continued. "By 1833, when she was forty, Catherine had nine children. There was Bridget, Eliza, Johnny named for his father, then Katie named for her mother, and – "

"I have sisters and a brother!" Rose exclaimed.

"Yes, more than one brother, but don't stare as if your eyes are anchored by a killick. I don't know where they be. There was a scattering."

Rose's eyes softened into a dreamy look. "They are my own flesh then, brothers and sisters who were in the same chummy warmth of my mother's body."

"Come on then," Anastasia urged. "Get up and out of your nightclothes. Put on your warm duds and my oarsman will take us to the place where your family lived. Across the bay you'll be going then, to Salmon Cove. Cover that yarn of hair you've got there, girl. 'Tis like the leavings of a knit garment that's been unravelled.

If it should happen that once we're out in the bay, we get in the wind's eye, it'll turn your hair into hag knots – stirrups for witches."

The mistress put her hand on Anastasia's arm and steered her to the outside. She understood more of Rose's station now that she'd heard the names Catherine and John Snow. She spoke in a low voice. "Perhaps I acted in haste. I can't go having the girl hear the truth of what I supposed to be claptrap. 'Tis too much for the maid who's been delicate. I took her as a favour and lately she finishes only a half-day's work, and that on a noon to midnight shift."

Anastasia looked at her evenly. "You forget that she was in the midst of this torment, though she was too young to know all that was happening around her. Some things I'll not want to tell, but I'll take her to someone who will."

Rose slipped from her featherbed and hesitated before going to wash her face in a small basin. Then she gathered her clothes and dressed with determination. She hastened to grab her warm, red, hooded cloak hanging on a hook. Then she followed Anastasia downstairs. The mistress closed the bedroom door behind them.

They met the maid coming up the stairs with a tray. She stopped and asked, "Not tarrying fer a sup of tay, ma'am?"

Anastasia shook her head. "Thank you, but no. It's not a whole day we've got to catch the wind and sail around the bay." She took a cup and a swallow from it, then placed it back on the tray.

"You'm lucky then," the maid said, "for you've got the wind to your backs, and 'tis only a stun breeze anyway."

"That it is then," Anastasia answered, nodding toward Rose. "Let's hurry, Maria, before the wind changes its mind and sets the sea on us with a fury."

Maria, thought Rose. *She called me Maria.* She followed Anastasia without a word.

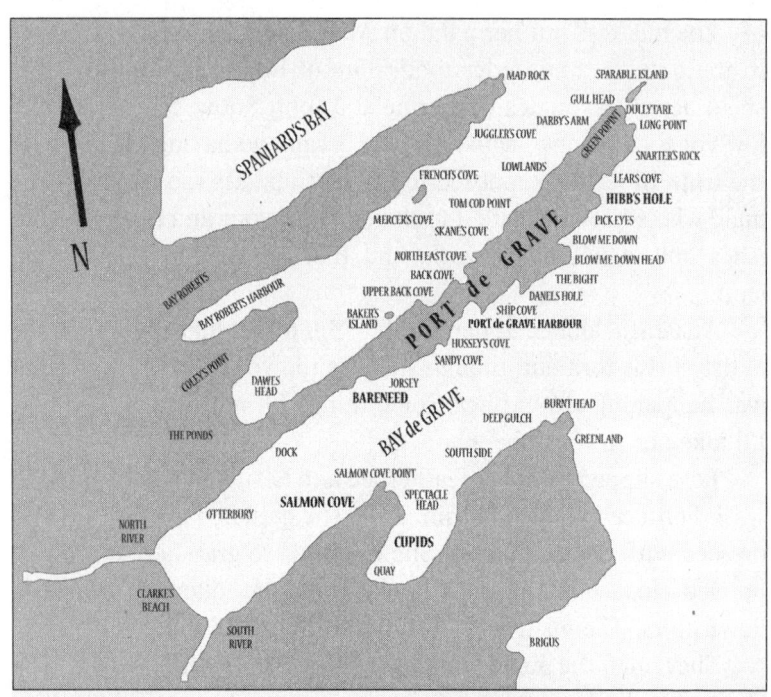
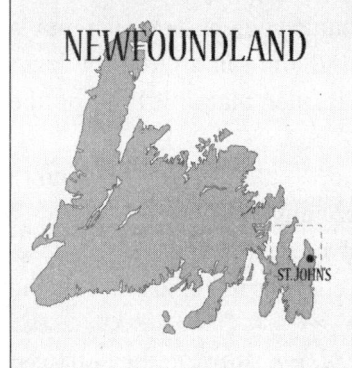
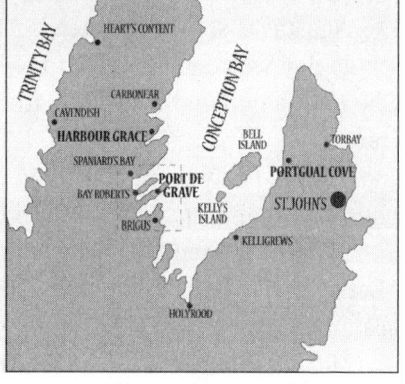

Book I

The Birth of
Caitríona de Móinbhíol – Catherine Mandeville

"I'd as 'lief take a bear by the tooth' as attempt an Atlantic crossing."

Durand of Dauphinè
A Huguenot Exile in Virginia

One

VILLAGERS were told by Celtina, the midwife, that inside the bedroom of her small cottage, Mairi de Móinbhíol turned white as a cut tatie when she took her first look at her new grand baby. No one – not even Edward, the baby's father – could draw out of her what destiny she had seen for the child. It was enough that he witnessed his bed bled into, the soaked rags and the splashes of blood on the walls. The midwife had dragged the baby feet first into the world, leaving Edward's wife, Bridget, to bleed in silence until she was empty . . . still . . . and turning icy cold in the summer warmth.

At first the child didn't draw breath even under the might of a slap – a first slap that was destined not to be the last. Celtina was not one to tamper with God's work and risk forfeiting her own life by giving her breath to the child. She waited for God to breathe the breath of life.

"*Ochón* – Alas!" sighed the grandmother, looking on. Then, as if nudged by her gran's sad sigh, the child let out a mewl.

Celtina brought the tiny wretch to her mother's breast to take of the beestings, still warm. The baby latched on until she was full and then, with the umbilical cord tied but not cut, she fell asleep, lying on the cooling surface of her mother's body, still a part of it – death and life entwined in a new day.

Grandmother de Móinbhíol wept silently for her daughter-in-law. Then she laid her black shawl over the baby, her old scent mixing with the sweet scent of new life. She and the midwife locked sad eyes, as if they both had the same fears. They had seen milk ooze from the baby's breasts. Some of the villagers would have tried to convince them that it was a witch's milk and that Catherine was a changeling and should be let die. The white discharge disappeared after four weeks and the family kept the secret of it.

GRAN MAIRI AND Grandda Liam loved Catherine, a child with heavy, dark ringlets and blue eyes that turned stormy whenever her father's new wife, Ada, ordered her about. Mairi often whispered prayers that her second sight in the instance of Catherine would be mislaid. She watched her grow into a happy little girl picking daffodils in the meadow in early spring, and skipping through daisies during long summers. But she wasn't to see her grow up. Mairi was drawing a bucket of water from the well inside the hill when the bucket splashed back down. Twelve-year-old Catherine saw her gran's hand go to her chest and grab the shawl, covering it, as if some horror was gathering under the breast that had fed a dozen children, some gone to bountiful places across the ocean to mix Irish and foreign blood. The old mam fell, expelling a moan, it fleeing like a ghost, leaving her a corpse. The shock of her grandmother's silence reached Catherine. She ran through the grass, calling, "Gran!"

Catherine flopped down by the well beside the limp body. She lifted the old woman's head and sat holding it in her lap. She stared at a sky over which clouds drifted as light as pearl millet. But behind her eyes a darkness was gathering that she couldn't break through – a darkness as heavy as the silence of her gran.

During the wake, Catherine looked into the cold eyes of her stepma who believed that children should only be seen and heard doing a hard day's work. She scolded her for crying after her grandmother. "Your gran's gone and it's today you have to think of – not yesterday or tomorrow."

The woman's words worsened Catherine's feelings, and whenever her stepma was in a foul mood she tried not to think of yesterday – or today. She set her thoughts on tomorrow and the cheer it would bring if only she could wait.

Catherine lost her father and her brother a few months later. A motley group of war beggars came to drag them off to war. She had seen them coming down the *Boher slocht*, a dirt road, past the stone dyke that separated the neighbour's house from her grandfather's field, the village graveyard to the side of it. They reined their horses to turn and trample the little corner lot of corn that Catherine had coaxed with digging and dunging into a climb. The intruders had boldly stamped through the field of potatoes until the potato stalks broke and their beautiful white blossoms fell to the dark earth like snowflakes.

Catherine had heard a frantic call. "Open the latch!"

The wooden gate leaned into the wall in front of the door. Just as she lifted the latch, the gate was pushed back against her head. Her brother Richard ran past, leaving her open to a stranger's face. She slammed the gate so hard against the man's nose, his blood smudged her face as he passed her to chase her brother into the house.

Catherine had wanted to run away and hide, but she knew the men would catch her. She slipped inside the open door and over to huddle against her grandfather. The intruders eyed her boldly. One of them pointed a flint musket at her; then he lowered the gun and moved on. The strangers laid a tight fist on her father's jacket. He stood silently, as if surprise had overtaken his tongue. The intruders turned to Richard as he crouched beside the fire whimpering.

"You are called upon to fight a noble war against the bloody English," a tall, bold-looking Irishman told him. Richard responded, in a stuttering voice, that fighting starvation was the noblest war.

The leader then made a straightforward motion with his finger across his own throat. Catherine knew what that meant and her shuddering cry sent her brother and father scravelling to appease the fighters. Their quaking voices came as one: "What is it you want?"

"Fetch us food," the gun bearer shouted, his eyes boring into Catherine. Her heart sank as she looked toward the *fulacht fiadh*. Early in the afternoon, her grandfather had wrapped a joint of meat in straw and placed it into the stone trough and kept it cooking by adding heated stones. Now the lamb was ready to eat. Her grandfather could ill afford to spare the meat to strangers.

Catherine helped lift the leg to the table and ladle some juice over it. After the intruders had gluttoned on the lamb leg, they grabbed hold of the de Móinbhíol men and dragged them outdoors.

Catherine had tried to scream, "Poppa, don't go!" but the words froze in her throat. She could feel them there, and then they thawed and echoed through her head months after she had watched the strangers take her brother and father up over the hill. The sight of the men like black shadows against the sky came to Catherine and her grandfather time and again. They would often glance up the hill, waiting for the men to come down over it – back to them. Sometimes as the sun's shadows crept across the hills, Catherine feared that in the darkness ruffians would come and take her. Other times she felt a dread that the shadow of death would steal across her grandfather's bed. He'd be taken in his sleep, leaving her with her stepmother.

It was bad enough that she had lost her brother and father, but the weather appeared to be in mourning. Mist settled in over the hills and held for days. It sopped leaves and grass with dampness. Many mornings later, the sun looked out like a tease – a stranger with a smile on its face as it called children to play.

Smoke, from the chimneys of stone houses and small sod huts dotting the landscape, rose above the hills into the sky as Carrick's youngsters climbed out the half-doors of their homes and slid into muddy holes. They ran laughing and leaping down to dip their feet in the Suir River. Soon they would be slipping under its water as if it were a satin blanket, warm when they were wrapped in it, their bodies cold when they shed it. Catherine eyed the Fleming children. They were ronk Catholics, and well off. Their uncle Martin was the priest in Carrick. Young Michael Fleming, who was Catherine's age, always passed her with a lofty look. She had heard a farmer say, "That quare-looking young fellar has a weak chin but he'd make a fine priest, if he gits the call. His younger brother, Edward, is on for fighting the English. He don't mind the church a'tall."

Grandda Liam's mud-walled, thatched cottage with its beaten-down earth floor stayed dry even during rain. Dried rushes spread over the floor saved the dampness. Just off from the house was a bath place where water was sprinkled on a circle of heated stones to make steam to ease Grandda's aches.

The sun broke through the mist like a friendly face one spring morning, and Catherine slipped the catch on the door, hoping to get the spread of sunshine on her face. She ran out, her feet slipping in muck. She lifted her skirts and ran toward a greening meadow no longer hidden in mist. Her coarse cotton dress was already the worse for wear. But it was Saturday and due for a wash anyway. She turned to a stir, just in time to close her eyes before Daniel Kennedy, her second cousin, let a mud ball fly into her face. It rolled down over her dress in a brown smear. She picked it up, rolled it in the mud again, and ran after Daniel, her baggy white petticoats spotting as her bare feet splattered mud into the air. Daniel was far ahead, but she lifted her hand into the air and flung the ball with all her strength.

Ada was coming from behind the house along a tract of green. She opened her mouth in astonishment at seeing Catherine in such a mess with her arm flung out. The mud ball took the woman fair in the mouth. Ada rushed toward her stepdaughter. She raised a pudgy hand and brought it hard against Catherine's lips, making them bleed and swell.

The sudden glance of the sun on the grass before it was smothered by a hand of cloud was what Catherine tried to think of as she leaned to scrub her stepma's dress on an old furrowed washboard.

Her knuckles burned like something scalded as she strained to rub out all the stains. The outside air was too damp for drying clothes so she hung the dress by the fire in the hearth, hoping the woman would not blame her for old stains too set to wash out.

The rick of turf gathered and laid up against the winter had been burned. Grandda went off with his wheelbarrow, his old knees almost knocking together with the twisted malady that had overtaken his limbs these last few years. When he returned and dumped the turf, Catherine helped him pile it by the sweat house. He came inside, muttering that spring grass should be erect and lively instead of in a dull swoon, heavy with mist. He sat in the corner and picked up his *dúidín*. He reached the tongs into the fire, hoisted a cinder to the pipe and lit it, his lips smacking down again and again on the short-stemmed, blackened clay pipe. He settled in the comfort of his pipe smoke and the warmth of the coal and peat fire meeting cool May air. The sun would shine, but not today. Maybe not tomorrow. Maybe not for a hundred morrows.

Two

"CATHERINE, you're a petulant young girl, that you be then, but the apple of your grandfardher's eye. I'll tell you that," Liam rasped with a fond look. "There's news you'll be wanting to hear. Your stepma's gone off to Waterford with some tinker, left Carrick-on-Suir while you were off gathering *curr amilly*."

The sweetness of the honey root Catherine had picked from the grassy fields over the hilly reach minutes before tasted even sweeter now. She passed her grandfather a piece of the herb and the two sat by the hearth, enjoying the peace a hag's absence could bring to a place. Ada had been threatening to leave since Edward was carried off.

Catherine and her grandfather, who was all of sixty, were left alone, he to rage at the loss of his son and grandson and to worry about the damage to his crops. There were fewer vegetables to be harvested in the fall, but the man and his granddaughter were kept busy. Two lambs were killed, the meat cured. Their wool was yanked and saved to be added to spring wool already yarned and made ready to be knitted into stockings and sweaters and cotton-lined woollen underwear. Stools of osiers were cut in November and December and piled against a garden wall. Once spring came, the rods were boiled, allowing the skin to slip off in one peeling like a stocking off a leg. The skins were used for making very strong ropes to trade with other villagers.

Whenever Liam sat by the fire, his eyes seemed to float in tears, as if thoughts of the capture of Edward and Richard were like eyelashes stuck in the whites of his eyes, leaving a constant watering. Catherine sat beside him while he told her that she wasn't just an Irish maid. She was of Anglo-Norman descent. Her Mandeville ancestors had come from England with William the Conqueror. They had taken the lands of Balleydine on the river Suir, and survived through countless wars and feuds. "'Tis all one flesh and one blood we be – all of us on this earth – and those who fight inflict their oewn brothers," he said in a grave voice.

The fall turned to winter. Catherine scrubbed threadbare clothes against the wooden washboard as she gazed out the window to the cold landscape. She remembered how in springtime Daniel would slow to a walk on his way up the hill to plough his father's ground. In summer, he passed their house, going out to fodder the outliners. Hay had been tied with a rope and bunged on his back to a dry spot to feed cattle not stabled for the night. He slaved in bog and meadows, carrying stud baskets of water and milk. His gaze would pitch on Catherine, his eyes like brown butterflies. She had her sight on him too, but only when his back was turned. She had listened to the sounds of his *feadóg* penetrating the mist. Now she imagined his strong fingers playing the whistle.

She told Grandda about Daniel and he asked, "What kind of giggery pockery is that? Sure he's Church of Ireland. His destiny might not be a good one for you to have to follow after."

Destiny! she thought. *Whatever that is, I'll be having nothing to do with it.*

CATHERINE AND LIAM had good luck with them. They survived many winters alone. This one passed with only a shadow of snow. Spring came early, with a gentle laugh of wind under the bright smile of the sun. The grandfather, despite his malady, and the young girl scampered out the door and kicked up their heels on the green like dancing elves. The growth of new life was all around them.

In a short time, wild Alexander and mushrooms grew large enough to be ready for the pot. "The strength of any land lies in how well she can nourish her people like a mudder nurses her children," Catherine's grandfather told her. Sometimes Catherine lay on the grass as if the land was her mother, she, her child. She loved her little spot of Ireland. It held all that was familiar. The potato stalks grew green and sturdy and promising, while Liam sat working hazel rods to make himself a cylinder basket. He had done the weaving and was finishing up the binding when he looked across at Catherine with a clouded look. "You'll be going away come late spring."

She was leaning on the half-door and eyeing the early spring sky, deep blue and cut into by dark limbs of trees motionless against the silent stealth of night. An owl, like a white cloud, feathers light and ghostly, flittered to the eave of the barn. In its mouth was a small mouse, a kiss of food for its baby.

"And where will I be going then?" she answered in a strong, even voice.

"To a new land where some of your kin already are. They live by the ocean and fish from the sea."

"And you, Grandda?" She gave him an intense look as she waited for his answer.

"An old Irishman likes to keep his legs on his oewn land and his feet under his oewn table, girl," her grandfather told her. "Besides, new experiences bide well with the young. I won't be leavin' here." Her grandfather knew something was coming to dispossess them, to take their place and their peace, and he, in ill health, knew he had not the years nor the will to start over.

Catherine looked at her grandfather, the last knot keeping the fabric of her life in Ireland from unravelling. That knot could only hold so long. She did not want to leave Carrick-on-Suir. She loved the place nestled in a lush valley against gentle mountains. Though she knew Ireland to be surrounded by water, she had never been to a seaport. It was hard to imagine the new-found land her grandfather told her about – land rising out of an ocean almost as deep as the sky.

Catherine had heard idle men, as they sat around a keg of *poitín* in her grandfather's house far into the night, talking about the island across the pond. Daytime, they often gathered at "The Tell" and squatted on a rock wall just out the road. They lit their *dúidín*s and squinted against the smoke in their eyes as they yakked over the day's doings and the morrow's worries. They could get passage to *Talamh an Éisc* by promising two or three years' labour to a plantation owner. There were places in the new land that had not had the print of a human foot. People who left Ireland could have land all to themselves.

Catherine was watching for Daniel as she had been doing for days without seeing him when her grandfather's voice cut into her thoughts. "You're best to be setting your mind in gear for leavin' this place, girl. Don't be pitching your sights on Daniel." Liam's voice was stronger than it had been for some time, though there was a thickening black spot on his face that was drawing the skin tight. It seemed to pain him when he smiled. He sat beside the small fire in the grate, holding coins in his trembling hand. They still held traces of the ground from which he had dug them. It was money he had laid aside for his coffin and to buy seed for next year's planting. Now it would pay for Catherine's voyage to the land of fish.

He no longer wanted a grave box. For all he cared, he could be wrapped in rags and slung down into the earth. He had seen a foreshadowing of Catherine's destiny in the midwife's eyes as she left the house when Catherine was born almost twenty-three years ago. He had said nothing, not wanting to know his granddaughter's fate. He knew that before his son and grandson returned he would be in the earth with no one to protect Catherine from the wild dogs that some of the young men in the place were. Even now there were glances toward her, and familiar looks like ones he once had toward young women when his body was on the surge. He wanted Catherine away from here before she got rooted to the place with a young Irishman. She was going to a new land where war had not the chance to take a foothold as it had in Ireland. He wanted new beginnings for his darling, grand girl. He hoped that the evil eye would not be able to follow her across the sea.

"You best go on the boat," her grandfather said in a haggard voice. "I've no life left to speak of and the warmth of this house will soon follow the smoke. I don't want me granddaughter caught up in the Irish rebellion. There's to be a lot more unrest in this place. You'd best be away to a new land where prejudices won't have deep roots. Your cousins from Kilkenny are already in the island country. Mind you don't get yourself in with the English. Keep the Cartlic faith, and find an Irishman who will keep a warm house with plenty. I'll give you a bag of potato eyes to set. God rest them and make them grow."

Catherine looked toward the greening land; then she eyed the tarry clouds. She could already feel the cold stealing in like a monster to swallow the warmth of the house, the warmth of her grandfather's body. It was as if winter, instead of summer, was coming.

"But Daniel?"

"Gone," her grandfather said abruptly. "I'm not sure what's to become of him. Maybe he's gone with one of them secret societies trying to oust the English. I've laid by enough money for your passenger ticket," he added, his voice choking, his eyes misty. She stared at the coins in his hands. Then she looked toward the River Suir cutting through Carrick like a silver scar. The 114-mile river, alive with brown trout and salmon, flowed from Devil Bit Mountain, passed like a traveller through Cahir, then Clonmel, through Carrick-on-Suir and on down to the mouth of Waterford into the Atlantic Ocean. Sometimes the hills and sky were painted on its calm waters. Boats moving down the river scrubbed away the scene. A blow of wind brushed the river grey.

Catherine had one last time on the hills. She picked some tiny, white bog flowers for the grave of the mother she could only imagine. Afterward, she lay across the grassy knobs above the meadow, tightened her arms against her body and let herself roll, as if she were in a barrel going faster and faster down the hill, just as she and other children had done when they were younger. A large rock wall brought her to a jolting halt. She lay still, wondering about that other land. *Will the grass be green and will I find the same flowers?* She got up and hurried to pick the root of the shamrock.

"The fairies have wanted you, Caitríona," her grandfather said as she came inside, her breasts heaving from her romp over the land. "Once, when you were little, I felt their breath mingling with the sweetness of yours as I stooped to kiss you good night. I have heard the whisper of their wings against the walls after you've settled in sleep. Don't even take the belief of them, dear heart."

He remembered his wife having bad dreams. One of them surfaced before he could slam his mind against it. Mairi's recurring dream had frightened her to tears. She had seen Catherine as a moon cut into pieces, turned to blood, and a dark night descending forever. Liam had brushed her dreams aside by exclaiming, "Pure augury. Pay no mind to it."

On a muddy, spring morning, they left home, the old fellow with Catherine's hand in his. The boat keeper was impatient to be off the north banks of the River Suir for the seventeen miles down to Waterford. Catherine pressed her lips on her grandfather's furrowed cheek wet with the brine of his tears. She pulled in her lips unconsciously and tasted salt – her tongue taking inside her the last bit of her grandfather she would ever have. Her own tears stayed sealed inside her, inside a body that was coming alive to a sense of intrigue, even while she shivered with thoughts of her dark journey. She could not even imagine the rise and size of the new island that would bear her footprints.

Liam had pulled a soft, woollen shawl from a place in the wall before they left. "Your mudder's shawl to be in your keeping. The hag was making off with it, but I yanked it off her. 'Tis yours now to wear. Your mam's scent is still in it, for 'tis never seen water since she laid it aside. She wore it over her belly while she carried you for 'tis not proper to show oneself with child."

Catherine took the varicoloured shawl without a word and buried her face in it. Then she pulled it over her heavy dress, dyed red from boiled *sraith na gcloch* – the hard moss she picked off dry fences and in stony places.

CATHERINE THANKED THE oarsmen as they helped her down from the pier to the passenger boat. She nodded a greeting to the few people seated on the thwart and then called to her grandfather standing on the banks. "Send word, Grandda, if me fardher and Richard show for the land." She pressed her arms to her side, feeling the shamrock and a wild Irish flower trailing wispy brown roots in pockets she had sewn in her coat sleeves.

Liam's face brightened. "The promise is there, Caitríona, to be given as soon as the lads break over the green. I'll send word by someone passing to that land." His face darkened. "But I'll be fearing the land grabbers. Sure they're in the works everywhere." He wiped his eyes and then waved his large, brown handkerchief. "*Slán leat* – goodbye," he said softly. "I'll place you under me wishes and prayers."

He called after her, "*Glac bog an saol agus glacfaidh an saol bog tú* – Take the world foine and aisy and the world will take you the same."

Struck dumb with grief, Catherine felt her eyes plim with tears. They overran her lids and plopped down her nose like large raindrops. Tears were her only way to say goodbye to her grandfather.

The Suir River's currents pulled the boat down – on down between dark hills shadowed by lively clouds – taking Catherine away from familiar ground and everyone who had ever loved her. She would soon be sailing to another island – *Talamh an Éisc*.

Three

OARSMEN rowed the boat down to Waterford to its river sucking the feet of the hills on one side and the beach on the other. Residents trudged down from high in the hills through paths flanked by Irish ivy and morning glories, to pick sea kelp from rocks on the beach, and to buy fish from fishermen on the wharf. They watched relatives give up on their homeland for a land far beyond their gaze. Irishmen, many with wives and children, left for North America, hoping for betterment. Young single males looked to make money. Some of them would return to the Emerald Isle and to waiting sweethearts.

Only now could Catherine imagine Ireland as a massive rock anchored in an ocean, surging waters stretching beyond her vision to touch the shores of another gargantuan rock. She had no time to think on it, for she was hurried along toward a long wharf by a rush of passengers and relatives seeing them off. Out from it, several large schooners lay anchored. Not far from them, fishermen stood in coracles, jigging fish from the river. Birds, meandering through the sky, pitched on the hills of Waterford as a young woman hurried down a narrow lane. Looking frightened, she rushed to the arms of a waiting lover.

Catherine tripped over the girl's ragged skirt as she rushed away from her coosie and back up the lane, sobbing. The girl's companion fingered his fare with one hand and ate a potato scallop with the other, his blue eyes clouded as his gaze followed the girl.

Catherine looked down at her rough hands, well-worn clothes and buttoned boots, a button missing from one boot, and thought, *I'll do good over there in a new land ripe for the likes of me.*

Bobs of conversation drifted across her ears as she shifted her bag over her shoulder and waited with other passengers to board the ship.

"The Irish Sea, the Celtic Sea, and the North Atlantic ring Ireland," a man with a white beard was telling a little boy standing solemnly beside him.

"'Tis not like going to Belfast then, or England. We don't know what we're doing – going off on that wild sea," a woman complained.

"That 'tis not then. There's land waiting for us to set the first hoe in it. We'll claim the land, sure. No one can take it from us. If they try, we'll split their arses."

A young woman, leaning on the arm of a man looking twice her age, whined, "I never wanted to leave Ireland. I should have had an inheritance of hand and thigh."

The man grunted. "You mean there were no brothers and you come in for everything. Why didn't you have it then, instead of going off with the likes of me only because I'd pay your passage?"

"I've told you before. When me fardher died, me uncles claimed everything."

The man scowled. "What's gone is gone; don't prate to the world." The man pinched his disgruntled companion and she let out a yelp.

Catherine heard a rough-looking man mutter, "I didna want to sell ya, maid – you bein' me sister – but 'twas how I got me passage and yours in advance. Do this or the two of us'll starve. You'll be gotten a good price for, so you will, and a little of it will go back in yer own pocket. If you don't get yourself fertilized by a hot-blooded Englishman, you might get away to do your oewn will."

A man lumbered toward Catherine, scuffing dirt under his

gaitered boots. "No time for daydreams, girl. 'Tis to a new land you'll be going. See that speck of ship coming in. Her name is *Cambroila* and to the land of *Talamh an Éisc* she'll be setting course, once she's off-loaded the supplies she's brought back."

Catherine nodded and got in line for the custom house inspection. She felt a stir against her skirts as she stood waiting. She tried to move but the crowd pressed against her. She didn't know until she got to the wicket that someone had stolen her money. The officer at the open window dismissed her and she was pushed aside by passengers reaching with ready money. She moved to a side of the wharf, her heart pounding in fear. She would be left at Waterford without means to find her way home. The savings her grandfather had worked so hard to garner were gone. She stood motionless, tears dripping down her face.

THE *CAMBROILA* HAD let off supplies and was now ready for its passengers. Captain Murrey straightened up from checking a rope in the fairlead. His rough face hardened into a scowl he was likely to keep through the voyage as he eyed his passengers keenly. He spied Catherine, not a slip of a girl, but a sturdy, full-hipped, full-bosomed female. "'Tis a pleasure this one'll be," he muttered, barking an order to one of his men to hold the rope. He stepped ashore and tipped his cap. His voice was gruff. "So you'll be wanting to be aboard me ship, will yer?"

She met the captain's sea-bleared eyes, and dropped her gaze, not wanting to be part of the look he gave her. "My grandda said so, sir," she hiccuped, "but ruffians stole me sovereigns." Her words tumbled out. "They must've been watching me before I came on the wharf. I checked me skirt to make sure the money was safe."

Captain Murrey's look shifted from Catherine's bright, tear-soaked eyes to the cut hem of her skirt where the money had been sewn. *She's been well-fed*, he mused. *The juice of life is in this one.* He turned from eyeing her body. He nodded toward the boat. "In you go then, squat yourself among the passengers and we'll see what's to become of ya."

Catherine scrambled to get to the gangplank, relieved to be getting away. Hope rose in her, tingled with an excitement that made her glad, though her legs felt weak as she walked the gangway. Someone called, "Don't look down as you cross to the ship."

A man's voice murmured against the ear of a young girl he had his arm slung around. "Sure over there in the new land silver grows on trees."

"Money?"

"No, silver."

Another young fellow raised eyebrows that had thick scars above them. "I've been there. It's nothing but freezing rain coating trees on a cold day with a bright sun. That's all. It's a silver thaw."

"It wasn't easy on the boat the last time I crossed the sea, I can tell yer that," another passenger said. "The ship was on mad water. Passengers were stowed three to a bunk and given a rat's ration of food once a day, pea soup and the kind. There were sixty hands on board, including a dozen girls to be sold. One had a fever on her and died. A storm broke the hoops of the last salt pork barrel. Mildewy biscuit was left to eat with water that was rationed. I hope 'tis better this time."

Catherine stepped down the rope ladder into the hold of the ship. She got herself settled in a dim, lantern-lit underbelly with strangers. A mixture of excitement and apprehension slipped inside her as the ship moved out into the ocean away from the steady flow of water lapping the shores of Ireland.

"We should look for a shelf to stow ourselves," one young girl said, dragging on the hand of a red-headed fellow.

The heaving of the ship as it sailed into deep water upset Catherine's stomach and a tide of fluid came up her throat. She pitched forward into the lap of a scowling man. Vomit went down between his open legs. He pushed a keg in front of her and she spewed into it, her blue eyes, defiant and unashamed. "I tell yer now, maid," he threatened, "you had better keep that slop in your own mout' or else."

Catherine thought she had spied Daniel on the ship as she came aboard, his thatch of blond, shoulder-length hair tied back against the high collar of a thick, blue jacket. Now she looked up to see familiar long legs coming down the ladder. "Daniel," she whispered, "what a surprise on me!"

He ducked his head and, smiling, said, "Catherine," and she knew she was no longer alone. She had a friend and he was going on the same journey to the same place. A familiar sight, he would be – she hoped – for all her live-long life.

Daniel did not get seasick like some of the other passengers. He set about emptying the wooden slop pails with their hinged covers, twine knotted over a nail to keep them tight. The pails were kept yoked inside a water closet hardly big enough to hold an adult. Daniel cautiously held a slop pail as he climbed up the ladder. He pushed up the hatch and drew in brisk, salty air, closed his eyes and listened to the roaring seas, the cracking masts and the whistling winds, the likes of which he'd never heard before – all as one. He emptied the pail, careful not to have its contents splash back in his face. He filled his lungs with fresh air before descending the ladder to the hold of body odours, stale breaths and the musky smell of fish oil burning in a lantern.

The ship's rations got fewer and fewer as the weeks went by and contrary winds kept the ship out to sea longer than was expected. Water rations were mixed with vile-tasting liquor. Rats scurried through the ship, seeking sweat from the faces of sleeping passengers and saliva from any snoring passenger's open mouth. "It's good luck to see rats on a ship," a kind sailor told the passengers as he passed down a keg of rainwater. "Don't be afeared of them."

Someone muttered that rats would soon taste good. The looks on some passengers' faces suggested that they had already eaten the rodents.

THERE WAS NO water for washing and Catherine watched one mother sprinkle arrowroot powder from a stuffed muslin bag onto the raw urine burn on her baby's bottom. The baby cried pitifully. Another passenger hoarded a wedge of cheese, already mouldy. When she wouldn't eat it or share it, one woman's hand, studded with sores, reached for the cheese as if to dig into it and take what she could get under her long, broken fingernails.

The boat rolled and lurched in storms of wind and the billowing seas, bringing passengers rolling into each other's faces, some to encounter the bile spilling from seasick guts. Young passengers cried from hunger. A mother's milk was the only sure food, and grown men eyed nursing mothers as if they were tempted to go after their milk. Their looks grew so intense the mothers cowered. Children's eyes seemed to slip deep in shadows as each day passed with no sight of land. Babies dragged on their mothers' breasts for milk that was drying up. Daniel feared the women would die and their babies follow them. "I'm goin' to the captain," he whispered to Catherine. "There's got to be food somewhere. People paid for it with their passage."

Catherine eyed him, wanting to urge him not to go, that he was only one person, a bold one, and that the captain was likely mingy and wouldn't listen. Still, she let him go without a word.

She waited for Daniel to come back, listened for his step on the ladder. She stayed put until the next day. Then afraid and angry, she mounted the ladder, lifted the hatch and climbed on deck.

"Go back down," a deckhand warned, "or you'll roll yourself into the sea – or worse."

"I'm looking for Daniel Kennedy," she said confidently. "He's not come back down after goin' to speak to the captain."

"Spoke to the captain, did he? What was that about?"

"Food and water," she answered. "We've little and the nursing mudders needs to be fed to keep the babes in milk."

"Leave the captain be," he warned. "He don't relish hunger fer hesself, and hes mind is dumb from drink. Your Irish boyo was likely what went over in the bundle last night."

A fellow with pus-filled eyes added, "I heard tell of the captain havin' a skirmish with someone complaining about conditions. No one can be telling him how to treat hes passengers and crew. The sea'll likely cover a few bodies never to be accounted for."

Catherine fell to her knees, her dress and petticoats soaking with salt spray. She screamed over and over, unable to bear the thought that Daniel had gone to a deep-sea grave for trying to save the other passengers from starvation.

She was sobbing hysterically when she felt a sting across her face. She stopped suddenly and raised her head in fear. The captain stood above her, his short, knotted fingers stroking a dark handlebar moustache.

"'Tis time you paid what ya owes," the captain told her, reaching to pull her to her feet. He slipped his arms under her body and lifted her against him. She stiffened as he moved quickly across the deck.

"She's in fer something now," the deckhand smirked, "suppin she likely won't forget."

The captain held Catherine tight as he descended down into a lantern-lit cabin below deck.

"Daniel!" she screamed over and over.

Four

HEAVY-EYED with sleeplessness from a terror she could not think on, Catherine wondered if life could get any darker. Another thought surfaced. *Will I ever ag'in feel the sun's beaming smile on me skin? Will I see land, or will the sea sweep the motley lot of ship voyagers into its frothing mouth?* She imagined her lifeless body washed ashore, her bones cleaned of flesh by wild birds. Wind and tides would sweep clay and pebbles into her skull, a bone vessel for primitive flowers. Her morbid thoughts scattered as the ship came to a shuddering halt. The passengers heard shouts and loud movement above them as the ship was made ready to anchor.

Presently, a voice barked down the hold of the settled ship. "All off board, the lot of yers." Catherine followed the swarm of stumbling feet up the ladder. She stopped while other passengers crossed the deck to the rails and a ladder dangling over the side to a punt below. A fisherman kept it steady with a sculling oar. The small boat shilly-shallied under the weight of each passenger stepping to the gunnel and jumping down into the boat. Other small boats followed to be loaded with passengers.

Catherine stared at the place, her dry lips parting at the sight of the poor-looking land with its wooden houses and huts. If Ship Cove had ever been wooded, it was now razed. There was hardly a tree. Here, grey, jagged cliffs, some holding fish flakes aloft, fenced the sea. Grey sheds leaned into cliffs, their legs like long fangs biting rock. Above the cove, seagulls flashed through the sky, and dropped to the land. The odour of dead fish and salt spray mingled as skiffs, loaded with catches of cod, pulled alongside fish stageheads sitting out over the cove, their weathered legs standing in water among floating fish offal and seaweed.

Catherine felt as if she were inside the cove's open mouth, damp breath around her, its rock jaws ready to snap and swallow her as she was rowed with other passengers to shore. Wind, with a temper, blew her blue bonnet off her head. It ran around her neck on its strings and would have likely gone if she hadn't secured it in a bow knot. "Have an eye now. Don't fall," a shipmate called after the dazed and famished passengers.

Livyers waited on shore. Some hurried toward the wharfage, their looks taking in the faces of women aboard the punts. Bold looks met shy ones. Catherine had never been so filthy. In Carrick-on-Suir there was always clear, clean water flowing over the rocks, even in winter. Now the filth of a beastly captain was on her. She tried to free her thoughts, but her mind was impaled on the act. The sight of male eyes scanning women immigrants made her cringe.

Soon the bewildered passengers were standing on solid footing, trying to hold steady to the sudden stillness under their feet. Some of them went off with people who greeted them. Others stood nervously fingering the straps of their bags while they waited to see what would happen to them.

A muscular young fisherman swaggered along the wharf as the captain grabbed the gump post and swung himself onto the wharf. "'Tis late you got here," he complained, running a tanned hand through curly black hair, his eyes like speckled brown stones.

"Good to see you ag'in, John Snow. Sure 'tis contrary winds we've been havin'."

"I've heard of it," the fisherman answered with a shrug, whiling shillings in his hand. "But gettin' to the point. I want a woman who's not too slight – an Irish maid to work her tail."

The captain shook his head. "There's hardly a plump one now –

haggard-looking the whole lot. But sure 'tis aisy to fill 'em out one way or anudder." He let out a raucous laugh.

John Snow walked to the end of the wharf with the captain, an arm slung over his shoulder, the two men deep in conversation. After a time they turned back, coming directly to Catherine standing on the wharfage clutching her bag. Her heart lurched with fear as John's eyes met hers. She protested to the captain. "You can't sell me to any man. My grandda gave me money for me fare and – "

"Your grandfather's on another island with a sea between," the captain grunted. "Beside, your money was stole – "

"By thieves in your employ, no doubt," John cut in. He raised an eyebrow toward the captain. "She's not yours then?"

The captain looked at Catherine, her blue eyes bold under dark, high-pitched brows. "Let's just say I broke her in," he grinned. "There's more like this from the green, but not on this voyage."

"I'll let the girl decide for herself," John said with a wink. "She'll have to put up somewhere, and I've as big a house as most planters and a board floor in it – likely, something she didin have in Ireland."

Catherine drew back and protested. "A relative named Nicholas Mandeville is comin' for me. My grandda sent word...." She squinted to see up the road, her hand over her eyes.

John grunted. "Nicholas Mandeville. Sure he's ben gone off to Grates Cove a twelfth month. He won't be back. His woman's father giv' him hes boat."

The captain turned back to the planter. "There's a brazen look to this one. No meekness a'tall. By jove, you'll relish it. She'll make a row to quicken yer blood, that she will."

John eyed Catherine up and down, as if warming to the look of her deep-set stormy eyes and high cheekbones in a soft, white face and enquired, "Are you well acquainted with the business of a servant girl?"

"I am so," she answered in a strong voice. "Not only can I farm, but I can keep house, cord, spin, knit, and dye."

"Die!" He lifted his eyebrows mockingly and added, "A lot of women do that here in this colony and early in life. Come on then. Up with yer."

"If you go with him," a raspy young voice warned, "you'll be no more than the Englishman's spit before he's done."

Thomas Snow tightened his lips against more words as John glared at him. "Hold your tongue, do!" He looked at Catherine and laughed. "Me brother, Tom."

Catherine took in the straggly look of young Tom, his face sallow, and his grey eyes bloodshot. His words meant nothing. Her belly was rumbling. She was near dropping down for want of food and drink. She knew what servant girl meant the minute the bold-looking Englishman had looked at her. He must know she'd be stinking in her hinter parts like a dead fish after she was banged by the captain and not a drop of water to wash with these past six weeks.

"Drop the coat, why don't you!" John said abruptly. "Your country clothes hangs around yer like thick drapes."

She let her outer clothes slide to the ground and stood ragged, her mother's shawl clutched in her hand.

John's look raked her body, making her feel as naked as a maple tree in autumn. "That settles it," he said, and slapped his hand against the captain's palm with coins. He nodded for Catherine to pull on her clothes. At John's nod, she climbed aboard his horse cart and sat down on a sack of straw. John leaped up on the bench and grabbed the horse's reins. Now and then he'd turn his head to tell her about himself. He was a fisherman and a planter who had a skiff and punt and two servants to help him with his work. Edward, his brother, was gone to Labrador to make his wages to buy his own boat, leaving his wife, Ruth, to mind their half-dozen children. Just then, rain came fast and furious, playing circles in puddles already in the potholed road. Catherine lifted her face and opened her mouth to the refreshing shower.

They passed dull, red-ochred box houses waterproofed with a foul-smelling mixture of ochre and cod-liver oil. Catherine felt favoured not to have been taken by a poor fisherman who lived in them. It would be the lot of other passengers, she felt sure. She drew in a sharp breath at the sight of a high-standing house facing Port de Grave Harbour. It was a wooden castle unlike the stone castles in Ireland. "Butler Castle," John said, noting a sign on the gate. "I can't read it, but I've heard it said often enough." He turned to glance back at her. "It's not there you'll be, nor on the Snow property anighst a valley of small houses in front of Jailhouse Mountain. You can see the jailhouse for evildoers and insane mortals. I bides farther up over Bareneed Hills and down in the valley."

Catherine felt a tremor as she looked toward a rough-looking stone dwelling in front of the mountainous rock. The horse and cart climbed a steep hill, and lumbered along a level stretch of land high above the sea and dipped down over a steep hill to a valley. John pulled back on the horse's reins and called, "Whoa!" The animal stopped by a house walled in wide planking. "There's already a woman in the house," John said with tight lips. "She'll be lying for her wake in a short time. Her eyes are on to closing."

Catherine gave him a startled look and exclaimed, "A woman who's on for dying!"

John answered with a laugh. "'Tis me old Irish mam. But me, I'm my father's son – an Englishman."

A hen clucked for her brood to scatter at the approach of John's heavy boots. The chicks had found their bellies on his toe before this. Lambs bleated and sheep baaed behind a garden fence beside a pigpen where two pigs grunted and rubbed noses.

Inside the house, Catherine stood on the planked floor. She looked down and John said, "You're lookin' at puncheon timber. It'll keep your feet warm in winter."

An elderly woman smoking a pipe sat on a wide stool to the side of the fireplace. Long, grey hair as thick as a scarf fell around a face as wrinkled as old potato skin. She raised her lids, loose skin bunching as she struggled to see Catherine under milky pearl blue eyes. Then she drew in nearer to the hearth, as if to guard her spot.

John grinned. "Old woman, you've no fear of losing your place to this young one. Sure she's but a servant girl. Her name's – well, I don't rightly know."

"Catherine Mandeville," said Catherine primly. "In Irish it's Caitríona de Móinbhíol."

The woman glared at her son. "This Irish Kit will charm the knickerbockers off you, no doubt, you with a body bursting with randiness." She added a warning to Catherine. "John's free with his wiles, always was, though a woman's scent was never as strong as the scent of grog on him. He's one for drinking, that son is, I can tell you that." She raised a gnarled finger of warning. "When the drink's in, the sense is out."

John grinned at Catherine. "Don't mind the old mam. She sleeps a lot and dreams more." He nodded for her to take a birch chair in the corner. Its knotted legs were straight in places and crooked in others. John smiled. "The legs on that chair are as natural as if they walked out of the woods be themselves."

Catherine stumbled on sea legs toward the chair and sat down, feeling its crosspieces under her behind like someone else's bones. John sat in a twig chair. "Made from alders," he told her. "They're not much good."

Catherine smiled absently, her mind on food and sleep. "The chairs could do with a little dressing, maybe some stuffing – a pillow for its bottom and its back."

"I'll have better in a few years, I can tell you that," John bragged. "To be a moneyed fisherman and planter is my aim. For the next house, I'm ordering furniture from England. I've promised myself that – a Windsor chair, one with a saddle seat and spindle back and sprawling legs." John added, "The foretellers have claimed this year of 1816 as a year without a summer. It's gettin' into summer, and the wind is mostly bitter. There's talk of fewer European markets for the fish, and lower prices at that, what with the Napoleonic Wars now ended. But I'll make my mark, just like me English da did before he died."

The old mam half turned, muttering to herself.

Catherine wasn't listening. She had sunk into a deep sleep.

HOURS LATER, SHE woke with a start. A rich aroma crossed her nose and she swallowed in hunger. Fire sputtered under a pan hanging from a hook over the hearth where John stood turning over flat cakes.

"'Tis a good smell there," Catherine murmured, now hungry enough to drag her tongue down her throat.

"You'll be fed," John promised. "'Tis fattened up we need to get yer, and we will."

"What is it?" she asked as John dropped food into a small wooden plate and handed it to her.

"A mixture of softened sea biscuit, grounded onion, spices and beef blood," the old mam told her. "John's oewn concoction."

John handed Catherine a mug of water and she drank it down without stopping. Then she dug into the food. When she finished, John refilled her plate, remarking, "Before the summer's out you'll be making a blueberry grunt."

She squinched her face. "How do you make a blueberry grunt? Do you pinch it?"

John threw back his head and laughed. "You got the wit about you then. A blueberry grunt is a bagged pudding boiled in hot water."

The old mam looked at Catherine. "It's a strange place you've come to, a colony full of little islands sticking out of the ocean around one big island. There's Offer Island, Pea Island, Kelly's Island, Belle Island, and Little Belle Island. . . . To name all I know would take me breath. There's nicknames on dwellers too – Queer Eyes, Foggy Eyes, Webbed Eyes, Long-legged Joe, Black Jack, Johnny Tosh, and Three-fingers. There's ever so many people gets off the boats from the old country with branded flesh and missing fingers."

When John went to his fishing room, Catherine asked, "The earth closet – where might it be?"

"If 'tis only water you want drained, you can sprinkle on the bushes out back. For the other job, the outhouse is partitioned to the henhouse. Whatever you do, there's someone to watch. There's Ada Manning up on the hill. She's got the place covered. Every move draws her look – an open door, someone on the path, a full clothesline. Allie Mugford on the side of the road has her sights on the meadow and the men comin' off the water. Then there's a few more idlers. They all know when a baby is comin' before a woman even has her barrel up. They come together to pass the news."

Catherine almost fell over her own feet hurrying out. Her stomach was cramping. She shifted the wooden knob on the toilet door and opened it. She sank down on the largest hole in the seat, eyeing the smaller one. Blue flies were buzzing up from it; a couple of stouts pitched on the rim. She hastened to finish before she got a nasty bite. A cloth and a pail of water hung on a large hook. She ignored them and scravelled back out of the toilet, pushing the wooden fastener across the door.

As soon as she came inside the house, John's mother took her in hand with warning words. "Catherine Mandeville, you're in service for lodging and grub, but he'll soon be after you."

The old mam's clouded blue eyes could not see the fear that filled Catherine's eyes. Without saying a word, Catherine hurried outside and pulled from her dress pocket the root of a wild Irish flower, and a sprig of shamrock, its root a dusty brown thread. She planted the roots in clay beside the door, hoping there was the chance for growth, a part of Ireland making roots in a new land.

Afterward, she bathed in a wooden tub kept in the linhay off the house. She slipped down into the warmed water, carefully holding a shiften of clothes from her bag to keep her covered. After her bath she dressed quickly, fearing there were spying eyes about the place. Then she scrubbed her dirty clothes, enlarging holes already in them. *Why,* she wondered, *wasn't there someone of me oewn flesh and blood to meet me at the boat? Hadn't Grandda sent word of my coming?*

Five

CATHERINE was given a bed in the old mam's room. Her body shook from fear of John the first few days, but he was busy with the fishing business and barely acknowledged her. He gave her mostly nods instead of words at the end of the day. She drew back from the sweet scent of rum on his breath as he passed her for his room off the pantry.

Catherine listened to John's mother rambling as she sat on her stool by the hearth. "'Tis aisy for young ones to forget that I had me time as a young girl. But I did. I danced me shoe taps thin."

Catherine flashed her a look. "I don't doubt it."

"Yes, I wouldin want to tread me life ag'in." Her face darkened. "There's such a thing as livin' too long." She drew in her lips, then relaxed them. "You can handle it all now then, girl. I'm worn, that I am, in mind and body. The Maker has me on Hes mind. I'll go aisy." She smiled, her gums a pale bend under thin, white lips.

"I'll get you your tea," Catherine offered. "You sit there and rest."

The old mam tipped back her head and closed her eyes. "And that you can, and that I will do."

She's already halfway in heaven, Catherine thought as she stirred the fire under a big, black kettle. She eyed the old mam's head already bobbing toward her chest, eyelids dropping as she fell asleep. Catherine rushed to lift her head back. She picked up an old feather pillow lying on the floor and pushed it under the woman's head.

Then she put on dinner as the old mam had instructed: "Boil your fish under a gentle hand, but let your potatoes gallop."

Catherine went to the window and looked out over the harbour where a string of boats, like charms on a bracelet, swung on their collars in the wind. Beneath the stage, the sea folded under, then rolled over itself, its milky green waters fringed in lace-like forms constantly changing shape, falling apart and coming together over and over. White floating spots rocked gently in the water.

At first, Catherine helped milk the cows and feed chickens and hogs. John had a man come to help him set the gardens. After a fierce wind, kelp fronds clung to beach rocks like old rags jibbered to pieces. The briny scent filled Catherine's nostrils as she gathered tubs of it for the potato grounds. *Summer in this new land is going to be a time of great tiredness,* she thought, looking out over the harbour wharf where young boys were sculling flat-bottomed boats known as flats. They leaned over the risings to stab dabbies – small flatfish that moved like white moons under calm water. Now and then they glanced toward the open bay as if they were waiting for their fathers to come home with a load of fish.

Long before dawn, John and his hired men had sailed out the bay in John's skiff to trawl codfish. They brought back a load. Michael Manning was swift in throwing the fish up from the pound of the boat, keeping in stride with Joe Taylor pronging them from the stagehead into a fish box. John stood beside a roughly made wooden table and grabbed a fish by the eyes. He slapped it on the table and cut across the throat and down the belly in a blink. He was about to gut the fish while he waited for Michael to empty the pound and give him a hand, when he saw Catherine coming down the path. She came on in through the stage and he called, "Get yourself a barbel hanging on a nail in the stage, and I'll show you a thing or two about gutting fish."

Without saying a word, Catherine found the linseed oil–cured apron and put it on. She slipped the barbel collar over her head and tied the apron strings around her waist. Joe and Michael eyed her skeptically as she came reluctantly to where John stood holding a bulgy-eyed fish, its back brown-spotted. He moved, making room for her at the table. Then he gutted the cod while she watched. John slid a cut cod to her and she took hold of the slippery fish and gingerly reached a hand inside the white belly. She pulled out ropes of cold guts and a slab of liver.

"Mind the gallbladder," John warned, just as it burst, its green fluid squirting in Catherine's face. She sputtered and backed away from the table, dropping the fish. John stooped to pick it up, telling her, "Make sure you drop the liver into the cask beside you." He cracked off the cod's head. Then he pushed the fish against a board nailed to the table for holding fish in place while he removed the sound bone, leaving a perfect crease mark. The fish landed in a large puncheon of water. Overhead, wheeling gulls dropped white dabs on the stagehead. Catherine shivered and pushed her hair up inside her bonnet.

"You'll be helping put the fish in cure," John told her after the load was washed and barrowed into the stage. John and the men lifted it from the barrow and began spreading it in layers over fish already in salt. Catherine was given a bucket of coarse salt. Soon, salt crystals fell like showers of hailstones from her bare hands stiff with cold. It was a long time before the day's catch was salted. When it was finished Catherine washed her barbel and her hands in a puncheon of clean, cold water.

"Go on with you now," John said with a grin, slapping her behind. "Be up to scald some milk and skim off the cream to go with me bread and jam for a mug-up." She left in relief and scurried up the path back to the old mam who was sitting by the fire, nodding off.

She came to with a start. "That you, girl? Be up and doing. Git the broom and brush out the house. Sure you'll be wanting a house one day and won't know how to keep it clear of the outdoors. Don't be lollygagging."

CATHERINE DIDN'T MIND gutting fish on the stagehead when sighs of westerly winds swept in over lapping, shining waters, but when there was an upwind, and dark waters lashed the stage and damp, cold air crawled over her face, she longed for Ireland.

Waves of sunlight often slipped through cracks in boards of the stage like light on dark waters as Catherine helped spread coarse salt on layers of wet fish. The murmur of the sea caught her ears, its water crawling in across beach stones, tides dragging it back out as she worked through the day, building up layers of fish from John's daily catches, adding to a wall of fish climbing higher and higher in the stage. Sometimes if John went trawling or hauling nets twice in one day, work went far into the night. Then John hung a bib stage light – a kettle with a wick placed in the spout on a stage pole.

Three weeks later, while the hired hands took the skiff out on the water, Catherine helped John wash the fish in a puncheon of fresh water to scrub away surface salt. She and John barrowed it up the steps to the cod loft over the stable, and out its back door onto the bough-covered flake. The flake rose high above the ground on stilts to keep animals away. John told Catherine, "I won't be spreading fish on beach rocks like some fishermen, where goats can tramp on it and dogs lift a hind leg to spray it."

They spread the fish under warm breezes sweeping in over the land. Before dark, the fish was stacked and covered in rind for the night. After a few days spread under gentle winds and the sun's golden cast, wet fish that had covered the flake like a blanket of snow lay like a field of golden leaves, each nape a pearly grey.

One evening, as Catherine piled fish to cover for the night against rain already pecking, she heard a small voice: "Might I have a fish, ma'am?" She straightened with a large fish from the top of her pile. She looked down from the flake into the upturned face of a little girl.

"What's your name then?" she asked.

"Jessie Rose Newell, ma'am. I'd like a fish, if you please."

John was at the other end of the flake and didn't see Catherine drop the fish down to the girl as quick as a flash. The little girl was so startled, she fell back, and the fish landed at her feet. She grabbed it up with a quick look toward John's back and ran off.

Catherine shrugged. *One fish won't add much to John's account in the merchant's books, but it will mean a lot to a hungry family.*

EARLIER IN THE month, John had sent Catherine down to Hussey's Cove to sell butter she had helped his mam churn. She had trudged up over the hill on the neck of Bareneed when she heard a muffled cry from inside a cottage. It was less than a cottage and more like a sod tilt – a frame of slabs and bark covered with sods, its walls chinched with moss. The transparent membrane from an animal was stretched across a window opening to allow light in while keeping cold out. Catherine lifted the latch on the door and made a cautious entry inside. She walked across a beaten-down earthen floor to a small room off the main one. Huddled under a blanket lay a young woman on her back in labour. Catherine had run outside, calling for a midwife. Someone found Granny Tilley and she delivered twin boys while Catherine helped. Afterward, Catherine went to John's house to bring kindling to light a fire.

John had jawed Catherine for meddling in other livyers' lives. "There's many a house here," he said, "neither wind nor watertight, and there's many a tarred shack with only a window grate in the wall. People all over the colony live in dwellings a long ways from what they should be livin' in, and dressed in tartles. We can't have our minds dragged on and troubled over them."

Catherine stared at him, too full to answer. She had helped twin babies be born, sweet creatures, christened Josh and Abe, whose best shelter so far had been while they were inside their mother, Rachel Newell.

John stood up with his last yaffle of fish and came toward Catherine. His voice was stern. "When you sew a new brin dress to wear on the flakes, Catherine, get some beach stones and stitch them in the tail of your dress. There's men in this place peeling their eyes in the hopes of seeing up a woman's leg."

"No one more than you," she lipped. She looked down at her dress tail billowing in the wind, her petticoats showing. *Jealous, is he*, she thought, as she finished spreading a covering over the fish.

She had dropped the brin dress she'd worn over her regular dress into a water barrel by the linhay door and was washing up in the scullery, wiping her face with a cool cloth, when John strode into the house and hove himself on the kitchen bench. "Hurry on, Catherine," he called. "Git the food on the table."

The old mother was sitting by the hearth, smoking her pipe. She took it out and looked at John. Then she raised her eyebrows and nodded toward Catherine. "You be the servant now."

Catherine got the meal and settled into housework still to be done.

SHE CAME UP the path from the stage one evening, looked down and caught her first glimpse of the tiny unfolding leaf of a shamrock. It had pushed up through earth it could hardly penetrate, so scarce had been the rain. Over the weeks, the clover-like plant spread, shooting little sprigs up through hard clay. She carried water from a small stream and let it trickle over the ground. Soon she picked a tiny shamrock and placed it between the leaves of the Bible John kept in the shelf. She had never seen him open the large black book and he didn't know she touched it. The old mam told Catherine that many people believed the Bible was too holy to be opened unless someone was born or died. Then their names were inscribed therein, but only if they were relations, not bastards. Catherine had not learned to read, but she could count the names of people who had died by the black symbol of a cross beside each of them. John's mother explained that a twig sooted in the fire was used to mark the black crosses.

One day when John sailed into the harbour, Catherine was standing on the stagehead, the rouge of red berries on her lips. She pretended to be looking at a ship sailing out in the bay.

"Looking to see if there's a familiar Irish face, is yer then?" John called as he threw a rope over the gump post of the stagehead.

"I bees looking for you," she answered with a quick tongue.

"I'll have you and that's fer sure," he said with a saucy grin. He climbed the rails and grabbed at her; he licked off the berry juice, leaving her mouth reeking with salty saliva.

"Stop it!" she protested. "'Tis in broad daylight and perhaps there bees eyes watching in this place, their oewner expecting to have you for herself."

"And she will. 'Tis play I'm having with you. For all I know your belly could be rising from the captain's bastard. I'll bide me time and see."

And that's why he hasn't come after me, she thought. *A gentleman he's not. He wants an empty womb he can fill hes own self, if he minds to.* She wouldn't let on that sometimes, without cause, she passed a month or two without shedding blood.

When Catherine showed a white face and a hand on a cramped belly, the old mam spoke to John. "The maid is free of the captain. Her blood is cleansing her, if that's what you're waiting for."

After her blood days ended, John grabbed Catherine's mouth with his. She felt its harsh thrust, and winced at his touch, remembering how the captain's reeking lips had closed over hers. He had drawn her lower lip to his, the suction bringing terrible pain. The soft flesh had been bruised and swollen for days.

John moved back to take in her face. He smiled at her healthy curved cheeks. "You'll draw me to your bunk, Irish girl," he said, as if she wanted him. A bit of her did. "You'll be warmer under my covers. Please me," he coaxed.

Something turned in her and her heart hardened. She wished she wouldn't think of what had been done to her. It should be left to the past like yesterday's dirt washed from her body. Instead, it had gone inside her heart, turning there like a heavy, sharp stone whenever she thought of it. She went to John reluctantly, captured by the fleshy pout of his lips and pirate dark eyes, their boldness dragging her into their depths as if to never let her out. Seeing John in his pelt was a shock. Having to show herself to him filled her with shame, its flame rising along her cheeks.

John was heavy-handed in his strokes inside and outside of her, like a fisherman trying to gut a cod. He was almost as rough as the captain in taking her; he killed her interest with his roughness. When he was finished, she pulled away, feeling wounded.

For a while she kept her distance, brooding on the sorrow of her new life. *If only Grandda knew what has happened to me!* She cringed. *I'm glad he doesn't.*

Then, on a warm Sunday afternoon, with the fishermen's boats all sleeping on their collars, John grabbed Catherine's hand and towed her down to the beach under the legs of the stage. He coaxed her to a huge rock peeled bare by outgoing tides. The pitted rock held a place for them to sit and let their legs dangle into the water. When the tide began to rise, it covered their toes and came to their knees. It began to pool over the rock toward their crotches, tickling them, soaking their clothes, already pulled up to their knees. John grabbed Catherine's hand. She giggled as they jumped to dry ground. John pulled her toward a sheltered area of the beach and they slipped down, flattening grass and flowers. John surprised Catherine by picking a blue bellflower from a damp bed and running it across her nose. When John had laid Catherine that first time, she had opened her mouth to scream and he had closed it with his strong, fierce lips. Now, as he bent toward her, she bit her lip and let out a strangled protest. His lips softened, but his body didn't. Catherine would think back to that day as the day she knew she had the chance of having a baby come from her very own body.

When they climbed the rocks from the beach to the path and opened the door, John's mother, her wrinkled face blotched with the heat of a blazing fire, sat papping on her pipe with her toothless gums. "Yesterday," she said mournfully, "I was a beautiful young girl. Today I'm an old hag with a glim on her eyes like there's on the eye of a weathersome moon."

John shrugged and glanced at Catherine. "Don't mind Mam. The old harridan spent her young days in better spirits. There's people around here believes she's a dark one, once in with a pirate, and many times taken by fairies. I don't believe any of it."

Six

ONE morning, the old mam's ears picked up the young girl's movements, her feet light as they stepped to the work. It was as if young life stirred in the old mam and she mumbled, "I'm wishing I could make the bread." She rose above her stool and tried to walk to the bowl Catherine had made ready with flour and barm. Her body appeared to be shrinking while her feet looked to be growing larger and turning away from each other, as if one was going one way and the other another way to avoid that straight path taking her toward the end.

John laughed. "Sit, Mam! Catherine is good fer it." The woman moved back to her stool and sat down, sighing.

When the dough had risen, Catherine said gently, "You'll be wanting to knead the dough and roll the buns for the pot. Come here then." She lifted the frail woman by the hand and brought her to the bowl. She took a wet cloth and cleaned the woman's hands. The woman's fingers reached to the dough, her arms shaky, and when she tried to fold her hands against the bread to knead it, she could not bend them into fists. Catherine saw how weak they were, the veins running under the thin skin like ravelled strands of yarn.

"You've done your work, sweet Mudder," Catherine said.

A tear stood in the corner of one clouded blue eye. The old mam was likely thinking of her bygone days of clammer and klitter, trying to squeeze out of a summer day time for house tasks and children and making fish in the stage. Her trembling hands reached for her crucifix and Catherine saw then that the woman was looking beyond her wasted body, her spent life, and getting ready to make her soul.

One Sunday morning, the old mam keeled off her stool right at Catherine's feet, as if death, itself, was bowing to a new mistress. Catherine tried to lift the body, but her slender arms shook at her instant recall of her gran's death. The dead weight was beyond her strength. She stayed by the old mother until John came home from securing his skiff against dragging its grapnel in high winds. With a curse on his lips he lifted his Irish mam gone to be with her English husband. He laid her on her sleeping mat by the fire to wait for Granny Tilley who always came in a tear to deliver the livyers' children. She took her time coming to wash the dead.

"The old dilly is dead, and that she'll bide," Granny Tilley said with a grim look on her face. She set about skivering off the woman's clothes and laying them in a bundle. While the granny washed the body, Catherine got her the burial gown the old mam had sewn for herself.

"What was she like?" Catherine said suddenly as John sat down to dinner. He shrugged and went on eating. She already knew that John hadn't thought much about his mother's life.

When the old mam had shown Catherine an Irish jar she'd cherished, and a cayla – a quilt holding squares of cloth cut from articles worn by her mother and John's father – John had shut her up. "Stop the blathering, Mam, about what's gone."

John's mother left a mourning brooch. John threw the keepsake into the fire, and listened to the sizzle of hair woven into a flower – hair from John's mother, his grandmother, and his baby brother who had died of scarlet fever.

Catherine felt then as if the road the old mother had travelled had fallen into the earth with her. She shut away the thought that this could happen to her. She'd have children, grow old, die, and when someone asked about her, her children would shrug.

One Saturday evening, not long after John's mother was

buried, John came home with a young horse. It splashed through a pool of muddy water, kicking up its heels like a child. "You get to ride it on its first undertaking," John told Catherine. "The old horse is sold – gone to make a lot of salt beef. I want you to take this horse down to 'Ibbs 'Ole on the morrow. I've some kegs of spirits to deliver to Esau Bishop."

She went to rub the horse's head, brown with a streak of white above its eyes. Its tail batted the air. "I'll tie a knot in its tail to ensure us luck," she said with a smile.

"That you'll not then," John said scornfully. "That Irish custom is nothing but Catholic witchcraft, likely steeped in Druidism."

When John went down to the fishing stage, Catherine reached under the horse's tail and took several strands of hair and tied it in a knot. "There you are then," she said. "You'm in luck with your new oewner. Your name is Luck."

On Sunday afternoon, Catherine climbed into the seat John had built and fastened to the front of the wagon he'd bought with the horse. John had tied down the kegs and covered them with an old sail. "No need of people knowin' my business," he said.

Catherine picked up the reins in her right hand. She patted the horse with her other hand and it started up. She liked the movement of horse and wagon, the whir of wheels, and the clop of hooves against paths trenched in the steady hold of hills, over rock-strewn cliffs. She would have visited Cat Breen, a young mother who had brought her a meal after the old mam died, but she had moved to Cupids. Instead, she stopped in to see Mary Britt, who often came down to the Bareneed wharf looking to trade eggs for fish. She unlatched the storm door and walked in where she found Mary making a rose cake – kneading raisins and currants through dough.

Mary looked up, pushing out her bottom lip and blowing blonde hair away from her brown eyes. "I can't stop to talk," she said. "I'm fair harrished trying to get this cake baked for Joe's brother and wife comin' to make company for the night."

Catherine nodded. "I'll be off then. I wants to see Lucy Petten, anyway. The poor girl lost her first baby." Mary nodded, raising a hot hand to her forehead.

Catherine thought of horses and carts moving through winding, narrow lanes edged by stone walls in Ireland, as she drove the horse and wagon down through the lane, past the harbour with several boats on collar, their sails furled. The little horse took her up over Dawe's Hill and tipped down Taylor's Hill on the other side. It trotted along the winding cliff road past the Church of England's place of worship and down over another hill beside stages, wharves, and ships anchored in Ship Cove.

Catherine rode up hills, beside Blow Me Down, and followed a path as winding and as dusty as Ireland's roads. To the side of the narrow path, land seemed to have burst out of itself, spilling grey boulders and white rocks, holding deep, dark cracks. When the wagon lurched over the rocky surface that was part of the lane, she felt its jolt in the pit of her belly, as if the earth, under deep waters, had reached up to alert her to a world that was before her beginning, before the mountains pushed up from the deep. Here, on top of hills that seemed to have their heads in the sky, she was far from the valley of Carrick, and yet waters stretching out from this land mingled with waters flowing from Ireland's shores.

She jerked the horse's reins and called, "Whoa!" The horse slowed to a stop. She let the reins rest while she scanned the ocean and the mist of the far land edging it – St. John's, Portugal Cove, and a place inhabitants called "over on the shore." She patted the horse and turned down the lane by Foxes Rocks. She came to No Denial, its path edging a high scarp of overhanging cliff. The horse minced its steps as it took Catherine down to Pick Eyes in 'Ibb's 'Ole overlooking the sea where the sun's gold stars twinkled and danced off gentle waves.

"Don't go marming about the cove, I'll want my supper," John had said when she told him she might drop in on a mother who had lost her baby. He'd added, with an impish grin, "Watch for abductors hiding in the hills."

She had laughed and asked, "Indians, French, or English?" She thought of what the old mam had said: "'Tis peaceful these years, but it wasn't always that way." Looking down over the quiet little cove, it was hard to imagine that Frenchmen with their Indian slaves had burned out the residents of the place, along with the rest of Port de Grave. One attack had set the Avalon on fire, taking houses, huts, and food supplies. Some English settlers had fled to Kelly's Island, named after a pirate. Brave ones had fought off the enemy twice – once in 1695 and again in 1705. Using lighted blubber-smeared logs, the inhabitants had driven the French and Indians out of the cove.

Catherine shook her head as if to scatter unpleasant thoughts. She brightened, knowing that though all the trees were gone, bushes had slowly crept back, growing berries that were used for making jams for the inhabitants' bread, and wine for the stomach's sake.

She tightened her hands on the reins and called, "Giddy-up!" The horse raced down the lane to the cove, the wheels of the wagon rushing past patches of gowithy bushes and sweet swallow.

Esau Bishop looked up from where he was sawing logs on a wood horse. "Now mind the cliffs, maid," he warned, leaving the logs and coming to the wagon. He lifted off the three kegs. "I'll deliver them around," he promised. "I'll be talking to John later."

She nodded yes and carefully guided the horse down the cliffs into a valley edged by the same cliffs. The Petten house was on a brow of land with rock walls built high across the cliffs so a child could not wander and fall to rocks prowled over by white manes of rough seas.

Catherine found Lucy Petten curled up on the settle with a worsted blanket around her shoulders. Her thin, blonde hair hung down as dry as straw. Catherine had seen her minding Ruth and Edward's children when Ruth was tending the gardens. John's brother and family lived only a few doors away, but the summer was too busy for Ruth to be handling everything herself with Edward gone to Labrador on a fishing schooner.

"You'll have more children, Lucy," Catherine said, offering to get the grieving mother a cup of tea to go with the blueberry muffins and fresh cream she'd brought.

Lucy turned her head from it and whined, "I've a husband who won't come anighst me. He can't forget the blood on the white counterpane and the shrimp of a babe in it, and me as white as a cut halibut gone into a trance. If old Susy Lear hadn't spelled me with her charms and roused me with her herbs, I'd ben gone. I know his body aches for me. His member rises like a trout to a hook. But he's afraid."

Catherine stayed as long as she could, but she knew she could not take away a young mother's grief. It had to have its season. Her hand went to her own belly.

When she came back home, John gave her a dark look. "Don't be gone so long next time."

The next day John told her, "You can go out on the water with me today. Michael Manning and John Boon are sick to their guts. A long wake over Sunday did them in. I'm just taking the punt to do some jigging."

"Leave me on land," Catherine said. "I'd be wise to bide home and see to the work here. My hands are nish enough to be broken into at the first line."

"You'll harden 'em up then; have no more talk about it."

Catherine unhooked the jigger from its reel along with a length of twine and threw it overboard. The line ran through her hands like something alive out over the gunnel of the punt and down into the clear blue waters off Burnt Head. She pulled it back length by length, dripping cold water under a tepid sun, leaving breaks in her skin with a smarting that made her tongue tiss. After a few tries she learned how to jerk her line and pull it up quickly. Water fell away like curtains of gold thread as a large cod flapped in over the boat. She let out a squeal. John, jigging fish as fast as he could haul them in, glanced at Catherine. "Haul, Catherine! Shut it up and haul!"

She licked salt water off her lips to keep them from blistering as she hauled in one codfish after another, and dropped them flopping against each other in the bottom of the boat.

On the way ashore she sat on the gunnel of the boat and held on to the rising. She tipped her head out over the water, her long dark hair combed by a light breeze.

"If we hit a wave, you're gone," John yelled.

She threw back her head and let out a long, lively laugh.

They reached the stage and John pulled the boat alongside. Water sloshed over its gunnels as Catherine jumped to the rails and climbed up to the landing. She picked up her skirts and hurried across the stagehead past Ruth's children thumping through the stage playing hide and seek. "Off, on home with yers," John roared.

The children fled through the stage and scattered – all except ten-year-old Ann. She looked up at him with a frown. "Uncle Jack, don't be so mean."

He laughed and pinched her cheek. "Watch your tongue or I'll bite off your summer moles." The little girl took off and John chased after Catherine. "A bite to eat and then we'll take care of the fish."

IT WAS JUST after the old mother was buried that Catherine had found the money. She was telling Mary Britt about it afterward. "I was about to gather the old mam's clothes for someone in want when I heard a clink. It was the shifting of shillings, sovereigns, guineas, and other coins. That old mother must have surely held a pirate's heart in her hand and squeezed the jingles out of it. She had the money, I tell you, all sewn up in underclothes kept unworn in the back of her storage chest."

Catherine took Mary's hand and laid a coin in it. The woman looked at her speechless. Then she confessed, "I've never had money."

"Keep it for a rainy day," Catherine urged.

Mary glanced toward the window and laughed. "'Tis peltin' rain now."

"Go on then – dance in the rain and feel the warmth of the guinea in your hand for a real rainy day."

Catherine watched Mary hurry up the hill, her worn brown skirt picking up the mud. The poor woman's husband farmed and fished with whoever would have him. Catherine turned to scrub the place. She was carrying a withy basket of hers and John's garments to the clothesline when John, coming up the path, called, "I hope you've washed and stitched me old mam's clothes to fit over for yourself."

She stopped and gave him a long, piercing look. "Your mudder's garments will lie on any body but mine."

He let out a laugh. "Spitey, idn't you then! Just put everything in the poor box at the Society for the Promotion of the Gospel. You are now the woman of the house."

"*Bean a' tí*," she said in awe, "the woman of the house."

"Leave your Irish be, woman. 'Tis not for here. I'll not answer to that tongue."

"The tongue of your mudder," she retorted, "likely stripped from her mouth by your English fardher."

She heard a whistle outside the door and she murmured, "*Buaine port ná glór na n-éan, buaine focal ná toice an tsael.*" She laughed heartily, unwilling to let John dull her spirit.

"What is that you say?" John asked, his voice traced with annoyance.

She repeated the phrase in English. "A tune is more lasting than the song of birds, and a word more lasting than the wealth of the world."

"The wealth of the world I'll take then, and no tune or word in exchange," John said, his full lips curling in scorn. "None of this romantic clobber to live on."

That night he complained, "I don't want you wearing winceyette in my bed."

"But I like flannel underclothes. I'm warm against you and so's me woollies. The winter'll be bitter."

He shrugged and settled in bed with his back turned. He sank into sleep, his snores making Catherine wish for a nightcap that would keep out the sounds.

One night she was startled out of sleep by a sting of pain across her face. John's hand had hit her so hard, her teeth came through her lip. She had mouthed the name Daniel in her sleep, John told her. She tried to defend herself. "He was only a friend I lost on the ship, drowned by your friend, Captain Murrey."

John didn't seem to care about what the old captain had done to her. He slipped back asleep, while she lay awake, glad she had not told him about the old mam's coins she had hidden away. She sighed. *Hope and despair can be as close as two strands in a rope and just as likely to unravel, and let one's life fall to its doom.*

That night John sat across from her at the table and eyed her critically. "The first scent a man wants when he comes out of the fishing stage is food steaming in the pot. Once his belly is full of grub, then he turns to his crotch, and to the scent of a woman. You, my Irish girl, have the chance to fill my belly and empty my groin."

Catherine pretended not to hear him. *His belly, his groin*, she thought. *Does he think the sky changes colour for him? It's me oewn belly that'll be filled with his children.*

He got up and went to the mantel. He pulled out a stone in the wall and came back with his hand full. He opened it to show a rosary of garnets on his palm. "My mam's Celtic cross, plain and heavy like she was. Wear it for luck," he said, passing it to Catherine, adding, "when you give birth to our first child."

She wrapped it in John's black handkerchief and put it in a drawer. There were times when she felt she would need much luck.

Seven

CATHERINE slipped away from John's snores and got up one morning to find the windows frosted and the sashes frozen, sealing the windows. She eyed the crystal pattern on the window facing the sea. Then, like a child, she licked a hole in the frosted landscape of ferns and willows and saw that the bay was caught over.

Wrapped in a red cloak lined with sheepskin, she pressed hard on the front door and eased it open to crackling noises as it became unsealed from the frost. She ran outside and whirled in tumbling snowflakes, catching the fluffy crystals on her hands. Snow melted on her lips, her breath a warm mist as she walked along the path, her feet shattering discs of bubble-patterned ice. Soon livyers would stir the place awake as they stoked banked fires, sending smoke up chimneys and out to meet the morning frost. They would open creaking doors and eye the day, drawing in cold air before turning back to the fire crackling in the hearth. For the moment she alone was held in the majestic beauty of a perfect winter morning where land and sea lay as one, asleep under a white blanket.

By mid-afternoon, Catherine watched as the dark shapes of children patterned the platter of ice. The children scooted over it under a bright, cold sun, and not a breath of wind. Their shouts and screams filled the air, mingling with the calls of mothers warning them to stay close to shore. Catherine leaned against the doorpost, smiling. Soon, some of the children running and screaming in joyful abandonment would be hers.

AS WINTER DEEPENED, high winds beating against sea and land and the *kek kek* of seabirds were sometimes the only sounds heard in the bitter air. On days when the winds settled, children slid down the snow-covered hills on wooden sleds. Except for feeding the barn animals and poultry, the women stayed indoors, raising bread and caring for the family. The men worked with twine and nets in their fish lofts, some of them finding comfort in a pipe and a swig of homebrew.

March brought days when the sun showed a warmer face. It licked the bay ice ragged. Surly seas pushed through the ice, breaking it into shards. Older boys dared younger boys to venture out, despite calls from parents warning the children about rotting ice. Rain came, leaving snow dirty and tattered like white sheets blown off a clothesline and muddied.

Sometimes the scent of burning peat crossed Catherine's nose like a stray wind, and thoughts of home came like the quick stab of a toothache. In Carrick-on-Suir, snow gave the land only a cursory glance. The sun licked it up almost as soon as it came; clouds sent rain instead. Here, winter was quick in coming and slow in going.

Catherine let out a gasp when she opened the door one morning to a dazzling scene. Trees pierced the sky under silver skins beside crystal grass and pearled rocks. It was a silver land caught over, holding its breath while the blue sea moved on. She looked over her shoulder at John filling the wood bin by the hearth. He turned his head. "You've never seen the likes of that, now have you! We call it spring thaw."

John pulled her away from the door and into his arms. "Let's have our own spring thaw."

He rolled his tongue around her lips.

She gave him a flash of her eyes and pulled away, teasing him with her words. "Don't you know the Irish blessing and curse that goes hand in hand? If women goes to their men on Monday, Tuesday, and Wednesday, their men'll love them and the women – their oewnselves – will live longer than their men. If they goes to the men Thursday, Friday, and Sunday, the men won't love them. Saturday is a common day, lucky for both of them."

John pinched her and laughed. "No Irish wrinkle will decide when my bed goes into the shakes. 'Tis a warm body for a cold day you'll be giving me, Irish girl."

MARCH LET GO and April came, bringing the strong scent of spring and the sounds of water rattling its way downhill over rocks into brooks. Birds flittered around opening tree leaves, their songs lauding a new season.

"The waters are surly, but 'tis a good sunny day, and last year's berries bees sweetened with frost," Catherine said to John. She took her bucket and went a little way over the hill to pick enough partridgeberries for their Easter Sunday dumplings. Blobs of snow like newborn lambs still lay on cliffs, and by the time she came home her fingers were frozen.

A gentle air swept in over the cove, filling Catherine's nostrils and stirring her senses to life as she made her dumplings the next day. It drew her mind away from John. He had come home from the grog shop the night before after drinking hard with two young planters, John Jacob and Thomas Martin, on their way to forming a business partnership.

"'Tis a Saturday night," he had mumbled, "and all a man needs is a brew with his friends, a bath by the fire, and a woman to give him his dues."

After their baths, and still soaking wet, John bent to lick her from her lips to her breasts. He drew in her nipples until she let out a searing cry. By the time his tongue dug into her belly button, the pain had subsided and he tickled her into laughter before wandering down her belly to her fork, where he had no shame in tantalizing her.

"You imp of Satan," she had laughed boldly. "Your tongue is longer than your tail."

"And I suppose I have hooves too."

They both laughed, and for that moment Catherine felt good.

THERE WERE HUNGRY times for many people. "In with the spring and out with the dieters" was the chant once there was news of a seal hunt under way.

Spring brought hope to the place. Men caught in the lethargy of winter, and dulled by it, felt the same surge that was in the ground stirring with life in the roots. Catherine felt it too. At first it was as if a butterfly had spread its wings inside her and was poised to fly. She cupped her hands around her belly, as if it were a chalice holding a precious gift.

At first she told only Mary Britt about her merry-begot. Mary was a Catholic. *Like minds makes good friends*, thought Catherine.

"I'd have expected John to have gone to St. John's for a woman and gotten one with English and Protestant breeding," Mary said bluntly.

"And maybe he was planning to do that after having fun with his servant maid. But I'll be having none of that. A maid is as good as a queen in God's eyes. Once a man gets a woman abed and with child, he's nabbed, I should think," Catherine told her. "And it's all his own doings. Meself, I would have settled for an Irishman and ben glad to have had a caring one."

"Sure your mind is always on the end of your tongue," Mary said, shaking her head.

WHEN CATHERINE TOLD John she was carrying life, he responded to her wide-eyed look with a grin. "It had better be a boy then." He was already hurrying out the door and down the path toward the stage. She watched him go, knowing that John's success would be measured by how well he could supply the merchants and how generous they were in payment. She knew he was already visualizing the fish stage and flake filled with fish. Soon his shed would be emptied of homebrew stored in kegs on the loft and in the cellar, to be sold to the owner of the first transatlantic schooner sailing into the harbour.

John turned and saw Catherine as she came outdoors. He called, "Bring the reddening box."

She brought the container holding a paste of ochre and water, and John dipped a string to mark a straight line on a piece of timber he was sawing to repair planks in the punt.

Catherine drew in the tangy smell of oakum rope as she helped John with a corking iron to squeeze a long stretch of oakum into seams of the punt. John rose up from where he was corking along the boat's waterline to look out the bay. He turned to Catherine. "The kind of day 'twill be for fishing is told in the face of the sea every day. The sea is more settled, kinder now and the days bees lengthening. Tomorrow I'll be down in Port de Grave Harbour helping the hired hands get the skiff ready. Between the fishing and the planting, we'll have a lively summer."

THE PROMISSORY NOTE that had lain in sodded, rock-walled cellars all winter in the eyes of potatoes and in turnip and carrot seed brought the livyers outdoors to set their gardens. Catherine helped John turn the sod and dig the ground for beds of carrots, cabbages, and turnips, and the potatoes they would set by the middle of June. She smiled down at her belly mooning under her brin apron. She and John would have a child long before the year was out. She stood up to give her aching back a stretch and stayed watching John, his calloused hands on the garden post, twisting it to make sure it was solid. It was, and with quick strides he went to the next post. It had been bitten into by rot, so he worked it out of the ground. He had a new post laid out in no time, skinned and white like a limb that had never seen the sun – a whitened rod. John lifted the stake maul, called justice, and came down on the head of the post, driving it deep into the ground. Catherine turned away from the echoes of the maul against the post, feeling its violent vibrations go through her.

Barking pots were being stirred under fires along the beach, and John and Catherine brought gallons of water to pour into John's iron pot holding spruce bark. John boiled it over a roaring fire, until the preserve was ready for him to steep his nets and sails. On a fine day he spread the fishing gear on the meadow grass to dry.

In between, gardens had to be sown and kept. Catherine would soon be transplanting cabbages and thinning turnip tops. She swallowed in longing for the greens she would be pulling for the dinner table. She could fair taste them. Her belly was growing big and hard, stretched around a baby with a strong kick. She quivered with the pleasure of each gentle turn the baby made inside her.

CATHERINE CARED FOR the hens and the animals. More than once her meal ended up beside the horse's oat bag. Sometimes when she was milking the cow, the knobs falling beneath its hoisted tail was enough to lift her stomach to her mouth.

John came up from the stage one morning to see Catherine outside the barn dancing and screaming, "Don't you come near me!"

"Who are you talking to?" he called.

"Wasps! They're going to sting me. I struck a nest."

John grinned. "Try talking to them in Irish. They don't understand English."

"If I'm frightened by a wasp the baby'll be born with a birthmark shaped like a wasp," she whimpered.

"The mark of a wasp on his arse!" John exclaimed, and roared with laughter. "A midwife's tale that is – pure pisogery."

SOUTHWESTERLIES SCENTED THEIR way into Bareneed and filled children with the joy of running and leaping in warm, sunny air, their bare feet on hard, dusty paths, their voices like birdsong in Catherine's ears. The children raced across the beach, stomping on starfish they called devil's fingers. Other children jumped on a stranded dead whale beneath a saucy show of gulls beating the air for a feed on the carcass. Young boys climbed cliffs to find birds' nests holding babies. Lambs bleated outside the houses in the valley. Human and animal sounds mingled. Everyone was outdoors, as if blowing off a spring that had come with too many cold days. Women laughed and gossiped while pinning clothes on lines that quickly galloped in faddering winds. Catherine lifted the cleft pole against the clothesline. It wavered in her hand before she got it stuck in the ground. She looked toward the sea where brown sails played in the wind. John was on his way ashore. As he came closer, she saw his hair curled with sweat, his face creased in a grin. She imagined muscles rippling in his arms as he pushed a sculling oar through the waters, bringing the boat close to the stage. He hooked a gaff into a longer and pulled the boat alongside the stage. Then he threw up a rope for Catherine to tie. The other men started to follow him up over the stage.

"Throw up the fish first," he told them. "I'm off for a cup of tea and then I'll be back, and you can go for a mug-up."

Summer warmth and winds playing with Catherine's clothes drew John's mind to her fresh and warm body, hips and fine thighs widening. He smacked her on the behind and his grin opened into a hearty laugh. He pushed her into the house with a hand up her dress and a squeeze on her breast. "I'm promising myself this for later," he said. "Right now I wants me dinner, and after that there's fish to cure."

IN AUGUST, JOHN bought a western boat. "A thirty-ton schooner with a forty-foot keel and a fifteen-foot beam," he bragged to Catherine. "If we finds plenty of fish, and the weather holds, we'll be gone for three weeks at a time. We'll cut, gut, split and salt the fish aboard the boat."

The ship took John and his crew far out into the bay. Catherine waved goodbye, missing John as soon as the boat went out of sight. "There's plenty to do," she told herself, knowing there was more than plenty, and she too tired to do it.

CATHERINE SNOW

WHEN CATHERINE CAUGHT a glimpse of the schooner, its barked sails billowing in the breeze on the way home, a warm feeling stirred her. John was coming home! She took off down the hill, her feet sliding through slippery wet grass and landing her on her behind. She pushed herself to her feet, holding on to her rounded belly. She hurried to the Bareneed wharf, where John's boat had gone to tie up. She eyed John as if she had never been his, and a sense of wanting to have him as hers by God's and man's law assailed her. She wanted him to be hers as much as she had already been his.

John glanced up from his ropes and called, "Put the pot and kettle on, girl. I'll be up the minute I settles me boat."

He strode off across the deck and she stood still, anger rising. She tossed a heavy cloud of hair back over her shoulder and eased down over the rails and onto the deck. Her eyes, wide and bold, flashed as she blurted, "I wants to get married."

She expected any instant to have John's hand across her face. He hardly turned to look at her as he lifted a net from the boat and slung it up on the wharf. She carried on. "In this place, men thinks they're the ruler of land, sea – and women, slummy or highbrow. I'll not be one of these women. I wants to be made higher than a servant who licks your boots and whatever else you wants licked. I wants to be wedded."

John lifted a damp hand across his forehead beaded in sweat and, to her surprise, grinned at her. "A shameful woman you be, and spirited. I like the Irish mouth on yer. But marry the likes of you when there could be someone more of my breeding in St. John's!" He raised an eyebrow.

"And she'll want you too. You're just a crackie from around the bay. We've crossed bloodlines in making this babe, as your fardher and mudder did in making you. Don't be holding it against me that I be Irish by blood and Cartlic be me parents' faith. Will you not marry me? No! You'll make me your whore and your children bastards. I'm telling you now – I'll not born a bastard."

Catherine looked toward a small boat coming into the cove, and John, following her gaze, said, "Now there's a bastard."

"And it is then," Catherine answered, knowing that a small crudely built boat was a bastard. She decided that she would never use that word again no matter whose voice branded children born out of wedlock as bastards. *God gives life*, she thought, *and one life is no purer than another. I'll not be insulting Him or the babes. Our children may be born outside the law, but not outside God's grace.*

Without another word, she climbed back up on the wharf where Ruth stood, her hip stuck off with Frances, her youngest child. She had come looking for a fish for supper and had overheard the conversation. Now she cautioned Catherine about accepting her lot. "If you're hes woman in bed only, what's to stop him from kicking you and your baby out the door? I tell yer I'd have hes name."

"He's Protestant and I'm Cartlic. He thinks we can't mix oil and water."

"Bodies aren't oil and water. Your bodies did well to mix and will make a pack of weans before he's finished with you. Now be after him with the marriage vows. Till death you do part. I'd have that." Her soft, freckled face lifted in a smile. "I'll stand at your wedding."

Eight

JOHN made a cot from pine he'd cut on Kelly's Island and put barrel staves under it for rockers. He carved out flower shapes in the barred sides so the baby would be able to see out. Catherine made a mattress for the cot out of flannel stuffed with dry grasses and soft moss. Then she stitched flannel diapers. She picked arrowroot, dried it, and crushed it into a powder. She put it aside to heal the baby's belly button after the cord was cut.

As Catherine's time drew near, her mind was on Susan Tucker buried down in the harbour. She died, leaving a newborn, saved from being smothered in his mother's blood by Jake, his able father.

When she asked John what he'd do if she died in childbirth, he answered casually, "Think what I'd do with a baby – you gone. Sure I'd be thinking it was the young one's fault and I'd not want it."

She was shocked. "What? Your own flesh and blood and you'd not want it."

Ruth, who had dropped in to borrow a cup of molasses, spoke up for John. "It's only talk he's having. He's not meanin' it." Catherine stared, sullen-faced, as Ruth backed out the door murmuring, "I must be on home to feed the young ones, and afterward get me feet up for a spell."

While John finished a garden beer he'd brewed from home-grown hops, Catherine filled the half-puncheon with water she had heated over the fire. She softened the water with blueberry soap she'd made and John dropped his gurry-grounged duds and climbed into the tub. He was on Catherine quick after that, hardly noticing her belly in the way. He plunged himself into her, not heeding her protests against his roughness. That done, he jumped up, and hurried to the outhouse to rid himself of beer-laced urine. He came back for supper and then he was off to the grog shop. Catherine watched him go, her eyes flashing in anger. He hadn't even taken time to cup her hard, ripening belly and feel the baby's kick.

That night, her belly tore with pain and she dropped to her knees, praying in a trembling voice. "Hail Mary, full of grace. . . ." She stayed on her knees while tides of pain gripped her, let go and came back to grip her and let go over and over.

She stood up as clear fluid began to run down her legs. She was looking down, unsure what to do when she heard John's voice. "Lie down! I'll fetch help."

The baby girl didn't have to be pulled from Catherine by Granny Tilley. The mite slipped out all by herself, shivering like a leaf in barbarous winds. She let out a mewl, her scrunched face as yellow as a flowering gill-cup.

The thin-faced granny smiled cautiously and wrapped the baby tight in blankets she'd been warming by the fire. "A little early," she observed. "We'll put her facing the sun during the day to clear up the jaundice." She passed the baby to Ruth, who had spied John going for the granny and had hurried to be with Catherine until she arrived.

"I want to hold her," Catherine said quietly, reaching out her arms. Ruth hurried to place the baby against Catherine's breast, urging her tiny lips toward the nipple. Catherine felt the baby latch on. She looked down at the tiny creature and thought, *She's mine!* Then the most joyous feeling she'd ever known swept through her body and settled inside her heart.

The midwife pressed on Catherine's stomach and she groaned.

It seemed that her insides were slipping outside her body. Then Granny Tilley lifted a beefy, bloody substance.

Catherine shuddered at the sight, and the old granny assured her, "You can eat the afterbirth, my dear, in a stew."

"Eat me oewn body!" She felt bile rise in her throat.

"It's not your body, but what your body made from itself. It'll nourish you."

"I'll take nourishment from the fish in the sea, and the food on land," Catherine declared. "The crows can have this."

The midwife shrugged. "I'll take it for myself." She dropped the placenta in a pail she had brought with her. "It's a good healer for burned flesh."

Catherine shook her head and turned back to her baby, sighing. Her look went from the baby's raised arm to a scar, like a speckle down her own upper arm, where a flanker had burst from a fire and pitched on her skin when she was a child. She hoped no harm would come to her daughter. "Bridget is what I'll name you – after me oewn mudder, and after the patron saint of Ireland. You'll have an Irish saint to protect you," she murmured.

After Catherine was washed and settled with a bellyband tightened around her middle, the granny told her, "Pull tight now, and keep pulling tight." Despite her soreness, Catherine willed her belly to pull to her backbone, hauling herself tight, letting go and tightening over and over. "You'll need to keep a good, strong body for other babies," the granny advised her.

John came in and Catherine lifted the baby for him to hold. He looked into her face as if stunned. "You don't look like me then."

"Not in certain parts," the granny said bluntly. "You've got yourself a little girl." The granny turned and smiled down at Catherine. "You're at the beginning of children. Get your rest now."

John passed the baby to Ruth and went out. He came back with a large knife. He reached toward one of the heavy beams in the ceiling and made a cut. "I've chopped me first beam to mark the occasion of my eldest child," he said proudly, looking toward his daughter. "Next year, I hope to chop the beam for a son. Sons belong to themselves; daughters belong to other men."

Neither woman answered. Instead, the granny set about getting the baby washed and oiled and settled in the cot by the hearth. Ruth made Catherine tea and soup. Both women promised to be back in the morning. The granny left a parting instruction. "Nine days abed. That's the custom here and we bides by it."

John was getting into bed when he turned startled at the sight of Catherine holding her head back with a cloth to her nose. Blood poured down her face. He rushed to an alcove in the wall and pulled out a wooden box.

"What's in the box, John?" Catherine asked, swallowing the rusty-tasting blood.

"Something belonging to me old mam," John answered. "She used it to stop nosebleeds and cuts, and to keep a baby from comin' too early."

John lifted the cover and brought the box to her. She peeped in, her eyes bright with expectation. She drew back puzzled. "A green string with a lead on it."

"It's a slug beaten in the shape of a heart and a hole made in it to hold the green string. You hold it between your lower lip and your gums while you recite a proverb penned there on brown paper at the bottom of the box. I can't read it, but I knows it by heart. You can't be havin' nosebleeds."

She gave John an amused smile. He scoffed at other people's superstitions, never acknowledging that he had some of his own. He placed the lead heart inside Catherine's lower lip and, holding the green string, he whispered in her ear words she couldn't decipher. John smiled in satisfaction when Catherine took the cloth from her nose and the blood had clotted.

Despite John's show of superstition, she decided to wait until he was nowhere in sight before she sewed a tiny pocket of salt on the baby's nightdress. She wanted to keep her baby safe from fairies that may have followed her from Ireland.

The next day, John went down the lane strutting like a rooster chuffed out. Catherine watched him through the window. *Even if John does not want me as a true wife, I am a true mother*, she thought defiantly.

The newborn's pure scent helped assuage reminders of Captain Murrey. She'd never tell John that sometimes when he came home with the smell of brine, fish, and cod oil on his clothes and skin, she had to push away reminders of the captain.

Soon the baby was letting out bubbles of laughter, drawing John in, drawing the three of them together. Catherine sighed in relief. *Now I have me very oewn family.*

ONE SUNDAY, GRANNY Tilley came to see how Bridget was doing. She followed Catherine into the room with a ready smile for Bridget in her cot, now three months old. Just as Catherine bent down to pick up the baby, Bridget let out a deep, cutting cry.

"She's gathered on the chest," said the midwife, hurrying back out to stir the fire under the pot. As soon as the pot boiled, she took a sprig of dried herbs from her apron pocket and dropped it into the cauldron. She poured a cupful and lifted it to the baby's face. Bridget's quick breaths drew in the steam and she settled. "Do this for the baby every time she gets fussy," the granny told Catherine.

What if something happens to her and she not baptized? Catherine thought, staring down at her sleeping baby long after the midwife had left. She made the sign of the cross over her, forgetting the Irish belief that it was bad luck to make the sign of the cross over a child not baptized.

She leaned against the doorpost, her lips parted with the question John knew she was about to ask. "I'll not have the baby baptized," he told her stubbornly. "We're not married."

"But we live in one house, lie in the same bed, become one whenever you want," she cried. "You will taste Cartlic flesh and spit, but you won't have a Cartlic for your wife."

He turned a stiff jaw toward the fireplace and Catherine decided then that she would not have another baby unless John gave his word that the baby would be baptized.

That night, Catherine sat on the gaze, thinking about moths as a host of them flittered through the air. She wondered what would happen to Bridget if she died not christened. The Irish believed that piskies took the souls of unchristened babies. These lost children appeared at twilight as little white moths.

"My flower-of-an-hour," she murmured, thinking of the bright mallow flower back home. Bridget's little red lips puckered when she was full of milk. Her blue eyes seemed to follow Catherine. Soon she would be saying, "Mam, Mam." To be spoken to by the child of her own flesh, and feel the warmth of soft arms around her neck, these were the treasures she had been looking forward to, and wouldn't be able to stand losing.

After nights of waking out of her sleep with a wail that startled John awake, and he tired from being on the water the day before, he made a promise to her, that should there be other babies, he would have them churched.

"To keep the peace," he later told his brother Edward, now back from Labrador.

"Sure b'y, John," Edward answered, knowing it was Catherine who would have to keep the peace in that house.

THE NEXT SPRING brought a disappointing start for fishermen. Despite the cold weather, John readied his nets early and got them in the water. He cursed when he saw schools of jelly squalls moving along with the tide, turning the water white. As John and his men pulled the nets, streamers of the sea nettles came across their arms, stinging them and leaving painful red welts. John brought his dirtied nets ashore, grumbling about the gelled white squalls he called sea blubber. Deep sea wrinkles fastened to the nets showed thin shells – a sign of scarce fish. He told his brother, "I think, Edward, 'tis on the Labrador coast I'll be headed to this summer, along with yourself. There's no fish to be had in Conception Bay with all the cold water. I'll be sure of fish in Labrador. I'll look around to see if there's a chance of me starting a fishing premises there."

John promised Catherine, "Once we have a good fishing season, we'll start a bigger house, one without the spirit of the old mam in it."

Catherine didn't want to forget the old mam, who had come from Ireland as a young girl with apple seeds sewn into her pockets. She had set the seeds in the ground and spread caplin around them. It was years before they sprouted and grew into trees that bloomed with apples. Catherine picked them for her cakes and tarts. She blessed the old mam for other things. She had shown Catherine how to put in hop barm to get her bread started. Then there was her money.

Catherine remembered the old mam telling her, "A woman spends herself hanging on to life – her knuckles at the washboard – reaching to hang and gather clothes on the line – fighting with fierce wind and rain while her frozen fingers gut fish. She runs through her years under a man, begetting his children and pushing them out. She spends her life, and at the end she dies alone. Everyone else bees busy getting what they can from life – never thinking their end is around the bend."

"But a woman often leaves someone, Grandmudder," she whispered now, as she bent to the soft scent of her baby. "She leaves someone to carry on the colour of her eyes, the sparkle of her smile, the pith of her oewn self. No one is ever truly done with life. I'll carry the memory of you from my first summer here."

John cut into pine to make a Labrador box for the summer voyage of 1818. "I'll not be making a habit of going to Labrador," he told Catherine as he attached rope handles and connected the lid to the back with iron strap hinges. "I'll soon be staying home to handle me business, and this box'll come in handy for me money and books. This summer, though, I'm letting John Jacob and Thomas Martin use the western boat in exchange for supplies."

Catherine cautioned John, "You know the proverb, 'Don't get into a puncheon when a barrel can hold you.'"

On the tenth day of June, all the fishing vessels geared for

Labrador sailed away. Catherine watched the boat carrying John disappear from the horizon. With John gone, Catherine had time to marm about the place wheeling Bridget in a baby buggy, and chatting with other young mothers having an idle moment. She nodded to mothers who carried babies laced to their backs while they lifted and spread salted fish on rocks and flakes. Those whose bellies were full again showed the strain of growing a baby while carrying a baby as they helped make fish to feed their families.

Catherine took milk and eggs to Cat Breen who had just lost her husband, Jude, on the fishing grounds. Now Jude's brothers were harassing her to get out of the Breen family home with her young son. The young woman trembled as she told Catherine that she was looking to go back to Brigus and stay with an elderly aunt. She had lost her husband and everything belonging to him, even a share in his late father's fishing premises.

John was gone a month when Catherine woke in the dead of night, to wind screeching against the windows and swirling around the house as if it would carry it off. She looked out the window at a mad sea. Bridget whimpered and Catherine took her in bed beside her. She thought of the house nestled in the hills of Carrick-on-Suir, and not a wave of sea to be seen.

Nine

WHEN John came back from Labrador, he had his nature all the time. Catherine gave herself to it, biding her time. Then she freed herself from him and he fell back into a spell of snores, his sea legs on the twitch.

One Sunday morning, she tiptoed to the door, opened it quietly and shut it behind her. She stood on the gaze, taking in the calm scene of a bay with not a breath of wind to make the water shiver. The quiet haven lay like a looking glass, mirroring little boats resting after making their way out the bay all week. Now their little canvas sails were tightly lashed and their owners lay asleep.

Wild birds flittered about and pitched on the boats, undisturbed by sudden noises that often made them take flight. A crow, in an apse tree overhanging a barn, let out a loud, thick caw, startling the birds into flight.

Catherine sighed and went back inside the house.

That evening, she looked toward John asleep on the daybed by the fire. She sat beside him and rubbed her hand across his forehead and through his dark, curly hair. He stirred, and she murmured, "So far, this has been a good year." She turned a tender look toward the cot where Bridget slept peacefully.

Later, as she lay in bed beside John, she felt wind tunnel through the house as if it were her grandfather's voice warning her not to marry the Englishman. For one moment she wanted to run. *We are good together sometimes*, she told herself. *Before next summer I hope to be wed.*

While John was on the water, fishing for herring and mackerel to smoke, Catherine had Granny Tilley baptize Bridget. "She's baptized in God's eyes, but it's not in the books," Granny told Catherine.

"God's got Hes oewn book," Catherine said as she made the sign of the cross over her child and recited the rosary. "Bless you, child," she added in earnest. "May you always be in health, and left to bide on earth until your full years be spent."

The baby's crystal blue eyes opened wide and her lips pursed as if to give a kiss.

"A koob you're wanting to give your mamma," Catherine said, bending to fill her baby's neck and face with noisy kisses.

One night, Catherine stood outside and watched the place darken as home fires were banked and lanterns and candles in houses around the meadow were quenched. At a window here and there, a soft flicker of light spoke of hands relighting a lantern or candle. The glow steadied itself to burn brightly, showing a mother or father standing to a family's needs after darkness had crept over the place. Catherine stirred to the ocean yawning and heaving like a beast too restless to sleep, its innards stirred by living creatures, its skin licked by gentle winds.

October came and went, its days closing fast. Soon another winter would come. There was a cozy settling as the earth fell asleep. The smell of woodsmoke rising in chimneys all over the harbour brought a tangy scent to the cold air.

John had the cellar stowed full of vegetables by November. The smoked salmon and herring were staked in the smokehouse. Wood brought from Kelly's Island was piled in the shed to ensure that the wood bin by the hearth would be filled all winter.

Bareneed fishermen had their squaring-up day with the merchants, and no matter how hard they worked, many fishermen could not balance their accounts. Some of them grumbled that they had brought enough fish to the merchants' warehouse to pay their account, but most of them could not read or write; they could not prove their complaints. Sometimes a fisherman lost his land to the merchant. John grimaced wherever he heard of another fisherman losing his property. "That won't happen to me," he told Catherine. "I'd take a man's head before I'd have him take me land."

ONE MORNING, AFTER John had been to the barn to feed the animals, he came inside, stamping the first fall of snow off his waddies. "The devil's blanket is out there this marnin! 'Tis snowing be the rip," he muttered, "and only November. A long winter's comin'."

That night, Catherine drew the heavy curtains around the bed and tied the string at the bottom of the curtain box, to keep out cold air from frost gathering on the window. Then she tied a curtain box for Bridget's cot.

Mid-December, John leaned against the doorpost and eyed Catherine as she sat knitting mittens and socks for Christmas boxes. "I've made a dancing master for Bridget's Christmas box," John said. Without another word, he went out to the shed, and came back with his present. Catherine smiled as he set the wooden puppet in motion. She thought, *Maybe he loves his little girl as much as he would have loved a boy.*

As they sat for supper, Catherine smiled at John. "We'll have a grand Christmas. I'll make creamed salt cod for the eve of Christmas and bake a duck, pudding, and Irish bread for Christmas Day."

"Thomas Butler is having a grand party – a New Year's party at The Castle," John said casually.

Catherine looked up, her eyes dreamy. "A place I'd like to get inside," she said, thinking of the large mansion with its conservatory, fine peaked roof, and widow's walk. "You'd want to be a Butler, wouldn't you, John?" she asked, thinking, *Livyers look up to those with money, and the power it gives them.*

He shot back. "No, I wouldn't then. The Snows have been here as long as the Butlers. Samuel Butler controlled Butler Island between Ship Cove and Port de Grave Harbour as far back as anyone can remember, and had the best farmland on the Avalon Peninsula with three plantations. But," John bragged, "my forefathers were the Western Adventurers. They sailed from Devon through seas infested with pirates to build fishing plantations here. Maybe it's true that me father rescued the old mam from pirates – and she but a little Irish girl stolen from her home."

John believes a story when he wants to impress someone, Catherine thought. Still, she wondered where the old mam had acquired coins that included ducats.

John shook his head, his eyes showing admiration. "You can't take it from the Butlers though. 'Tis in the Butler logbooks that by 1677 the kingly Butler had fifty-three servants."

"Sure," Catherine retorted. "It was easy to get penniless and starving young men off the ships coming from England and Ireland. Samuel likely fattened them with cod britchins and sounds, and drew their sweat every day of their lives."

John went on. "He built a stone castle in the harbour – the talk of the place. It went to ruins after Old Sam died. But here he is now – Thomas Butler – taking after his ancestor and building a wooden castle. He puts off a party every New Year."

"The likes of us would never get invited to that big house," Catherine murmured wistfully.

John grinned. "If you're biting at the bit to go to the party you'll be going, I can tell you that."

"I will?" Catherine's eyes widened in disbelief.

John gave her a smug look. "I'm comin' up in the world, you know. I'm doin' business with Thomas Martin and John Jacob. I've got the invitation and Ruth has already agreed to take Bridget to her place."

Catherine smiled down at Bridget. The little girl looked up through a fleet of dark curls falling around her face and babbled, "Mam, Mam."

Catherine turned back to John and tilted her chin. "I'll be goin' on your arm, John. Don't be thinking you can have me hired out as a servant. I'm your woman now and I'll not be someone's maid."

On the eve of New Year's Day, John went up to the attic and came down with a high-collar black jacket and black pants. He pulled out a white shirt from under the jacket. As he buttoned it up and hooked on a starched collar he sliered at Catherine. "Since we met, time has gone with a gallop, hey Kit."

"More like a trot," she retorted, looking at John dressed in his best clothes and as handsome as you please, while she pulled out her best blue wool dress. She would wear it with a silk shawl John had brought her from St. John's last fall.

John cocked an eye. "You can do with something better than that frock. Look under the bed."

"Under the bed?" Her dark brows lifted.

"Yes, there's a New Year's box for you, kept for this very night, and fittin', seeing you're not bulging with child."

"And that I'm not then, but 'tis no thanks to you." Her blue eyes flashed and she dropped to her knees and lifted the woollen counterpane. She pulled out a wooden crate and raised its cover. The sight of a damask dress as bright as spring partridgeberries made her gasp. She lifted it out and the skirt unfolded into scarlet red swirls. She had always made her own dresses. Now she had a ready-made new dress, and as far as she knew she wasn't carrying another baby.

Catherine slipped the new dress over her head. It dropped fluidly over her belly and hips and fell in elegant folds to the planked floor. A white lace inlay in the bodice set off Catherine's full breasts. Sleeve trimmings at the wrists showed off her long fingers. John's look flicked over her face and dropped to her belly where it lingered. "There's something about you," he groaned, "the way you pushes out your hip – a healthy thrust it is to put the heat between me thighs, and I'm thankful for loose brigs more than once."

Her look swept over John's face in a moment of tenderness.

He can be kind and thoughtful, a man I could love. Taking in his handsome face and muscled body, she felt a stir. She dismissed it as she swirled the dress around her.

She passed John a black choker to hapse at the back as she lifted her hair above her long, white neck.

"Not too tight now, John. Don't choke me."

After a few clumsy efforts he fastened the clasp. He came around to face her. "You're dancing *only* with me, tonight," he told her, his jaw tightening, and his eyes taking on a dark look. His hands went to the black choker around her neck and dropped to the tiny crystal hanging from it.

Her eyes, under soft, thick lashes, clouded like a weather moon. "If you want it that way," she answered quickly. She sat on a chair to pull on her long black boots and button them. Tendrils of hair trailed down her forehead as she looked up and asked, "Will I do?"

"Do what?"

"Do you."

His hands slipped to her waist. "I can no longer span your waist with me fingers. Sure when you marled off the ship, I could have wrung you in two pieces."

"A lot of good I'd ben then."

He laughed. "I'd take the half without the tongue."

"And lose me heart," she teased.

John glanced out the window and called back to Catherine, "I hear carriage bells. John Jacob is on the go to the party, or. . . . Wait now," he added indulgently. "There's a carriage stopping outside."

"A carriage?" Catherine said, puzzled.

John turned quickly from the window. He picked up Catherine's coat and set it around her shoulders. She hurried her arms into the red woollen coat and tied on the matching red bonnet. She slipped her hands into her gloves, and John grabbed her hand. "Come on, why don't you, Irish girl."

John hurried her from the room. They stepped out the door, laughing for their lives.

Catherine's eyes widened at the sight of the Butler carriage. It was the grandest thing, and rarely seen outside the large porch off the Butler castle. "Well, the like of that!" she exclaimed. "The Castle's not far, John. You needin have done that. Sure we could've walked."

"What! And have you mess your dress! We'll do good business this year and every year after, and we'll have means," John promised. "You should be glad not to have to live like Clarice. Sure she works at whatever she can. She'd live in a pigsty with Frank Coveyduct, a Jack of one thing or another."

Catherine had sold eggs to Clarice last summer and sat with her for a chat. She had eyed Frank as he darkened the door, read his look as he lowered his lanky frame to get in under the lintel. She could see that he looked forward to coming into his tiny house, his look pitching on Clarice with a soft twinkle. She met his look with a saucy one. She always had a saucy look about her, and she used it on Frank, to his delight. "Always the same, dear Frank is," Clarice had told her. "Never having mean spells like some men."

Like John, Catherine had thought.

The Butler carriage was upholstered in royal blue velvet. Animal skins lay folded, ready to cover the passengers and keep out drafts. Frank, a man of various jobs, was the coachman for the night. He lifted his hat with a smile that reached his eyes, his agreeable face showing under the soft light of one of the two lanterns mounted on the carriage. Frank lifted Catherine's hand as if she were a high lady and helped her step up to the cushioned seat. He settled her dress and coat and wrapped her knees with fur rugs. John caught the brass rail to the side and swung himself in beside Catherine. Then Frank hurried to his own round seat in front and, with a crack of his whip, the horse was off, its feet clopping the packed snow.

The harbour was in a restless mood, its air fresh and cool as the horse and carriage stopped by "The Castle," alight with lanterns from the road to the door. There were thick railings along a walkway to the house. Inside the first door to the side of the mansion, Catherine noticed a sleigh as beautiful and as comfortable as one could ask for, just brought back from the Butler youngsters' randy around the harbour.

"The Irish Butlers got the English way of trying to lord over all their eyes espy," John said as he helped Catherine from the carriage. Frank called after them, "I'll be back fer yers by midnight whether you're ready or drunk." He turned to yank the horse's reins. "Giddy-up!"

As John and Catherine walked up the path, a simpleton everyone called Webbed Eyes went by, a Jack tar on his head – a tarred cloth hat he'd likely gotten from a sailor. He muttered, "A roomful, a houseful, and they couldn't catch a spoonful." He laughed and laughed and then he yelled, "Smoke, that's what they can't catch."

"Aye then, keep your mouth shut," a passerby told him. "'Tis mummering you're not, with that bare-arsed face on yer."

His look darted about, and he ran off, muttering to himself.

Clarice was in uniform, offering polite greetings as John and Catherine entered the house. She explained that the mistress was laid up with a sick headache, but the master was present. Catherine's look pitched on Thomas Butler who was talking business with John Jacob. Catherine recognized other guests. There were Thomas and Emma Martin, Robert Pinsent, Robert Prowse and Jane Woodley, John Bowes, the Dawes, Andrewses, and Taylors. Amy Taylor's pinched face was yawny-looking, as if she hadn't seen the sun for a good while, though she had lovely hair flowing down her back like the soft, shiny fur of a muskrat. Sarah Winthrop's forehead held tendrils of hair drifting from a heavy flow falling on both sides from its centre part, reaching her shoulders in waves. An eyebrow flared upward when she saw Catherine. *I can stand to the best of them*, Catherine thought haughtily.

Catherine was eyeing the Brussels carpet, the haircloth reclining couches, and the marble lobby table holding silver candlesticks when Clarice brought a tray of assorted drinks. She passed the drinks around, stopping for Catherine to take a glass of swanky – a hot drink made from cranberry jam. Then she turned to the gathering. "I've a poem a lady on the Avalon has published."

Robert Pinsent gave her a derisive look. "I have a poem for you," he said in a slow and deliberate voice. "A silent tongue, my dear, is sweet to hear."

Clarice's mouth dropped shut. Her eyes clouded and she pressed the book to her bosom and walked past him into another room.

Catherine looked at the young fellow, his eyelids loose above rope-like rings under small eyes darting about. *An arrogant Englishman*, she thought, *the son of a merchant*. He was someone, John had said, who wanted to secure his financial position in the community. He gave Catherine a slight nod of his head as he went past her.

Catherine noticed a small book on the side table. She let her fingers roam over the brown cover and thought, *Clarice learned to read, and so can I.*

"It's the first book of poetry anyone in this colony has ever seen," Clarice whispered after she came back into the room. "A poet named Robert Hayman published *Quodlibets* in 1628."

Catherine was about to ask her what quodlibets meant when she heard the call to come to the next room for the first dance. She hurried to join the gathering and hear instructions given for those who had not done the square dance before. Her mind wandered off when she saw John giving Sarah Winthrop an attentive eye. She wondered if Sarah had been one of John's women before her – if she was still a woman he saw on the sly. ". . . hold hands; go left; go right. Ladies come in raising hands. Shout Hurrah! Ladies go out; men come in. . . ."

Catherine pushed aside her thoughts and looked into John Jacob's dark eyes as he danced toward her. She smiled at him, though she had an uneasy feeling – as if he might try to do her harm some day. She knew he disapproved of John carrying on with a Catholic. He had come with Rebecca Maley, a slim young woman with a shapely, delicate face and a small nose above full red lips. Almost stumbling, Catherine turned back to a voice: "Grab your partner, swing around. Stop! Stomp! Hurray!" When the dance ended, she sat down light-headed.

Catherine felt like a spirited creature as she got up for the second dance. She let her body loose. Her hands rested on her hips and then slid down her flanks as she danced across from John, their looks latching together. She sat down after the lively dance and was letting out a satisfied breath when she felt a quick dizzy turn. She closed her eyes and let her heart settle.

Clarice passed around a second tray of drinks. She looked at Catherine and asked, "Will you take a glass of claret then, a more respectable drink than port this year?"

John came from behind her where he and Sarah had exchanged a quick laugh. "Will a fish swim?" he asked, winking.

"It's a fish's nature, so he will, but what's your excuse for drinking?" Catherine said, her eyes flashing at John for inferring that she was the drinker.

John scowled and barbed, "I could tell you had enough tongue to fill out your face the first time I clapped eyes on you."

"And I knowed you'd have enough acid in your tongue to burn a hole through the sides of your oewn face," she lipped. She hurried away before John got ornery enough to fight her with more than his tongue when they got home. She wanted to be starting the new year in peace.

She looked back to see guests gathering around to watch a challenge. Each man was to stand on one leg while drinking calibogus – a mixture of rum, molasses, and spruce beer. The man to stand the longest would be the champion. Catherine knew that if John failed the test and another man with a more steady leg beat him, she would suffer his foul temper. Each man raised a glass and drank it to the king, and then another. John gulped his glass and emptied two more. His leg began to shake after the third drink.

She wanted to call, "Stop it, John! Put down your hand before you go legless." Instead, she closed her mouth on a truffle she had taken off a tray Clarice was passing around.

John Jacob had missed out on the challenge. Now he swaggered across the room. Catherine glanced at the planter. Then her eyes widened as he knocked John on the back, sending him sprawling. The man's thin face spread wide in laughter. John didn't say anything. His friend might have saved him the embarrassment of losing to a merchant.

No one, it seemed, was a match for Protestant merchant Robert Prowse, the last man standing. He was an accomplished boxer and a distance walker, used to tackling the almost half-a-day trek from Port de Grave to political meetings in Harbour Grace. He was on the hand of establishing a business on a knob of hill overlooking Port de Grave Harbour, land owned by the Butlers. He boasted that one day the area in front of his house would be paved with cobblestones. He was already raising livestock and producing hay and oats on a large marsh everyone called Prowse's Marsh.

It was late when John and Catherine left the Butler castle for home. Catherine lifted her skirts and climbed into the carriage. Then, as the *clap clop* of the horse's hooves sounded and the carriage bells rang out, she felt her stomach churn.

Catherine stepped from the carriage and threw up.

Book II

"The ancient saying is no heresy;
Hanging and wiving goes by destiny."

William Shakespeare
Merchant of Venice, Act II, Scene IX

Ten

LIFE slowed again during the dark winter months. There was little to-ing and fro-ing between settlements. Doors to domestic dwellings weren't opened as often. Paths that were filled with people going about outdoor work when the ground was bare were now narrowed by piles of snow and used mostly by people on horse-drawn sleds. Women dwelt on housework and fishermen worked in store lofts, readying themselves for the spring fishery. It was early to bed and late to rise for the livyers who looked forward to the end of winter's early nights. Catherine enjoyed the time she and John spent together rising out of a late sleep to each other's needs and to Bridget's chatter.

Bay ice thinned under a spring thaw and disappeared. Then, after hard gales from the northeast, Catherine opened her door to the dawning day. The sun, a banked fire behind the night sky, broke behind clouds in soft, muted light. She stared at the ocean of northern ice spread out as far as she could see. The icy dome of the sky met the icy seascape seamlessly. "I could walk my way to Ireland over that land of ice," she told John.

He grunted. "The ice come down from Labrador and is not nigh Ireland. Ice is not what I wants to see unless it's bedded with seals. We could be asleep at night and it come in quick and take the legs off the stage and leave with our barrels of fish blubber."

John hurried down to the stage and out over the stagehead with his spyglass. He knew that seals napped in a familiar place on ice, each creating a cradle from its body's heat. He was disappointed.

Then the ice broke and the sea, seeming to sleep under a quilt stitched in ice blocks, awakened, stirred, rose up. Patches of blue-hued ice slammed against each other and rose in uneven chunks. By afternoon, ice had loosened and pulled apart to bob and shift its way out, leaving the bay holding orphaned bergs. Pieces of ice driven onto the beach by easterly winds melted slowly.

John grumbled when spring rains came slopping down windows and eaves and popping holes in the bay, as if gunshots were raining down.

Catherine smiled. "Spring rains'll bring timothy grass and clover for the fall harvest." She eyed a bunch of purple crocuses already bursting through the ground of straw grass. She imagined wind sweeping clay into open pockets of cliff, and tongues of wind lifting flower seeds and dropping them into the drifts of clay. Rain would press them down to burrow underneath. The quiet warmth of the sun would coax them to life, to spring up in a yellow nod or bluebell – to dance in winds that helped them be.

A summery day surprised everyone one morning. Doors opened and children scooted out. Dogs followed. Laughter and barking mingled in the salty air.

Children called to each other, "Hurry on!"

Dandelions were sprouting through the grass and Catherine and Ruth filled their baskets, eager for the greens to be boiled down for a spring relish. Old Martha Porter was digging for the root. Libe Porter had been yellow-faced of late, and she believed that an ingested dandelion root was the only proper cure. She struggled with the root, complaining that it was as deep as a fairy's hole. She soon held the gnarled root up in triumph. Then she kept going back for more.

Livyers like Lene Lear often went over the hills, children tailing her with pooked lips, vexed at the task their mothers were calling them to. Lene would be all in a crump, trying to wrestle stumps from the bogs to keep her fires going during the chill of early summer.

John settled his wooden lobster pots in the bay, their parlours ready for mornings and evenings, when there was no sea or swell and lobsters came out of their holes to feed. John liked to catch lobsters on a full moon, a time when the meat was packed tight. Fishermen who didn't have lobster pots worked their gaffs – poles with hooks attached to catch lobsters. The green crustacean was a poor man's food, the merchants claimed, and they didn't want to buy it. Catherine boiled lobsters until the shells turned as bright as an apricot sunset. She and John sat with a lobster each, slipping the white slab of meat from the slit tail and breaking the claws to get the claw-shaped meat. They drenched the flesh in melted butter or fried it in pork scrunchions. Catherine liked to haul "the old woman" out of the body, tear open the sac, clean it and turn back the veil. She imagined her as Mary, queen of the world, sitting in a regal chair, reigning forever.

One calm afternoon, following a morning when the cantankerous sea had kept fishermen ashore, Catherine took Bridget and climbed the shed loft to the strong, tangy smell of oakum and the lazy buzz of flies. Over John's shoulder she watched a spider in the window spin a web turning to gold under sunlight. A fly strayed too close to the waiting spider and was soon tied and wrapped in its gossamer web. *Poor fly*, thought Catherine. She looked past the web to the scene outside, of barked nets drying in careless sprawls on a grassy meadow under the hot sun, blades of grass sticking through the square holes, folding over themselves into triangular and parallel shapes.

John leaned against the wall. "You're here now then, Irish girl. Trawls are to be made ready and you'll learn." He showed Catherine how to knot a sud line and push it through heavier twine and loop back and down to sud it through a hook. She helped ring the trawls in a half-sized barrel after she watched John's strong hands make a sweep around the tubs, laying layer after layer until the tubs were full. Bridget sat on the floor, happily playing with an oakum rope.

Women watched punts and skiffs sail out into the bay with their sails abroad, waiting for their return with fresh fish to fry. The fishermen who came home with a fine catch bounced up the path, their eyes wide and bright, their strong voices ringing out news of their haul. The fishermen who had little or no fish, or had their nets torn into by sharks, came up the path on heavy feet, their eyes lowered, their voices low or silent. The fishermen who had lots of fish could only boast for the day. Tomorrow it could be them grieving and glutching in hunger.

"WHAT'S WRONG?" JOHN asked one spring morning as he came in from the stage to where Catherine leaned on the half-door, her face white. "What makes you get the heaves so early in the day?"

"I'm having another child. You know it."

"I do – and the piss-pot tells it."

"I've been throwing up me liver and lights almost every morning. 'Tis as sick as sick I am, and no cure for months. I'd thought I was in child after I threw up the night we left the Butler Castle, but that was not so. 'Twas likely the food then. But the baby will be here before November."

"Hurry then and get the pots emptied."

Catherine gave John a cranky look and then she went to empty the chamber pots into a slop pail. She carried it to the outhouse hanging over the cliff and dumped its contents to be swiftly flushed by the sea. She looked to the side of the road where mangy cats tissed and snarled at each other. Beside a tilt in the valley, young, curly-haired Tildie Hussey tottered outside a shed, running after a hen with both hands, as if she wanted to squeeze an egg out of it. "Don't touch the fowl, Tildie," Catherine called. "It will peck your hand." There was no sign of Tildie's mother.

That night, Catherine lay in bed beside John and imagined another cut in the beam to mark her second child's birth. *Another child coming,* she thought, *and I not wed.* Her lips tightened; her eyes looked anxious. *Jesus, Mary and Joseph help me. I can't fuss with John now. He'll hit me and frighten the baby out.*

Catherine slipped out of bed before dawn and stood staring out the window as day cracked open like an egg, spilling its yolk on the egg-white rim of the ocean. She looked out across the bay to distant ships passing, moving silently, it seemed. It was Sunday morning and the place and its people slept – except for Catherine. She stayed at the window a long time assailed by uneasy feelings.

SPRING SLIPPED INTO summer and the harbour filled with young children letting out ripples of laughter as they splashed ankle deep in salt water out from the beach. Older boys, wearing a string of corks around their waists, swam out into the bay, careful not to be in the path of an incoming boat.

Every time a boat came home with gunnels low, the Bareneed women's hearts gladdened that their men were drawing the season's treasure trove out of the sea. Each load of fish they helped clean and cure lessened the threat of a hungry winter for their families.

On warm days, Catherine hurried to the stagehead with Bridget in her arms. Now the little girl clapped her hands as John's boat drew near the stage.

"We've got a sagger of fish," John called proudly.

"A boatload, John?" Catherine asked.

"I tell you, the pounds are full and overtopped. John Jacob is gone to meet with merchants in St. John's to determine the price of fish according to market value. I hope 'twill be fine."

Catherine asked, "And what will you be gettin' for all your work? The merchants'll have the profit."

"Rest yer mind, Catherine. I'm adding up an account from me western boat."

Catherine remembered seeing John go off to the barn with a locked box under his arm that he wouldn't let her see inside. Now she sat Bridget, with her rag doll, in a playpen John had fastened to the stage. Here she could watch her father and mother work and listen to their voices. Catherine hurried to slip on her barbel as John's boat brought up against the stage with a gentle bump. He cast his painter ashore and climbed the stage to fasten it to a gump pole.

Catherine's hand went to her belly. *John is waiting for a son, a son to grow up and help him in the boat. If he doesn't get a son, he'll come with a face as long as a foggy day.*

SUNDAY BROUGHT AN idleness in the harbour that had nothing to do with inclement weather. Some fishermen stayed on land to give holy dues to their Creator; others stayed ashore for fear that the Almighty would set the sea on them if they didn't honour the day of rest. Secretly, many men enjoyed the respite from labour, to hold their women's softness against their hardness, some hoping to have the pleasure of a woman's body without springing a child inside.

John smirked when he mentioned to Catherine that the Reverend Nicholas Devereaux was on the Harbour Grace wharf asking, parishioners not to work on Sundays. "The priest is common like the rest of us."

Catherine bit her bottom lip, anxious that John not talk about a man of God like that. What if he got wind of it and cursed her baby?

In August, boats went out on the tide, the fishermen using bare jiggers. The cod had full guts from eating caplin. There was no need to waste good bait. Still, the cod often turned away from the jigger, staying close to the sea's bottom.

When the squid came inshore, John told Catherine, "Leave Bridget with Ruth. I'm takin' you squidin'. You'll be frying tails and rings for supper. There's nothing sweeter fried in their own juices."

Catherine sat across the thwart of the boat and watched the turn of John's oars as water rippled and giggled over them. She leaned over the gunnel and looked down through the wavering green water to smooth stones on the bottom looking alive and undulating. As the boat moved out into deeper, denser water, she turned back to look at John's healthy, tanned face above the rolled neck of his guernsey. She thought, *I could be happy.*

Boats were lined up all along the bay, ready with jiggers for a school of squid to come like orange globes shining under water. Suddenly there were shouts of "Squid O!" Catherine felt a tug on her jigger. She began to pull furiously, hand over hand. "Watch your face," John called just as the squid came out of the sea, sending black ink into Catherine's face. She sputtered and spat out the vile fluid, wiping her sleeves across her eyes. John grabbed her line and flung the pulsing squid into a fish box. Then he went back to pulling in squid as fast as he could work his line.

When John and Catherine came ashore, Catherine hurried to the linhay to change her clothes and wash. Then she went across to Ruth's house with a bucket of squid. When she brought Bridget home, John tried to put a squid in the little girl's hand. She squinched her eyes and pulled away. Catherine gathered the squid, their translucent orange skins turned grey, their lives gone. She cut off the heads and tentacles, cleaned the insides and peeled the skin, leaving the flesh lying like white sleeves to be cut into rings. The tails lay like kites.

John dropped all the leavings in a tray for the pigs to slobber through.

CATHERINE'S BELLY WAS rounding out, and as she gathered fish she had spread that morning on the flake, she thought of little Bridget having a brother or sister. She heard a soft, timid voice. "Mammy says you'm havin' a baby."

Catherine straightened up, rubbing her fist down her spine gone as stiff as a rod. She smiled at Jessie Rose, dabs of dirt stuck to her brown face. The little girl scuffed the dirt with her toe while she picked scabs off her head and ate them. Last summer, her heels had hung out of her wooden shoes, her bare heels scarred by stones and seashells. Now her woven brown dress danced in the wind around her bare calves above shoes too big.

"You've grown an inch," Catherine said, smiling at her. She thought, *My Bridget will never be as poor as Jessie Rose.* Wisps of hair blew into the child's mouth. Her white teeth clamped down on a strand as if it were food. She let go of it and pushed the wet hair away from her face as she answered Catherine shyly. "'Tis me new wooden shoes, ma'am, me fardher made." John would say there was not enough flesh on the girl to bait a hook, but it was likely her nature not to be fat no matter what she ate. Catherine knew the little girl might not have a chance to find out.

John was doing well enough. He could help the family, along with merchants like the Prowses and the Butlers who should show more coin to the poor. For now she'd give the child a fish. She climbed down from the flake and picked a fresh, uncut cod from a bucket John had left from his catch earlier that day. "Here," she said. "Stick your fingers in the eyes and run on home with it."

Jessie Rose grinned and grabbed at the fish. Catherine watched the little girl run across the beach, her heels criss-crossed with dirt and cuts. She ran, calling, "Mammy, Mammy," the clammy cold tail flapping against her legs.

Catherine smiled as she finished the fish and climbed the path to the house. She set about making dark Irish soda bread to go with the molasses beans she had left cooking for John's supper. When she was finished she stood in the doorway, watching John lather his brown, hairy arms as he washed up in the linhay. She blew stray hair off her forehead, thinking, *We live under one roof, sleep in one bed, have a child and another coming, and we're not wedded.*

The next day, easterly winds came fierce and John stayed on shore. By mid-morning, the winds had died down. Ann Snow, now twelve, came to mind Bridget. Catherine took the berry bucket to go over the hills to pick berries for jam and pies. She went on past John who was out by the wood horse sawing wood and piling it for winter. He called, "Where yer off to?"

"It's a foine day for berrying if 'tis not for fishing, and I've got the berry bucket," she answered saucily. She swung it by her side, her pockets holding a piece of hard bread to keep away the fairies as she followed the path to the berry bushes. Soon she was in over a neck of hills, her skirts and petticoat tails lifted to keep them from getting caught on gowithy bushes. She walked down a wide, dusty path cut into by horses and carts and dwellers centuries ago. It remained a living path for berry pickers and for planters looking to bring home sheep and goats left all summer to roam the hills and valleys.

Catherine stopped on a grey, ridged cliff forming the path on a knuckle of land. Here she felt as if she were standing in the blue depth of the sky. It surrounded her as she looked across the bay.

She walked down the point, its land spread like a lonely moor, little dips of land holding berry bushes. Now and then she spied someone's head bent to pick berries. Playful winds whispered through the grass like ghost voices tantalizing her ear, murmuring tales of buried treasure. The berry-scented wind roamed her face with its soft, refreshing touch. As she bent to grab a handful of velvety blueberries, she looked up to see sheep standing on the headland. In the distance she saw Jane Hussey's boys picking woollies from bushes that sheep had brushed against. Over the summer and fall, the animals obliged them with wool enough for their widowed mother to make wool stockings for the winter. "That crowd," John complained, "would steal scraps of food from the pigs."

Catherine had filled her bucket and was almost home when she saw John coming.

"Vamping about the place, eh?" he called with a mean cast to his voice.

"I was busy picking berries for the blueberry pudding you likes, and holding them in the wind to scatter leaves and twigs. Pick and clean berries at once, is my way."

She lifted her head from the berries, holding one velvet blue bead between her finger and thumb. "See, a nice and plump berry we're getting this year."

"'Tis high time you were home gittin' the supper on." John chased after her. She ran, lifting her skirt and petticoats, feeling the gowithy bushes scratch at her legs. She had left off her cotton stockings, knowing the bushes would needle them. Now she had skin cuts in stitches of blood. She fell, and John was on her, sucking the juice off her fingers and muttering, "I've got yer now, Irish girl." He thrust his hand up under her clothes.

She looked down at her rising belly. "You'll have to wait then. I'll not risk losing this baby or dropping it too early because of your nature."

His jaw tightened and his hand smacked against her cheek. She ignored the sting and got to her feet holding the bucket, not bothering to gather the berries she'd spilled. She pressed the cover down just as

John gave her a push. She went back down on a wide, flat rock. Wildflowers she had picked, careful to leave the roots in the ground for next year's flowers, now lay squashed on the rock. She left them lying there like a knot of spiders' legs while she picked up the covered bucket she had dropped. She made quick steps ahead of John, expecting any minute to be grabbed. To her relief he left her alone.

Soon Catherine was in the pantry, measuring the ingredients for a blueberry grunt. John lay stretched out on the daybed, waiting for supper, his eyes closed. Bridget toddled around, sometimes going to her father and crawling up on his chest.

"Hold her, John, don't let her fall," Catherine cautioned as John lay with his hands by his sides. As soon as the water was galloping in the pot she threw in the bagged blueberry pudding. It plopped down in water, swirling around salt beef that would add to its taste. In a half-hour, Catherine added new potatoes and a dark green cabbage, its sweet, pale heart split.

After John had eaten his supper, he looked at Catherine. "I'm on the bust, and it's your doing."

"I'm on the bust too, and it's your doin'." They both laughed. Bridget's lips pooked out. "Koob," she called, and giggled. Then she smacked her lips in a kiss.

After supper, Catherine bent down to scrape ashes from the fireplace, thinking how good she felt when the three of them broke into laughter at the same time. It didn't happen often, but when it did, Bridget was happier and less fussy.

Catherine filled an old pot with the ashes and water, bringing the mix to a boil to make blueberry soap. She put in a stick, and when it turned yellow and slippery she strained the ashes through a piece of thin muslin. She soon had strong, clear lye. Into it she dropped bits of seal fat and blueberry juice. She stirred the mixture into a taffy spin, careful not to let it boil over and start a fire. "We'll soon have our new batch of soap," she told John. "Lots of soap bees needed in this place where fish gurry sticks to clothes like turpentine."

Three days later, when Catherine dropped a bit of cold lye into the mix to make sure it was done, the soap floated to the top. Her soap was ready to cut and portion and let harden in the sun. John sniffed the air as he came into the pantry. Instead of a strong smell of lye soap, his nose caught the soft, muted scent of blueberries.

By September, John was keeping after Catherine to go in over the hills to pick partridgeberries for winter jam. She was getting too big to squat down and fill her pail with the berries John loved, so she knelt or sat every time she came to a thick patch. On her way up the path from the point, her skirts brushed past withe-rod berries, misty blue on shiny green leaves in summer, dull under crimson leaves by autumn. She slipped her fingers under soft heather and picked marshberries to pop into her mouth. They made her think of small cranberries wearing freckles. She stood up, squinting as she looked across the sea, as if to follow the path to Ireland. There was a sadness in this new world, but it was her home now and the place where her children would make their way. "With not too much hardship, please God," she whispered in the wind.

When Catherine got home, John was outside. He had Bridget standing in a small barrel to watch him as he sawed wood. He had already made a new wood horse to hold his logs while he sawed them in lengths for the hearth. Now he was building a wood gallows – a framework to stack the firewood. He glanced up as Catherine came toward him. His damp, curly hair, tangled with wood chips, clung to his forehead. A frown crossed his face as he stopped to unbutton his shirt, sweat clinging to dark chest hair like raindrops.

When Catherine got closer to the woodsy scent, she lifted her mouth for a kiss. John grabbed her head and smacked her hard and quick on the lips. He pushed her away so hard she almost went off her feet. She had likely been gone too long for his liking.

Eleven

CATHERINE was pinning clothes on the line the next morning when the sight of Mary Britt hurrying with a long face down the path made her drop the wooden peg she was holding in her mouth.

Mary called in a hoarse voice, "Aye, there's three dead down in the harbour this marnin. Freda Bussey lost her children."

Catherine turned, stunned.

"Yes, boys born and dead. All, clear one. It stirred to a breath but lost it. Stillborn they lie, and their mother with her hands over her belly is as pitiful a sight as her blue babies."

"Three less mouths to feed, I suppose," John offered as he stood diddling Bridget on his arm.

"Three less boys to grow up and feed her when she's left alone and can't feed herself," Mary retorted.

Catherine finished pinning the clothes on the line. Then she pulled off her apron and went down to see the babies. One baby had been chrisomed by Granny Tilley – wrapped in the shroud of a white cloth as a sign of innocence, and consecrated in the oil of baptism and sacrament. The corpses of his two brothers lay in a rough blanket. The dark-haired young mother lay white-faced and dazed-looking, her mournful eyes shadowed. She looked up, her face screwed in anguish. "I've nothing to show for me pain," she whispered.

Catherine rushed to console her. "'Tis not in vain. You've made bodies that God will fill with souls in heaven. Your babies will be right there with God. His angels will mudder them."

The latch on the door lifted and Ada Bussey from The Marsh rushed in. "I hear there's been babies born, but not sucklings. My milk's not in and me child is starving hungry. Will you give up your beestings?"

"Will you give up a shilling then?" the father asked harshly.

"Would you think I had as much as a shilling with the man on his back, his feet idle from sickness? I'm asking for charity instead of death for the babe. I'll find a way to give back."

"Here." Catherine pulled a silver coin from a little pocket in her dress.

"Thank you, ma'am," the woman said and curtsied in gratitude. She passed the coin to the father and he took it.

Catherine looked at Ada's mangy child hanging out of a tattered, dirty blanket, his legs scabbed. "Pick arrowroot, powder it and rub it on the baby's skin," Catherine advised the mother.

Ada just looked at her and Catherine shook her head. "Never mind. I've some at home you can have."

"Pass the child here," the grieving mother said, her voice wet with tears. She slipped out a breast, and a tiny mouth latched on. A tear rolled down the stricken mother's cheek, and then tears rained on the baby's head. The baby guzzled until he was full and then he shuddered and let go, as if falling away into himself. The nipple lay naked, like a raspberry under dew.

Queer-eyed Tom, the undertaker, scuffed his feet against the doorstep as he opened the door. He looked around the room, one eye glazed over like a cooked egg white. He'd been stabbed by his brother when they were children. The boy hadn't known his brother had fallen asleep in the hay he was pronging. Now the eyelid was covered in beads of flesh. Tom doffed his stovepipe hat with the words, "Sorry for yer trouble." He paused before asking, "What's the length of the corpse?"

"There's no length to be measured here," the father answered, looking up from where he sat on a low stool. "We'll do the deed ourselves."

The undertaker looked disappointed as he backed out the door, leaving it open. Catherine got up to close it. She came back to kneel by the bed of the childless woman who sniffled, "Why, my babies?"

The granny shook her head. "Too many babies crowded each other. 'Tis a healthy body you have; you can bear more children."

"I don't know what it's like to have a baby born to his own silence. I know there is life after, and hope," Catherine said softly. The words ended like a promise to herself, her hands moving down over her belly, cupping it.

Later, from her bedroom window Catherine watched little boats rocking across the water, white and brown sails holding a gentle wind. A peaceful sight. But the sounds of a mother crying for her lost babies still rang in her ears. She turned back with Bridget in her arms, her eyelashes fluttering under a gentle sigh as she slipped into sleep. She laid her child in her cot. Its staves creaked against the planked floor and settled. Catherine drew in the most peaceful sight of all – a sleeping baby.

CATHERINE'S SECOND DAUGHTER was born in October. "Sweet, sweet child," she murmured as she held the tiny being against her breast. "May you have sweet dreams."

Ann Snow had been down on the stage, waiting for John to come off the water. She called to him as he was tying the boat to the stage. "The baby's ben born."

He climbed the rails and smacked a kiss on the young girl's face. Then he rushed up the path and into the house, past Ruth who was stirring the fire, and on into the side room. He looked at Catherine hopefully and asked, "What have we here?"

Catherine hesitated, her voice caught in her throat. Then she spoke hardly above a whisper. "A girl."

John turned away with a back remark. "You can name the maids. I'll name the fellars, if we ever get them. You've got the hips for cradling babies, so there's hope."

"Eliza Frances is named for your mudder," she said, hardly breathing for fear he'd change his mind and slap the names from her mouth with his own choice.

He turned back. "I'll have a son yet."

She smiled. "You will, that! Hold her," she urged, pulling the cayla back.

John took the howling little mite, his face softening. "You've got the lungs of a strong wind. I dare say you'll be me sally boy."

"I want her christened by the church," Catherine told John.

"And she will be," John promised, "once you're over the birth, and the harvesting is done. It'll be right after the western boat is back. I'll have me trip to St. John's first. Women bees waitin' on yard goods and ribbons, and the men twine to mend the nets and trawls, and oakum to caulk the boats in spring. You'll be wantin' raisins to soak in rum for your Christmas cake. I want to be the first boat to reach St. John's and the first boat back home. But we will christen sally boy."

TOWARD THE END of October, burnished red hills looked as if a fire had swept over them, and easterly winds took on a fierce bite. Gulls made harsh cries in the early morning air as fishermen sailed home with their catches. There were fewer boats out now that fall and winter work was on the fishermen. John was getting ready for his last catch of the season. This time he wanted a load of mackerel and salmon to smoke for the winter.

"Last night the sky showed for winds today," Catherine warned. "You best stay on land."

"I won't then!" John snapped. "I don't plan on gettin' in a tight spot like Jude Dawe down in the harbour. He's got a week before his plantation is to be auctioned off beneath his feet."

Catherine sighed as she laid Eliza in her basket. "There's always people with enough wanting more. Then one day they try to reach beyond their grasp. They end up in a little bit of ground sealed with sod."

"That's all I'll own if I don't get out in the boat," John answered.

Catherine thought of their conversation after John left. Bridget followed her around while she gathered vegetables from the garden. She stood up, weak from a heavy flow of blood. She took Bridget inside the house. Wind, carrying rain like streamers of ghostly cloth, howled around the windows, its mournful voice cutting into her until she felt herself open to a cold draft. She muttered, "Bansheé winds, and John out on the water."

The thought that John could be lost to the sea brought a sweep of loneliness. If he didn't come home, his brothers would likely come down on her for the land and fishing room. John had told her, "We don't bother much with each other. None of us Snows do. We needs our hands for work instead of at each other's throats."

Catherine couldn't think of her and her babies turned out of doors. She dropped her head to the sight of her children. John would be home. He was strong, energetic, alive. She couldn't imagine him any other way.

Catherine scraped a salmon, its scales clinging to her hands like tiny silver moons. She washed it and dropped it, with onions and fatback, into a pot and hung the container on the cotterel above a roaring fire. She lifted it on a high notch to let the fish stew simmer, knowing John would be on the sea longer than on most days.

Catherine's forehead furrowed with worry as she sat at the window, holding baby Eliza to her bosom while Bridget played with her doll on the floor. That afternoon, she saw a vessel that looked like John's boat cutting across the bay. Its sail cracked like a whip as the boat blew into the harbour. It wasn't John. Catherine went outside and stood calling his name as if he could hear her, the wind blowing her breath back against her nose in a smothering gust. She put her daughters to bed and came back out, her lips stiff with cold and grief. She wasn't up to being a sea widow! *A widow*, she thought in consternation. *I'm not even a wife!*

She thought about Pasche Efford whose husband Nicholas was lost in heavy seas. She had heard that a giant squid had stirred from the depths and swept its tentacles in over the punt, found

Nicholas and dragged him into the deep. He had left Pasche and several children to fend for themselves. John had shaken his head and muttered, "That man was always on land when luck was on the sea, and on the sea when luck was on the land."

She quivered through the night, the wind's moans swirling her emotions. She fell into dreaming. *'Tis galing. John is lost . . . the wind took hes sail and capsized hes boat. . . . Full sea. . . . Empty sky. . . . Seabirds blown into their nests in cliff pockets. . . . Empty boat. . . .*

Her dough was wet with her tears as she mixed it the next morning. When she had wrapped it and put it aside to rise, she moiled through her work, keeping her eye on the bay.

That afternoon, she was standing outside, wind whipping her skirts between her legs, when she saw John's boat cut through black depths, feathering them white as he sculled into the harbour. John was casual. He had put into Redman's Cove and stayed, the grapnel dragging but holding.

Lawrence Lundrigan, a young fellow from the harbour, had gone fishing with John and his men. He came ashore with his dark hair spiked like an autumn pussy willow, a sea boil showing above straggly chin hair.

"Get yourself on home," she told Lawrence. "Your mudder is wringing her apron by now, and you her only son."

He went, his body slouching along the road.

Between mouthfuls of stew, John told Catherine that he and the men were pulling in the last net when they noticed the sky staining red and spreading out. The red disappeared in an instant and John knew he had to be wary. At first they didn't hear the wild wind. Then, all of a sudden it came, a northeasterly beating into them. "Drop the net," John shouted. "Throw it overboard." They covered the fish pound and started for land, trying to scull in.

"The northeasterly wind was a dirty one, blowing waves into the boat," John said, shaking his head. "Lawrence kept bailing with the piggin. I got the boat along by Redman's Cove by wedging the gaff in the rocks and pulling in until we got in the lun of the cliff. From there we watched the water boiling in the bay. We were too full of water to be hungry."

That night, Catherine drew John close to hold him tenderly, but in an instant his tongue was in her mouth, tasting like a stale scallop. He went into her body again and again, as if he wanted to prove he was alive and able. It was as if Captain Murrey was on her, banging her insides, his sweat and seed and her blood mingling. After John fell asleep she went to the linhay and scrubbed her body until it felt raw.

The next day, Catherine told John she needed a servant girl to put the house to rights, knowing she'd be getting in child again before long.

He shrugged. "You can have a girl to help with the children and the wash."

"I'll have one of James Lundrigan's girls from Cupids," Catherine said quickly, remembering the time Ruth came to her house, her apron tail lifted to wipe away tears spilling down her face, the bun on her head tottering in indignation. "A most awful thing! James Lundrigan is being whipped and his children and wife, Sarah, watching and they crying."

"That poor planter! What did he do that was so terrible?" asked Catherine.

"The law was after hes property after he'd had a poor season and couldn't meet hes payments to the merchant for fishin' supplies. He was taken to court but he wouldn't give up his property."

John had grunted. "Too many planters lose their boats to the sea and their lands and dwellings to merchants."

"Where would you be without a merchant such as myself?" John Jacob had once asked John.

He replied without hesitation. "Where would you be without fishermen like me who works their flesh to the bone to keep from starvin'?"

"A merchant is a good banker and a bad steward," said John. "No one knows that better than the Snows, and as soon as I can I'm gettin' me own accountant."

"Sure," said Ruth, "Sarah was blamed for the beating. She was saucy with the constables who showed up at her door to take the house, and she with two children huddled against her skirts. 'Be gone or I'll blow your heads off,' she threatened. Captain David Buchan, the acting governor, was nar bit pleased with Sarah for puttin' her family's welfare above her regard for the law. 'Her husband deserves a whipping for his lack of control over his wife and her contempt for the law,' he said.

"Poor James was one for having fits. By the time Captain Buchan and John Leigh, an Anglican priest, had given James fourteen lashes, he went into convulsions and fainted. Dr. Richard Shea, a surgeon who had been in Port de Grave since 1790, hurried to save the man's life, the little stands of whiskers on the sides of his mouth bristling in indignation. The punishment ended – for James. But there's ben more beatings, and James still carries the stripes."

CATHERINE FOUND BESS Lundrigan timid at first, but the young girl caught on. When she was sluggish or a little delayed in arighting the place, Catherine tried to remember that she, herself, was first a servant. *And still a servant*, she thought.

At the sight of Catherine working hard, John retorted, "Why keep a dog and bark yourself!"

"A servant is not a dog, but there's plenty of work for both of us," she answered.

John went to St. John's for a few days, passing off some of his cod, smoked herring, and salmon to the inport merchants and buying merchandise to sell to people on the Avalon. He bought Catherine raisins and yard goods.

"You've been pestering me all fall and now's the day," John called as he came up the path to where Catherine was standing dallying Eliza on her hip.

Despite his setback on his last trip in the skiff, John had made a good harvest from the western boat. His mind was full of well-being, and he made no quarrel about taking the baby to the Harbour Grace Catholic chapel for baptism.

They sailed into Harbour Grace, the sun strong and warm like a smile, though it was November. Catherine could see the top of the one-hundred-foot tower of the wooden chapel from the water as they rounded the point to a sparse-looking port. She looked down at the babe asleep through the whole travel. Catholic priests had paid well for the privilege of taking Catholic children to be baptized in their own faith. She had heard stories of the priests having to escape with their lives, their dwellings burned just like they were in Ireland. By the time they got to the chapel, Reverend M. Cronin was ready with witnesses Patrick Mackey and Catherine Mullowney.

Catherine made a note in her head. *November the first in this year of 1820 will mark the baptism of my babe.* She was determined that if she had other children they would be baptized in the chapel.

That night she dreamed of more children. Names, like little feet, tiptoed through her mind – *Johnny, Catherine, Martin, Emilia, Maria, Thomas, Johanna, Richard.*

Twelve

CATHERINE leaned against the wattle fence after John and his men left the stagehead to go fishing one May morning. She took in the sight of the sun rising out of the sea turning ocean crests to ruby gems. She had scrubbed her clothes and was pinning them on the clothesline when Mary Britt showed up. She stared at a strange contraption Catherine was hanging. She screwed up her nose. "What is it you've got there?"

Catherine laughed. "'Tis two cloth cups with strings and a band to hold up me breasts when I'm bouncing from one thing to another."

The other woman looked at her, aghast. "You should let them hang the way God meant, not have them shamelessly perched, their shape plain for all and sundry to see."

Catherine shrugged. "God's got more to think about than my milk jugs."

They turned to watch as a young woman came over the hill, just off a boat up from Harbour Grace, confidence showing in the swag of her dark heavy clothes. A white cut parted her hair in the middle. The sides of it fell down her breasts and swung at her waist. She grabbed one tail of hair and swung it over her shoulder as if it were the end of a scarf. If the girl had seen the sun it hadn't been for some time. She turned in the lane to John Jacob's house, nodding to the women as she passed.

"Sure that's Margaret, William Denning's daughter, the manager of a large company," Mary said. "I've heard she was coming to court John Jacob who's making good in this place. He'll make better now that he and Thomas Martin have formed their own company."

"John Jacob's ben to see Margaret time and ag'in. John says they're getting married," Catherine offered. *John would have wanted Margaret likely*, Catherine was thinking, *though he was not up to her breeding.* She looked at her own roughened hands, as brown as the skins of potatoes with as many nicks. Her eyes lingered on her bare finger. *Until a woman is married she doesn't know how long her man will be hers,* she thought. *I'll never know if John's all mine. He keeps his Saturday evenings for roaming.* "Doing business with the merchants," he told her. *What if this woman – Margaret Denning – is about when he's in with hes friends and in the liquor?*

Mary laughed. "That one won't have any gurry under her fingernails."

THAT NIGHT, JOHN hove himself down on the feather mattress, ropes squeaking under his weight. He raised himself on an elbow and said, "John Jacob's gettin' married and I not far enough up in the world to get an invitation. I might be, though, if I had a merchant's daughter in me bed."

Catherine slapped him across the face. Then she jumped out of the bed before he gave her worse. Her insides began to roll and she grabbed hold of the water basin on the dresser and retched into it until her eyes and nose watered. She curled up on a wolf rug on the floor, her body shaking in sobs until she fell asleep. Bridget climbed out of her little bed the next morning and shook her awake.

John sat up and looked down at her in disdain. "Look at you! You're not the one for stirring the bed in that state."

"And not the one wanting to," she retorted. She jumped up and began to retch again in the water basin.

"A son we'll have this time," John said, lying back on his pillow, one arm slung behind his head.

THE NEXT MORNING, Ruth dropped over with a loaf of fresh bread. John looked at her and announced, "I'll be gettin' a son to carry on the Snow name."

"You will if God wills it. Still, there's many Snows on this peninsula, and enough John and John Junior Snows," she said bluntly, going out the door.

"They're not mine," John said to Catherine. "A man lives only so long, and makes only so much money, and gets only so much land. Not a bit of it adds to his life. A son is hesself all over. My son'll be there to harvest the sea and land after I'm gone, holding to my plantation. I'll not have me brothers take it. John'll be his name."

Catherine smiled. "If we have a son, he'll be baptized John, and I'll call you Jack to make no mistake between the two of you."

"If you have him, we'll get married."

"Words they are to you. Knives in me."

"You do what you want with me words."

"I'd like to make you eat some of them."

"I suppose you would then. But what if I said the words 'marry me'?"

"Marry me!" She let the words sound on her tongue as if she could taste them. She flung open the door and ran down to the beach, dancing in her stockinged feet. She called to the wheeling gulls, "I'm getting married!"

The wind veered up, lifting and filling Catherine's bonnet. It sailed on the wind. She ran after it as it tumbled along the beach.

"'Tis coming on a livin' gale. Come inside," John called. "I didn't mean we'd get married right now. We will, sometime."

"Sometime!" she retorted, coming to a stop. "'Tis sometime, is it then?"

THE MORNING THE baby came, Catherine awoke with a quick squeeze of pain and then another. John ran for Granny Tilley who came dazed from sleep, breathing heavily from her rush. She'd not long gone to bed after delivering John Jacob's first child. "Margaret's own self," she told John, who smiled, looking relieved that John Jacob's first child wasn't a boy.

"Now the talebearers can stop counting the months on their fingers to see if John did the work on Margaret before they got married," Catherine said, clenching her teeth in pain. "I'm not married and John's done the work on me a few times, and I bear no shame for it. I've borne the Almighty's creations. God's breath is in each one."

"Mind now, don't be talking," the granny chided her.

John's son rose from Catherine's body just as the sun rose above the earth and poured itself through the window, filling the room with liquid gold.

This time, John kicked up his heels, exclaiming, "There's nothing I've wanted more than a son." He added with satisfaction, "John Jacob is there with only a daughter."

Catherine would never forget that day with John claiming, "One son is worth two daughters." Her heart hardened against him then. He had dismissed their first daughter and belittled their second child. Her third child was his glory.

After the baby was washed and wrapped, John took him and strutted around the house like someone who owned the world. He almost stumbled over Bridget and Eliza playing on the floor. He laid the baby against Catherine's breasts. Then he grabbed the granny up in his arms and whirled her around, calling, "I have a son, me very own son."

The granny made Catherine comfortable between fresh sheets. She lay with her baby tugging at her breast. For a time she listened to the happy voices of the children playing outside the room. Then she and her first son drifted into sleep.

A FEW WEEKS after Johnny's birth, Catherine went to a little blue box on a shelf to one side of the fireplace. She raised the cover and lifted out a tiny, linen petticoat and a dress. A scene flashed before her.

"Here," John had said, a month after Bridget was born. He reached from behind and placed his hands over Catherine's eyes. She heard the start of hinges as a cover was lifted. She smelled wood and oakum.

"Open your eyes."

His hands fell away and her eyes flew open. "A beautiful blue box!"

"For your keepsakes."

That's where she had laid one of her most prized keepsakes – the garment her daughters had worn the early weeks after they were born.

Catherine sat by the fire, holding the garment. She looked at John. "Johnny needs to be baptized if he's to be goin' on the water or the ice when he's old enough. What say he gets drowned? Hes body, hes soul. . . ." She stopped abruptly.

John scoffed, "Go on, woman. The sea can be anyone's bed, even mine or yours when we bees crossing the bay. I'll do it, though, after the fishin's over in the fall. I'll have him baptized."

But that week, John gave in and Johnny was baptized the twentieth of May, 1824, by Reverend Nicholas Devereaux. *Baptized by Newfoundland's first ordained priest*, Catherine thought proudly as holy water, cupped in the priest's hand from the baptismal bowl, splashed on the tiny face.

Catherine looked at John after the christening and suggested they go to the first playhouse ever opened in Harbour Grace. "The priest says it opened just this spring and there's 'A play on words.' You don't have to know how to read. It's all aloud."

John looked at her and grunted. "I'm too old for play."

ANOTHER DAUGHTER FOLLOWED two years after Johnny. "She'll be named after me," Catherine said.

John looked at her, his voice even. "That she will be, though I'll call you Kit and her Katie." A week later, Catherine smiled as she sat rocking Katie by the chimney corner. The other children sat on the floor, playing with wooden blocks their father had cut for them.

John went down in the harbour to see how other fishermen were faring in lobster catches. He came back with a worried face. "There's bad news on the go," he said, wiping a grainted hand across his forehead.

Catherine lifted her head. "What then?" she asked hesitantly.

"Dr. Shea died today."

Catherine's mouth dropped open. "Of what?" she asked.

"The pox, perhaps. It's been about, and the doctor was around people with it."

Catherine pulled her newborn closer to her breast. She felt a surge of fear, thinking how the Irish surgeon had come mere days before to deliver her child after it was a long time coming; the granny was down with a fever. Dr. Richard Shea had married Bridget Kennedy from Carrick-on-Suir. "Bridget is your second cousin," the doctor told Catherine, "on your mam's side, gone from the place when you were little."

"Will you go to the wake?" Catherine asked John.

"That I will! And a fine wake 'twill be," said John with satisfaction. "All the money people'll be about. It's a chance for me to make business connections since Shea was a buying agent and fishing crew operator. John Jacob will likely have the chance now to send a crew to the French Shore and to the Labrador Coast in Shea's stead."

"They won't be showing the doctor's face if he's got smallpox," Catherine said.

"Well, he won't be breathing on anyone, that's for certain," John answered.

Catherine mused, "Dr. William Appleby Brown will have to stand for all the sicknesses now, and he not young and not our kind, having come from Copenhagen, wherever that might be. The dear man is not as swift as Dr. Shea was. There'll be less sleep for him with the pox, galloping consumption, grippe, and diphtheria. Such don't let go of a place for long. Then there's pauperism, and that as bad as anything and as hard to cure, though there's fellows who can help and won't, like yourself, Jack."

John gave her a mean look, turned on his heel and went out the door.

TWO YEARS LATER, on a May morning, a second son was born. "Who will we name him after, Jack?" Catherine asked, tossing a braid back over her shoulder and away from the light-haired baby she was cradling.

John pondered a bit and then he answered. "Martin is a good business name. Sure 'tis a name from the family. Uncle George Snow married Patience Martin in 1800."

"Martin you be then," said Catherine, tracing her finger over the little face. The baby sighed, his hands shooting into the air, fingers spread.

"Sorry I startled you, little one," she said tenderly.

A few days later, John came home sighing heavily and wiping his hand across his forehead. "Smallpox is broke out ag'in and taken the first person since the death of Dr. Shea. John Dawe of Ship Cove will be buried on the twenty-third. His wife, Patience Kennedy, after these twenty-eight years married, is heartbroken, and his poor, widowed mother out of her mind with sorrow. Job Dawe's wife, who bides near them on Red Baich, is sick too. The doctor thinks she mighten make it."

"And she so young," Catherine murmured, "and so well-looking."

John trudged up the path a couple of weeks later, his face clouded. "Jacob Dawe of Ship Cove is another one dead of the pox and buried June thirteenth. His poor widow left with the children is beating her breast and wantin' to die." He shook his head. "Then there's Isaac Porter, son of Robert Porter, Blow Me Down. Sure he was buried two days after Jacob, and young William Andrews of Ship Cove. We could all be in the grip of pox." His look went to the children playing on the planked floor. Catherine felt a tremor. *What if something happens to John!*

She looked up at John. "It's time we got married."

"Married, and have you contend for me holdings if I falls over the boat one day!"

"Learn to swim!" she retorted. "If I contend it will be for your children to have your holdings and not your brothers or the merchants."

"Johnny, me namesake'll have everything when I'm gone." Catherine snapped. "If I'm left, I s'pose he'll bring in another woman and turn me out."

"If that's his will to do. That tongue of yours won't ever meet another woman's in silence."

Sometimes Catherine wished John would just hold her hand, stroke her face, rub his hand along her back, treat her other than for his use.

ONE SATURDAY AFTERNOON, John sauntered up the path, singing, "Spring has come for sowin'; grass is green and growin'; soon I'll be amowin'; then I'm on for marryin'." He grinned at Catherine looking through the kitchen window. "Have yer got fourteen pence there in your skirts?"

She looked at him blankly.

"That's what's to be paid to the Governor for a Cartlic marriage. I guess I'll marry a Cartlic. I'm only a half-Christian, seein' as I was never baptized meself. Not much of a chance when I was born. We'll be married right after the business is clued up in the fall."

Catherine flashed him a cynical look.

That night, John told Catherine, "We're not the only ones gettin' married. The magistrate, hesself, Robert Pinsent, is planning a grand wedding with Louisa Broom Williams on the twelfth of December in St. John's town. We'll have ours first."

I got married, she thought later, *even if John never married me in his heart. Hes oewn self – if not hes heart – is baptized into the Cartlic faith. On the thirtieth of October, 1828, we were married at the Harbour Grace Roman Cartlic Parish by Reverend N. Devereaux. Our marriage was witnessed by Ruth and Edward*

Snow. John and I signed our agreement with crosses. Neither of us knows how to write. Catherine Mandeville is still me name. I never giv' it up. The reverend wrote in our names and the names of our witnesses. I would like to write me name, if someone would show me how. I would like to be able to read everything I'm signing.

She'd never forget John lifting his glass to the small gathering at their wedding and muttering, "Me old man left Madeira wine for me marriage toast. He didn't know I'd be pulled into marryin' an Irish wench with youngsters comin' on the quick." He tipped his glass to Catherine. She tried to excuse him, to remind herself that he had loaded himself up with liquor and now his tongue had taken leave of his brain.

When John got home he kept on in a slurred voice, "John Jacob married a merchant's daughter, Robert Pinsent's marrying the chief magistrate's granddaughter, and you had me marry the likes of you."

"You've already had me body for yourself and to carry our children," she shot back, her eyes stormy.

"I didn't take thought for so many youngsters."

"When you set the seed in your potato beds, what do you expect?" She didn't wait for him to answer as he slumped down on the daybed. She went to bed, trying to keep the tears filling her insides from spilling into wet sobs and waking the children. She decided then that the greatest threat to her contentment was herself for letting John vex her.

FOUR DAYS AFTER Robert Pinsent's wedding, the whole of Bareneed was awakened during the night. About three o'clock, Old Teck, a Bareneed Hill fisherman, was banging on John's door and shouting, "Fire! All up! Fire!" John stumbled to the door half asleep. The man explained rapidly that he had been going into the woods when he noticed fire bursting through the back end of John Jacob's home. "Heavy winds," he panted, "must have blown fire and ashes throughout the house."

"Hurry on then!" John urged. "Shout the people out of their beds."

Old Teck went on down the lane, rolling back and forth on arthritic legs as he hit each door, shouting, "Fire!"

John could see, as he ran for his water bucket, other inhabitants storming out of their houses in nightshirts. They were too late to dout the fire before it took John Jacob's family. The house had burned so much that the roof had already fallen in, burying everyone inside. Sparks still flew into the night air like fireflies. There were sighs of relief that the wind had veered off the land in time to save other dwellings, all except the Martin & Jacob store.

Women and children were driven indoors as John and other men searched for the victims. Catherine hurried to get her newly sewn caylas to wrap the remains of Margaret, only five, Mary Anne, halfway between two and three years old, and John Charles, in his mother's bed, only five months – born just two months after Catherine had Martin – and Margaret, their mother, only twenty-four herself. Then there were two young maids, Sarah Taylor and Ethel, Mary Britt's sister.

ALL DAY, BOATS pulled up alongside the wharf and stages and threw their painters up for young boys to tie to gump posts. Michael Manning's dour look met questioning looks. "'Tis hard news it is," Michael said, turning to look toward the meadow and the sight of the blackened remains of John Jacob's house and store. "Poor Margaret and the three children were burned this morning, and the two maidservants – all devoured, gone to bone and ashes, and John not home. Sure he's in St. John's, picking up supplies. He'll be shocked to death hesself, he will."

Abe Taylor had climbed the rungs of the stage only to get the news that his daughter, Sarah, was one of the victims. He looked at John stone-faced. "I'll tell Amy right away." He untied his boat and hurried down the rails with his painter in hand and flung it into the boat. John heard gruff, heaving sounds as the bereaved father sculled away from the stagehead.

John turned up the path to his house, looking stunned. Catherine came toward him, letting out a deep sigh. "What can we do?" The tone of her voice drew the children around her as John answered in a stilted voice, "There's little anyone can do."

Mary will be off her head with grief, she thought as she walked up the hill to Mary's place. Joe met her at the door, saying his wife wasn't speaking to anyone for now. Catherine hurried back down the hill. She stood outside her house, shivering with her arms folded across her breast. She stared at the men sifting through the ashes. Magistrate Pinsent was a small man with tiny eyes in a nondescript face under heavy-looking dark hair combed flat and crossing to one side of his head. He stood at the site with his collar held up against the wind, little wisps of curls edging his scarf at the back. "Looks like the fire started at the back of the house," he said. Constable John Bowes, his thin hair stuck off like horsetail fern, stood next to him, blowing out his cheeks and his belly. "Yes, sir," he agreed.

John came down to where Catherine was standing. His voice was heavy. "They can't be sure what or who started the fire – or maybe they can – what with all the tension between merchants and fishermen." He sneered. "Irishman Bowes – now he's been made a constable. Sure he's so far up Pinsent's arse only his toes bees showin', and they tryin' to find a solid footing to push him up farther."

"Hush you blaigard, do!" Catherine told him. "There's no quarrel you've had with either of them – that I know of, and there's mourning goin' on. I feel the melancholy, meself." Her face broke apart in a cry, her voice waterlogged as she murmured, "A mudder and three little ones gone, and two young girls. Hold me, John."

"Aw, women." He shrugged and strode off.

Catherine went inside and sat at the window, unbuttoning her dress to feed the baby. She found herself staring at the empty space in the meadow, dirty snow and ashes scattered about. Loneliness swept through her like the slam of a sea wave. She thought of the past summer when she'd watched five-year-old Margaret picking buttercups and piss-a-beds for her mamma while Mary Anne giggled in the grass beside her. John Charles slept in his pram, a sheepskin drawn up to his chin. Now and then, Margaret turned from the clothes she was pinning on the line to smile at them. Catherine pictured Margaret inside the house, cooking John Jacob's favourite foods. Now everything was gone, even the threshold over which Margaret's glad step had met John's quick step.

Catherine remembered Margaret's piercing cries sounding through her open window one summer evening. Knowing she was quick with child, Catherine had called Ann over to mind the children. Then she'd gone for the granny. She had stayed to look after the little ones and to help the granny. Now she held images of the slight young mother bent in pain. Someone had found John Jacob on the Bareneed wharf. He hurried back up and out to his store, as if he was trying to keep clear of Margaret's cries. After a time, he came inside the house, shaking his head. He asked Catherine why Margaret was screaming – so unlike her, always so composed. Catherine pulled herself to her full height and told him bluntly that childbirth pain, for many women, was akin to having their buttocks held over boiling water or a brisk fire while their legs were being pulled apart to the breaking point – over and over – until the baby came. "You were away the last two times. But that's likely the way it was then too," she assured him.

When Margaret's cries stopped and a wee cry was heard, and then a lusty bawl, Catherine pushed the door ajar. The granny held up the newborn, telling him, "You're bawling with your fists swinging as if life is out to do you injury, but with your father's ambitions you're on your way to wealth."

Catherine brought in a pitcher of warm water for the basin. The granny rubbed down the newborn and washed him to bring out a soft fresh colour. John Jacob followed Catherine into the room, his face white and drawn. He brightened when he saw the granny swaddling a healthy-looking son. Granny Tilley eyed him and gave him a blunt warning. "Margaret is only slight and she's given you three babies with not many years apart. That member between your thighs when cocked is as menacing to your woman as a loaded shotgun. Keep it out of her, for another child could kill her." John had looked beyond the granny to his wife, her eyelids closed and fluttering. Margaret had recovered to proudly show off John Charles.

Now Catherine noticed Robert Pinsent, John Jacob, and John Bowes coming down the lane from John Jacob's premises. They all glanced toward her at the window, three cold looks as one, sending her body all abiver. She held her baby tight, thinking how empty she would feel if she lost her children and her home, and if, like Margaret, she lost herself. Her mind spun in the agony of such thoughts.

MARK HENNEBURY AND Joe Britt held shovels that had, earlier in the year, been used to dig into soft, rich earth to sow seeds and to harvest vegetables. Now they dug into dark, unyielding earth. It finally gave way, opening up reluctantly to the sharp thrusts of their shovels, making way for the box holding the bodies of John Jacob's servants. After the service for the two young girls, the single pine box was quickly lowered into the earth, and the grave filled. Mary Britt clung to Catherine, fair out of her mind about her sister gone, and not much of her left for the pine box. Catherine had watched the two young girls playing with Margaret's children in the garden. Maybe they imagined having their own children some day.

John Jacob had sailed back to news of his whole family burned to death. He dropped to his knees in a whimper that rose in a wail, long and harsh, so deep that it pierced the hearts of people listening until they were sobbing, as if they would break apart.

"It's too much for a man to lose his whole family," Ruth said as she came into Catherine's house with her hand to her breast. "Sure the scene would stun even the heartless."

John refused all ministrations and offers of an abode, though

Robert Pinsent strongly urged him to stay with friends. He retreated to the cuddy of his boat, staying there alone, it rocking gently on its collar, as if it were sobbing its loss of children who would no longer climb all over it, and a woman who lovingly painted it each year and put things to rights after John had strewn everything around the cuddy.

The inhabitants spoke well of the stoic way John handled himself, standing by the grave sombrely looking down at the casket holding his whole family. Thomas Martin and Robert Pinsent stood by his side, each wearing a black crepe band on their right sleeve. The widower stared at the icy mound of clay left above the earth. Then he tightened his lips at the sight of children and their families. Suddenly he drew his dark collar high, pulled down his hat and walked away, leaving outward expressions to lesser mourners.

John Snow had seen John Jacob look at a pin, a lucky charm in his lapel that Margaret had given him to ward off disaster on his voyages. He was fingering it mournfully when John caught up with him, telling him that the men around the place planned on erecting him a shelter until spring when he'd have a proper dwelling built. John offered his friend the best words he could find. "A man's got to scull through life the best he can in all kinds of storms."

The grieving man nodded, his face breaking open in a sob.

It had been a fierce day with northeasterlies sweeping the bay when Margaret and her children were buried. Catherine had stayed by the hearth, thinking of them in the cold grave. She thought of her own life. *Sometimes I'm afraid I'll be put in the grave by John's hand, the way he yells at me and bangs my head with his fist, and keeps the gun always loaded.*

Thirteen

EMILIA was born the next September, a dark-haired mite squinching his puffed eyes and gasping for air while Catherine lay, her head like an overturned white jug, wine pouring out of its spout. John let out a gasp at the sight of Catherine's white face. He tilted her head back and put a rag, dipped in a bucket of cold brook water, to her nose while he rushed to get his mam's charm. He pushed the heart-shaped slug inside Catherine's mouth, unaware that her blood was also seeping into the bed from her birthing place. She had almost lost the baby two months earlier. She had slipped and fallen while lifting a bucket of slop over the pigpen. The bleeding subsided and finally stopped after she went inside the house and lay down. Now Granny Tilley urged her to keep the baby at her breast while she mixed a herb concoction for her to drink. When the children came with smiling faces to look down at their tired mother, she could only cry. Every day she got a little better, reaching weak arms to hold her babies against her.

Mary Britt came to tell Catherine she had urged Reverend Devereux, who had sailed to Bareneed on his travels from Brigus and Cupids, to drop in to baptize the tiny baby. Catherine was grateful that he came, and relieved that he recorded the baptism in the old mam's Bible – Emilia Snow, baptized the twenty-second day of November, 1829. The priest could have added a cross beside Emilia, for later that month Catherine went to the cot to pick up her baby. He was struggling to breathe, his little fists tight. A tint of blue spread over his white face. Then his eyes grew dark and staring. Not a blink! Catherine felt a thud inside her as she lifted the warm body tight to her chest, her mouth holding in a scream. There was no movement – only a dead weight. Her pent-up scream broke through, and Mary Britt chanced upon Catherine's outburst just as she was opening the door to come inside. She reached to take the infant but Catherine would not give him up. Mary quickly made the sign of the cross.

John never said a word when he saw the tiny, lifeless baby, not then, not later. He acted as if he had never had a son named Emilia, even though he went to the shed and hammered boards into a coffin. He picked up his shovel, went up to the vegetable garden and dug a hole beside a sturdy pine tree. Catherine held the still body close to her warm neck, her pulse beating hard against the baby's cold forehead. She murmured, "I'd done with having merry-begots. You were my wedded child. Why did God take you?"

The baby was pried from her arms, washed, dressed and laid in a little box lined with muslin. She looked at her child as still as a newly fallen snowflake, as distant now as her own mother. "*Dia Duit* – God greet you," she said, her voice choking.

From a shelf she lifted the skin-bound Bible, its pages as uneven as slates in the cove's cliffs. She marked a cross with soot from the fire beside a name she knew to be Emilia's. She blessed herself and murmured, "May Mary and her Son guard you, and God in heaven keep Hes eye on you while St. Bridget spreads her cloak under God's eye."

John came into the house after laying the baby in his tiny grave. He looked toward Catherine with the Bible in her hands. "Shut it up," he said. "I take no comfort in that. We've put the child in the grave and I don't know where he's gone from there." His back was already turned to her, his feet on the move out the door, to find the comfort he was used to from the grog keeper's hand.

He came back late that night, glanced at Catherine and muttered in a slurred voice, "Don't be an ash cat – always huggin' the fireplace."

John had taken Catherine still bleeding after Emilia's birth. She was already carrying another baby and fearing the worse for it. Bridget whispered in her mother's ear that she had seen her father make the sign of the cross at Emilia's grave. Catherine thought, *Maybe he is a true Cartlic, as all our children will be.*

The priest visited Catherine and John after he heard about their loss. He sniffed the air. "Is it a rabbit I smell in your pot and on a Friday?"

John gave him a deadpan look. "No, sir. It's fish."

"It smells like a rabbit." The priest lifted the cover off the pot.

John reached with a cup of water. "Once a rabbit now a fish." He lifted an eyebrow and with a mocking smile added, "When you baptized me, you used your holy water to pronounce, 'Once a Protestant now a Cartlic.' It's just as easy for this rabbit to become a fish as it is for you to turn me into a Cartlic with your holy water."

The priest drew his lips tight and departed without another word.

After he left, John stormed, "It's enough that I let you yoke me to the Cartlic church, and give me children to their blessings to save your peace of mind."

"You'd not done it if you weren't at odds with the Protestant church," Catherine snapped back.

"You're nothing but an Irish harridan," he yelled. His hand stung her face.

CATHERINE VISITED THE baby's grave often, snowflakes falling on her face and melting like tears as she whispered, "*A mhic mo chroí* – son of my heart. You'll be held inside my love forever."

Thoughts of her lost child dragged on her heart like a stone until Maria was born the next year, healthy and bright-eyed.

Catherine wasted no time in having her baptized on June twentieth. The baptism was witnessed by Catherine's young cousin, Tobias Mandeville, and Margaret Murphy. Catherine had discovered a cousin on her father's side who had come from Ireland and was living in Harbour Grace with his family of two sons, Tobias and Thomas. Catherine asked the elder Thomas, who had married Dr. Shea's sister, Eleanor, to stand as witness for the baby. He refused, his voice harsh. "I don't hold with Orange Catholics." Instead, he sent his son, Tobias, and a family friend to witness the baptism. Tobias's uncle, Richard Mandeville, in Brigus, was a well-off esquire and merchant. He had seen to Tobias's schooling, knowing the bright young fellow had a mind for figures. He had learned from the merchant how to make barrels.

"You've come from the old place," Catherine said.

"A while back, and glad of it," Tobias told her, running his fingers through curly red hair.

Margaret Murphy, coming behind him, stopped to tamp tobacco into the bowl of her pipe before saying, "'Tis been trouble there these many years and his father took his family away. If 'tis not famine, it's war. Famine is a curse man can't help, but war, 'tis man who makes it and waters the earth with the blood of good and bad. 'Tis in the Good Book sure."

"You know the Bible?" Catherine asked.

"Some of it, to be sure, from what the priest told me."

Catherine held her baby close and cried as Maria was baptized. All her feelings about Emilia's loss came back to slam against her heart in waves. When she came home, Bridget and Eliza, who had been minding the younger children, said nothing as they took in their mother's strained look. Johnny and Katie, seeing Catherine's sadness, came to her, bumping against her and leaning on her arm until she was forced to think on the children she hadn't lost. She let them hug her, let their touches heal her.

CATHERINE LOOKED THROUGH the window toward John on the fish flake, spit curls against his sweating brow. Her look went beyond him. Wind had settled into a whisper on flat water; underneath it pebbles lay shadowy in gold dust as a sunbow arched over the water like a promise.

John finished making up the fish and covering it. He came into the house, his face creasing into a smile. "Ah," he said. "These are the finest sights – a wife's belly full of another child, her hands holding the hands of children by her sides, a smile on her face and food in the pot."

"Not another child I'll want in me yet," she retorted. She lifted her chin and caught his eyes with hers. "These *are* a woman's foinest sights – a boat low at the gunnels, a man who takes water for ale, and bides by his woman while the night idles."

John's look got dark. "You mean for me to stay home on a Saturday night?"

"To sit by the fire with me and the babes," Catherine told him. "There's no need to be off tippling with the merchants. Your kegs are full of spirits."

"There's business to be talked with me suppliers," he said, his tone harsh, his eyes narrowing. "I've got business you know nothing about."

IN DECEMBER, JOHN came back from Robert Pinsent's schooner anchored in the harbour with winter supplies brought from St. John's. He handed Catherine a clock. "It's a James Hann bracket clock," he said proudly. "You pull a cord, and it tells the time of the latest hour and minutes."

Katie looked up from play, tucking a lock of dark hair behind her ear. "I already know how to count minutes." She began to clomp with her tongue. "Sixty times and one minute is passed."

The children came to sit by the fire as John pulled chocolates from his pockets. Soon their little cheeks bulged with sweets. Snow swirled outside. The lantern light in the window shone on ice crystals, patterning the pane in gold. It was a gentle night, and John's spirit seemed to be mellow. "Sit by the fire, Jack," Catherine coaxed. "Be with the children on Christmas Eve."

"I'll be with them tomorrow for the Christmas bird," he answered, tramping out the door. He came back after Catherine had gone to bed. She lay awake, her thoughts drifting to poor Margaret Jacob and her children. She imagined one of the servants, asleep and under the spell of the old hag, swinging an arm, causing a lit candle on a crate beside the bed to drop into bedclothes. It may have been a spark from the fireplace in Margaret's room. Possibly, fire erupted from a cinder pan laid on the floorboard. Catherine was nagged by the thought, *What if John Jacob kept records in the store, never thinking there would be a fire? Maybe someone lit a fire in the building to destroy records of debts owed to John Jacob, never thinking the winds would take a fire started in the store to the dwelling house. Who knows what goes on in a place!* She felt guilty for her thoughts and quickly quelled them.

Fourteen

"WE'VE got too little land here," John said one fall morning as he and Catherine filled brin bags with potatoes for the cellar. "A lot of me old man's land was pinched by merchants for debts. John Jacob will buy the bit of land I have here to enlarge hes own. He wants room to extend hes fishing rooms and to build a fine cooperage."

Catherine glanced toward the large two-storeyed house John Jacob had already rebuilt on the land that took his family. Now he had a fine home, and a new wife, Hannah, who was expecting their first child.

She didn't say anything, and John continued. "John said he'd write me up a request for a government grant of six acres at the tip of Salmon Cove."

"Salmon Cove!" Catherine exclaimed.

John placed his arm around her and pointed. "See, Salmon Cove Point, face to face with Bareneed. It's got a long stretch of grassy meadow inland, with roaming horses, cows, and sheep feeding on it summertime. It's a wild place in winter, but it calms under a bright sun and gentle tide."

Catherine stared across to a point of cliff poking its pitted head out into the bay. Though there was not a breath of wind, the sea rose against the cliffs like a great white mammal, hissing and spouting and falling flat like a melting snowman, only to rise just as furious.

John went on. "Just over the ridge is Caplin Cove. It's got cliffs with cracks deep enough to lose a man if he strays in the dark. But the place is blessed with a gravel beach. Over on the other side of the cliffs is Goats' Cove, and up toward the meadow is Rip Raps beside Spectacle Head on the north side of Cupids."

It was late December when John swaggered into the house holding a piece of paper in triumph. "I've got the land," he shouted. "Governor Cochrane signed it on the fifteenth of November – six acres 'to have and to hold until the end, John Snow, his heirs and assigns forever.' John Jacob read it to me. We'll get it registered in the new year." He grabbed Catherine and swung her around. "We're having a new home, bigger and better, a little higher, a little longer and a little wider than this one. That place'll be an inheritance to pass on and no merchant's goin' to find a way to grab it. Edward's got hesself a grant too, three acres up the higher slope of land just beyond ours and facing Caplin Cove. To the side, in from the tip of Salmon Cove, is a fine place for a fishing stage. People living farther up Salmon Cove cut their houses out of the woods, but there's little more than shrubs down on the point. We'll clear the land, and build up rocks for our plantation."

He grinned. "You, a little cailin come from an earthen floor in Ireland, will always have a floor under your feet with the earth under boards, stairs to climb and a landing above it."

"And a widow's walk, I s'pose, for me to pace while I looks for the long-delayed sight of you comin' in the bay," she said in a low tone.

John smiled broadly. "The wait'll stir your blood."

They left Bridget, who was now fourteen, to mind the younger children, and sculled across the bay to see the place close up. In the golden dance of sunlight on the bay, gulls sat like black shadows in nests of moving waters. There came a sound like rushing wind as they rose in a flock to perch on the high point of Salmon Cove.

Mary Britt, who had already moved to Caplin Cove to care for her ailing father, had warned Catherine that from the cliffs of Salmon Cove there was only a narrow, rock-filled path over steep terrain to Caplin Cove. Still, Catherine had no concept of the rugged landscape until they were nearing the place, which was now under a scant spread of snow. She was struck by its desolation. *A gloomy place to be*, she figured, *worse, likely, when it's smothered in fog.* A strange feeling crept over her, like the sun's dark shadow over a place before it goes dark.

"From a distance I thought the land in from the head was flat," she said, her disappointment keen. Now she saw that it was an uneven stretch of frosted, empty land. Beside the area where John planned to build a fishing stage and head, land dipped to the sea like a tipped, crinkled plate. She turned to John in alarm. "The younger children will be in danger of rolling over the bank to the rocks below and into the sea."

"We'll have the place yarded," John assured her. "The woven fence will go up, starting from the lip of the cliff." He pointed to a ridge of land above a steep bank. "We'll build the house up a ways from the sea, and away from the stage. Farther up, I'll have a shed and barn."

Catherine nodded, but a feeling was growing that the move to Salmon Cove would change her life beyond anything she could imagine.

JOHN HIRED MARK Hennebury, Michael Manning, and John Doyle from Bareneed to work on the house and surrounding structures. They worked hard, sweating through warm spring days, and shivering through days with the wind blowing easterly. They dragged large rocks for a drywall to be built along the house. John and the men sailed to Kelly's Island and cut huge stands of trees. The small island, close to St. John's, rose out of the sea like a dark, mammoth creature. It was an island rife with stories of ghosts, pirates, and buried treasure. The men sailed back home, laughing and shuddering as each told his own ghost story passed down through generations. John and the men made numerous trips to the island. They cut and skiffed enough logs for John's use. Others John took to the Martin & Jacob warehouse as a credit for spring and winter supplies.

On good spring days, Catherine sculled over in the punt to watch as chips, scented with the strong smell of newly cut wood, flew into the air. She lifted her face to draw in the warm, refreshing scent of cut pine. She listened to the ring of the hammer as John nailed the timber, his dark hair in a sweat. Her heart gave a lurch as John and his hired hands raised the frame for the two-storey house. *How strange it is,* she thought, *that humans can bar a place against wind and rain, and portion it off from the wild tread of animals and the flight of birds – their life having inhabited the land and the air for centuries.* Her hand went to her belly where another baby curled. She hoped – dear God – this house would be christened by the birth of a healthy newborn.

Soon the house was standing overlooking the bay. John set a ladder up one side of the house to meet a ladder on the roof for climbing to tar the roof or, if need be, to put out a chimney fire. A shed was built on Salmon Cove Head with an outhouse fastened to the end of it, the toilet holes hanging over the high cliff. John intended to dig an underground cellar off a barn in the meadow by September.

Slates were brought from Green Point and settled into the hearth. The chimney was lined with rocks. A dark mahogany wood mantel rose above the stone fireplace. Soon fire would crackle under the bake pot.

On a spring day, the Snows moved to their new home. John had a broad grin on his face as he brought the punt alongside the Bareneed stage. Bridget's blue eyes clouded as she helped the younger children down over the rails and into the boat. Her lower lip was pushed out, as if to show her father how vexed she was to be leaving her home.

"Don't be havin' your lip out far enough for someone to sit on," Catherine said. "Sure we've all got to get used to the place." Eliza looked at her sister and rolled her big brown eyes. She frowned at her mother under stray strands of hair falling from thick hair loosely braided like strands of oakum.

"You too," Catherine scolded her. "You needin be down in the mouth about something you can't change."

When they were all settled, John untied the painter and threw it down into the boat. The punt rocked under John's heavy boots and the children squealed.

"We're loaded to the gunnels, but it's not with fish," Catherine remarked, looking behind her at Bareneed, the place she was leaving. She turned her back and looked toward Salmon Cove. The sculling oar in John's strong hands knocked against the punt as it crossed the bay through lively waters. Bridget and Eliza sat sullen-looking on the thwart beside Katie. Johnny trailed his hand over the side and through the water. Catherine held Martin standing against her knee and Maria in her arms. Her heart lurched with the thought of leaving Emilia. *You are in here*, she thought fiercely, her hand going to her breast, a mhic, mo chroí – *son of my heart*.

As they neared the plantation they could see a freshly hewed path sloping down to the new stagehead that reached out over the water. Sea rushed against its knobby legs. John said he was going to keep the stage door locked for fear of thievery. A shed leaned above the bank like a long slug, its many legs leaning into the rocks haphazardly, as if the weight was too much. Farther up past the house a barn stood, painted ochre, a pig pound and a henhouse attached to it.

Katie and Johnny clambered up the wide, laddered stagehead shored at the centre with a vertical post. Their feet made thundering noises as they dashed over logs forming the lap of the stagehead. They scravelled in through the stage and up over the steep path.

Catherine waited for Bridget to get her bearings as she reached one foot to the stagehead rail while keeping the other foot on the gunnel of the boat. John held the boat steady and tight to the stagehead while Catherine passed Maria up to Bridget, who tightened one arm around the child as she looked to the side of the stage at the teethed rocks and the large ledge of cliff sticking out of the water, its uneven plateau a rusty red. Martin's freckled face screwed into a cry as Catherine passed him to Eliza. His arms tightened around her neck as she followed Bridget up to the landing.

Catherine climbed up to the stagehead, turning to watch John's punt swing in a breeze against his efforts to moor it. He called after her with a sweep of his hand. "This is your Irish castle, not towered like the castle in the valley of your kin, and not stone, but better than the bothy you were raised in."

She settled her misgivings about the place as she started up the path, thinking, *This is my family's home, not the Snows' family home. A new beginning, and a new home that'll take a bit of getting used to.*

She smiled as Johnny yanked open the outside door to the house, and then a door inside. It opened to a narrow set of steps. The children raced up the stairs which led to a narrow landing and the servants' quarters – a small room on either side, each with a narrow window. John had put in bed cabins – wooden bedsteads with interlacing ropes attached to frames to support each mattress. A bucket by the bed, a pot under the bed, and a washstand with a water basin and jug by each window gave the simple rooms all else they needed for comfort. The rooms would hold a cooper, a shipped man, a servant girl or two, and visitors – not all at the same time. Catherine's girl would help cook and clean, and John's girl would work at the fish and grounds. The servants would eat with the children.

From the servants' passageway, Johnny and Katie came across the landing and down the family stairs to the pantry and out into the kitchen to stand by the hearth.

John had shaved wood into small pieces of tinder to go with a handful of furze. Soon fire leaped up in a warm flare to burn the damp air. The scent of new wood afire in lively, zesty strokes stirred Catherine's nature as she eyed John bent toward the fire with an armload of kindling. She breathed in his woodsy scent, and her feelings for him brought her body to life for the first time since she'd lost Emilia.

Catherine took a nub of Irish peat from a small box. She broke it into pieces and sprinkled it over the fire to christen her new house. Then, holding Maria, she leaned back on the hinged seat of a barrel chair John had made. She closed her eyes and forgot about her surge of feelings for John. She fancied herself back in Ireland. Irish words danced through her mind like clothes on a line in gentle winds. She didn't speak them lest they sail away on the wind of John's tongue. "'Tis not a learning language in this country," he had warned her. "The lower tongue carried it here and will drop it here."

Catherine laid Maria, now sound asleep, in her cot and filled a pot with vegetables Bridget and Eliza had peeled. She hung the pot and a kettle of water on the cotterel.

ON HER FIRST night in the new home, Catherine woke with a scream, her hands holding her neck. She grabbed hold of John and he growled. She could not remember her dream, but its lingering effects left her unsettled, and she lay awake waiting for daylight. Her fear settled and her face spread into a smile at the sight of Johnny standing by her bed, up and ready for their new day. Through the window she watched the sun pop above the horizon like a live coal, sending a trail of firelight across the calm water.

John came up behind her. He said playfully, "'Twon't always be so calm. Sometimes it will be so windy you'll have to sit on your feet to keep them from being blown away. Other days the fog'll be so thick you'll think it's pea soup and you'll try to catch it in your pot." He got serious. "This day is too fine, too calm, too warm, and with the barometer falling it's a weather breeder. I'll stay at home out of its way. There's as much work to be done on the land as on the sea."

Catherine's heart lifted when John was in a civil mood. She smiled. "We'll have to make the most of it."

"Just be ready with your hands for the garden," he told her.

Fifteen

ICE came, filling the bay and cobbling against the shore, chilling the air. It left a few days later as abruptly as it had come. Then the place began to warm up. A few trees standing toward the meadow were late in showing signs of spring. Now, silver-grey buds as soft as a rabbit's foot surged into green shoots.

One afternoon, Catherine looked up from her clothesline. John was sculling across the harbour from Bareneed with a stranger aboard.

Johnny looked up from where he sat on the stage with a clasp knife his father had given him.

John called, "Now boy, stop your idleness. You can't be cutting pieces out of the stage."

"I'm rounding out the knotholes and rinding off the bark left on 'em, is all."

Catherine ambled down the path with a wooden peg in her hand. "Leave him be. He'll tire soon, and then he'll be off out of sight. Then you, with your hands in fish guts, won't be able to find him to throw fish in the box."

John shook his head. "Here we is then," he called, throwing up the painter for Johnny to catch. He eyed Catherine. "We've got ourselves a green boy come over from your side of the pond. I've paid his passage on the *Black Flag* and indentured him to help with the farming and fishing, a fine strapping fellar. He'll work off his passage and earn a little over this summer and the next. Then he'll be free to stay or go."

Another man would come in handy, now that John's men were on his western boat for three weeks at a time, and there was no telling when Catherine would be called to leave the stage to straddle the birthing stool. She didn't want to be making fish this summer.

Catherine looked down from the stagehead into the dusty blue eyes of a young Irishman – not a day over twenty, she figured, and not much to look at. He lifted a heavy face, his sloppy-looking mouth open as he climbed up from the boat to the stagehead. Rough, threadworn trousers shaped big, knobbed knees. His baween, a loose jacket made from undyed flannel, looked filthy-white.

"Arthur Spring's me name," the young Irishman said, extending his hand to Catherine. He had a tight grasp.

"What've you brought with yer?" called Johnny, seeing the bag over his shoulder.

"Just an empty ditty bag," Arthur answered. "I'm lucky to have hung on to that with all the thievery on the schooner."

Catherine nodded at him. "Where is it you're from then? Is it Waterford?"

He smiled. "I come from Kilkenny, and glad to be away to better meself. I lived there all me days, in not much more than an Irish crate for shelter."

"Come on then," Catherine urged him. "You're off the boat, so you'll need to be slapped with lye soap. It's to the wooden half-puncheon you'll be taking yourself with a shiften of John's clothes, though they'll be a little big for your frame."

"You'll not be sitting on your haunches here," John warned. "There's work to be done, back-breaking work all around. I need cod cured properly. Otherwise, we'll not get a good market for our best fish. Gardens have to be kept and harvested. Rocks have to be dug up, weeds rooted out and thickets of gorse cleared for another garden. Fences will need to be overhauled now and ag'in to make sure they keep out roaming animals, and keep in roaming youngsters. You won't own a gun, but you can use one of mine to frighten off wild animals."

John likes his guns, Catherine thought. He had built a gun rack above the hearth. "Always on the ready," he'd said, pouring powder from a small bulb case into the mouth of one of his four guns. He dropped a ball down the throat of the gun and pressed tow down on it with a rod. He then laid the gun aboard the rack. He was ready for thieves, wild birds, and animals or a seal in the bay. Catherine had protested. "No need to keep a gun loaded, John. It's dangerous. You're not needing to use one unless you go bird hunting or sealing."

He had given her a mean look, and Catherine had backed away, thinking, *It's not only John's britch-loader that's always cocked.*

After John finished telling Arthur all he expected of him, the hired hand looked at him and asked, "And afterward, sir, when I've paid off me passage and spent me summers and winter, there'll be money for me?" Arthur's question buzzed through the air like a wasp.

"I'll think on that then. Only a fool makes promises for a morrow not sure to be his."

"Fair enough." Spring held out his hand, but John went past him up the path toward the house.

Arthur looked up at Catherine watching him. "A foine cut of a woman, you be, missus." Then he called after John, "'Tis bold of me, sir, but my will is to offer you an Irish blessing. 'May you never live to see your wife a widow.'"

LATER, AFTER ARTHUR had lumbered off to get a wash, John turned to Catherine. "Silly Irish tripe, makes no sense a'tall." He sent a scornful look in the direction of the impudent young man. "I'll thank him not to be using silly words on me."

"Proverbs, John." Catherine laughed. "Don't you be worried none. If the fellar's got a lower grade of brain than yourself, he'll likely make up for it with brawn." Arthur would understand her mind better than John did – how it held the belief of fairies and piskies. *Likely Arthur'll be getting back to Ireland,* she thought. *He'll feel like a shorn lamb here.*

After Arthur came to the table, Catherine passed him a bowl of fish stew. Johnny and Martin, not the least bit shy, sat on the long stool with their elbows on the table and their palms under their chins, taking a good gander at the new man. Their looks took in a dark purple bump on his forehead showing through his wet coppery hair. Like someone famished, he didn't look up while he ate his stew and fresh bread, crowned with cranberry jam, and gulped his mug of molasses tea.

Once he'd finished eating, Catherine told him, "You'll make a bed on the loft of the barn and sleep there until winter. Then you'll have a bed in our house loft."

After Arthur had helped with the animals and he was settled in the barn for the night, John came into the house and wiped his forehead with the back of his hand. "I've decided to give Arthur twenty pounds for two summers, and a winter's work with a few quid off for his passage and the grub from our table."

Catherine wondered if John didn't know more about Arthur than he was letting on. She thought, *He likely got him in exchange for a deal with the captain of the* Black Flag. *No one knows what dealings John's got going on at the Bareneed warehouse, what trade goes on between it and sinister-looking ships like the* Black Flag *right under the nose of the custom house.*

AFTER ARTHUR'S AND John's first haul, Arthur helped prong fish up from the boat to the stagehead. Catherine stood ready to gut the fish. When Arthur climbed the rails and slid the knife across his first fish on the splitting table, cutting the head off, Catherine told him, "Don't cut the head off before you slices the belly. You makes a cross – a slit across the throat, and then, while you holds the head by the eyes, you makes a slit down the belly to the tail. Then you pulls out the insides and takes the head."

"What then?" he asked. "Tell me the whole thing."

"Then you cuts out the sound bone and your fish'll lie flat like a leaf. But John looks after that. There is no one with his clear cut. He hardly takes a bit of flesh with the bone. After you've left the fish in salt for a few days, you washes it and spreads it on the fish flake, napes to tail, then tail to napes, always in that order, with the flesh facing up to get a nice creamy look. When you makes up the fish in piles for the night, or in the day against rain or hard sun, you places the skin up with its napes out and its tail in. You covers the pile in rind and canvas and holds it down with rocks. You needs three days of wind and sun."

Arthur listened carefully. He was ready to work, ready to spend his time making money to take home.

CATHERINE EYED ARTHUR Spring the next day as he worked with John on the boatload of fish they had thrown up on the stagehead. "And what was your occupation in the old country?" she asked.

He answered quickly, "I was a dyker."

"Your hands are cut into then."

"They's so."

"Mind if I look?"

Spring lifted thick hands. Their stiff, stubby fingers and palms were criss-crossed with lines enough to confuse a palm reader. "Building rock walls is what I was doing in Ireland. Sure you know how the lanes run up and down with walls built from rocks taken from farmers' fields. You've ben there, you, an Irish girl."

Catherine's eyes got misty as he told about piling cairns of rocks. "I think of home often," she said. "The thatched house, its rafters made of black and white thorn, roofed with oaten straw. It was warm in winter and cool in summer."

Arthur nodded. Then his tongue loosened and he rattled on. "You've got to make your trench and then lay in the stones and the packing. If you get a man on one side and you on the other side, you don't have to bother about jumpin' over the rising wall. Stones have to be laid well so that the wall can be something wonderful to see. On rainy days 'tis well to stay home and let the cuts on your hands heal. Otherwise, the rocks'll be slippery. I lost me livin' to an Englishman."

"Don't you worry," Catherine said, patting his hand. "I lost me oewn self to an Englishman. He's the same man you'll be gettin' a living from. You'll get cuts on your hands here too, once you're trawling fish."

BY MID-MAY, CATHERINE was setting her vegetable garden with turnips, carrots, beets, and cabbages. In her kitchen garden she set chives, sage, thyme, savoury, and parsley. Beyond the kitchen garden, bulbs and seed she had saved from lilies of the valley, phlox, and sweet-smelling rockets were taking root. White waxberry bushes and mock orange bushes were already thriving.

Ruth and Edward Snow's house was up from Catherine and John's new home, at the end of the path on a hill that faced the cliffs of Caplin Cove. Edward had gone off to Labrador on a schooner. Ann helped her mother set in the gardens while her younger brothers and sisters played in the yard.

Beyond Edward's homestead were lowly houses built on rock foundations here and there. Any fertile land was kept for kitchen gardens. Above them were meadows where cattle roamed and grazed. John's horse, cow, and sheep grazed on his own land. The horse and sheep would be let out farther inland on the commons during the summer months.

Bridget and Eliza were called out of their beds as soon as the sun rose. They gathered kelp, cow paddies, and ordure from the fowls and animals to fertilize the gardens. If John went into the barn and Arthur lay curled on his straw asleep, he kicked him in the rump and rasped, "Be up with you before the day leaves the sky." Arthur hauled himself up, splashed water on his face, and began mixing the pig meal fast and furious. The thudding of the spade against the wooden tub brought the pigs squealing for their breakfast.

John expected Catherine to be ready to help with the fish whenever he needed her, ordering her to leave housework and the young children to Bridget and Eliza and Kitty White, a slim, soft-spoken maid he had hired from Cupids, to live in.

A rugged island this Talamh an éisc *is*, Catherine thought as she stood on the stagehead, listening to the sea roar and dash against the stage's legs as if it were trying to bring them down. Little boats rocked, swirled, dipped, and choked on water as they swung from painters tied to stagehead strouters along the cove; punts and skiffs, held fast by collars of rope moored to killicks, turned on lively seas. When the seas settled, seaweed lay tangled in rocks and scattered among jagged and round stones as if it were the ocean's hair caught in a storm and flung ashore.

John came up from the stage one evening as the sun sank, taking the blush from the sky. He let out a sigh. "'Tis the third week of June and the sun is starting to back up and me with not enough daylight as it is."

ANN BROUGHT KATIE and Johnny smooth round stones she'd picked up in a rippling stream beside her house. Sometimes Catherine listened to the children laughing in the evening light as they played a game of alleys out on the grass, tossing the stones into the air and catching them on their hands. "Tickle stones," Ann called them. "They make the water laugh."

Once, when Ann came to see the children, John pinched her breast. "All grown up," he said with a grin. "Twenty or more years old, I suppose you is!" He slapped her behind. "Mind the young fishermen lookin' to have a solid rump fer a jolly romp."

Ann backed away, giving Catherine a self-conscious glance. Then she turned bold. "You watch yourself, Uncle Jack, or I'll spit in your face."

John laughed as if he liked Ann's boldness. Sometimes he had her helping on the flakes and in the gardens. He never snarled at her, no matter how careless she was with work.

Ann's got a way with him, Catherine thought. *If she wants a salmon or a coin she's bold about asking and he's free about giving.*

When Catherine asked him why he was so generous to Ann and mean with other people, he shrugged. "Her da's away, idn't he?"

"If a man looked at Bridget's budding breasts and pinched them you'd threaten to skin him alive. I've seen you drive off young boys with your looks," Catherine said, giving him a dark glare.

John scowled and went down the path to lock his stage for the night.

Sixteen

"SMALLPOX has struck the place ag'in," John said with a deep sigh as he looked down on his newborn. "It's been about two years since we've heard of it."

Bridget looked up from washing supper dishes. "What is it, Fardher, a small pox on the face?"

Catherine explained. "It comes in the way of small bubbles filled with pus breaking out all over the face and body. It can scar and, at its worst, kill." Her eyebrows drew together as she followed John's look to baby Thomas who had been born in August.

That day, cold wind had swept in over the cove, dragging salt water into beads of dampness against Catherine's skin as she stood on the stage. She shivered from her poll to the backs of her legs. Then pain surged, gripping her, and she let go of the fish she was gutting, her lips tightening. She looked toward her house, wondering how she was going to get up the hill without dropping the baby. Then her lids crunched in pain; she felt swept away by it. Her body opened, urging the baby out while she tried to hold it in. *I can! I will! I must!*

John prompted her with a push to her back. "Up you go!"

"Carry me!" she whispered.

"Take her head, and I'll take her feet," John snapped at Arthur who was mopping gurry off the stage.

Bridget looked out the kitchen window just as the men

grabbed Catherine. Her mouth dropped open at the sight of her mother being carried like a barrow. She ran outside and up the path to find Ruth.

Catherine moaned as the men laid her on the bed. Then she let out a scream. John barked at Eliza to heat the water and bring some swaddling clothes.

Cat Breen, who often came down to the stage for a meal of fresh britchins, had just come over the hill with a pail when she saw Catherine being carried into the house. The woman ran, her brittle hair flying away from her face like a birch broom in a fit. "Hold on, Catherine," she called.

By the time Cat got to Catherine's room, the baby was born and wrapped in warm flannel, his tiny ruddy face scrunched up in a weak cry.

Thomas was baptized on the second day of October, 1831, two months after his early birth. Now, dread coiled around Catherine's heart, squeezing it. "The pox's not gettin' our babies."

John grunted. "'Tis not only babies goin' to their graves. There's older people too."

John's words slammed against Catherine like an icy wave. *What if I dies of the pox and me children bees left without me?*

One night, Catherine hurried to the sound of a harsh cry from Thomas in his cot. She stared in horror at the sight of a blister on his face. She drew in a sharp breath as she gathered him to her breast. She didn't tell John that night, but the next morning, when he looked at Thomas, he frowned and glanced at Catherine. She caught his look and started to cry.

Neither of them spoke as John went to light the fire. Then he got ready and sculled to Port de Grave for Dr. Appleby Brown. When the doctor came, he asked Catherine to shorten the baby. Catherine unpinned the clothes swaddling him from his feet to his armpits. She took off his nappy and removed his bellyband, and the coin placed beneath it to keep his belly from a hernia while the navel healed. When the doctor finished his examination, he looked up at Catherine and John's anxious faces. "Keep the other children at a distance," he advised, "and only one of you tend to this delicate child. I wish I could help him."

"But you can." Catherine's voice came out strained. "Didn't you tell me a long time ago about a Dr. Jenner who brought a cure for smallpox to Trinity as far back as 1804?"

The doctor nodded. "Dr. Jenner gave the first smallpox inoculation in North America at Trinity and it worked. He used pus from a blister on a cow's udder in a scratch on the patient's arm."

John was skeptical. "I can't see how that could work."

The doctor looked at John. "As strange as it may seem, cowpox inoculations made people immune to smallpox. The disease is dangerous from the onset, but once the throat swells, the victim can't breathe and – " He drew his lips tight and looked down at the baby. He shook his head. "I'm not sure I can save your baby. I'm still waiting for the vaccine. The child's too young to have the root of the pitcher plant administered to him, and it doesn't always work."

Catherine watched her baby's face break out in blisters like a fire burn. His trembling legs drew up against his blistered belly, his face tortured. She was relieved when his face settled and his cries ended, but then sorrow burst inside her and she ran from the house and across the head of the cliff. She stood there, her legs like white pillars fastened to a rock, her face cracked in grief. Wind came to life against the dead stillness of her body. She clung to her shawl, its fringes skipping into the air as tails of wind swirled her clothes around her. Caught in the eye of the greatest storm of a mother's life, she fell to the ground on the high cliffs of Salmon Point. Amid the liveliness of the wind and the fury of a mad sea, her body lay as still as if it had turned to marble, until she heard John's heavy voice dragging her to her senses. "The constables'll come and take you to the gaol across the way if you stay like this."

She turned, her clothes wrenched around her as if grief had wrung her body in a brutal twist. She stumbled to her feet and ran home to the children. Martin and Maria came to place their little hands in hers, looking up with troubled faces at her tear-stained face.

Katie held her doll tight. She touched the porcelain face, and then she reached a finger to the baby's cold cheek as he lay in his pine box. She looked up at her mother and asked, "Mamma, is Thomas a doll now?"

"He's an angel," Catherine said softly.

Martin laid down his wooden truck. He came to look at the baby. "I wanna see hes wings."

"Sure he's a baby angel," Bridget told him. "He won't have wings yet."

Catherine let the children talk and bring a smile against her grief. She would keep the memory of her baby's peaceful face, hold it against the rage she felt.

The next day, Mark Hennebury came from Port de Grave. He met John on his stagehead with news that Dr. Appleby Brown's vaccine had arrived and that the doctor had built a makeshift hospital to treat his patients. He was keeping them hospitalized until they were well, hoping to slow the spread of the disease among families.

John turned away as he told Mark that Thomas had died. Mark's grey eyes showed concern as he offered John condolences. He followed him up to the house, telling him, "Blow me Down has lost so many people it's ben called Poxville. A man with the dead cart bees waiting outside for those dyin' inside. Ship Cove's people have set up a graveyard over Pond Road Hill for smallpox victims. The graves are marked with black wrought-iron crosses."

John opened the door and Mark went inside. He looked toward Catherine who was in the parlour getting ready for Thomas's burial. He shifted uncomfortably. "Ship Cove mourners have made glass-faced, whitewashed boxes tapered at each end and holding dried everlasting flowers to lie above the graves of their babies. If you'd like a box...." His voice trailed off.

Catherine dragged her breath up through grief as heavy as wet sand. "I don't want to hear about it."

Thomas was buried in a corner of the meadow facing east. That night, Catherine tucked the children in bed, their eyes swollen from crying for their baby brother left out in the dark night under the ground. Johnny looked across from his bed to where Catherine was sitting on Katie's and Maria's bed. "Mommy," he whined, "I don't want to close me eyes. I'm afraid I'll fall asleep and disappear."

"Only for a few hours," she said gently.

"I'm afraid I'll stay gone," he whispered, "like Emilia and Thomas."

"None of us will ever be gone. Even when the time comes for us not to wake up, we won't be alone. We don't disappear from God. He carries us in Hes mind while we're here on earth, and when we goes to heaven He'll carry us in Hes bosom."

The first night after Thomas was buried, Catherine got up from her bed and looked through the window. She stared up at the full moon. It seemed to look back at her like a cold, uncaring eye. When John scolded her for getting up from sleep, her face grimaced in pain. "I wake up forgetting. Then it's as if some beast pounces on me, and digs its claws inside me chest."

"Come to bed," John coaxed. "You'll have more youngsters. Me britch is always loaded."

"Sometimes your tongue is longer than your britch," she snapped.

Catherine's body made a dizzy lurch, and she knew that another baby's heart was already beating inside it. Her mind spun like a buoy in the ocean on a wild day, dragging and whirling flotsam.

Seventeen

BY the summer of 1831, Martin and Jacob had taken Tobias Mandeville into their business as a cooper. Tobias worked from Monday morning to Saturday evening to meet the demand for barrels to hold not only fish, apples, and pickled cabbages, but a variety of goods.

Catherine was pregnant with her ninth child when she saw Tobias for the second time. She and John had taken salt fish to the Bareneed warehouse, as they did every Saturday to free up room in John's stage for the next batch of fish he was salting. They tacked across the bay under sail with northeasterly winds kicking up a swell.

As they approached the warehouse, Catherine noticed Tobias and another young fellow turning the handle on a heavy cover to press cured codfish down into a barrel. When it was tight, they nailed the cover. They hardly glanced up as they hurried to finish the day's work.

John Jacob, tall and long-shanked with a lazy-eyed look, came out of the store, wiping his hands on a piece of brin. Catherine watched as he laid a thin stencil on the cover of the barrel and brushed tar across it. He removed the stencil to show the letters SHIPPED FROM NEWFOUNDLAND. He looked at Catherine, then nodded toward Tobias and drawled, "Here's a young fellow who's got your maiden surname. Sure he's likely your cousin one way or another. I hired him to make barrels, and I've let him lodge with me."

"I know him," Catherine said with a smile, taking in the young fellow's tousled, golden red hair and bright blue eyes in a lightly freckled face. "Sure he stood at me daughter's baptism. A cater cousin – one not far removed he is, a grand cousin by the looks of him."

"He's a good cooper. Sure he can make a tight barrel for wet merchandise and a loose barrel for dry goods as well as ever you've seen. He's a smart young fellar, right handy with reading an' writing, and quicker with the feather pen than a fisherman is with a hook and line." Jacob looked at John. "Sure you can hire him to do your books at the week's end. I'll spare him."

Tobias gave John a confident look. "I've worked off me cobbler's tools. Now I oewns them," he said proudly. "Coopering takes a full six days, but I can spare Saturday night."

JOHN AND CATHERINE were back home having supper when John said, "Tobias is a good hand at figures. He can tally and write up me books and make sure I gets me dues from all the fish I lands at the warehouse the end of every week. He can record a right assessment of all the supplies I orders at the store, and all the rest of me dealings with people buying from me."

John had a familiar method. He used a group of slant marks tallying five in a group – four slant marks with a line through them to count five quintals of fish. Between his head and his pocket he had the rights of how many quintals of fish he brought to the Martin & Jacob warehouse. He had thought no one could sell him short, not even a keener like John Jacob. But lately he'd been wondering if everything had been kept straight over the fishing season. The merchant never gave him a write-up. Then there was his own business. He needed his own records. Catherine could wash Tobias's clothes, feed him his Saturday night supper and Sunday's fare, and call their business square.

If John Jacob has Tobias in his pockets and John leaves the tallying to him, we could be shortchanged, Catherine thought. "Keep what you're doing, John," she advised, "tallying your own business."

"Sure merchants can do what they like with the books if there's no one lookin' out for the fishermen and planters," John reasoned.

Catherine lifted her eyebrows. "True, but will Tobias look out for you? He's already got one master."

WINTER HAD BEEN long in going and spring late in coming. "So cold it is in some homes this morning, John," Catherine murmured, "and little children without sustenance and warmth."

"You're not fretting on other people's children."

"That I am then. Ruth come with news of Joseph Knox down in Carbonear – sixteen months and dead for want of proper nourishment."

John dismissed her concerns. "God's got the say in it all."

"He giv' us hands to tend to our own comfort and other people's if we have the means and the will."

One May evening, John came home, complaining, "In Conception Bay candles light every pane of glass in every Cartlic house. At Harbour Grace beach, a bonfire is climbing the skies. 'Tis fed with barrels of pitch and tar. I counted sixteen, and hundreds of loads of wood. There's talk of a parade and Thanksgiving Mass. I tell yer now, it's caused by the Benevolent Irish Society and the Mechanics' Society. Sure that's run by the Cartlics. The harbour's full of boats with flags flying and guns discharged. I didn't know the minute I'd have me head blown off."

Wouldn't I like to celebrate Cartlic Emancipation Day! Catherine thought. *Cartlics should have the right to vote as humans equal to other humans, and that includes women.* She said nothing. It would only keep John going.

The next day, she stood at the window. Under a grey sky, an iceberg sailed against the horizon, a white rock of ice roaming the ocean. Two small bergs lay close by, as if birthed by the larger one.

Sheen and shadows marked their variegated forms. *A woman and an iceberg show only a small part of themselves*, she thought. *But they don't always roll over quietly.*

JOHNNY WAS SITTING on the quoin that John had built to keep casks from rolling over the stage when he saw Tobias get out of a small boat and climb the stagehead. He ran up to the house to tell Catherine. Bridget came outside and took in the sight of a young fellow coming up the path. She looked at him intently as he blushed under a spray of dusty freckles. His open shirt showed hair on a chest as coarse as a tacker. He shifted his supple young body and looked away.

Catherine watched as he went past Bridget and came into the house. The way he crinkled his eyes against the sun, and the way they opened in a sparkle reminded her of her people back home. John had ordered, for his ledgers, a fine hardwood desk with a rope-and-braid motif and crystal knobs on its drawers, and a red walnut, slat-backed chair. Now he pulled out the chair for Tobias. "I'm thinkin' I should be doing a bit o' learnin' me letters," John told Tobias as he watched him make his first mark in John's new ledger. "Sure anything could be written in a will or on a land claim and you'd have to depend on other people to tell you what was on the paper before you signed your X. You could sell yourself out of house and land, and not know it."

John said Tobias could stay the night and he'd scull him back over to Bareneed by Sunday night to be ready for Monday's work.

Sometimes Catherine sat at the desk, wishing she could write. *Tobias is learned in putting figures and words on paper. Maybe he'll teach me to write me children's names.*

OVER THE MONTHS, Catherine's grief deepened over losing her two boys. As her body grew heavy with another child, her mind grew heavy with the thought, *I've been wearin' out carrying babies, and never knowin' if death, itself, would crawl out of me body – come to claim me child.*

Another daughter was born one May morning. Catherine drew laboured breaths as the lively baby lay in her arms. She touched the tiny face under a cap of soft, light hair. Then she let out a sigh and resolved to think of the children she had and be glad for memories of those God saw fit to take. She let her heart fill with gratitude.

Johanna, named after John's sister living in Redman's Cove, was baptized while Catherine was still in bed. She watched through her bedroom window as Ruth came across the path, along with Mary Britt and other women. "I'm not to rights yet," Catherine told the women as they sat around her bed, sharing the groaning cake Ruth had made for the christening.

Catherine was soon out of bed and sitting by the window, watching the children in the yard while she nursed Johanna. She called to Kitty White who was hanging sheets on the clothesline. "Mind that the rope is over the gatepost to keep Martin and Maria in." She was always afraid that they would wander down over the bank and into the water – or over the cliffs. Sometimes she dreamed that the children were running toward the cliffs, and she was running after them trying to call. No sound came as they disappeared over the edge.

The weather warmed and soon Katie and Johnny were racing down the path to Caplin Cove and paddling in the salt water. Buoyed by strings of corks around their waists, some of the young boys in the cove swam around the point to John's stagehead.

John came back from the Martin & Jacob warehouse one Saturday evening and looked around for Bridget and Eliza. Catherine could see that John's blood was boiling as he rushed to the top of the cliffs and looked down to Caplin Cove beach where the girls were skipping through salt water, their skirts and petticoats pulled up to their shapely white knees. A Noseworthy boy and an Anthony boy from Rip Raps were running over the beach and through the water, ducking under and grabbing the girls' legs.

John let out a roar. "Git on home!"

The girls dropped their skirts, soaking them in the knee-deep water. They ran up from the beach, crying for shame and running so fast their wet skirts were like their father's hands slapping their legs.

"Don't hurt them, Jack," Catherine called from the doorway. "They just took a bit of time for fun, and the boys were only having play with the girls." Catherine knew that John was often in the stage or on the cliff, having an eye out for young fellows eyeing his daughters.

When the girls hurried up over the steep path with sour looks, he slapped them hard on their behinds. "Don't you be knockin' about with young fellars. You'll be like your mam – saddled with a brood of youngsters."

AS THE DAYS went by, Catherine could see that young Arthur was a busy and steady worker. Alongside Mary Connolly, he went about his work in the stage, piling and salting wet fish. Mary lived a ways up the road with a father who was in a distressed state. She had been given summer work helping clean and cure the fish John's skiff and western boat brought in. The damp, salty smell of fish flesh was so strong Catherine could fair taste it from her doorway. Arthur worked unheeding the young children running through the narrow pathway between the layered walls of salted codfish. The hard edge of the flat, headless fish fanned out hooking the children's clothes.

By late July, Arthur had the sive stone out and was sharpening John's scythes. He cut the grass early the next morning while it was wet from dew. He was soon hauling hay from the back garden to the barracks, hardly stopping for a cold drink.

Mary had started giving Arthur her eye. Soon to be an easy nod, Catherine suspected, taking in the buxom girl with her wide mouth and ready smile.

Once, when John noticed Arthur's look flick over Mary's blooming bosom restrained with a leather camisole, he pulled down his mouth in a grump and raised his eyebrows. He looked at Mary. "Don't marry a short person. Hes brains's too close to his rump."

Arthur's face turned red. Catherine noticed his hands tighten into fists by his side.

Mary seemed to get along well with John. Earlier that spring, her father had gotten her work with a man in Harbour Grace. She'd been glad to get out of Salmon Cove to live in a place where there was more of a chance for fun. "My daughter, Mary, is a strong young maid to work," James had told Edward Moores.

Edward had eyed her and nodded. "Fer four pounds then." He nodded again, and started walking away.

"Go on then," her father said, pushing at Mary. She reluctantly followed the man, noting his scowl. Her new boss turned to see if she was coming and she met his surly, dark eyes. Through the spring, hot days and cold, she filled stage racks with codfish to be salted, washed and dried on the flakes. Then the caplin struck in on the beaches like a mass of live silver. Everyone hurried with their buckets to gather the flickering silver-bellied fish arching their iridescent green backs. Mary helped load the caplin on wheelbarrows and carts. She was moving a cart up the steep path to the stage when it hit a rock and overturned. She was hurrying to gather the caplin, trying to be quick in filling the cart, when she felt a pain in the back of her head. She turned and got another blow across her face. Mary's father hauled her away from the place with only a shiften of clothes that Moores gave her. He had torn her clothes, trying to get at her while she was in the stage, laying out fish to be salted.

Her mother didn't want anyone to know. "Just keep yerself to yerself, and don't get in the shade of flakes or stages alone. T'reaten to tell the man's wife on 'un, if it happens ag'in," her mother said.

ARTHUR'S UNDERSHIRT AND woollen drawers hung on his body, salty with sweat. One afternoon, he flung his drawers on the fence under a hot sun while he wore bare overalls. His hands were chafed and his palms as dry and powdery as cured, salted fish, as he sweated with the work of weeding the land. He'd have to wait patiently to have his passage money for home. The fall beyond this one would be slow in coming.

"I'm planning on working to store up before I have a woman," he told Catherine in a tight, crisp voice as he turned to the sight of Mary eyeing him, and his drawers on the fence.

Later, Catherine listened in the cooling night air to John ramming commands down Arthur's throat. Just as he was ready to call it a night, John shouted, "Get out there now, Arthur, and crop a wing off that saucy fowl so it won't fly into the gardens and ruin the plants. Be ready on the morrow to cut yokes to keep wild goats out of the gardens."

Catherine chided John. "Don't be using Arthur so hard, forcing him into constant labour. Sure he's fair pickled in hes own sweat. Yesterday, he got so overcome he flung off hes drawers."

"He's a servant, Catherine. A servant earns hes keep. The food's on the table for him as well as us. You know he can eat until the food fair pops out of hes eyes."

"Arthur is not beholden to you. I'm sure he could live out of a barrel of water if he had to."

John's look turned soft. "Now, Irish girl," John coaxed, as his arms went around her, "you can leave your softness for me."

One September day, for the first time since Johanna was born, Catherine went with John to the Martin & Jacob warehouse with a load of fish. She sat in the prow of the boat, soothed by the turn of John's sculling oars as water rippled and giggled over them. As they neared the Bareneed wharf, John rested his oars, and threw up the painter. A Taylor boy grabbed it and tied it to the gump post. John Jacob sauntered out to the wharf. He shook his head and grimaced. "I thought 1832 would be a good year. Instead, the potato crop is not going to be what it should be. And the fish. I wish it was like when John Cabot come."

"Sure he was speaking of caplin. John Cabot took them up in buckets. We can still do that when caplin swims in schools and when they rolls on the beaches," John answered.

John Jacob shifted his galluses over his shoulders and said, "I've just heard that the English Government has granted us a representative assembly. Now Port de Grave will have a representative speaking on its behalf at the political level, and we'll have a voting centre here."

"A lot of good 'twill do us," retorted Catherine. "There'll be money for political positions for the likes of Robert Prowse, but nothing for the commoner. There's people starving in the colony, and dying for need of money or something to barter for flour, barm, and molasses. A crime it is that men in power have the best of wine and food while urchins die in the roads for want of shelter and a loaf of bread. A wonderful thing 'tis to do well in life, but 'tis better to do good."

John turned to Catherine. "Hush, woman. Do." He gave her a look that stung as much as a slap. He turned back to John Jacob who was saying, "John Bowes, Thomas Butler, William Mullowney, and George Cranford will administer the election with the voting at John Bowes's house."

"Two good ones, John Bowes and Thomas Butler," scoffed Catherine. She thought of how Irishman Bowes had come to Sandy Cove as a blacksmith and, under the nod of Robert Pinsent, had become a gaoler and a constable. Irish Catholics didn't trust him to stand with them on Irish Catholic issues.

ARTHUR APPROACHED JOHN at the end of his first year. "I'd like a shilling or so," he said.

"You'll get your money when the time comes," John answered. "For now you've got food and rum – and Mary Connolly, I'm sure, if you wants her."

Arthur, looking embarrassed, turned away. Mary was after him like a dog after a bone. He hadn't been taken by her bold looks and her smooching around him evenings when it was time for her to have gone home. Catherine watched him put up the new barrack for dry hay, knocking in the four posts with a heavy swing of the maul. His shoulders hunched, his neck dropped as if he was readying himself to meet an enemy. He swung the maul over and over until the posts were solid. Then he built a roof over the posts to protect the hay. He stogged each netted bag with one hundred pounds of dry hay and lifted them into the barn, up to the hayloft, all the while holding a brooding look.

Arthur was strong. He could grab up a hundred-pound bag of potatoes and load it on his back as quick as you could look at him, then swing the heavy barn door open in a blink.

"He's a worker," Arthur overheard John tell his brother, Edward, one November evening. "But he's got the brains of a starfish."

"He's got brawn, and that's all you'll ever need from him," Edward said, letting out a chuckle.

Catherine knew Arthur had overheard John and Edward talking. She saw his fingers curl against his palms and thought, *He's a luckless wight to have got in with the likes of Jack.* She knew that Arthur's temper matched John's, but he had no way to express it, except to kick and shoot wild animals on the prowl or wring the neck of a hen wanted for dinner. Once he lifted a gun from its rack and went outside and fired at the chickens. They went off clucking except one. Its head lay scattered on the ground.

"I'm glad he didn't point the gun at me. I'd be afraid it would go off accidentally," Catherine later told John.

He shrugged. "It's for sport, and he's got a good aim."

"He can use a slingshot to fight off stray dogs," Catherine said, knowing it was no good to talk to John. *I'm hes wife, and he's raised the loaded gun to me with a coarse laugh, let his finger slide along the trigger. It's enough to wreck me peace.*

There were harsh words between John and Arthur as time went on. One morning, Catherine watched from the window as Arthur twined twigs to a birch rod to make a besom for sweeping the barn. John must have wanted him to be doing something else. He knocked him across the back and the two shouted back and forth. Finally Arthur spit into his hand and extended it to John. They shook hands – a truce for the time being.

John came across the path, shaking his head and muttering, "That one's got sawdust between his ears, and a brain as thick as fog."

Arthur heard him; his eyes narrowed and he gritted his teeth. Catherine could see his hands ball as if he would like to puck John in the head.

"Sometime, he'll find someone taking his oewn gun to him," Arthur threatened under his breath.

One Saturday night, as Arthur sat riffling playing cards for a game with Tobias, cups of rum beside them, Catherine tried to make light of Arthur's quarrel with John. "Arthur, me man, don't pay any mind to that cripsy old fellar. Words you haven't got to heed, and if John strikes you, and you strikes back, there'll be the Devil to pay, so try to forestay a fight."

"I'll oewn a gun and be me oewn man in time," Spring said with a saucy grin. "You can bet on that."

"Don't get on the hard side of John," Tobias warned, glancing through the window and catching sight of John going down the path.

Arthur looked after John's back and uttered a curse under his breath. "May you live to see your oewn funeral."

Catherine caught his words and felt a tremor.

JOHN HAD ORDERED spices for the Christmas pudding, and their scents soaked through the house on Christmas morning. Catherine called out the door, "The duck is on the fire and the chowder is set to the table. Come along and eat."

The children came running over the snow-covered path, snow fluffing around their boots. Their rosy cheeks were stuck out with knobs of molasses candy Catherine had put in their Christmas stocking. They danced across a puddle caught over beside the door, stomping their feet until the ice cracked like glass.

Eliza went to fetch Arthur from the barn where he was tapping his waddies with tar to keep the water out. John came home from Edward's place, lucky to have his gun already loaded. He stood in the doorway, pointing it toward the sun. He was too drunk on flip to fire the gun straight up to start the Christmas dinner.

"Sure he'll have a hole in the sun," said Katie in alarm. "It'll break apart and drop down on the ocean, and then the day won't ever be warm." Martin looked at her, wide-eyed.

"Silly," Johnny scoffed. "It's too far away to shoot."

John stumbled to the table and lifted his cup to a Christmas toast. "Here's to a clean conscience, and a guinea in each pocket." He took one look at John McCabe seated next to Bridget and frowned. He had hired the young fellow to help out around the farm during the fall harvest, but he wasn't fussy about Catherine having him come for Christmas dinner, even if it would keep him from spending the day alone in the small cabin his father had left him. "You never know what he's thinking about Bridget," John told Catherine later.

"It's enough that Bridget thinks nothing of him," Catherine answered. Bridget didn't seem ready to latch on to any boy, though there were times when Catherine saw her look flicker over Tobias. But not when her father was around. It was as if John couldn't imagine men doing to his girls what he had done to other men's daughters.

After dinner, Arthur and James rigged up the horse and sleigh and took the children up the path to Clarke's Beach for a ride.

"'TIS A PITIFUL place this is," John muttered, coming into the pantry one January evening where Catherine was making a pot of soup for supper. "Spare the taties," he cautioned. "We're better off than some livyers, but the taties won't last."

"What's anyone doing about the need?" asked Catherine.

"I heard," said John, "that a Mr. Brown presented a petition from Port de Grave to the government stating the distress of this place. He said that the government got no funds for starving fishermen. But there's to be a committee struck, and the Governor, hesself, will adopt measures to relieve sufferers. The failure of the potato crop'll remind you Irish crowd of your own crop failures."

"No thanks to the English invaders. *They* didn't starve in Ireland."

John lifted his hand as if to strike her. She gave him a mean look. "I've got the knife." She went on. "The little Newell children, Jack. They're on the neck in that drafty hut in bitter cold winds. Their father's without a boat and all their crops were bitten off with frost before they had a good start. It wouldn't take much skin off your nose to help them. Your western boat did well. You've got money laid aside."

John gave her a look that showed his contempt for such a notion. "Nature's way is to help the strong and break the weak."

SPRING WAS NEAR, and the place dazzled under sunshine on snow. The branches of evergreen trees, holding handfuls of snow, slipped free, sending showers of flakes against crusted snow. Conkerbells, hanging off roofs like crystal tongues, broke off and tinkled in the clear air as they struck the ground. Gulls pitched across the headland like the last blobs of snow as John fixed up his punt for the spring cod. There had been leaks in the punt the year before, and the piggin had been used often to bail out the boat. Now John set about replacing rotting timbers.

Arthur helped caulk open seams with oakum. Then the two men painted the punt black. They tarred and ochred it inside, making it ready to be loaded with the ten quintals it could take on its inshore voyage. John was letting his hired men fish the western boat. He was staying close to home for now, keeping a close eye on his daughters and any young fellows coming too close.

Eighteen

ARTHUR waited impatiently for the fall, when John would fix up with the merchants and have his wages ready. Catherine noticed that he seemed grieved, as if he was afraid he might not get enough money to go back to Ireland. Tobias had been instructed to mark Arthur's expenses in John's ledger. "You're beholden to me for everything but a drink of water," John told his servant. That made Arthur glum, his temper ready to boil as the summer wore away. Catherine had seen him take a stick to a wild dog. The animal, lively one minute, keeled over the next with frothy blood on its lips.

It was the twenty-ninth of August, and John was putting his boat on collar when a fisherman sculled by with the news that William Hele, a Cupids fisherman who was John's far cousin, had died that morning, and he but thirty-nine. John strode up to the house to tell Catherine the news. He wiped his brow on his sleeve. "We'll get someone to go up to Spectacle Head. He'll be buried in Cupids on the first of the month."

Catherine turned quickly. "I guess you won't be selling any more jugs of grog to him. How did he die?"

"He just up and died," said John. "No particular reason, it seemed. The man's back was so bad he was down in a double of late. But that wasn't a thing to kill a mortal."

Catherine shook her head. "Sad it is then. Kitty will go with

Mary Connolly. She'll like a night off to see what's going on and to get a yarn with her chums."

"That'll do," John said.

Catherine turned from the salted fish roasting on the hearth to get a cloth. Blisters had formed from salt coming to the surface. She wiped off the slub so the fish would not be too salty. Then she stuck the flesh fork into the boiling cauldron. "The taties are done," she said. "We'll have supper."

THAT FRIDAY NIGHT, the sky was like a field of pale bakeapples, spreading into an orange gleam as the sun slipped away. Saturday promised to be calm. The sounds of dogs barking broke through the gentle sighs of Catherine's sleep, awaking her. She hoped John didn't hear them. It was nothing for John, or Arthur, to get the muzzleloader and fire at wild dogs that John claimed were part dog and part wolf. Sometimes Arthur filled John's blunderbuss, a short, large-bored shotgun, with glass and stones to frighten dogs away. Other times he had Johnny and other cove boys using slingshots on wild goats. Arthur stuck a round beach rock in the kid of his slingshot one evening and challenged Johnny to shoot it up the hinder end of a wild buck. When the boy found his target, Arthur laughed so hard his eyes closed and his shoulders shook.

Catherine awoke the next morning to an open window and the sound of voices carried across the waters. She and John were soon up. Catherine went to get Arthur. "Up you get for breakfast," she called through the closed barn door. "The ground is laden with dew, a sign there'll be no rain. Fish can be spread."

After breakfast, Arthur and John hurried to the flakes to spread codfish needing another half-day drying. By midday, they were packing up the fish, dry and stiff. Good powdery fish, the kind John was proud to have made. The soft, cool sunlight and the gentle wind of late August had been perfect for making fish. John would have his best price. He always washed fish so that blood clots made by a prong in live fish would not show. Sometimes he cursed his men for not pronging every fish through the head.

Catherine spent the morning tending to housecleaning and changing beds, and after midday making a pot of pea soup for supper. She had taken off her bibbed apron and was smoothing her braided hair when she heard John call, "Kit, make haste!" He was hurrying her up to come load the fish in the boat.

Catherine called to Bridget in the parlour. "Mind the children. We'll be back before dark." Maria toddled across the floor, her golden curls bouncing. She held out a finger showing a tiny cut. Catherine stopped to soothe her. Then when she opened the door, Martin ran across the yard, calling, "Mamma, I got the egg cups."

"Hiccups, it is." She smiled and stooped to hold him tight. "I won't be gone long. Be good for Eliza and Bridget." The little boy nodded.

By mid-afternoon, John and Catherine were ready for the boat trip across the harbour to Bareneed. A salty scent permeated the air as Catherine settled in the bow of the boat. "A few more dollars for your money box then," Catherine remarked as John sculled the boat through quiet waters.

"There's no smell on the money," he said with a grin.

"You could give Arthur a few shillings," she coaxed.

"And have him run off on us. You know there's times he'd sooner see the Devil than me."

"And with good reason," she said under her breath. Then she steered their conversation to the wake. "It's Saturday, and William Hele, your very own relative, is being waked for the last night. You should go."

John shrugged. "That I'll think about."

Catherine remembered one day when she was standing on the cliffs above Caplin Cove, watching children skittering over the beach, arms stretched like wings. William Hele had come with coin to get a jug of mountain dew from one of John's kegs he kept in the shed. As he came up the hill to go home, he followed Catherine's glance to the children. "Their day will come," he said. She had turned back to stoop and cradle a bush, slipping off its handful of blueberries. Then she started back to the house. She stopped to listen to young voices rising above Caplin Cove. The disembodied sounds sailed through the air, met, clashed, fell away to silence, then echoed again, swallowing the silence.

Now, as Catherine and John reached the Martin & Jacob wharf, she thought, *William's day has come and gone, and life goes on. No one knows whose day is coming next.*

The warehouse door was open, and Catherine could see Tobias at the ringing table quoiling soaked saplings. He glanced up from fashioning the runner hoops to go around the middle of barrels he was making. He finished twelve hoops and tied them in a bundle. Then he lifted an elbow across his face and grinned at Catherine. She called, "You'll be over later with Jack, will you?"

He nodded, and when Catherine and John left Bareneed, Tobias was on the mare – a six-foot-long bench-like stool used in making barrel hoops and staves for casks. He waved them off with the marehead, a press-like tool.

On the way back from the Martin & Jacob warehouse, Catherine tightened her shawl against a nip in the air rising above waters slopping against the boat. September was coming, and already there were signs of green leaves turning yellow. There wouldn't be many more trips to carry cured fish to the merchants' warehouse. Once the western boat came back with her three-week load of salted fish to be washed, cured and delivered to the merchants, she would be making a trip to St. John's to be loaded with supplies for families who had no way of getting to the inport. John would bring back cases of Bohea tea, barrels of flour, molasses and butter, drums of Sultana raisins, and bales of cloth for women wanting yard goods.

John had told Catherine that St. John's Harbour was in a flurry during October and November. Ships flooded the place, their canvas sails rising into the air like a swarm of moths. Schooners lined the waterfront as boat keepers sold "made" fish to residents to get money to pay debts to the merchants at home and to have money for winter supplies.

Foreign ships winched baled goods up to buildings beside the water's edge. Residents came with coin, wanting to lay in barrels of apples, flour, vegetables, dried lentils, peas, apricots, and prunes.

The head of Salmon Cove lay in the bay like a sleeping animal as the sun slipped behind the hills. Catherine had taken the lantern in case they got held up at the warehouse and had to cross in the dark. Now she lifted it from the boat's tommy stick.

John cursed under his breath. "Leave it, woman. You know I needs light to go across to the warehouse."

Catherine had been going to put the lantern on the stage pole. She let it bide. Then she pulled the boat alongside the stagehead. As she climbed the rails, one foot slipped and her body was flung out; her legs swung back, one striking a rail. She let out a cry of pain. She got her footing and her hand went to her stomach. She'd been nauseated of late. *All spawned out, I should be by now*, she thought wryly.

She mounted the stagehead and limped across it up to the house. John followed, calling for her to fill the half-puncheon for his wash.

Kitty White was up in the house with the younger children, except for Johnny, who had gone on John's western boat, and Katie, who was staying with Cat Breen to ease her memory of losing her boy a year ago today.

"Why is she sad?" Katie had asked back then.

"She lost her baby."

"Did she find him?"

"He drowned, and he wasn't found."

Over tea, Cat had sobbed to Catherine, "He won't get a finger's breadth in the earth."

"He'll get his place in heaven," she had responded softly.

Cat, a faraway look on her round, sad face, said, "I think of the times we sat for tea, leaves swirling in the cup and settling to the bottom like a dark cloud while we went on talking and laughing. No one could read the leaves and reckon the times we would cry over my Jacob lost at sea and your children lost after they were born."

Earlier in the day, Catherine had watched Mary and Katie go

up the path on their way to Cat's place. Their feet dragged, showing reluctance. She called, "Now Mary, Aunt Ida Doyle is doing poorly by the sights of it. There's no smoke in her chimney. Along the way back from Cat's place, go lay the fire. Draw water and heat it so the poor dear can wash her face and hinder, it being Saturday. She'll want to be clean for Sunday. Make a pot of porridge to get her through the day. Tell her I wish her health, and smack a koob on her lonely cheek, and I'll see that you get your dues for it."

Now Catherine looked toward the bay as she filled her arms with junks of wood to carry to the woodbox in the porch. She hoped Johnny wasn't seasick on his first trip out on the water with Skipper Taylor in the western boat.

John finished his bath and came upstairs to shave in the wash basin on the bedroom dresser. Then he hurried to dress in his good fustian trousers and blue, striped shirt, so he could be on his way to Martin & Jacob's place where merchants and well-off planters often went on a Saturday night. They yakked over business, politics, fish, and Catholics, and told stories, warmed by Jacob's grog. Catherine, like other women, stayed home and tended to the children. "Saturday night is the time to get away from spiteful women and bawling children," John told Catherine.

Catherine often sat on the younger children's beds, holding her babies, rosy-skinned and fresh. She stayed to watch them in sleep, their faces flushed from their baths or from a day running in sunlight. She was grateful that they always slept through the night.

Now she heated water and poured it into the wooden tub. "Come for your wash," she called to the children playing in the yard. "You likely got enough dirt under your fingernails to grow flowers."

Martin came running. He stopped to call to a piglet, "Here, chucky, chucky."

Catherine looked toward John as she went to get towels and clean nightclothes to take to the children. "We are well off, aren't we, Jack? I wants to go to St. John's. I've never ben there."

He stopped her with blunt words. "And you're not likely to be there very quick. There's no room in the western boat. I need every scrap of space for my fish and produce. On the return, the boat will be loaded with merchandise. I'll bring you a Christmas box."

He pulled on his best blue waistcoat and left with parting words over his shoulder. "Tobias will be back over with me to do the books."

INSIDE THE FAMILY'S large kitchen, Kitty pushed back her stool from where she was eating with Arthur and the children. "That's it for suppa," she said. "I'll take the dishes to the pantry." She finished washing the dishes while she waited for Bridget and Eliza to get ready to leave the house for the last night of William Hele's wake.

The girls wanted to go to Cupids to have a night out. Catherine tried to hurry them up before their father got home. Kitty was uneasy about going with the girls, who were sure to feel the lash of their father's temper once they came home. There was a stormy tension in the house when everything wasn't done John's way. On times she wished she was deaf, when there was a roar from John and a screech of pain from Catherine or the children.

Bridget and Eliza hurried down the stairs, and Kitty called to Catherine, "Off we go then to the wake before it's fully dark. Sure it's dark now by half past seven."

"Don't be gone too long," Catherine answered.

"A couple of hours," Kitty assured her. She crossed the floor to the window and looked out. She came back, smiling at the girls. "Sure I wanted to settle me mind that your fardher won't stop yer."

Just then, Mary Connolly lifted the latch on the door and came in. She'd come back from seeing Katie to Cat Breen's, and now she was ready to go to the wake with the girls. Bridget and Eliza, their faces tight and anxious, scurried after Kitty and Mary out the back door and up over the hill.

IT WAS LATE that night when Catherine, holding fifteen-month-old Johanna, hastened up the path to Ruth's house. She turned to look toward the dark bay, unable to see the stage sitting over the water like a grey skeleton. She turned away, hurrying to rap on the kitchen door. She waited awhile, and then she heard Ruth shuffling toward the barred door. She opened it, her eyes in a sleepy daze.

"What time in the night is it?" she asked.

"After twelve, but not yet one," Catherine answered.

"What's the matter?"

"Jack's temper is on the boil, Ruth. He went to settle with the dogs turning on the salt fish bulked on the fish flake, and then he come back and was chasing the pigs from the door. I waited until the children had settled in their beds, dead to the world. Then I left to give him time to stay hesself."

"What did you say to make him so angry?" Ruth asked, still dazed with sleep.

"Nothing!"

"So much the better," Ruth told her. "You had better come in and lie down."

Catherine shook her head. "I'll sleep up here in the kitchen on the daybed." She laid the sleeping baby on the small bed, saying, "Jack's mad about the girls gone to Bill Hele's wake and smouldering now that they're not back. They've likely stayed the night with Bill's girls."

Patience Boon, Ruth's young neighbour, whose husband had gone to fish on the Labrador coast, was sleeping in a bunk beside Ann's bed when she heard voices. She came out, rubbing her eyes. Catherine was taking off her clothes when she noticed the woman. She said, "Oh Patience, if I'd known you were here, I'd have asked you to come down to sleep with me. Jack can sleep his spite and spit off on the kitchen bench."

She turned to Ruth. "I'd be grateful if Ann spoke to her uncle Jack. He's rough on the girls. Sure they can't move out of hes sight."

Ruth didn't look surprised. "You don't have to tell me a thing about it. You and the young one stay the night then. Get some sleep. Sure Tobias and Arthur will handle Jack, and the girls will handle the youngsters. John will, hopefully, have settled by morning."

Ruth Snow would later tell the court that she had heard a shot earlier that night while she was having tea. She thought it was fired near the flakes – as usual.

Nineteen

CATHERINE was awakened by Johanna the next morning. She breast-fed her daughter and left the house while Ruth's family was still asleep. The sun was lipping up over the far shore, as bold as brass, spreading its light against the fading night as she hurried down the path to her house. She faintly remembered that Bridget and Eliza had come to Ruth's house during the night, looking for tinder. Catherine stopped suddenly as a dizzy spell took her; her stomach rolled. It was usually the same while she was carrying her babies; sickness came along with them. Now here she was again, dizzy and retching. Inside her mind, she cried, *No more babies!* Her need to have an empty belly meant nothing. John was having his seed in her, and that was that.

"You can go down on your bendings and give me my dues," he'd told her with a laugh when she complained that she'd had enough babies.

"I'd sooner suck the eyes out of a codfish," she had shouted.

KITTY WHITE WAS making porridge when she heard the creaking of the front door. She hurried out of the kitchen, exclaiming, "It's yourself home, ma'am, and the master nowhere in sight. I sid his boat early this morning, loose near the rocks at the stage."

Catherine frowned. "He was about the house when I left,

chasing pigs away from the door. We'll have a look to see if he's fallen somewhere. He may be curled up in the barn among the straw."

"The porridge is on, ma'am."

"Yes, yes," Catherine said absently. "See that the children are fed. And get some sleep. Sure you've been up most of the night, all of you."

Catherine went upstairs to where Bridget lay asleep after her late night. She woke her, saying, "Your fardher must be abed somewhere snoring off whatever drink he had in him."

Bridget raised her head, wiped a hand across her eyes and yawned. "I didn't see him," she said.

Catherine hurried outside to the barn and hauled open the door. "Arthur," she called. "Wake up. Have you seen Jack?"

He woke, his eyes heavy with sleep and the dregs of his night at the wake. "The master?" He looked up. "No, I never sid he, not since last night."

"Well, look for him then. See if he's not slumped in the hay in the loft."

She walked through the barn while Arthur climbed the ladder for a look. John wasn't in the barn, nor the shed. Catherine went down to the stage and out on the stagehead. She took a deep breath and peered down into the water. There was no sign that John had fallen over. The punt swung on its painter. She stood pondering this and the sight of the unlocked stage doors. Then she came back to the house. "The boat's not anchored and the stage's not locked," she said, looking toward the pantry to a bare nail that usually held the stage key.

Martin looked up at her, his sunny-brown eyes wide. He seemed to sense a quietness that was not always there on Sunday mornings.

Kitty hesitated. Then she said, "When we got home I heard people talking and cursing under the bank."

Bridget, who had hurried downstairs after her mother awoke her, looked up from where she sat at the table. She stopped eating her porridge. "On my way home from Aunt Ruth's I heard the sound of oars, but no voices."

Catherine looked toward Arthur and Tobias coming from outside. "Come on," she said. "We'll go look for Jack." They stopped in for Ruth and Patience to help in the search.

When they got to Mary Connolly's house, the girl's father suggested that John could be off somewhere up to Eli Noseworthy's place, sleeping off whatever brew the two might have shared.

They stopped at the Noseworthys' house. No one there admitted seeing John.

As the morning stirred abroad, John's absence came against Catherine's senses like a deafening silence. *There were times when I knew if he be laid out somewhere, I could stand a chance of living to raise the children. But I never expected this. I don't know what will be.* . . . With her thoughts hanging, she went to sit against the window, her arms folded, her hands under her elbows as if shielding her stomach while her foot rocked Johanna's cot.

By the time Kitty laid the table for midday, and Catherine set doughboys on boiling water to rise like white bergs on a turbulent ocean, she found herself wondering if John had left his family. His pipe was missing. *Jack is where it is*, she thought. *But he's left his hat and his best blue waistcoat which he had on the early part of yesternight.*

"Come on," she called to the children, trying to keep a steady voice. "Tear the doughboys abroad." She poured molasses over the warm fluffy balls of boiled dough. The children ate them with a cup of warm milk, all the while eyeing the lemon curd their mother had promised them for their Sunday afters.

Catherine was washing Martin's freckled face of the leftovers of soft custard when Arthur and Tobias pushed open the door. "We ate at Mary's place. Now we'll be off to the funeral," Tobias told Catherine.

"And taking Mary, you'll be." Catherine's look went from Arthur to Mary, who was standing behind him, her soft, round face flushed.

"We'll come back if we hear tell of John," Tobias promised. The door shut behind the men and Catherine's hands went to her belly. *I'm not sure what it is I'm fearin'. But it's Sunday, and John is one to leave the work for drink and rest, though there's ben nights he's tarried at John Jacob's for the night blaming the weather, but he did come home the next day.*

Catherine had settled Johanna for her afternoon nap and was leaning her head against the back of the chair when Martin asked, "Where's Fardher?"

Catherine whispered, "He's gone." Her lips began to tremble and she couldn't say more. She pulled Martin into her lap. *If John would only come back from where he's gone, we could try harder. . . .* Her thoughts trailed like smoke into the air.

Bridget sat stoned-face as she told Catherine about their night. She and the other girls had come laughing over the hills, their arms linked. Tobias and Arthur began telling ghost stories until the girls were so scared they huddled against each other. They stopped abruptly, thinking it strange that the house was in darkness, not even a lantern light in the window.

The hearth was cold, and Bridget had exclaimed, "Oh 'tis bad luck this is; the fire in an Irish hearth should always be moored. But 'tis good luck that Fardher's not up, ready to smack us for being so late."

"So early," Eliza had answered with a giggle.

There was no sound of their father's snoring, no squeak of ropes as was sometimes heard when their father moved in the bed.

Bridget turned to the others. "I'll go to Aunt Ruth and get some tinder. We don't have to go to bed."

"I'll come with you," Eliza said and followed Bridget out the door and up the path. Bridget tried her aunt's door, but it was fastened. She knocked. Then she pushed hard and the door opened.

Catherine remembered how the knock had stirred her from an uneasy sleep. She had lifted up on her elbow beside Johanna sound asleep. The usually timid Bridget stood above her with a bold look on her face as Catherine asked, "What did your fardher do to you for being so late?"

"Nothing," Bridget had answered. "We didn't see him. The fire's out, so I've come looking for tinder."

"Never mind the tinder," Catherine had said. "Go on to bed and draw the blankets over you before your fardher comes back from where he's gone."

Bridget told her mother that, after she came back to the house, Tobias or Arthur had already struck a light with powder. Then they said they were going back to the wake. They went away together.

BRIDGET AND ELIZA went about with solemn faces, quietly taking charge of the younger children while Catherine went upstairs and lay down, her belly unsettled. A lonely feeling washed over her. *Jack had likely sat to brood and drink after frightening off the pigs, getting angrier and angrier when the girls didn't show. If he'd gone up over the cliffs he could have tripped up and fallen over. If he went looking for the girls and dropped by the wayside, the men will come across him on their way to the funeral,* she reasoned.

The day disappeared under the weight of a night that seemed to smother Catherine. Thoughts of her fight with John the night before closed around her like darkness. In her bedroom, she picked up a coral-shell brush from a brush-and-comb set lying on the nightstand. John had brought it to her from St. John's last year. She gazed hard at the brush; then she faced her image in the looking glass and whispered, "John's not come home, and I don't know what to say – what to do. I don't know how I feel."

"I've bought you a present," he'd said with a grin.

She'd taken it and opened the soft cloth holding the set. "A comb for your crown," he said. "Turn up your hair and confine it in its teeth. I won't have you out on the path with the wind playing with that shock of hair."

"You don't want me hair hanging loose."

"No, not with it dancing about and teasing the minds of other men."

Now she swept the comb under her hair as dark as the bark

that stained John's nets. *I don't know what's ben done to Jack – if anything.* A shudder went down her spine.

By evening, there was hardly enough strength in her legs to carry her downstairs to breastfeed Johanna and to bring her up to her cot. As she turned the blankets back from her featherbed, she rubbed her fingers along the mattress cover. She fingered the scar of thread where she had sewn it back together after John had put a load of shot in it, sending feathers flying. Johanna, in her cot, had screamed to match the noise while Catherine sang a cradle song over and over to settle her.

If he's gone, that won't ever happen again, Catherine thought. *Maybe Divine Providence has removed Jack from our midst.* Guilt followed that thought. Then her lips softened into a smile. *When I see him tall and muscled coming up the path, and I hear him call, there is something that makes me see him apart from his temper. If he would only be as handsome in his behaviour as he looks when he's dressed for a Saturday night, the place would be more pleasant. Even though he's getting on in years, his hair's not thinning like Edward's. He's still got dark curls and a face as healthy as you'd see, and he's as tanned as a Spaniard.*

A flicker of wind blew against a candle in a holder by the open window and the flame went out. She had brought a lantern from the parlour upstairs. Now she held it on her knees, feeling its warmth and letting its cheery light comfort her while she watched Johanna asleep in her cot. In the next room, Martin slept alone in the bunk he shared with Johnny when he wasn't in the western boat. Maria and Katie slept in a side bunk. Bridget and Eliza shared the third room. The children's minds were now forgetful of everything. Catherine smiled when she thought of Katie. "We're the three K's," she'd said. "Fardher calls you Kit, and there's Kitty White, and I'm Katie."

A cool breeze touched Catherine's face like a fairy breath, lifting soft tendrils of hair off her forehead as she pulled the shutters against the night. *I don't know how to raise the children and tend to the work and another mite to be born.*

She took the lantern and went down the stairs and out the door to the cliffs. She stood there as still as a pillar while a strong wind came like a cold hand pushing against her. Her grandfather had believed that the auld witch keened on the wind when there was a death. Now Catherine listened . . . waited . . . feared. She turned away from soft sighs of the sea breathing through the night, and away from what she didn't know, what she couldn't suspect, back to her children.

Upstairs, Catherine lowered the wick in the lantern and sat a long time, letting the world breathe around her while she listened to the frantic thumping of her heart. Could John be gone? Could something have happened to him, or would he come through the door in a rage? A soft whimper broke in on her thoughts, and she picked Johanna up from her cot and brought her to her own bed. She held her gently in the curve of her body. Now and then, she woke to a stir in the dark house, a creak on the stairs, a snore from one of the children.

Finally, Catherine and the house slept – not for the first time – without John.

Twenty

MONDAY came with rushes of wind against the windows. Catherine lifted up on her elbow. She was startled to find the maid beside her in the bed.

"You were crying in your sleep, ma'am, something awful. Besides, I didn't want to sleep up in the room across from Tobias and that fellow, Wills, who stopped in for the night. Though Wills could be a Molly man, for all I know – and Tobias too." The maid jumped out, promising, "I'll dress and then I'll fetch the children breakfast. You lie abed for a while."

Catherine didn't answer. Her head felt swollen and achy. She pushed the counterpane aside and sat up, feeling a tremor through her body. The room spun around her and she lay back down for a moment to get herself to rights.

WIND SHADOWED THE sun with dark clouds as Catherine went to the stagehead where John's boat was tied. Rushing water swelled against the rocks, its foam falling into piebald circles. Turrs pitching on the water went belly up, bobbing like white buoys. "'Tis the scowl of a dark sky and the temper of a wild sea we're having today, and Jack nowhere in sight," she said to Ruth who had come down behind her. Ruth nodded without a word.

All morning, the sea reared like a wild animal roaring and hissing, then dropping as if to crouch and spring again, snarling and biting. Toward noon, it rolled and yawned and settled. Catherine could hear John's voice: "The sea can be as cold as fire is hot, and just as dangerous."

Catherine came back to the house to attend to the children's needs, all the while feeling her strength petering. She was sitting for a rest in the parlour in the afternoon when Constable John Bowes showed up. He stopped by Arthur in the path. "'Tis rough handling in the sea today. It delayed the crossing."

Arthur shot him a glance. "And that it is then, rougher here though with the master missing."

"And how be you?"

"Good."

"Sure you is." He paused. "Now there, boy. Do you know where John is? Has he been done to death?"

"We haven't heard tell of that. He's just missing."

"Is that so then?" Bowes banged Arthur on the shoulder and tramped up the steep path.

High on the door ledge outside the house a row of bells tinkled on dancing springs. Then a knock struck the door like a shudder. Kitty drew away from stirring the fire, her lips tight. She went to pull a curtain aside, then called to Catherine in the parlour. "'Tis the constable at the door, ma'am, come with his billy knocker and with the sternest look you ever sid." She let the curtain fall and hurried to open the door just as John Bowes lifted the draw latch and strode in.

Catherine rose unsteadily with Johanna in her arms. She stood mute, her small finger in the mouth of the child just settling after crying from teething. Ruth and Ann, Mary Britt and other neighbours, along with Tobias had gathered in the parlour. Now they followed Catherine out.

Constable Bowes's look met Catherine's. "Magistrate Robert Pinsent and John Jacob have sent me to make enquiries regarding John. The old fellars at 'The Tell' says he's missing. They thinks he might have been murdered or that he made away with hesself."

Catherine knew all about the men at "The Tell" sitting out on a rock wall against an old shed, the strength to do a day's work gone. They managed to hobble a little work here and there, finding fodder for their gossip as they sat drawing on their pipes or taking in a laboured breath.

The constable went on. "Magistrate Pinsent is concerned with John's whereabouts, and the business. He knows he has a large sum of money laid by."

"He has a money box, but it's not in my keeping. Perhaps it's with him. I don't think Mr. Pinsent should be meddling in John's business."

"It's his duty to do so," Constable Bowes answered before turning his back.

Catherine muttered, "The business of John's money is not hes to know."

The constable asked bluntly, "Have you seen your husband of late?"

Kitty stepped toward Bowes and said eagerly, "He did come for supper, sir. He had it with Arthur and the missus. That's what the missus said. Mary Connolly and me went off to the wake with the girls."

Constable Bowes didn't take his gaze from Catherine. "So you did see your husband last Saturday evening?"

"I did. I saw him late Saturday evening. We went to sit for supper, the three of us – John, Tobias, and meself. Tobias had come to help make up the week's accounts, but before we got to our meal, Tobias said something John didn't like and they got into a squabble. There was also some business with John Jacob's tally and what John wanted written in his books. Then, when John knew the girls had gone to the wake where there could be young fellows eyeing them, he ranted and raved, his temper heated with the liquor he'd taken at John Jacob's. He took hold of a shotgun on the rack." She paused. "'Tis always loaded on the ready. He was waving it around threatening to kill me and the girls. But then he heard wild dogs barking. He thought they might be digging into the salted fish pile down on the flake. Arthur and Tobias were behind him as he took off down the path with his shotgun. They came up before him and went on to the wake. But he did come up. I heard him behind the house driving the pigs from the back door as I bundled the baby who was woken by the squabble, and she not long got to sleep from teething pain. I took the child to Ruth's for the night."

The constable narrowed his eyes and unbuttoned his waistcoat as if to tarry awhile. His tone was harsh. "You know that his boat was found bumping against the rocks by the stage and no sign of him. You had no cause to want him dead?"

Catherine answered with a heavy sigh. "I'd not say I had no want to see him gone the times his choleric temper roused mine. But he stays our children and meself, though I do my share. Other than on the Lord's Day I hardly slackens me body on a chair. Summertime there are days when I works from dawn to dark in the fishing stage or turning fish on the flakes. Then there's work in the barn and in the house. Plenty of times a child is draggin' on me insides. But there's no cause to lay on me. I bees afraid of Jack on times. Saturday night I took me youngest to Ruth's place to bide the time while Jack's temper settled, the same as I've done a few times before."

"You knew John would be mad, and still you sent the girls?"

"I did."

"And your reason?"

"Respect for the dead. Jack wouldn't go hesself. Beside, the girls needs time with their chums, and wakes are good meetin' places."

"You have how many children?"

"I've borne nine babes. That's all I'll have to say about that."

"With Katie at Cat Breen's, you had three children at home. You took only one to your sister-in-law's. Why did you leave the two behind?"

"They were asleep in their beds for the night. The children sleep till morning. That's their habit. I had no fears of Jack hurtin' the babes. He was more apt to hit the older girls or me."

"Wasn't it a little late for your daughters to be traipsing home?"

"I've had no worries with them. They don't often have the chance to go to gatherings on a Saturday night."

"You said you were afraid to go."

"I was afraid to go be meself. No one knows who or what is about the place. In the back of me mind were thoughts of wild dogs or wolves about. It wasn't that long ago when livestock was killed by wolves. A white wolf was killed in Turk's Gut and stuffed for Magistrate Pinsent. I wouldn't have minded going to the wake, but not alone."

"Now I ask you, in the most solemn manner, if you had a hand in the death of your late husband, John Snow."

"He's late, that he is. But stretching the truth won't make it go any further. If he's dead, you knows more than I do. I'll be obliged if you find him."

Tobias looked at Bowes and asked if he could get across the harbour to be at his place of work for Tuesday.

"You can then," he said.

Catherine closed the door behind the two men, mumbling to herself. "He's an Irish copper, that one, who's given to favouring those who favour him. And Pinsent, he's into business – other people's." She laid the baby back in the cot and sat fanning her face with a handkerchief. She swaggered as if faint. *That Black Protestant, Robert Pinsent, has it in for the Micks and is using Bowes. The less than a hundred Cartlics can't keep ag'in the thousand Protestants in this place. John, a Protestant, takes hesself off somewhere, and I, a Cartlic, am held accountable.*

Mary scuffed in from the parlour on short, heavy legs. She held a stone vase in her hand. "I'll get rid of those white flowers, ma'am. Deadman's flowers, we calls 'em. 'Tis said that when children pick these their fardher'll die, and Bridget picked 'em yesterday. Last night I dreamed I heard the auld witch keening on the wind, and this house with no death kit – no holy candles and holy water to be kept in the house fer laying out."

"Hush yourself," Catherine scolded her. "'Tis a common yarrow and a cure for the piles. Nothing else! And we don't need a death kit for Jack. Now go on home and keep company there until Jack comes back from wherever he's taken hesself."

All that day, gulls screamed and wheeled about in the heavy winds above waves rolling into each other spurting up like little fish. *Jack is gone, gone, gone. . . .* The words banged through her mind like empty casks against each other on the stagehead on a windy day.

Sounds were all around, filling the air, but Catherine felt a deep silence in John's absence, and a fear as sharp as the edge of his splitting knife.

The sun set and night fell like a shroud.

Twenty-One

ARTHUR was working in the barn when he glanced up and saw through the open doorway Magistrate Robert Pinsent's boat sailing into the cove. It pulled in to the stagehead and several men climbed up to the landing. Arthur knew all the men. There was John Bowes, who'd been there the day before, Robert Pinsent, John Jacob, Mark Hennebury, and three or four planters.

Arthur wiped his hands on a rag and lumbered down to the stage. The men hardly gave him a glance as he told them that he had found a pile of fish on the flake near the stage disturbed on Sunday morning. He said he thought robbers had been there. He broke off a piece of salt fish from the pile, chewed it and washed it down with water he'd gotten from a barrel of rainwater sitting on the stage. He splashed his wooden cup into the barrel and gulped a second cup as the men started up the path to John's house.

Catherine and several of her neighbours were sitting in the parlour when a knock came on the door. The maid opened it and several men went past her. Johanna looked up from where she was lollying across the floor. She let out a screech at the sight of the strangers and tried to get to her mother. Catherine rushed toward her, cooing, "Hush! Hush, sweet baby." She pulled the child into her arms and gave Pinsent a tense look.

He was blunt. "We're here to make enquiries about the mysterious disappearance of your husband. State all you know and we'll be off to commit it to writing."

Catherine told the men the same thing she had told Bowes. Then Pinsent turned to Kitty. "You'll come with us to Bareneed. We'll take Eliza too, and Arthur Spring."

Thirteen-year-old Eliza sat on the stair landing, biting on the tip of a blonde plait and listening to livyers talk about her father's disappearance. The house was more comfortable now. Her heart had jumped like a scared animal more than once as her father jawed her mother or herself and the other children. She tightened her arms around her body. She had often been more afraid of him than she was of the loaded gun on the ready in a rack on the wall. Now she was afraid for her mother. Her face was white and she'd been throwing up, though she wasn't spitting blood. Eliza knew she didn't have the consumption. Her breath caught in her throat as she heard the men say they were taking her to Bareneed.

Catherine protested. "Why would you want Eliza? She's only thirteen, and Kitty White, why do you need her?" She did not say what she was thinking, but she had a swift image of her daughter being hurt. There were so many older men out to do unmentionable things to young girls.

Eliza got up and came down the stairs. "I'll go, Mamma," she said in a tight voice. Magistrate Pinsent took her by the arm. She went, her face pale and drawn. Kitty White took off her apron, grabbed a shawl for herself and a sweater for Eliza from a hook behind the door, and followed them outside.

The men surrounded Arthur Spring as they were on their way to the boat. "Sure you could have brought your friend, blacksmith Kenny, to handcuff and chain me," Arthur said with a glare.

"You're up for questioning. That's all it is – you and Tobias, and the girls here," Pinsent said.

Catherine watched Pinsent's boat cross the harbour, tacking its way, its barked sails leaning into the wind, then against it. She turned back to the house, filled with worry. All that night she wondered when she would get her daughter and servants home.

Arthur and the girls were brought back the next morning, the fourth day after John's disappearance. Eliza was silent, thinking how, at the warehouse, John Jacob had been nice to her, gentle and friendly. He'd never spoken to her before, not a word anytime she'd gone to his warehouse with her father. He listened as Magistrate Pinsent questioned her. Yes, she missed her father. No, her mother didn't know where her father was. Yes, her parents fought. Yes, both of them had slapped her. No, she didn't know if Arthur knew where his master had gone. Yes, Tobias liked her mother. He was friendly to her. She washed his clothes. He liked Bridget too. No, she didn't know where her father's money box was. No, she didn't believe Arthur and Tobias had taken it.

"Maybe me fardher took it and left us," Eliza had answered boldly. "He could be gone off to Irish Water Cove for all I knows, or up the Northern Coast with a woman."

John Jacob had frowned and stood up. There was no more talk after that. Eliza had lain on the hard bench in his kitchen all night, scared of the darkness, scared of the day that would come, not knowing what it would bring to her family.

Arthur came back angry. He said that John Jacob and Robert Pinsent had looked at him and Tobias as if they knew where John was. He told Catherine, "We made a statement that we knowed nothin' of John's disappearance. Tobias spelled his letters and I put X under the words Tobias wrote. Pinsent and Jacob looked at each other and then at us, as if they were on two minds about lettin' us go." Arthur added, "I wished John dead on times when he mistreated me, and there were times I said it. But half the world would be killed by the other half if words were deeds. I worked hard for John, I did, and glad for the hope of me wages."

Arthur didn't say much as he sat for supper. He looked up from his plate and took a gulp from his glass of water. He gave Catherine an intense look. "What will you take for me clearance?"

"Don't mind about that now. When your time's out you'll have your wages," Catherine promised.

Arthur's eyes looked determined. "When Richard Taylor

comes home with our oewn western boat, as she's goin' to St. John's, I'll put me box on board and go with her."

"John never allows room for passengers," Catherine told him. "You'll have to find a way by land when your time's out, but you can put your box on the boat when there's money from John Jacob settling John's account. There's work to be done till then."

On Thursday, Richard Taylor and his crew came home in John's western boat. He tramped up over the stagehead, the longers shaking under his boots as he went to look for a grapnel he'd placed in the stage when he left.

"That could be gone with John," Dulcie Noseworthy, a farmer's wife, spoke up as she came toward John's stage. Her husband never found time to fish, and now she and her husband were wanting to buy fish to store for the winter.

Richard's sunburned face took on a perplexed look. "Gone where?"

"Ah, merciful Jesus, the pity of it," said Dulcie. "John disappeared last Saturday night. A right well-off man – gone – murthured entirely, not a sight of him to be found."

Richard looked stunned as he pulled on strands of white moustache curling under his lip. He had intended to speak to John about having another haul in the boat, maybe two if the weather held until late October. Now he didn't know what to think.

He went back to the boat, where he and the men brought up the cod they'd already salted. Then they threw up a few hundred pounds of fresh fish caught on the way to shore. They worked on the fish, watching all the while as specks in the bay grew into boats full of men. The boats did not come into the cove but settled in the middle of the harbour.

"Draggin', they are, for John's body," said a Caplin Cove fisherman after he'd come back from rowing his rodney out to the boats.

Catherine listened from the house, leaning on her half-door. She watched as the boats dispersed, sailing away without catching John on their hooks or in their nets. Richard and his men finished gutting and washing their barrel of fresh fish. They bulked the salted fish in the stage. Then Richard brought up a bucket of britchins and cod tongues for Catherine. They looked at each other without saying anything about John. "I'd be liking for you to have a meal out of the bucket for your missus," Catherine said.

"And so I will," Richard replied. "I'm full of fish, meself, but the missus would be pleased. I only wish the best for everyone," he added solemnly.

Catherine nodded, pulling in her lips, tightening them to keep from breaking down.

AFTER THE CHILDREN had gone upstairs to bed, Catherine sat by the fire, its dancing flames pulling her into its warm glow while she listened to a quietness that had followed noise as seamlessly as night follows day. She got up and unlatched the door and went outside. The chimney was spitting golden sparks into the night air. They lingered for seconds against the wind's cold breath. She shivered as a cloud crossed the moon, blinding its path on water.

I'll make sure the fire is moored for the morning, she thought. *John was supposed to have raked the fire and covered it Saturday night.* She turned toward the door, with a backward glance at the stage. *John has not come home and I don't know what to think, what to feel, what to say. Here he's gone and I'm left like a widow, and with all the work there is to be done for winter.*

The next morning, Catherine came downstairs and went to the chimney breast – a square hole on each side of the chimney for odds and ends – that John had built. She clasped the old mam's rosary and bowed her head toward it as she touched each bead, her lips moving without a sound. Then she said aloud, "May God and the Virgin Mary who brought meself and the children from sleep bless us through the wakefulness of day, and bring us to the night with a clear conscience. Let our souls and bodies be free from the dangers of this life. Have John come to hes senses, wherever he be."

She smiled. *When I first saw John Snow, his hair was black as a crow and as curly as lambs' wool. He sauntered toward me, he did. There was something between us in that instant. I don't know what it was, but it began something I swear I never finished.*

She took the old mam's rosary up to her room and placed it under her pillow.

Twenty-Two

THE sun shone over Harbour Hills, dipped low, and evening shadows crept down over the small stone jailhouse set against a mountain in a valley facing Hussey's Cove. The Methodist building was not far from it, and on a clear night the shouts of its occupants would strike the ears of any transgressor caught in the gaol cells of Jailhouse Mountain.

The jailhouse would be a temporary place for Arthur and Tobias, questioned and placed in cells partitioned off from each other by planks. Constable Bowes stood in the doorway of Magistrate Pinsent's office with his thumbs stuck in the narrow pockets of his vest. A candle flickered in a holder on the outside wall as he moved to speak to Arthur Spring sitting on a thin mattress spread on the clay floor of his cell. "There's not a sight of Catherine Snow, and she with her husband missing. Didn't she try to send a message to you through Mark Hennebury, telling you to speak only in Irish?"

Arthur shook his head. "I got no word from the missus."

Constable Bowes lifted his bushy red eyebrows. "And a good reason too. Mark Hennebury, being the Christian man he is, chose to espouse good and ignore Catherine Snow's conspiracy to evade justice. He did his duty and reported her words." He paused, then added, "There's a finger of murder on John's stage in a trail of blood. Gashes in rails show where other spots of blood were cut out."

Arthur stood up slowly, as if in pain. He pushed his hands into his pocket and limped to the grate in the door. He sounded defiant. "Fish blood it is then. I never shed any man's blood. 'Tis a common thing to have fish headed and gutted on the stage. As for nicks, young lads are always idling their summer days shibbing with knives."

Tobias heard the conversation from his adjoined cell. He agreed. "I've ben told that fifty men in ten boats dragged the harbour without a show of John's clothes – or the least bit of hesself. Some article of clothing would show on the tides if John was in the deep."

"We don't need a body to know what you've done," countered Constable Bowes. "There's been numerous sharks circling in the bay."

"Basking sharks," scoffed Tobias. "You know they're seen in the harbour every August. Forty feet long, they be, and they feed on plankton and swim slow and close to the surface. They don't go to the bottom in the harbour. There's enough bloody fish offal to draw gulls and sharks anytime."

Bowes goaded the men. "Everyone knows, Arthur, that you and your master didn't see eye to eye about your wages, and you, Tobias, there bees rumours that you played with John's wife while John drifted down into the silt of the seabed. Have you ever heard the like? You and Arthur Spring'll be on your way to St. John's to face your crime." He smiled, adding thoughtfully, "Maybe there's blame to be saved if it's put on Catherine."

Arthur looked at Bowes with a hopeful look on his face. He didn't speak.

Tobias's voice was sullen, his countenance pitiful. "I want to be at the warehouse doin' me work."

Constable Bowes turned toward the door with a twist to his lip. "You could have thought of that before the deed. I'll leave you to stew for a while." He blew out the candle that had shown the two men's bruised and dirty faces. A door slammed and a key turned in the lock to the sound of sharp cries coming from the dark cells.

AT "THE TELL" on the knob of Bareneed, old men, crippled with "the arteritis" and fighting the pain of bunions, "himrods," and other ailments, helped spread rumourtitis. They sat against the shed, squinting and papping on their pipes, or chewing tobacco as they looked across the bay to Salmon Cove.

"What do you make of it, nar sight of John Snow?" Old Teck asked.

He got a quick answer from Tite, his next-door neigbour. "He's ben kilt!"

"He likely took hes own self away," said one old planter squinting his eyes above the trail of pipe smoke.

Another retorted, "That's what he didn't, kill hesself. He was a sound-minded man who feared God. He'd have to be gone in the head to have done the likes of that, and he with a crowd of young ones and a strong, fine-lookin' woman."

One old fellow lowered his pipe and leaned in to his buddies. "When you come to the rights of it, I wouldn't put it past 'un to've gone to be a free man, living in another cove, hes money gone wit' 'un. Either that or his wife done away with he."

"There's no lack of tongue in this place," a young mother called as she wheeled her baby past the men. "Sure the Snows fought, but it was all spit and temper, no body to it. 'Tis only for a rumour to get a head. Then it grows a tail as long as anyone wants and sweeps the harbour with it. The next thing they'll be saying she committed adultery."

"What?" one old fellow exclaimed, leaning forward with his hand to his ear. "Did she say Catherine Snow committed adultery?" He leaned back, shaking his head. "A shameful thing, that is."

Women, hanging out their washed clothes, stopped to talk over their fences. Amy Taylor nodded toward the men. "There they bees, yakking their heads off. Sure they'll talk enough to sod a field."

Ida Hussey, whose only work seemed to be clodhopping around the place passing the news, stopped by Amy's fence. She shook her head in consternation. "There's talk Kit Snow had John killed, and there's talk of her cousin and she. More went on in that house than anyone knowed."

"So it's Tobias who's ben havin' her," another said with a grimace. "The closer the kin the sweeter the skin."

Joe Mugford's servant girl left her clothesline and came toward the women. "He's aback of it all, that Tobias, I tell yer. He's been eyeing the Snows' holdings and the daughter. If he gits hes way he'll have the wife done away wit' and go off wit' Bridget."

"What? Kill someone, he?" exclaimed a neighbour coming off her fish flake. "Sure Tobias's got no more guts than a flake full of codfish. I've heard he's a Molly man, and he can't take to women, and he a forked relative. He'd not have ferked with hes cousin, and she gettin' ter be twice his age. But Arthur Spring now, sure no one knows hes mind."

Catherine had sculled across from Salmon Cove after hearing that the men had been taken to the jailhouse on suspicions of murder. She hurried from the stage to the road, lifting a worn hand to her bold forehead. Her face was white against dark hair, windblown and tangled, flowing back over her head and down her back.

A ronk Protestant, with a bedsheet lifted to the line, nudged her daughter standing beside her with a clothespin between her teeth. "There she is, on the road as nice as you please. And she with not a bit of shame in her cheeks. 'Tis said she killed him with a maul. I tell yer now, she did it, and if she's clear of the hangman, sure we'll all be looking at our backs."

"As bold as they come," a woman called from next door.

"She mightn't've had a hand in his killin'. She likely had her tongue in it," someone added.

Catherine passed them, stopping to speak to Hannah Jacob sitting with her baby in a wattle chair out on her gaze. Hannah clicked her tongue and tutted. "There's always someone to run away with your character. Here rumours have more tentacles than a squid. More so if you're not born in a place."

Catherine's blue eyes narrowed. "'Tis for sure a place where truth's got as many legs as a codfish."

CATHERINE STARED THROUGH her window at boats in the bay, their owners carrying on with life as if nothing had changed. A screech of wind broke the quietness. Coarse weather was on its way. The evening sun, pulling its light off the sea, was quickly muffed in clouds. Catherine's mind felt suspended like a dark cloud reaching nowhere, touching nothing. The next day, it landed like a stone, became imbedded in her heart, when Kitty, who had been hanging clothes on the line, dropped her pin and came running into the house calling, "Ma'am! Ma'am!"

Catherine knew straight away that trouble, deeper than she had ever known, was on its way. Kitty was panting for breath as she told her that a boat had come across from Bareneed with John Doyle and Abe Newell. They were there with the news that Arthur and Tobias had confessed to killing John. Kitty shook her head. "Who knows the cross work done to get their confessions? What if they snare you?"

"But I'm innocent!"

"Hump! So was the Blessed Saviour, and He was spread and bled with nails fer bein' good. Rumour has it that the men said you helped 'em."

Her hands felt heavy in the leaven tub as she mixed barm with flour and water. She quickly kneaded the dough and made the sign of the cross over it. Three-year-old Maria was hanging around her skirts for a chaw ball. She rolled the dough between her palms and put it into the little girl's open mouth. Then she covered the dough, washed her hands and went to the kitchen window. She turned away, frowning. She grabbed John's spyglass off the window leaf and rushed out the door to the high land above the bay. There she could see the magistrate's boat from Harbour

Grace sailing across Port de Grave point through green squalls. Sails fluttered, luffing into the wind. She knew the boat was coming for her and that there were hands ready to shackle her if she didn't go willingly. She was an Irish maid, not an English lady. She would never be a lady.

She ran back to the house and stopped to bury her face in Maria's warm neck, feeling a strong pulse against her forehead. She was relieved that she had already given Johanna her breast. She had to leave Bridget, sixteen, Eliza, thirteen, Johnny, nine – and he just back from the western boat – Katie, seven, Martin, five. Emilia would have been four. Maria was three. Thomas would have been two and a half. Johanna was fifteen months. The children's names bled her heart – Bridget, Eliza, Johnny, Katie, Martin, Emilia, Maria, Thomas, and Johanna.

Catherine had no time to plan the children's care. She had to worry about her own life. The law was after it – the wolves were circling. She had to stop thinking about John gone and start planning to save the plantation and fishing room and keep her children together. She had to get ready for whatever was coming.

She called to Bridget. "Fetch me some hardtack and water. I have to be off. Keep a good hand on the children. Don't let Maria and Johanna wander over the doorstep. Help the girls and see that Martin and Johnny eat well."

Bridget turned from the broom and stopped its sweep. She stood still, biting her lip and looking as pained as if her teeth had pierced it. "I'm afraid for you, Mamma. Afraid for us."

Catherine turned away so her first-born wouldn't see her wet eyes. "Do your best. I hope to be back before long." Her mind felt as scattered as shot fired from a gun as she went upstairs. She had taken the last few sovereigns and shillings of the old mam's money. Now she secured them in a bundle of clothes she shoved down in a brin drawstring bag. She worked quickly with her bodkin to stitch a flannel-lined hood on her cloak. A sodden mess she'd be under streams of rain, but if it held off she'd be warm. She was hurrying to get into extra clothes when Kitty came up the stairs. She looked in as Catherine pulled on an underskirt with a heavy dress over it.

"Where is it you're off to, ma'am? Sure we'll be needin' to know in case we've got to get in touch."

"I'm off to do some business," Catherine told her maid as she let down her braid and pulled her hair apart to keep her neck warm.

Kitty drew in her lip and pushed it out with a sigh. "I don't think yer done it, ma'am. Most people aren't thinkin' you killed the master, if he be dead."

"No one can say what's been done, dear girl." She took a deep breath, swallowed hard, and blinked to keep back her tears. "There's not a sight of the man, and he such a strong one and able to see the work done. 'Twill all lie fallow if he's not found. We're not done for winter. I hope to be back, but if misfortune stays me, there's the pigs to kill and salt; there's the cellar to fill. Oh there's so much to do." Her hands flew into the air. "I'm hoping to be back to do some hiring for the outside work if Arthur is kept away all month."

She hurried downstairs to the children waiting to see her off. As she tightened the strings of her bonnet under her chin and pulled her hood over it, Johanna lifted her bright, round face. "Mamma, Mamma," she cooed, reaching her hands toward her mother.

Catherine's face strained to keep from bursting into tears as she buttoned her boots. She tried to smile as she bent to kiss Maria's palms and fasten her arms around Johanna. Her tears dropped on her little girls' heads.

Eliza rushed to take Johanna, gushing, "You'll be back, Mamma. I know you didn't kill Fardher."

The baby held on, her hands in her mother's hair, as if she sensed the tension in Catherine's body, the fear in all their voices. Eliza pried the baby's hands away, leaving Catherine's head stinging as if a thousand needles had pierced her scalp. Katie sobbed in a chair, refusing to hug her mother goodbye. Catherine put her arms around her, whispering a promise. "I'll be back."

Eliza and Bridget stood looking at Catherine as she nodded at them. "I'm off to Brigus to get some papers settled."

"Go for the good of us all, Mamma," Bridget urged. She blessed herself.

Catherine's look met her daughter's. "You'll have to mind the children. Don't be off lollygagging with the Noseworthy boy. You don't have to think your fardher's dead – not unless he's found without hes breath."

Bridget held her gaze; then she looked away. "I hope to never cause you trouble." Her voice trembled. "Never!"

"'Tis that I know," Catherine said, reaching to hug Bridget. The other children, sensing something new – dangerous – came toward her. The young ones cried, "Mamma!" She let them cling to her, felt the soft warmth of their bodies as arms reached around her. Guilt rose in her throat like bile. She wiped her eyes and stowed her handkerchief in her sleeve.

Catherine grabbed Martin and Johnny, pulling them to her. She was already starving for the sight of them. She pulled away and Martin's eyes welled with tears. *Will this be me last image of the children? Will the baby I'm carrying live?*

This house was christened with life's passions, Catherine thought. Her look gathered all the parts of the scene before her: the short-handled birch broom for sweeping the hearth, the iron kettle on its stand, the belly soup pot hanging from its black bar, the long forks and round spoons hanging from the side of the mantel. The clock showed eight o'clock, but it was as if time had no measure.

Bridget hurried from the pantry and pressed food and a flask of water into her mother's hands. "Be off before the law gets to the stagehead."

She nodded. "Look out for your brothers and sisters." She turned to the maid. "You will stay to help, won't you?"

"Indeed, ma'am. I won't leave off now, with such a time it is."

"Tell anyone who comes I have quit the place," Catherine said as she opened the door and hurried away from the house with Bridget and Eliza staring after her.

"You'll be gone only a little while," Eliza called.

"Not forever," she whispered. "Not forever."

Martin sat on a chair, wide-eyed and staring, one hand crossing the other to grab hold of his little feet. Catherine heard his voice as she gently closed the door. "Mamma's gone. . . ."

She looked back to see the children's faces filling the window.

Then the door flew open and Johnny was running after her, his bare feet stumbling over small pebbles and sharp rocks. She turned back to hug him. "I'll be back soon. I promise."

He looked at her, his eyes big and round and terrified. "What if Fardher comes home and you're not here, and I doos suppin he don't like?"

"When he comes home, I'll be home too," she promised.

Catherine remembered John whittling a block of wood with Johnny watching. *A chip off hes fardher's block, he is, the face and eyes of him,* she'd thought. Little chips of wood flew, some settling into their son's dark hair. Catherine had cautioned him. "Move away, Johnny, so the chips don't fly in your eye."

John had fun with his boys, tickling them until their giggles turned to cries. Once he grabbed Johnny arse over kettle. He kept him hanging by the heels as he swung him back and forth while tickling his feet. Johnny chuckled at first. Then it wasn't fun anymore, and he began to cry. Still, John didn't stop. "Don't be a wis," he said scornfully. Sometimes Johnny hid from his father.

One day, when Martin was rubbing the sleep out of his eyes, John told him, "Don't rub your eyes with anything but your own elbows." Martin tried to get his elbows to his eyes and John laughed. Then they both laughed and it was as if John was never angry with any of them.

Now Johnny pulled his arm out of his shirt and waved goodbye with his sleeve as he backed toward the house, letting his sleeve drop slowly. Catherine turned to look and got his last wave as she went over the ridge out of sight. She broke into sobs, tears dripping down her face like rain as she thought of the time Johnny was chasing after a hen. He had stopped suddenly, an uncomfortable look on his face.

"You want to do your job, Johnny?" Catherine asked.

Johnny nodded.

"You're standing there holding it in, Johnny. Go, go!"

Johnny raced toward the outhouse, but he wasn't fast enough and down it came – skutters running away from him.

Johnny lay on the ground caught between heaves and skutters. He was crying. "I was afraid that if I moved it would come, and it did."

John was behind him. He'd broken off the cane of a September mist bush.

"Don't, Jack! Don't!" Catherine called. "Johnny's caught the summer sickness."

Catherine reached to grab the switch, and it hit across her arm. She felt its smarting welt through her sleeve. Later, John kissed the weal left on her arm and blamed her for getting in the way.

Catherine had picked up her son and yelled at John, "I'll have your head when you least expect it." Then she went toward the house. She opened the door, calling to Bridget to take the pot of hot water from the fire and fill the tub. She cleaned Johnny and wrapped him up in a cayla.

"Don't be tormenting Johnny," Catherine chided John when he came to supper. "You wanted a son and you've already lost two."

John ignored her as he slipped a spoon into his pea soup and chanted, looking at Johnny, "Pea soup will make you poop down your leg and out your boot."

Johnny not only looked like his father. He was growing angry like him, angry with his little sisters and brother. She shook her head as if to shake away scenes she'd rather not think about.

Summer warmth was on the wane, and autumn's bleak, clammy wind crawled over Catherine's skin, dug into her body, gnawed on it as if there was no flesh on her bones. She hurried away from the house, looking back to where a globe of light showed in the darkening night like a clouded moon foretelling stormy weather. Johnny was nowhere in sight.

She glanced toward the bay, thinking, *If I dropped me cloak and shoes over the bank into the water, would the law take it that I'm drowned?* She couldn't do that – have her children mourn for her while she was alive somewhere. She had left the house without a torch, believing that a flicking light would trace her path for her trackers. There was not a star showing. It would be so easy for her to lose her way in the dark or stumble over rough, uneven ground. She passed the backside of Edward's house and crossed through a patch of swampland under soft heather. Her feet sloshed as she moved to dry land and down over the steep, rocky footpath to Caplin Cove where lamplight flickered in several windows. She trembled at the thought of going farther than Mary Britt's alone. She was afraid of half-starved roaming dogs, or a wolf venturing about the place with its eerie, mournful cries, its eyes glowing in the dark.

She knew that Mary Britt, who had moved to Caplin Cove, would hide her until the magistrate and his constables passed the house and she could find other means of shelter. Mary, holding a clay jar of spirits stoppered with a wide cork, was turning from her ailing father when the door swung open and Catherine rushed in.

"Hide me, Mary, until I can think on what to do. This is the sixth day since Jack disappeared and the constables had me for questioning. Now I'm thinking they're looking to bar me up." She stopped for a breath and Mary stood looking at her, her forehead creasing. Catherine went on. "I have to get to Brigus, and get papers to protect the children before Thomas and Edward Snow – or the merchants – lays claim to the business while Jack's gone. The constables will be on to this place in short order once they've searched Salmon Cove."

Mary's eyes clouded as she hurried Catherine. "Under the daybed then, until I can think. Lay yourself down till morn."

Catherine took one look at the sallow-faced man and asked, "How's your fardher gettin' on?"

Mary shook her head. "Not so well since he got the farmer's lung – got that from poking in mouldy hay, he did."

Catherine gasped as a tap came on the door. Her heart settled at the sight of James McCabe pushing it open. He eyed Catherine without a word. Then he looked at Mary. "I've brought a fresh codfish."

"Don't rob yerself now to give to me," she told him, adding quickly, "though a stewed cod with onions and fatback would be good for dinner on the morrow. A little broth off the fish will do me fardher good." She took the fresh fish and laid it in a pan to wash.

James said, "I'll be headin' on home now. The old woman'll be waitin' fer a fish." His look flickered over Catherine, as if he wondered why she was there. James worked on John's western boat and likely stopped off to see a woman after he and the men had stowed the codfish they had salt-bulked on the boat. Catherine hoped the girls would wash out the fish, spread it to dry and then have it over to the warehouse in Bareneed for credit.

Fearing a constable would lift the latch of the door without warning, Catherine raised the counterpane on the daybed and lowered herself to squeeze beneath the wooden frame holding Mary's father. She dropped the bedskirt around her.

Before Saturday's daybreak, there were voices at the door, and then a thunderous rap and the door swung open. Catherine tried not to stir, not a foot, while her heart thumped in her breast. Mary listened to Constables Bowes and Thomas Butler's accusations that Catherine had coaxed Arthur Spring and Tobias Mandeville to kill John with his own gun and throw him into the bay. Bowes threatened, "You'll be charged too, if you harbour this woman. So if she shows up, be sure to let us know."

Mary looked toward the sick man on the daybed. "I've other things to do than be protecting someone you say is a killer. So be off and find her elsewhere."

As soon as they were gone Mary spun around. "You've got yourself into something now, Catherine, and I'll not be a part of it." She dropped to her knees beside the daybed and lifted the skirt of the counterpane. She ducked her head under the bed. "I've heard the facts of the case from the constables and you'll not be hiding under my bed. I have you as a friend, but I won't have the law as me enemy."

Catherine crawled out, her hair falling down around her face. "But whose word will you have as truth?"

Mary Britt's face took on a stubborn look. "They said you helped them, Catherine. John's servant and his bookkeeper pointed the finger at you. You could have killed John. 'Tis not as if you never had a fight, you two. I'm turning you out of doors fer the sake of meself and me fardher."

Catherine gave her friend a look of scorn. "I'll not take blame for something I didn't do, and don't put it on me. For sure, Jack was me bread and butter, and he held me shelter, and didn't he remind me of that, as do countless men to their women who lip them."

Mary, her face showing determination, shouted, "Out!"

Catherine threw up her hands and left, muttering, "I'm aclear of it."

She took a hesitant step from the back stoop of the house as she looked into the blackness, hoping the law had shoved off in boat and there was no one left ashore to waylay her. Silence wrapped around her like a ghostly skin as she hurried up the narrow lane from Mary's house, not wanting to be caught in the awakening dawn.

Her legs grew tired as she trudged up the steep meadow along a gurgling stream that had cut a meandering path to the beach. She crossed it, her feet already wet from the marsh. She stooped and cupped her hand for a drink, grateful for the stand of trees all along the hill, left there by the settlers wanting to break harsh northeasterly winds that often swept through the cove. She skirted the trees for a while and then settled against brush and dry grass at the back of thick spruce to await nightfall. Shivering from dampness and fear, she huddled into herself, her head against a tree trunk. She fell asleep listening to the tickle of water over rocks.

Hours later, she awoke, the reality of her situation striking her like a stone. Sounds drifted up the meadow: voices mixing with the mooing of cows and the bleating of sheep still out to pasture. She listened to leaves rustling on trees, a harsh sound under the stiffening autumn air. Soon all was quiet under the shadows of night as wind, animals, and livyers settled.

The moon was beaming off the ocean as Catherine hurried up the rock-knobbed path keeping a steady step as she rose over the hill and down the valley to Rip Raps meadow past houses and tilts, silent and shadowed. She crossed to the side of Spectacle Mountain, a massive peak of rugged rock overlooking Cupids. Cold marsh water sucked her boots before she came to a dry path strewn with tilting, sharp rocks. It was only a short marl down the path to Cupids, but to Catherine, with fear on her, it seemed forever. She followed the path beside a stream running from the hills to the beach.

She let out a whimper as her leggings caught on a thicket of hawthorn. A starling's sharp cry blended with a moan escaping her lips as her foot slipped into a rabbit's hole and threw her off balance. Leaves flittered to the ground and bushes rustled under autumn winds as she got up and kept going. She came to Cat Breen's house all abiver, fearing she was being shadowed. Mary had sent her away on the magistrate's threat. Catherine's heart thumped for fear Cat Breen would do the same. She tripped in brambles as she rushed like someone with the Devil in chase. She pulled the hasp and opened the door. Her breath was heavy from her frightening trek. She stood still for a moment to let her heart settle; then she felt her way in the dark to her friend's room. She woke her gently. "I'm afraid I'll be taken by the constables. Let me stay here and I'll leave after nightfall."

She couldn't see her friend's face, but she imagined Cat's brows drawn together, her lips tight as she spoke. "I'll have you here for the day and when it comes dark you can move on. The constables will surely look here after a time, and then I'll be in trouble."

Catherine told her she knew nothing about John's disappearance. "Here I am being hunted, having to hide by day and move by night to reach Brigus. Richard Mandeville will be able to draw up papers to protect me children. If I'm taken by the law, I can't be sure of what will happen to them and the estate."

Cat threw back her bedclothes reluctantly and Catherine drew herself under the covers at her friend's back, relieved that Cat's husband had already left for fishing.

Long after daylight, Cat awakened Catherine from a troubled sleep. "Hearten yourself now with a drop of tea."

Catherine slid out of bed. "I'll have a tayscaun, so I will then."

Cat turned to blow on coals in the fireplace. She got the fire going with chobies and splits. Then she hung the kettle. Soon water boiled out from the kettle's spout and hissed on the fire. Porridge was cooked and dipped into wooden bowls. "Eat quickly, or 'twill not be your stomach that'll have the meal. You never know when the law will be on us. Make haste then to lie under my bed."

It was a long day for Catherine. Her heart quickened in distress at any movement outside the door. As the evening closed in, and the sky blushed in the evening light, she slipped her cramped body out from under the bed and stirred the curtains to look out the window. She could see across the dark waters to Salmon Cove Point where dancing white scarves of foam rose over skerries of cliff rock. Her heart lurched. *I should be dressing me children for night, gathering Johanna to me breast. If the little ones takes sick I won't be there to wipe their brows.* Her hands went to her bound, tender breasts.

As soon as darkness fell, Catherine left the Breens' house by the back door and skirted the back of houses and tilts, moving cautiously until she got to Denis Hartery's house. Tomorrow night she hoped to make it to Brigus. She looked around before she lifted the latch on Denis's door. Then she shouldered her way inside and stood there, panting like an animal after a long run.

Denis lifted an eyebrow as he grabbed his brigs by the stove and hove himself into them. "We thought you might be coming," he said. "I've nothing better to do than hide you for all the shame John put on me." Catherine didn't ask what it was about.

"The law is heavy against you, Catherine," Denis added.

"But I did nothing. Mary Britt listened to the hearsay of the constables and turned me out early Saturday morning."

He nodded toward the loft. "You can sleep in the garret. Just tuck yourself in beside Mary."

She followed his look to the rope ladder leading to the loft. The little girl, hearing voices, leaned out over the loft, rubbing her eyes. Her father looked up and nodded to his daughter. "Move over there, now, Mary. Let Catherine in. Don't stare. She's the same as she was before – a mother to girls like you – only now she's a poor mortal." He turned back to Catherine. "Stay in full clothes in the event someone comes searchin' for yer."

Catherine was halfway up the ladder when Denis's wife, May, a gentle woman, whose small head was kept in a tam day and night, called after her. "Blow out the candlelight, Catherine. Let darkness and sleep be one. I'll offer a prayer to Mary, Jesus, and all the saints. St. Jude will take your prayers, and St. Anthony will find John wherever he be."

Catherine looked back and nodded, grateful for May and Denis's lodging. She clutched the old mam's rosary strung around her neck. Then she blew out the candle in an earthen jar on a small stand and slid into the bed beside Mary, fearing that the greatest storm of her life was coming to sweep her away.

Twenty-Three

EARLY Monday morning, Catherine stirred to the sound of voices. She quickly stepped to the ladder and climbed down, going out the back way. She raced down over the hill and lifted the cover of a barrel beside an ochred shed. She tipped it and wedged her body inside, her heart pounding so hard it fair knocked against the wooden cask. She thought of Tobias. The young Irishman had likely made the barrel. She pushed out the bung and squinted through the hole. She watched as Patrick Walsh, Charles Cozens, and other men stood on the hill. If they came close they would hear her quick breathing, or notice her shifting when she couldn't stay in one position without her legs cramping. She eased out of the barrel, not knowing what to do. Then she rushed back into the house and up the ladder and into bed.

A few minutes later, she heard a banging on the porch door. She listened as Denis got out of bed and opened the door. She heard Patrick Walsh and Charles Cozens greet him.

Patrick's voice was stern. "I've been searching for Catherine for some days now. I have word that she's here."

Catherine had trusted Cat Breen. Now she wondered if she had betrayed her.

Charles raised his voice. "You'll bring her out, you will – or else."

Denis protested. "You've ben listenin' to gossipers feed other people's minds with their hash. 'The Tell' in Bareneed is busier than a nest of Protestant wasps."

Catherine scravelled from the bed and stepped down the ladder, not wanting Denis to have to defend her. She came up behind her friend and lifted her head over his shoulder. She looked past Patrick Walsh to Charles Cozens. "I'm here and I'll go, believing that the law is more just than the tongues of tattletalers."

Patrick Walsh rushed to pull her hands in front of her; he clicked on handcuffs.

"What do you want to be doin' that for?" she asked. "I'll not be able to get away."

Walsh told Catherine in a sombre tone, "Tobias and Arthur are after telling us all that happened. Now confess, yourself, to helping them kill John."

"I pray God, between us and all harm, that I will never confess to a lie. It's to send me to the gallows and the hangman's knot you have a mind. But I won't be having it. I'm innocent."

"Spring and Mandeville confessed."

"Perchance to save their skins," she cried.

"To hang yours?" Walsh asked.

"Arthur and Tobias had no quarrel with me. I heard tell of what was done to them in the jailhouse. Their skins were bruised and their minds were shaken by threats." She turned to Charles Cozens, pleading, "Me children needs me for their care."

"Bridget is there to mind the children, while Eliza can be off in service for her keep," Cozens told her. "John Jacob's wife is a new mother. She could use a maid or two."

"The girls'll have enough to do to mind their own brothers and sisters," Catherine retorted.

Walsh met her bold look. "There'll be places found for the younger ones if need be."

"Come on," Cozens said, grabbing her arm and rushing her down the path to the stagehead. She stumbled as he hurried her across the labry – a narrow wooden walk between the stage and stagehead – to Walsh's boat. She glanced down at the dusty green water over the seabed where rocks and sand lay in green shades. As Cozens helped her ease her way down the rails, her handcuffed hands folded as if in prayer, her boot slipped and she almost fell into the water. He held her elbow as she dropped her foot to the gunnel of the swaying boat. Walsh hauled on the painter, bringing the boat close enough for her to jump in.

Catherine caught sight of Kitty White hurrying down the path to the stage. She didn't know that Walsh's boat had first stopped in Salmon Cove, and that Kitty had heard Walsh tell Mary Connolly that he was there to arrest Catherine. Kitty had hastened into her coat, tied her bonnet and scampered across the path and up over the hill, hurrying to get to Cupids with a purpose. She got there only to see Catherine handed down into Walsh's boat. She was too late to tell her that Mary Connolly had told the constables where she was headed.

Catherine heard someone call from the gathering crowd, "*Go éirí an bothar leat* – Wishing you good luck on your journey.*"* Her heart lightened at the familiar words.

"Look on the water when you cross Salmon Cove," another fisherman called sarcastically. "See if your man'll bob up." She kept her eyes averted, as if John could come afloat – as if the men had really killed him. She let the thought slip in, *How do I know they didn't? John's money box is not to be found. Someone took it. Maybe John.* . . .

Walsh climbed down into the boat and a fisherman on the stagehead untied the painter and threw it down. As the sails took the wind and the shallop sailed down past Cupids, Catherine let out a cry, her voice reaching into the ears of bystanders who had gathered to watch in silence. "*La gra dé ní dein me é* – I did not do it!"

BRIDGET STOOD LOOKING through a window to the harbour where a shallop sailed, its topsail and jib holding a steady breeze. She watched the boat carrying her mother. It crossed the mouth of the cove and kept on going toward Port de Grave. She knew that her mother was gone without stopping in to the stagehead – gone for who knew how long. *Me and Eliza shouldn't have gone to the wake that night. We should've stayed home. . . .*

The younger children were unsettled since their mother left home. Maria, pale and heavy-eyed from her bout with a cold, kept twisting a long strand of hair around her finger and calling "Mamma" in a plaintive voice. Johanna wanted to be in Bridget's arms, often pressing her face against the soft flesh of her breast, as if to search for milk and her mother's scent. Katie played in the deep window shelf, her back against the wall at one end and her feet pressed against the opposite wall, holding her yarn doll as she looked out the bay with a sad, uncertain look. Martin was hanging on to the fence, watching Johnny down on the stagehead whacking a stick against oil casks or jigging smelts and conners off the stagehead. Johnny stopped to stare at boats crossing the bay.

Bridget stumbled, as if dazed, as she turned back to the children to whom she had to be mother and father. She blessed herself, her lips moving, her tongue mute.

CATHERINE SAT IN the boat, trembling. She looked down at her hands brought together by handcuffs. She eyed traces of bread dough caught under her fingernails, left there when she had rushed to clean her hands and be on her way. The dough had dried as thin as the wings of white moths. She thought of her children's faces as, over the years, each of them had reached under the pan cover to grab a piece of dough. She'd been sharp with them sometimes, smacking their hands to keep them off the dough. Other times she had been playful, warning them that their insides would stick together if they ate dough. Once she told Johnny that chaw balls would rise in his belly like a loaf. When she'd gotten big with Maria he had asked if she had swallowed a chaw ball.

Catherine was taken off the boat in Hussey's Cove and brought up to the gaol by Jailhouse Mountain. Magistrate Pinsent was waiting. "This is no place for a woman unless she's gone in her mind," he said, his tiny eyes narrowing. "But you've asked for it, yourself. We'll keep you locked up until we see what's to be done with you."

Catherine glared at him. "I don't know on whose word you've brought me here, but I intend to undo what's been done to me name." She drew back from going inside, but Pinsent put a firm hand to her back and she went. She dropped to the straw mattress on the earthen floor, her eyes swimming in tears. Then the magistrate left her, his look hard.

She hadn't seen inside the stone building before. The plank partitions may have been whitewashed once, but now they were grey, pitted and stained with dark splatters. She stared at what looked like bloodstains on the floor. She thought of Arthur and Tobias and her heart lurched. The jailhouse was a mystery place. She had heard of its inmates dying in a deplorable state of lunacy. One man was thirty-six, and down in his nerves since his wife died in childbirth only weeks before. When he was caught attempting to jump off the wharf, constables dragged him away to a jailhouse cell, where, it was said, he choked to death from the strength of his own hands around his neck.

Catherine quieted her fears of what could happen to her. *They'll know I didn't murthur Jack; they'll send me home.*

Book III

Catherine Snow in the Eye of the Court

"The Grand Jury have found true bills against the following prisoners . . . Tobias Mandeville, Arthur Spring, and Catherine Snow, for the murder of John Snow, at Port de Grave."

Royal Gazette and Newfoundland Advertiser
January 7, 1834

Twenty-Four

MAGISTRATE Robert John Pinsent sat reading the newspapers, squinting above the smoke of his pipe. In the September eleventh, 1833, edition of the *Times*, a St. John's conservative and Protestant-run newspaper, he read, "The charges against Arthur Spring and Catherine Snow are more serious than that against Tobias Mandeville. For a servant to kill his master, or a wife her husband, amounts to petit treason equivalent in lesser degree to killing a king."

Pinsent smiled as he took up the *Newfoundlander*, a Catholic-run St. John's newspaper. Thursday's September twelfth edition: "A most atrocious and unnatural murder has lately been perpetrated at Port de Grave, in Conception Bay. . . . We record the names of Spring and Mandeville who were lodged in the gaol in this town, charged as accomplices in the murder of John Snow of Port de Grave. It would appear from investigation that Mandeville shot the poor man at the instigation of Snow's wife."

The magistrate folded the papers with satisfaction. The information regarding John Snow's suspected killers was printed very quickly once it was sent to the papers. Word had spread. People were shaking their heads. A conviction was coming. He was certain of that.

CONSTABLE BOWES VISITED Catherine after she had been in the small jailhouse cell for a week. He stood looking at her. "It's goin' to Harbour Grace you'll be on the morrow. Robert Pinsent's young daughter, Mary Spear, is ben taken sick and hes mind's on her. 'Tid break anyone's heart to see the magistrate – he with his heart and soul in that child."

"You've hardened yourself ag'in me, you, an Irish blacksmith, paid by the English Protestants," Catherine said angrily. "Let Pinsent think of *me* mourning the separation from me children and me husband – perhaps deserted be him."

"Enough of your lip," Constable Bowes said harshly. "Arthur and Tobias already finds themselves in the St. John's gaol and you'll likely be there too." He went out, slamming the door and locking it.

The harsh sounds of crows cawing outside the jailhouse brought Catherine to the surface of another day. *I'm being forewarned, I'm sure of it and no hope.* She began to cry bitterly. A while later, Isaac Hussey, the jailhouse keeper, who lived beside Jailhouse Mountain, fitted the large, heavy black key into the square brass lock and opened the door. He brought Catherine water, a bowl of porridge, and a ship biscuit. She guzzled half the jug of water, saving some to wash herself.

The next day, Bowes showed up with a sad face. "There's bad news for Robert Pinsent this day. His little daughter died. A hard pain in her side took her."

Catherine stared at him, feeling sad for Pinsent. The anguish of losing Thomas and Emilia, her darling boys, washed over her in waves. Their loss had slipped inside her heart, as heavy as the round rocks she had carried to warm her children's beds. "I wants to see me children before I'm sent away," she said boldly.

Bowes shook his head. "I don't have permission to let that happen. You'll be goin' soon."

The next day, Catherine was taken to the boat, past dwellers on the path and wharf. Some of them called, "God be with you." Others watched her silently.

As the boat left the cove, she looked toward Salmon Cove, wishing she was close enough to see her children. She could barely make out the stage and the blurred image of the house. The place disappeared from her view as the boat rounded the head of 'Ibb's

'Ole, heading into open water toward Harbour Grace. Strong wind stirred the waters and filled the sails. Catherine's bones shrieked from lashes of wind cutting into them like a cat-o'-nine-tails. She bent her head to her shackled hands and held on to her bonnet and the hood over it to shelter her face.

She gulped hard as the boat came to the wharf in Harbour Grace and she was helped up the rails. She was handed into a small carriage while the small horse pulling it snorted impatiently. Fishermen lifted their heads from ropes and nets to stare as the driver took his seat. The horse cantered along the street past row houses and merchants' shops running together. When the driver reached the door of a small gaol, he called, "Whoa!"

John Currie, the gaoler, a tall thin man, took charge of Catherine and brought her through a hall where he knocked on a large office door. In response to a curt voice telling him to bring the prisoner inside, Currie opened the door to face Thomas Danson, magistrate of the Northern District. He looked up from behind a heavy desk as Catherine felt a hand at her back pushing her inside. She stood facing the small, wiry man. He eyed her.

"A fine mess you've got yourself in, haven't you, woman? Now we'll get to the bottom of it." He nodded for Currie to leave her there. The door closed behind the gaoler and Danson leaned back and gave her a keen look.

She looked back, unflinching, her voice sullen. "'Tis bad enough that I've suffered the loss of a husband; now I'm apart from me children."

"I'll thank you to show remorse for the time you're takin' from my day," Danson said. "Poor Mr. Pinsent sent you to me, seeing how he is grieving the loss of his daughter."

"Sorrow haunts us all," Catherine answered. "I was sorry some months past to hear bad news of Tommy Ambrose, your son. Was it in February of last year that he succumbed?"

Danson looked at her as if surprised.

"Words carry," she said.

"It was on the eleventh," Danson said. "Twenty-three he was."

He turned back to his papers. "I'll write your words, though I hardly need to. I've gotten the account from Mr. Pinsent."

"I'd want to read it if I knew how," she answered. "Betwixt Robert Pinsent and John Jacob there's trouble afoot and 'tis not all good what they bees up to."

"Are you accusing these respectable men?"

Catherine did not answer his question. She leaned close, drawing her shawl around her, and asked, "Can my words be placed in your keeping as I speak them? I don't know what Pinsent told you but he wrote nothing in my presence. His memory may be no better than mine."

"I'll write your words as you tell them," he promised. "Now for the examination."

He pulled a sheet of parchment from his desk and, with his left hand turned in toward him, he began to write.

"Why are you writing?" Catherine asked.

Danson's tone was relaxed. "I know some of your statement from what you told Robert Pinsent."

"But I don't know what he wrote. He didn't read it back to me, and if he had, I wouldn't know if he was reading what he wrote. I never signed a paper."

"Go on." He leaned back, waiting for Catherine to tell her story. Then he started writing. After he had finished, he said he would likely be a witness for the court, and he would give her version of events. Catherine thanked him and he opened the door and called for the gaoler to take her to a cell.

Currie released Catherine from the handcuffs and she dropped to the straw bedding on the floor, letting herself lie as if she were boneless. She looked up to the sound of a woman's loud voice. The woman rubbed dirty hands over a skinny bosom as she flirted with the gaoler, her lips drooping into softness as if to spell him. "You go on, I'll handle this hussy." She looked down on Catherine with scorn. "There you is then – a woman, and a Cartlic at that – with the tainted blood of the Irish in yer. You people should t'ink before you do." Her lips wrinkled into a frown and she lowered her finger in front of Catherine's face.

"You might have knowed you couldn't kill an English husband and get away with it. Sure the likes of yours had money, and friends in power."
 Catherine lifted a tight chin and spoke defiantly. "The law and me children will know the truth about me."
 "As you tell it," the woman muttered.
 "As it is," she cried.
 The woman brought Catherine a bowl of soup and made a gesture as if to spit in it. Catherine was relieved that she didn't. *Belly wash!* she thought as she bent her head to the watery cabbage and turnip mix. She was spooning the last drop into her mouth when she looked up to see Thomas Danson standing outside the cell. "You'll be on the packet boat tomorrow for St. John's," he informed her.

DAWN WAS BREAKING when Catherine was roused from sleep and brought a tin cup of water and a cold molasses cake. It was going on nine o'clock by the time a guard came to handcuff her and take her to the wharf where she saw the packet boat scunning into Harbour Grace. Its horn blew a raspy note once. Then it was silent. Catherine's shawl hung down her shoulders and brushed the backs of her legs as she was hustled to the edge of the wharf where the packet boat was pulling in alongside. Above it, gulls filled the clear, blue sky like white waves.
 Catherine's stomach churned with nausea as she breathed the cold, metallic smell of fish and gurry rising from the sea. "Mind now, you don't split your spraddle," the guard cautioned her as she was handed down to the boat. She tried not to retch as the vessel began its unsteady path through rough waters to Portugal Cove where a coach would take her to a St. John's cell. As the boat took her farther from home, her separation from her family came as keen as if a knife had cut through her heart. Her children were tucked inside her mind, fragments of their lives drifting through her thoughts – their smiles, the touch of their warm skin, the smell of warm milk on Johanna's breath. She looked down to where milk was leaking, soaking her bodice and chilling her. She fell asleep, her head falling against her chest. A lurch of the boat

awakened her, and for a moment she thought the snapping of the sails in the wind was from a line of bedclothes dancing in a breeze.

The boat neared the dismal inlet of Portugal Cove beneath a bald, mammoth rock and slowed to a stop. Catherine felt the tear of strong hands on her arms as she was dragged from the boat and up the rails of the wharf, her handcuffs clinking. She swayed in dizziness as waves flopped against the rails. She was hauled to a stagecoach with the name *Victoria* splashed in bright letters across the side facing her. The coach's large body was painted in red and trimmed in gold. Leather aprons were attached to the coach with brass tacks.

"We've a prisoner here, a Catherine Snow," the guard called. Bill Somers, the stout, red-faced coach driver seated in his box, was distinguished-looking in his long, black greatcoat, black cape, and a black top hat. He held the reins in one hand while he lifted his other arm. Catherine stared at it. There was no hand, just a leather covering over the wrist.

The two horses drawing the stagecoach snorted impatiently. Catherine stumbled as she was helped aboard the coach filled with passengers who stared at her handcuffs and then at her. She gave them a withering look.

A man beside the coach cracked a whip and called, "Git 'e up, Victoria!" Heavy yellow wheels splattered mud about as the coach rumbled along, banging over the crude road, the creak of leather constant. The thudding carriage was pulled by the fast-moving horses clopping through swamp and woods along a narrow, crooked and rutted path, and up a steep winding hill the fourteen miles from Portugal Cove to St. John's. Catherine's liver and lights shook with each bump of the carriage wheels.

She shrank inside herself as the coach neared Water Street and stopped. The passengers skittered out. Someone tripped in Catherine's heel, giving it a painful burn. She watched as the passengers waited for their trunks and packs to be unloaded from the top compartment of the coach. Some passengers looked at Catherine and pointed as they spoke to neighbours standing around.

Somers nodded at Catherine. "You'll be goin' up to Signal

Hill's holding cell for now. You'll be there for so long. Then you'll likely go to the bigger prison."

A harsh wind blew into Catherine's face and she closed her eyes against its force, but only for a moment. She was startled by shouts of "Papish whore! Orange Catholic! Killer!" Children, some of their faces and ragged clothes smudged with dirt, followed the carriage and taunted her, egged on by women with babies at their bosoms. A little girl whose hair sprang from her head in golden springs reminded Catherine of her own Maria until her arm came from behind her back in a fist. She raised her hand and hurled a rock at Catherine. It hit her lightly in the shoulder as the horses and carriage raced past garden patches green for harvest, on past a military fort at the base of the hill. Other rocks followed out of the crowd, some hard enough to knock her forward. An angry voice among them yelled, "The woman is to be gaoled, not shot with a poor man's pellets. You people could kill her before the trial. Let her be."

Along the Lower Path, the horses galloped past shacks, houses, stores, barns, and taverns. Catherine could see nets drying on fences beside stages, and fish flakes holding drying leaves of cod along the beach. A brutal wind, holding lashes of rain, swept toward Catherine. It carried the scent of salt cod mingling with the chummy smells of fetid mud, blubber, and fish offal. She stared in awe at the many shops and stores owned by chandlers, haberdashers, coopers, sailmakers, cabinetmakers, and ironmongers like Frederick Kenny of Sandy Cove who had made the irons that cuffed her wrists.

She eyed the Southside Hills across the harbour and the huts and houses dotting them as the carriage rose up the steep hill to The Battery, leaving the villagers and the hiss of accusing voices in its wake. The coach followed a rough, winding path gouged through rolling bare hills like lonely moors, past Deadman's Pond, a grave of murderers – and victims.

The prison, a grey wood and stone building, stood against the sky on top of bare land edged by cliffs above the Atlantic Ocean. Catherine looked toward the ocean and the far horizon, wondering if she would ever make the voyage back home.

Somers turned his head, his brow arched as he looked at Catherine. "You'm lucky," he said. "This makeshift prison holds a place for women prisoners. There's no dungeon on the hill like the one on the Lower Path. Sure if you get to go there, you'll have a deadwall all around, no windows and bars to the outside, just a locked door and inside a dung and piss pit." He turned with a sardonic smile. "There's no secret pit beneath the floor and a trapdoor to drop you to rot like there was one time. Still, once you're down there, ducky, you won't taste the salt of the sea on yer lips very quick."

The coach driver brought the horses to a halt and jumped down from his seat. He grabbed hold of Catherine, pulling her from the carriage with one hand. The other arm, with its leather covering, was kept to his side. Catherine tried to hold on to her shawl, her body trembling with unease. Winter would be cold on this hill with no trees to bar wind sweeping in from the spitting seas. She thought of her children having to get ready for winter without her. She hoped Bridget would remember to spread sheets of birch rind under and over the cabbages, and moor them with rocks so the vegetables would not freeze. Maybe Ruth and Edward would make sure the children had the potatoes dug and stored in the cellar and the late hay gathered in for the animals.

Somers called to the gaoler opening the gate. "I've a prisoner here, a Catherine Snow, widow of the late John Snow." He passed the guard a paper. Aside to Catherine he snickered, "They're binding you in the same gaol they use for soldiers who misbehave. I s'pose they won't get at yer."

The guard, a sour smell on his breath, unlocked the iron gate and yanked it open. Then he pulled open a heavy wooden door, its rusty hinges whingeing. Matron Newell, in a black wool dress and black mobcap, hurried along the corridor to take Catherine in hand. She turned a miserable countenance on her prisoner. Then she lifted a key from a string of keys at her waist and turned it in the lock to the door of the first cell.

The light from a lantern in the corridor shone inside the cell, its shutters closed over bars in the door. The matron removed

Catherine's handcuffs. Then she let out a snort as she dug her fingernails into Catherine's arm and thrust her into the cell. Catherine's bladder let go and she quickly straddled to keep her legs from getting splashed.

The matron drew her mouth into a scowl as she eyed urine soaking into the earthen floor. "A prison christening!" she uttered in distaste. She went out, shutting the door behind her, locking it, and opening the shutters across the bars to keep the cell in view. Catherine sank down in a huddle on a straw mattress, shivering as a gust of wind bearing rain pelted the window barred with iron rods.

Catherine got to her feet as the matron came back holding a heavy jug. "You'll get a jug of water a day to use for drinking, bathing, washing your duds, and – "

"One jug of water!" Catherine exclaimed.

"Don't complain. It could be less," the matron replied, tightening her thin lips. "You won't be as well off here. You likely had hogs to slaughter on yer plantation, making you well off in pork. Here you'll find yourself lucky to get acquainted wit' a piece of bacon. But you won't starve. There'll be bread, and oatmeal and scouse from cabbages grown in the prison yard by prisoners gettin' exercise." She set the jug down on a small stool in a corner beside a braided oakum mat. It appeared to be stained with dried, mouldy vomit.

Matron Newell continued. "I had a good man who drowned and here I be, sentenced meself, havin' to look after the likes of you to get vittles for me own table."

Catherine met her look without flinching. She answered boldly, "A good turn I'm doin' you then, if you're fed because of me."

The matron lifted a large, beefy hand. She swung it against Catherine's face. The blow sent her against the wall, her long hair falling around her face. *Jack was cruel but this place will surely lash me too*, she thought bitterly.

"'Tis cutting that hair of yours I'll be doing," the matron said sternly. "What a mess of it there is, a ready bed for crawlers and other vermin."

"Leave me hair," Catherine told her. "I'll need it to keep a warm neck if I'm here long."

"And that you will be," the matron promised her. "I won't be bothered if you pick up lice. They'll be left to die of old age."

Later in the day, Matron Newell opened the door and dropped a pair of shoes on the floor. "Here you be, Catherine, a fine pair of wooden shoes fer yer, left behind by a woman who died in this cell. They're the clever thing to squash bedbugs or throw at mice." She stooped and tipped up one shoe. "Ah, yes, there's many a bug died under this clog. You'll be well done by it."

Catherine stared at the shoes and then down at her own shoes, torn in places. "I'll thank you for bringing them," she said gratefully.

One of the gaol's walls faced the ocean and the morning sun. The matron took Catherine to an attached water closet that opened on the edge and emptied into the sea. She stood by the door impatiently, as if her prisoner could squeeze through the toilet hole to the outcrop of land below and escape by sea.

After Catherine was brought back to her cell, she lay curled on the mattress under a ragged, filthy quilt until she fell asleep. She was startled awake early the next morning by a blow to her skull. She had banged into the hard wall. Her eyes flew open to her surroundings and adjusted to them with a sinking heart. Only a flicker of light showed through the open shutters of the door. She blew on her fingers as stiff as icicles. They softened and she folded them into the palms of her hands, two angry fists against the winter of her life, a life that men were trying to weaken even as God grew a new one inside her.

Twenty-Five

TIREDNESS swirled her back asleep. Unfamiliar sounds beat on her ears, awaking her. She heard the grating sound of a key in the lock. The cell door squeaked open and the matron called, "Here's your porridge. Have it now and wash your bowl. There's molasses in it this mornin' fer which you ought to be grateful. Mind now to make your jug of water last the day. Every day you'll git breakfast and soppa."

Catherine took the wooden bowl of thick, cold porridge and a small tin spoon. She sank down on the stool and ate slowly. Tears bubbled in her throat and she dropped to her mattress, sobbing. *I never imagined idling away time – and I used to being so busy.* She closed her eyes and thought, *A woman can go anywhere in her mind, aclear of a gaol.* She eased her mind out of her body, as light as a butterfly freeing itself from a cocoon. She slipped away from the gaol and home to her family – feeding her babies, changing diapers, drawing in the scent of hops, and the aroma of kneaded dough and baking bread. She made clothes and mended them, knitted socks and cuffs, taking in whiffs of sea breeze between the whiles.

Just as suddenly, she dropped back inside her own body, to prison sounds vibrating through her cell. Unfamiliar dull and flat sounds mingled with shouts of pain or anger. Sometimes anguished cries split the air.

Catherine eased her limbs up from the mattress and crossed to the narrow window. Below the cliffs, steely claws of wind scratched the waves, leaving white marks stretched across slate-blue waters reaching like molten stone across the ocean to the shores of Port de Grave. She turned away and walked around the cell from corner to corner, counting her steps, purposing to make this a habit to keep her strength for when she went home.

She was awakened one morning by the gaoler pushing a slobby-looking young woman into her cell, a poor wretch of a woman in rags. She curled up on a stuffed bed ticking thrown on the floor. Catherine lifted herself on her elbow and looked toward her.

The woman's face came close to Catherine's. "Don't be lookin' at me," she snarled. "I'm Mary Hines if you'd care to know and I'm not in here for anything more than borrowing a counterpane and undergarments fer me two young ones. I knows who you be. So yer gonna hang is yer? Yer'll hear bones crackin' then, and feel 'em stabbin' yer skin like knittin' needles."

Catherine's eyelids flittered shut against the sight of the bold creature come to torment her.

The sheriff came for the woman a day later. Catherine never saw her again. Other women came, some with sullen looks and empty, sad eyes. All the women were charged with lesser crimes than Catherine was accused of. Some of them prated about their man, their children, and when they'd be going home. They gave Catherine saucy looks and dared to ask her if she had done John in. They left with quick goodbyes.

Women who got out of prison after sharing a cell with Catherine told of a worry-mauled mother concerned with her children's welfare. They talked about a woman who, along with two young men, Tobias Mandeville and Arthur Spring, were accused of murdering John Snow. They were – in their minds – three people likely to be caught in the eye of the rope.

CONSTABLE BOWES AND Thomas Butler made a visit to Salmon Cove after Catherine was detained.

"The magistrate from Harbour Grace was already here," Kitty White told them.

Mary Connolly came behind her and lifted a saucy face to Bowes. "What if I tells you I found a pair of Tobias's white, bloodstained trousers behind a trunk in the mistress's room?" She smiled at his startled look. "Oh the blood was covered in ink, but I could tell 'twas blood underneath."

"That's serious evidence, Miss, and I'd want to explore it further. Hand over the trousers."

Mary drew back indignantly. "Do you think we'd be having dirty clothes lyin' around this day? Sure that's been scrubbed within a thread of its life. 'Twas on the clothesline the Monday marnin after the mistress was taken by the constables."

Kitty turned in scorn. "Tobias's trousers had ink stains on them. Nothing more. I put them on the trunk with other articles to be washed. The mistress's petticoats and dress tails always carry gurry lumped like snot and splatters of fish blood whenever she's on the stage gutting fish. There's nothing to be made of any of it. More the fool a man would be if he wore white trousers to kill someone, if that's what you're gettin' at. The fishing boat's not always as clean as it could be on a Saturday evening. Fish blood is always about, and Arthur is not the hand to clean it spotless or find reason to, seeing that come Monday, fish blood'll graint the stage and gunnels of the boat ag'in. It wouldn't be the first time for Tobias's clothes to be soiled from the boat. White canvas trousers of a book-man and the grimy insides of a boat don't mix." In a firm voice she added, "Good day to you then, Mr. Butler and Constable Bowes."

They left without another word.

Bridget watched from an upstairs window. She had to get in to see her mother. "Not until after she goes before the judge," Pinsent had told her when he visited the house. "I've come to let you know of your mother's whereabouts, and to see how the children are doing." He didn't speak to anyone but Bridget. He spent most of his time sniffing about the place. "Consideration will have to be given regarding the plantation and the children, come spring," he said. Before he left, he stood on the stagehead, staying there a long time with his arms folded. *Looking as if he owns the place*, thought Bridget.

EARLY ONE MORNING, a prisoner who had been placed in Catherine's cell the night before screamed, "I can't see!"

Catherine rushed to open the wooden shutters over the window bars. "Your eyelashes are stuck with pus and your lids are swollen," she assured her. "You're not blind. What did you do to get here?"

"I stole some garments to keep me babbies warm."

"And your man, what ails him that he can't find cloth and wool for you to make clothes?"

"He's dead by visitation of God. There was a rough sea on and the stage legs went askew like the legs of a newborn calf trying to stand. Then the stage hove out with Bernard in it, and he not a bit able to swim. Since then, I'm that hungry sometimes, me stomach's reaching up to eat me tongue." Catherine felt sorry for the young mother, and when her porridge came she passed it to the woman who ate both bowls of food without a word.

One morning, as the gaoler shoved a prisoner into the cell, he winked at Catherine and clicked his teeth. "I heard you're in a rage for young fellars." He came close and pinched Catherine's breast. He let out a raucous laugh and Catherine pulled back, cringing.

Often Catherine awoke and for a moment caught the scent of John climbing into their bed, over her body, she wanting him as much as he wanted her. Who could be sure he was dead? He might have gone away from everything – shed her, their children, his old life like autumn sheds its old leaves and spring grows new ones. In between cellmates she was sometimes startled to hear her own voice, a disembodied voice raging against her plight. As the days shortened, sunshine rubbing along the walls of the gaol slipped through the iron bars and lay across the floor like a sliver of orange. She pulled her mattress under it and felt her life grow stronger in the light.

One morning, a whey-faced young woman was thrust into the cell, her brownish-yellow hair jibbed to her skull. Catherine's hand went to her own unwashed hair like oiled hemp, musky and heavy. The girl looked half-starved, and when Matron Newell handed her a small loaf of bread she grabbed it with both hands and ate with quick, furtive glances at Catherine. Her look flickered over Catherine's rounded belly and she sank to her damp mattress, moaning softly.

"What's your name?" Catherine asked. The girl didn't answer.

Later, the girl settled down. She looked across at Catherine. "Who's you – someone left here to git me in trouble?"

"I got me oewn," said Catherine. "You can keep yours."

When the girl babbled in her sleep, Catherine wondered if she was having dreams or nightmares. She'd cry out, "No, Da! Da, no!"

Ann was the girl's name. She trembled as she told Catherine she was accused of killing her baby. "My very own fardher threatened me, said he'd not raise a Protestant watered down with Catholic spawn. He took the baby, struck hes little head while he sucked on his knuckle. I won't forget me baby's cry. Da wanted 'un burned in the fireplace, just throwed dere. I covered hes little body in a shawl. I – " Her scrawny face broke open in a wail. "My baby was God's child as much as any other mudder's child. He let 'un grow in me, let 'un leave me body alive." She sniffled. "I tell yer now, the Church of England priest won't come looking for a confession. He knows what happened."

BY DECEMBER, WINTER pulled up alongside the prison like a cold shadow driving away a warm sun and a long day. Catherine shivered under her wearied shawl whenever the gaol door opened and cold air swirled along the corridor and into her cell. Though days were shorter, time seemed longer. She filled time with thoughts of home and the echoing laughter of her children filling the house. She pretended to be sitting by the galloping fire, drawing in the aroma of beans boiling on the hob and bread baking in its pans. Now and then she'd look across at John, a rand of twine running through his coarse, damaged fingers as he knitted a net or mended one torn by sharks. Later, there came a quiet rest as nighttime fell and the children were abed. John lay stretched on the kitchen bench, napping, while Catherine stretched a length of joined brin on a frame and dug in a needle, carrying a string of cloth from an old discarded petticoat or shirt.

Catherine's pleasant thoughts were scattered by the sound of keys rattling against the lock in the door. The matron came to take Ann Morrisey to an outer room to speak to a lawyer in private. A few minutes later, Catherine looked up from her bed, startled. "You have an attorney, Catherine," said the gaoler in a respectful voice. "A man from Governor Cochrane's office."

"Will he defend me to the last?"

"I will hear your story."

She turned to see a tall man looking down at her. He lifted a watch from the fob pocket of his long waistcoat, glanced at it and put it away. He didn't reach his hand as he introduced himself. "I'm George Henry Emerson, attorney for you and Tobias Mandeville."

"What of Arthur Spring? Who's to speak for him?" she asked.

"Bryan Robinson has undertaken the defence of Spring at the request of the court."

Catherine strained to get to her feet from the low mattress. Her breath came out laboured as she got up and sat on the stool. "So I will be in trial soon and proved innocent," she said boldly.

"You will go to court tomorrow with your fellow companions to hear if there will be true bills found against you. If so, you will be arraigned and charged with murder. Then a trial date will be set." He sat down on a stool brought into the cell by the gaoler. "I advise you to plead 'not guilty.' It is for the court to decide if you are to be tried on the charge of murder. You've been accused of a crime which is more offensive than if you killed a man other than your husband. If the court sees fit, you will be arraigned for killing someone analogous to a king. A man is the king of his home." He cleared his throat. "Then there is the matter of adultery. There are claims you carried on an intrigue with Tobias Mandeville."

Catherine stared at him. Her eyes flashed, and she asked bluntly, "Do you think I'm guilty?"

He crossed a leg over his knee and locked it with his hands. He looked her in the eye and stated, "I am not here to defend the truth; I'm here to win your freedom, regardless."

He slipped the stool out from under him and stood up. "You have to prove to the courts that you are innocent."

"And how am I supposed to do that with John gone from sight these last few months, and no show of life or lifelessness? You're the governor's oewn man. Does Governor Cochrane believe I'm guilty?"

He answered quickly, "We have not discussed your case."

Catherine remembered the snowy-haired Cochrane from the time John marked X for the land grant. He had a disdainful look and a purposeful nose. His nostrils flared above bladder lips, as if he was ever ready to tell the person in front of him where to go. Now she imagined him sitting at his desk, a high scarf resting under his cleft chin, as he wrote: "This woman must prove she is innocent of adultery and murder."

Emerson took out his watch and looked at it for the second time.

Catherine told him, "Don't you be mindin' the time. You have to help me."

"The magistrates have two conflicting statements from you."

"If that be so, whose fault is that? Whatever Pinsent asked me, and whatever I answered wasn't written down. Johanna was squirming in me arms, a bit cross with teething. I was nauseated and me mind was ragged from not knowing where Jack was. I tell you, I hardly knew what I said, but it wasn't anything that could convict me. If I had wanted to kill Jack I could have put a poison mushroom in his soup, or boiled gowithy leaves with his dandelions. I could have tripped him over hes boat. He can't swim. I think hes disappearance is connected to the men he had dealings with, something to do with money."

She asked, her voice shaky, "If the jury convicts me, is it possible that I'll be sent to the gallows?"

Emerson paused, pressing long fingers to his lips. "Eleanor Power was hanged in 1754 – the first woman to face that horror in this colony. In 1772, Mary Power was convicted of helping murder a man. She was sentenced to hang. When it was known that she was enceinte, the king was asked to interfere on her behalf and he did. Mary was banished from the colony." Emerson's look went to Catherine's belly. "If you are expecting a child, and it can be detected, I'll save you from the noose by citing pregnancy. To 'plead the belly' is a legitimate defence."

"Is that my only defence?"

"It is a legitimate one. No one wants to take innocent life."

"My life is innocent," she retorted.

"Humans often convince themselves they are innocent when they're not. It's a trick the mind plays when the conscience can't handle the guilt," he said slowly.

"I am innocent, and don't you go thinkin' something different. I fear God. It's not in me to kill one of His creatures."

"We'll see who says it's so. You have to face Chief Justice Henry John Boulton, a former Attorney General of Canada. He's been a judge in this colony for only a few months. You'll find him to be a stern judge with a raspy voice. He'll hook you with his eyes, until you feel as if you're sliding off his long nose into an abyss. John Prowse, a fine friend of mine, has remarked that, 'Boulton's views, both of law and legislation, are most illiberal. . . .' Personal meanness causes him to be hated as no one else has ever been hated in this colony. But you and he have a commonality."

"And what is that?" she asked quickly.

"He married a Catholic and you married a Protestant. You both crossed faiths to marry. Ah, but he married a spirited one. Sure Eliza Boulton has a tongue as long as a whip and she spies out the priests and bishop and reports any grievances she has. You'd want to have her for a friend. But, the woman is a disgrace to her faith. I can tell you that."

"Perhaps she's not a disgrace to God."

The lawyer turned the conversation back to Catherine. "If the court finds a true bill against you, and you are arraigned for trial, that will be a long day, and, at the end, you will be too worn and muddled to think what to say – except that you are innocent." He wrote down the names of people Catherine wanted called for her defence, should she be arraigned. He stooped, touching her shoulder gently. A shudder ran through it.

Twenty-Six

CATHERINE shifted in sleep, as if she was trying to break away from harsh, loud voices, the heavy tread of boots and the clanging of keys and chains at all hours. Sometimes she awakened from an uneasy sleep, forgetting where she was and wondering why her bed was so uncomfortable and damp. Her hand went to her swollen belly and its discomforting pull on her body.

She had slipped into a solid sleep after a night of wakefulness when there came the sound of someone banging against the bars.

"A new year is here!" Matron Newell called as she brought in Catherine's breakfast. She asked, "What will the year bring for you, Catherine?"

"A child," Catherine answered with a wan smile.

"If that be so," the matron said ominously, "it could go to the swingswong."

"You're one for cheerful words!" Catherine retorted. She cupped her stomach. "There's a chance now. I have a lawyer, and Dr. Fleming will help me."

"Dr. Fleming! Have you seen hide or hair of him? I haven't."

"He'll be along. The bishop'll come to help an Irish mother, for sure. 'Tis a deed done."

"T'ink what you will. The bishop'll save the child, not the mother, and have a hand in how the young one's raised."

"The bishop'll save me if the law finds aught against me," Catherine answered obstinately.

The matron's eyes widened. "If anyone can save you, it'll be the bishop. He's got more power than the Governor hesself. But his work might hinder him. He's raising God's building. There's talk of him building a cathedral that will make Protestants green with envy."

"God's already got a dwelling," said Catherine. "Nature, its oewn self, is God's cathedral."

The matron clicked her tongue. "You've got the Irish spirit. That's not ben knocked out of you. I'd be hopin' hard, along with prayers for the bishop's help if I was you. The bishop is as much a political man as he is a religious one. He told parishioners they need not beg for their rights in Newfoundland society. They should demand them. He's promisin' to help young Catholic men get a ticket on the sealers' voyage this spring. That's so there'll be a ready tithe of cash for his cathedral."

Catherine never wanted Johnny to go to the ice. Now she imagined him growing up and getting ready. There would be the moment when a captain would slap him on the shoulder and say, "Here you bees, goin' to the ice, you young gaffer. You are bone and health, me boy, and you'll do well." Johnny would have a proud look. He'd be thinking his captain's vessel would be first to come into port loaded with swiles. Catherine would be thinking of him caught on the ice in a snowstorm and freezing to death.

"Here then, if you're goin' to eat," the matron said, nodding toward Catherine's food. She left the cell. A few minutes later, she brought in Ann's breakfast.

The young girl pushed herself up on her elbow. The matron scowled at her, and she got up and took her food and water. She ate quickly while the matron watched. Then she lay back down without a word. She pulled the cayla over her and burrowed under it. Her thin body trembled as the matron slammed the door and turned the key.

The next morning, the gaoler pulled the shutters back and glared at the women. "Yez'll be goin' to court this very marnin – a fine pair you be. You two'll be lucky to keep your necks out of the swingin' rope."

The matron turned a key in the lock and came inside. "Tidy yourselves, fasten your capes and tie your bonnets. As the man said, you'll be off to the court this very marnin and goin' before the judge and the Grand Jury to see if there's cause for bringing you to trial."

Catherine felt a stir of hope. There was no evidence on her. A basin of warm water was brought for her and Ann to share in having a good wash. Then Catherine was given thread and a needle to sew her ragged dress and petticoats so there would be no show of flesh. She swallowed with the hope of being free, daring to believe she would see her children in a short while. She blessed herself again and again, whispering Hail Marys.

She dragged her heavy cloak around her pooked belly and held it with tight fists as guards led Ann and her to the outside. As the heavy gates slammed behind her, she stopped to lift her face to the broad blue sky. The vastness of the space around her sent shudders through her body. She had forgotten how broad and high it was under a distant sky, and how far the sea spread before reaching the horizon. Below the high cliffs the sea appeared to frizz as clear green water spouted white, then sank down into itself like slob ice. The lusty breath of northeasterly winds sifted tiny snow crystals against Catherine's face. She lifted her tongue to the cool fresh taste of the flakes. Then, just as she flung back her head and pulled a strong breath of clean, cold air into her lungs, a guard grabbed her elbow and steered her toward a black coach. Wind swirled her hair, whispering through it as she pulled her hood over her bonnet and climbed up behind Ann into the carriage. She cupped her belly with both hands, as if to cradle the baby from harsh jolts as the horse and carriage raced down the hill, taking her and Ann to the court. There were children all along paths leading from Signal Hill Road, some of them with fresh, healthy-looking faces. Others looked dirty as they dragged on the skirts of slovenly dressed mothers laden with heavy baskets and babies. One young child strained under the weight of an infant.

She wrapped a dirty scarf around its tiny, scrawny face, as if to keep it from the raw wind.

Catherine thought of her own children, and hot tears splashed over her cheeks. She wiped them away as the horse and carriage stopped beside the courthouse.

The prisoners were pulled from the coach as wild birds flew in graceful glides across the sky, rising and descending at will above the snow-clad hills. Catherine thought, *I never envied gulls before.*

She felt the weight of spectators' looks as she was led into the large courtroom and placed in the dock. The men were brought in, shackled. Arthur was smaller than the junky man she remembered. He and Tobias stared at her, held her look, and she drew into her mind the sight of their pale, drawn faces. Other prisoners entered the dock and settled on the bench.

The clerk of the court called for all to rise as the Honourable Chief Justice Henry John Boulton, Acting Judge E. M. Archibald, and Assistant Judge E. B. Benton took their places. Catherine tried to rise, falling back as a sudden dizzy spell took her. She blacked out. Then, just as quickly, she felt herself settle. Her sight returned and she took in the look of Judge Boulton as he settled on the bench pulling scarlet robes around him and adjusting a powdered wig that matched his grey sideburns. His drooping face held lines engraved from the sides of his nose to the corners of his straight mouth. Slack eyelids hung over cold, hard eyes.

All powder and horsehair! Catherine thought in disdain as she remembered what the matron had told her. "Judge Boulton believes that the upper class governs and the lower breed obeys."

After the swearing in of the Grand Jury, Catherine raised her head to attend to Judge Boulton's address. His bushy eyebrows winged above eyes that seemed to bore into the faces of spectators as he began his charge to the jury.

"Mr. Foreman, and gentlemen of the Grand Jury . . . to you who are living in a thinly populated island, where the kind and hospitable character of the people has hitherto shed a charm over the ruggedness of the hills and where to love one another seems to have been the leading principle of action, the sudden eruption of those vindictive and malignant passions which have produced the awful catalogue of crimes which are now become the subject of deliberation, must be truly appalling. . . ."

Catherine thought of happenings from the past that were not kind and hospitable actions. *French and English bayoneting each other . . . burning people out of their homes in the dead of winter . . . fishermen driven from their homes, bearing permanent scars from beatings in order for rich merchants to exact payment for supplies . . . children of the lower order starving to death while the upper class dined sumptuously. Even now, colonists risk losing their ears . . . and can be thankful it's their ears instead of their life, and here Boulton is saying that to love one another seems to have been the leading principle of action – until now.*

"If . . . any of the persons aiding and abetting the commission of a felony be altogether absent when the crime is perpetuated, they will be regarded as accessaries before the fact, and not principles. . . . With regard, however, to Catherine Snow, the widow of the deceased John Snow, it will be proper for you to enquire whether or not she instigated Mandeville and Spring to commit so unnatural and horrible a crime. In her case, you will observe that nothing said by either of the prisoners, Spring and Mandeville, upon their examination, can be admitted to implicate her in the act. If, however, upon other evidence you will find that she instigated one or both of them to murder her husband, you will indict her as accessory before the fact. . . ."

Catherine's body tightened against her heart beating like a caged animal as she tried to keep her mind on all the judge was saying.

The judge went on. ". . . some satisfactory proof should be required that the persons supposed to have been murdered are actually dead; for although we may entertain the strongest personal impressions that these unfortunate people have been made away with, yet we can only arrive at a safe conclusion by adhering strictly to clear rules of evidence, and fixed principles of law, and we must not allow our indignation to get the better of our reason, and indict even the most strongly suspected upon mere conjecture. . . ."

Catherine's attention drifted from the judge's voice, away from the proceedings to her own thoughts. *There's no proof I'm a widow.*

She came back to hear the judge continue his lengthy charge to the jury. ". . . let every man be assured that whatever his station in society may be, the merits of his case will in this court be decided according to the known rules and principles of law as administered in the land of our fathers."

Catherine tried to keep her mind on the judge as he droned on. Finally, he finished instructing the jury. A dread fell on her as Judge Boulton proceeded to read the charges against each of the prisoners in the dock, then ask how they pleaded.

Tobias, trembling slightly, answered, "Not guilty."

Arthur's voice was defiant. "Not guilty."

"How say you, Catherine Snow?"

Her voice was strong, her face tight as she answered boldly, "I plead 'not guilty,' Your Honour."

"This court will establish whether you are or not."

I know I'm not, thought Catherine. *The law can't prove I am.*

Other prisoners pleaded not guilty to the charges read against them, including Ann Morrisey, who was so timid in her response she had to be asked twice.

The jury left the courtroom to deliberate on the charges and the judge's instructions. They weren't gone long, and when they came back to the courtroom, Catherine heard her name listed among those whom true bills were found against. She was to be arraigned with Tobias and Arthur for the murder of John Snow.

Other prisoners, Peter Downing and Patrick Malone, were also arraigned for the murder of Robert Crocker Bray, his child, and servant girl, at Harbour Grace; Ann Morrisey, for the murder of her bastard child at Trinity; and Peter Fanning for the murder of his wife at Harbour Grace.

Catherine looked up when she heard the name Fanning. She remembered last May when Mary Britt came to her house telling her, "Sure there's a terrible t'ing happened in Harbour Grace a day ago. Poor Mary Fanning – me uncle Herb knows her – got such a smack, the back of her head was bate in to her face, and it was left like jelly. Her body was not only bate up, but her sweet baby, on the ready to see the world, was smashed to bits – and the handle of a spade broken. People heard noises and groans, and not t'inking it was nigh as dreadful, went to the quietness of their beds. The next morning, sure what a sight!" Mary's breasts heaved and her eyes closed. "'Tis not what I'd want to be seein' before me breakfast. I sid Peter come up on the wharf in Port de Grave only last week ready to sell his fish. He looked to be the nicest kind of a fellar. I never sid a murthurer before. And he with a face and eyes like everyone else. He'd been wise to have covered her up in the ground, to save livyers the sight. Blessed Jesus. Not his fault then, I suppose." She rolled her eyes. "The poor woman shouldn't have provoked him."

Catherine was to go to trial with Tobias and Arthur on Friday, the tenth of January. Her heart seemed to somersault with the thought. *What if the judge sentences me to die and he won't believe I'm having a baby, me long-waisted? It was a blessing how I carried some of me babies like a secret for eight months. Then in the last month, I burst open like a flower. This time, though, I'm so thin, I've shown a rounded belly for a while. It's not a belly stretched from having many children. I hope the judge can see that.*

Catherine felt flushed and heavy-headed, her body weary with the weight and movement of the baby as she was taken by the arm and led out of the courtroom down cold, stone steps to a dungeon cell. She closed her mouth against its damp, fusty air, and fell exhausted to a damp mattress. Ann Morrisey was pushed in after her. The young girl slipped to a mattress and lay curled in a ball, crying and shivering as the gaoler left with his lantern, leaving the women in darkness.

"They might have throwed me down in an ocean grave and ben done with me as to put me here," Ann wailed against Catherine's silence.

Twenty-Seven

CHIEF Justice Boulton's words echoed in Catherine's mind. "... some satisfactory proof should be required that the persons supposed to have been murdered are actually dead."

I will be found innocent, she thought, *on the strength of the judge's charge to the jury. Any fool knows that when no crime has been committed there can be no evidence of one.* She curled herself tight and let sleep swirl her away from tumultuous feelings.

Ann Morrisey was called away the next day.

"You'll be goin' to pay for the murder of your bastard son at Trinity," the gaoler said.

Catherine felt Ann's heavy silence as the young girl hurried past, her eyes downcast and her mouth glum. She went without a word to Catherine who wished her God's kind eye.

It was a long day for Catherine as she waited for news of the young girl's fate. She fingered the old mam's crucifix as night came and went. The lumpy, bug-infested mattress and the baby's movements added to her discomfort, waking her throughout the night.

It wasn't until the next morning that Matron Newell, who must have moved from the Signal Hill prison to be with Catherine and other women prisoners, brought news that Ann had been acquitted of the capital charge of murder – her life saved by a quibble. She was found guilty of burying her baby boy's body in the landwash at Trinity. The matron tightened her lips and shook her head. "She might have looked to be a sweet young thing, but she was an old offender, and now she's gone off to the Harbour Grace gaol for six months."

The matron warned, "Don't get yer hopes up, Catherine. Ann was Protestant, you know."

On Friday, thought Catherine, *I, a Cartlic, will go on trial for me life – and for me baby's life.*

She remembered a morning when John had just come in off the water with some fresh cod. A stranger, with low brows and sunken eyes and a tongue on the loose, offered John a quid for a brin bag of fish. Then he repeated something Arthur had said. "I'll offer your wife an Irish blessing, sir. 'May you never live to see your wife a widow.'"

A riddle from a simpleton, Catherine had thought at the time. *Now I know that John could be out there somewhere, alive, and he laughing his head off while I may be charged as his murthurer.*

Friday morning, Catherine was awakened by the sound of a key in the lock of the cell door. A woman with a kind face, her grey hair lifted and bundled up around her crown and held in pins under a net, came inside. "I'm Mrs. Perchard, the gaoler's wife," she said pleasantly as she lifted a candle to the sconce in a bracket on the wall.

Matron Newell came behind her, holding a large pot against her breast. "You'll have your porridge sure, a bit thick today for the trial will make a long day." She held out a large wooden spoon. "Hold out your bowl, why don't you? Sure your hands are shakin'."

Catherine was given the usual jug of water, to portion out in drink and toiletry, and a clean rag. She was told to make haste. She ate the lukewarm porridge as fast as she could, drank the water and shivered through her cold wash. She braided her long hair around her head and pulled on her bonnet. Then she sat waiting, expecting any moment to be taken to the courtroom. By the time the sheriff came, more than two hours later, she felt lightheaded and tired.

It was eleven o'clock by the time the Honourable Judge Henry John Boulton, Chief Justice of Newfoundland, the Honourable Edward Brabazon Brenton, and the Honourable Edward Mortier Archibald took their places on the bench.

ELIZA BOULTON, THE chief justice's wife, sometimes came to watch court proceedings from a front side seat reserved for distinguished citizens. Other seats were taken by well-off livyers while the riffraff stood at the back of the room. Eliza sat with her black-gloved hands folded in her lap. Her elegant mauve wool dress matched the hat veiled to her chin. She turned to see the room crowded by the time the three prisoners were brought into the court. She looked toward Catherine Snow and caught a glimpse of her ankles. Under black wool triheens, they appeared to be swollen. The prisoner staggered and her hand went to her rounded middle under a long red cloak covering a shabby dress. Eliza's hand instinctively dropped to her own belly where she felt the stir of another child. She hadn't wanted to be in delicate health so soon after her last child. It was not as if she needed children to do her work. There were enough starving youngsters to be hired and paid for in victuals. Eliza glanced at the men who were looking well as they were led by officers into the court. She knew what the jurors would think as they took in Catherine Snow's scrawny white look and the dark hollows around her haunted, plagued eyes. *What young fellow would go after the likes of that?*

Catherine was immediately placed at the bar with Tobias and Arthur. "Mind now, you don't try to communicate," the sheriff had warned Catherine on her way into the courtroom.

Arthur gave the judges a dark, sour look as Judge Boulton read the jury and witness list and told the prisoners they had a right to challenge the jury members chosen. He looked toward the prisoners and asked if they had any objections to the men chosen as jurors.

Tobias answered, "Your Honour, the jurymen are all strangers to us." Catherine and Arthur nodded in agreement. Only one juror, Catholic John Dillon, an elderly gentleman whose hearing was affected, was challenged and excused from jury duty. James Tobin was the only Catholic juror. The petit jurors were empanelled, sworn and charged. Messrs. Thomas Bickham, Thomas Eastrom, John Long, George Lewis, Patrick Byrne, William Buckley, James Tobin, Patrick Maher, Richard Treligan, Robert Radford, Valentine Merchant, and Andrew Stewart then took their places in the jury box.

There were too many names for Catherine's mind to hold. She raised heavy eyes to the jurors' faces. They blurred in front of her. She felt herself swimming with weariness, unable to concentrate on anything.

George H. Emerson, Esquire, Catherine's and Tobias's lawyer, nodded at them. Bryan Robinson, Esquire, was present to undertake the defence of Arthur at the request of the court.

The clerk of the court read the indictment against Catherine and the men. "You are therein charged with the murder of John Snow – the husband of the prisoner Catherine Snow – at Port de Grave on the thirty-first of August last – Mandeville and Spring as the principals and Catherine Snow as accessory before the fact."

Attorney General James Simms, in opening the case to the jury, observed, "Under the indictment which you have just heard, the prisoners stand charged with the wilful and felonious murder of one John Snow – the two prisoners, Mandeville and Spring, being charged as principals in the first and second degrees, and the woman, Catherine Snow, as accessory before the fact. Arthur Spring's and Catherine Snow's offence was, in its degree, technically distinguished from Mandeville's. His was simply murder, but owing to the relations of Wife and Servant, in which the Woman and Spring stood toward the murdered party, their crime, if proved against them, will constitute that species of murder denominated petit treason. The case I am about to unfold to the view of you, the jury, for your solemn consideration and awful determination, is in its character the most deeply atrocious and appalling that has ever fallen under my observation."

Catherine lifted tired eyes to the ruddy-faced man. *A most atrocious case*, she thought, shaking her head, *would be the beating to death of a mother and her unborn child*. Peter Fanning, according to the matron, had been convicted of manslaughter. He would not hang. She tried to hold on to Simms's words as he kept on.

After some time speaking, the Attorney General stopped to look down his monocle at papers he held. He drew in a long breath, pushed out his ample chest and continued. "John Snow, the person whom the prisoners are charged with murdering, was a respectable, industrious planter, residing at the south side of Port de Grave, thriving in his circumstances and, numbered among those of his class called independent, being known to have saved and laid by a considerable sum of money. The woman at the bar is his wife and they had no fewer than seven children, the eldest of whom is sixteen or seventeen years old, at least."

I have given birth to nine children and, God willing, I will have my tenth child, thought Catherine.

The Attorney General continued. "The prisoner Mandeville was by trade a cooper in the employment of Messrs. Martin & Jacob who carry on business as merchants on the north side of Port de Grave Bay, nearly opposite to Snow's plantation and fishing room. He was an intimate acquaintance of Snow's family, and particularly so of the wife's, claiming relationship with her in the . . ."

Catherine let out a gasp, missing some of the Attorney General's words. It was bad enough that she was charged with killing John, bad enough that there were rumours she had been adulterous with a cousin, and he practically a boy – but to be accused of it in a court! Fear wavered through her body. Such an accusation would turn the jury against her. She tried to follow as the Attorney General carried on. "He was in the habit of visiting John Snow every Saturday evening, to make up Snow's accounts of his dealings, which Snow, unable to write, could not perform for himself. Arthur Spring was a servant of John Snow, in whose employment in the fishery he had been for the period of two years. The leading facts which I expect to prove against the prisoners are these: that an illicit criminal intercourse had, during several years past, subsisted between the prisoners Catherine Snow and Tobias Mandeville. John Snow's existence was incompatible with the free exercise of their lustful gratifications, so they had for a long time past determined to murder him. They solicited and found a willing and ready associate in the diabolical plot, in the person of Arthur Spring. Several plans had been laid and resolved on by the prisoners, but they had been frustrated by accidental circumstances, until at the end of the month of August last. They then determined to carry their wicked purpose into execution on Saturday evening, the thirty-first of that month.

"On the afternoon of that day Catherine Snow accompanied her deceased husband in his boat to deliver to Messrs. Martin & Jacob, a quantity of fish at their stores at Bareneed where Mandeville was employed."

Deceased was he? Catherine thought wryly. *A hard way to deliver fish!*

The Attorney General cleared his throat, took a drink from a glass beside him, and carried on. "Catherine Snow here concerted with Mandeville the proceedings of that night's perpetration. John Snow, after taking home his wife, would as usual go alone in his skiff on the Saturday evening after Mandeville's work was done for the week, and conduct him to Snow's house to make up his accounts. As soon as John should leave home for this purpose, his wife was to send their servant Catherine White, and their two elder daughters to the house of a deceased neighbour named Hele, to attend his wake, at the distance of about a mile. The younger children were to be put to bed, and then Snow's wife and Arthur Spring would be prepared for the tragic scene that was to ensue. Mrs. Snow, the prisoner, was to give Spring her husband's gun, always kept ready loaded, with which he was to wait, in Snow's fishing stage, the return of his master with Mandeville, who was to land and leave Snow to secure the boat at her moorings; and as soon as Snow, himself, should enter the stage, Spring was to shoot him and the two men were then to dispose of the body, which in the event they carried into deep water and sank with a rope and a grapnel on or near the fishing ground."

The Attorney General raised his voice. "That this horrible plan was consummated to the letter, I will establish by the most positive and conclusive evidence. Regarding the prisoners, Mandeville and Spring, there may remain some doubt as to which of them actually fired the gun. The question upon that fact, under the present indictment, cannot, however, create any embarrassment in the minds of the jury, for if both men were present at the execution of the preconcerted plot, it makes no more difference in law than it does in morality which of the two parties fired the gun. Both are equally guilty of the murder. The confessions and admissions of these men will be borne out by various other proofs of immediate facts."

Catherine's thoughts drifted as Simms addressed wickedness and guilt. She was drawn back with his reference to her. "As respecting the prisoner, Catherine Snow, I have no direct or positive evidence of her guilt, but I have a chain of circumstantial evidence to produce against her, that, in my judgment, must leave in the minds of the jury no doubt on that point. I will trace her in her secret preparation and co-operation in the plot – in her movements immediately after the murder was perpetrated, and the false accounts she gave that fateful night to a near-relation and neighbour respecting her then murdered husband in such sort as to show that her conduct and statements could not consist with innocence. I will show that her paramour was sheltered in her house during the two days and nights next ensuing the night of the murder of her husband. It appears that at no time did she manifest by her conduct any endeavour to trace the cause of her husband's extraordinary disappearance, so calculated in its circumstance to excite distress and alarm, and awake suspicion and enquiry. Contrary to all that was natural and consistent with innocency, I will show that this woman, this *wife*, laboured to suppress all enquiry concerning the fate of her husband. She even denied a person sent to her by the magistracy to ascertain the truths of rumours prevalent the day after the murder. She informed them that she did not wish them to trouble themselves about her affairs."

That's not what I said. They were asking questions about John's business, wanting to know where his money box was.

"I will show that when Spring and Mandeville were apprehended, this *wife* laboured to prevent those disclosures which already had *had* their inception. Then this woman endeavoured to obtain the liberation of her husband's murderers; and, finally, when by their confessions the horrid plot and its catastrophe were unfolded, this woman was found to have abandoned her home and her children and had fled from justice."

Abandoned me home! Sweet Jesus, I was trying to protect the children!

"If these and other incidents equally weighty in the pale of her guilt are proved, and coupled with her own false and fabricated statements, I conceive that there can remain no doubt of her guilty participation in the horrid plot disclosed by the confession of both the male prisoners. But while those confessions cannot be admitted as evidence against her, yet her own contradictory statements and her own actions, would appear to be such, that they are to be accounted for on no other ground or principle, than that of her being a principal accomplice in the murder."

The Attorney General then observed that cases of murder sometimes occur wherein the guilty party subjects himself to the last penalties of the law, under circumstances that excite our deep sympathy. He said he was referring to those cases which do not involve what is vulgarly understood by malice aforethought – cases in which a party under the influence of sudden and violent anger uses a deadly weapon – or utters, under the excitement of momentary rage, expressions perhaps exceeding his real purpose or intention (in either of which cases the law infers malice) and causes the death of a fellow creature.

Simms lowered his voice and looked at the jury. "In such a case the monitor in our own breasts might whisper to us 'And are you, yourself, guiltless of indulging in anger; and might not this at some time have been your own case?' In lending our sympathies to others, we in such cases conciliate our own frailties. But in this case . . . there is no room for sympathy toward the accused, if they are guilty at all.

"If you arrive at the conclusion that John Snow was murdered, and that the prisoners at the bar are his murderers, you must also believe that his murder was premeditated through a period of many months – that it was repeatedly, deeply plotted, but still retarded – again brooded over and at last hatched into perpetration by *his own wife*, his own servant, and his intimate acquaintance. In proportion to the enormity of the crime and the severity and certainty of the punishment that awaits it, so ought your caution to be guarded by a more rigid and scrupulous examination of the proofs, on which a conviction is sought. And here I especially entreat you to thoroughly discharge from your minds and remembrance, everything you have heard or thought upon the subject of that solemn enquiry before you entered the court. You are bound by your oaths to deliver a just verdict according to the evidence. . . . I am confident you will scrupulously and religiously discharge yourselves of that obligation, and of the duties you owe to society at large, and especially toward the prisoners at the bar."

Twenty-Eight

FOR the Prosecution, Attorney General Simms called John Broom, Robert John Pinsent, Thomas Danson, John Jacob, John Bowes, James Shelly, Catherine White, Ruth Snow, Mary Connolly, Mark Hennebury, Patrick Walsh, Richard Taylor, James McCabe, Mary Britt, and Catherine Breen. They were severally sworn to give evidence and empanelled.

Catherine White, John Connolly, John Doyle, James McCabe, Bridget Snow, and John Jacob were severally sworn to give evidence for Catherine's defence.

JOHN BROOM, CHIEF magistrate of St. John's, was the first witness to be called and sworn. Catherine laced her long, thin fingers together and squeezed her hands tight, as if she were holding on to herself for support. John Broom's granddaughter, Louisa, was Robert John Pinsent's wife.

The man looked elderly, his eyelids heavy over small eyes in a jowled, sallow face. He testified that the day after Arthur Spring arrived from Port de Grave, he was brought before him in the Police Office. A confession he had previously made before Mr. Pinsent, the magistrate at Port de Grave, was distinctly and clearly read over to him and was acknowledged by Spring to be his voluntary confession.

Perhaps because it was aware of the controversial deal struck with Patrick Malone against Peter Downing, saving Malone's life and sending Downing to the gallows the Saturday before, the court asked the witness if he had held out a promise of a favour to Spring. Mr. Broom answered that he had not. He also stated that he was not aware of any inducement offered to him to make a confession. "In fact," said Mr. Broom, in an empatic voice, "I cautioned him against saying anything to incriminate himself, but he still acknowledged the confession to be his."

The written confession was handed to Broom who identified it as the one he had alluded to.

Catherine looked toward her lawyer sitting at the table with the other lawyers. She mulled over the fact that Arthur could not read or write. Therefore, what was read to him and what was on the paper could have been different. She sat back resigned, willing to wait for the statement to be read to Arthur by his lawyer so he could swear to it as his or dismiss it as made up. Broom was not asked to identify Tobias's statement.

Robert John Pinsent, Esquire, didn't look at the prisoners as he was sworn. He said he had lived at Port de Grave for the past twenty years and that he knew the late John Snow very well as a planter who had settled at the south side of Port de Grave Bay, about two miles from Pinsent's house. He knew Catherine Snow, John's wife.

When Pinsent was asked if he knew Tobias Mandeville, he said that he knew him to be a cooper for Jacob and Martin at Bareneed on the north side of Port de Grave Bay, about three quarters of a mile from Snow's home. He knew Arthur Spring to be a shipped servant to John Snow until August last. He said that on the second day of September, he heard that John Snow had suddenly disappeared two days before. Mr. Jacob who, as well as Pinsent, was a Conservator of the Peace, had called on him to say there was a report that John Snow was missing, and he was supposed by the people either to be murdered, or that he had made away with himself. Pinsent told the court that he and Mr. Jacob decided to send Constable John Bowes to the south side.

Pinsent gave Catherine a slow, deliberate look and said, "In consequence of his report, we felt it was our duty to go the next day, the third of September, to the south side, to make enquiries personally. We were accompanied by John Bowes, Mark Hennebury, and three or four planters." He lifted a freckled finger to scratch his nose and then he glanced at Arthur. "When we reached the stage the prisoner Spring came toward us and pointed out a pile of fish on the flake near the stage, which had been disturbed. He said it was perfectly sound on the night of August thirty-first, and on the following morning, he found the rinds and the toplines of the pile disturbed, and fish strewn about the flake. He said he thought that robbers had been there. We then went to the house and saw Mrs. Snow sitting with several neighbours in a small parlour which led off the kitchen. We told her we had come to make enquiries about the mysterious disappearance of her husband. We asked her to tell us what she knew about it and we would put it in writing. She then made a voluntary statement nearly as follows."

Catherine wondered which part of the statement he considered *nearly*.

"She said that on Saturday night, she and her husband were over at Bareneed, delivering fish, that they returned together about sunset – that about half an hour afterward her husband went across again to Bareneed, to bring back Tobias Mandeville who was a cousin of hers, and was in the habit of coming over every Saturday night, to enter up their accounts. They came over together about half an hour after dark. They properly moored the boat at the stagehead, locked the stage and brought the key up to the house. Her husband, Mandeville, and herself sat down to supper; Snow enquired for his two daughters, and being told they were gone to William Hele's wake he got into a passion, and told her he would take their lives and hers, if they did not soon come home. About this time, Mandeville and Arthur Spring went away to the wake. I asked her if she heard Mandeville say he would fetch home her daughters, and she said she didn't. She told me that when Mandeville and Spring left, there was nobody but herself, her husband, and their three children all together in the kitchen. Snow lay down on the bench for a short time after the men left, and continued in a passion about Catherine allowing their daughters to go to the wake. After a few minutes, he got up from the bench and took his loaded gun from the rack and went outside the door and fired it off. When he came in, he put the gun on the rack unloaded, and lay down again on the bench. I asked Catherine what she said about John firing the gun. She said that neither he nor she said anything. John then told her to go to the wake for his daughters. She said she was afraid, but that Tobias and Arthur would soon be home with them."

Catherine drew in a heavy breath, thinking, *I didn't want to venture out into the dark night be meself. Too, I was afraid of leaving Jack to tend to the children, not yet settled for the night, while I went for the girls. What if his temper got the better of him? I might think he wouldn't use his anger on the babies, but I couldn't be sure. I'd want them settled abed and asleep before I left for Ruth's. I didn't want any more rackets, and he'd be at it ag'in as long as the girls weren't home – and I was. 'Tis not as if it was the first time I left for Ruth's. . . .*

Pinsent kept on with what he swore was Catherine's statement. "Catherine said that after some time, John got up again and went out without saying a word. This was midnight. I asked her what he was wearing and she said he had on his hat, his best blue waistcoat but no jacket. She felt afraid to remain any longer in the house, as he appeared so moody and angry. In his absence she put the two elder small children to bed, and left the house with her youngest child. She went over to the house of John's brother, Edward Snow, who was in Labrador, and went to bed with his wife. She told Edward's wife all that had happened, and requested a woman named Patience Boon, who was in the home, to go with her to her own house for company. The woman declined. When she was going over to Edward's house she had heard her husband going toward his own house, driving some pigs from the door. She said from that time she heard nothing more of him. About three o'clock in the morning, her two eldest daughters came to Edward Snow's house, and told her there was no light in their house. Catherine said she asked her daughter what her husband had done to her since she came home from the wake, and her daughter replied that she had not seen him at all. Catherine said she got up at daylight and went home, expecting to find her husband there. She was alarmed at discovering he was not at home. She began a search all about the stage, flakes, and premises, and the neighbourhood. Tobias and Arthur and the neighbours assisted in the search, but from that time to this she has not been able to learn any tidings of him. She made the observation that a pile of fish on the end of the flake, near the water, had been disturbed, the covering of rinds being partly taken off, and some strewn about, but she thought no fish were taken away. She also saw the fish strewn eastward of the stage. She said she had no suspicion that anyone murdered her husband, nor could she account at all for her husband's disappearance."

Pinsent added that John Snow's hat and best blue waistcoat which he had on the early part of the night were found in the house in the morning.

The hat and waistcoat are still at home, Catherine wanted to say, *and free of gunshot and bloodstains. Maybe John's gunshot was a signal to someone doing business with him.* She never knew what transactions went on between him and the men at Port de Grave.

Pinsent was asked if he had observed anything particular at the time.

"No," he answered, then added quickly, "but later I saw spots of blood about the stagehead. It appeared to be fresh blood. Some of the longers had been cut with a knife, as if spots of blood had been cut out."

Catherine hoped Pinsent would be asked when "later" was and what was unusual about blood on a fishing stage. Instead, he was questioned as to when Tobias and Arthur were examined.

"They were examined on the same day before Mr. Jacob and me at Bareneed."

Pinsent was asked if the prisoners knew that Mr. Jacob and himself were Conservators of the Peace and had a right to make an enquiry. Pinsent said that they did. It was generally known in the neighbourhood. He had been Conservator of the Peace since 1826.

The clerk of the court stood to read the examination of Spring and Mandeville alluded to by Pinsent. It declared that they were utterly ignorant of what had befallen John Snow and knew not what to think of his mysterious and sudden disappearance. It was signed by both the prisoners.

Asked what he thought of the statement, Pinsent said it was evidently made up for the occasion, adding that Spring was arrested on suspicion on Thursday, the fifth of September, and committed to the lock-up house at Port de Grave. Mandeville was arrested on the same evening and placed in Thomas Butler's house in charge of a constable.

Catherine sighed. *Thomas Butler is a constable.*

Pinsent went on to tell the court that he accompanied Mandeville from Bareneed to Port de Grave. They met Mrs. Snow on the way. She had heard of Spring's arrest and had come to intercede for his liberation. She appeared very anxious that bail should be taken for him and that he should be let out. She said her hay and potatoes would be spoiled if he was not at home to attend to them.

"I told her," said Pinsent, "that it was of little consequence; for two shillings a day she could hire a man who would answer her purpose as well as Spring. She was very anxious that Spring should be freed, and at length prevailed upon Mark Hennebury, who was present, to become one of his bondsmen."

Pinsent told the court that he, Hennebury, and Mandeville then proceeded to Port de Grave. "I assured Mandeville if he could procure two respectable bondsmen he would be free on bail. He procured two such persons and was given bail on the evening of September fifth. Mandeville then exhibited considerable anxiety that Spring should be liberated, and went to Bareneed to obtain sureties for him."

Pinsent eyed the jury. "From the rumours which every moment were reaching Mr. Jacob and me, we thought we had done wrong in admitting Mandeville to bail."

Rumours! thought Catherine, looking toward her lawyer. *He needs to ask what the rumours were and who was spreading them.*

Pinsent went on. "We were determined not to receive bail for Spring on any account. Mandeville's bailsmen expressed an anxious desire to withdraw the bond they had given on his behalf, and I sent Constable Bowes to Bareneed for Mandeville. When he was brought down to my house, his bondsmen stated, in his presence, their desire to withdraw their security. They were afraid of the consequences, as reports were abroad that he intended to leave the place."

Catherine's mouth tightened. She mumbled to herself, "Pinsent likely ordered them to withdraw their security."

"Mandeville was given in charge to the constable who was directed to remain with him during the night. He was not confined to the same place with Spring." Pinsent turned to look at Judge Boulton. "It then occurred to me and John Jacob, the other magistrate, to endeavour, if possible, to obtain some clue to Snow's disappearance, which was involved with so much mystery. We thought it would be well – before we put Mandeville in the lock-up – to place a man under my desk to hear any conversation that might take place between the two prisoners who were in separate cells, divided only by a plank partition. A man was accordingly placed there, and Mandeville was committed to the adjoining cell. Upon our return to the lock-up house in about two hours, for the purpose of extricating the man from his hiding place, Spring accidentally discovered him through the grating. Spring appeared very alarmed and cried out, 'That man has been listening under the table – what did you hear? What did you hear?' The man, however, denied having been there, and slipped out of the lock-up to communicate what he had heard."

Pinsent wasn't asked who the man was and what it was he had heard. *If it had been significant, then Bill Richards should have been a witness; Arthur may have been merely cursing the magistrate for barring him up*, thought Catherine.

"In a minute or two afterward, Mark Hennebury, who had accompanied me and the others to the lock-up, came out and told me that Spring wished to speak to me. He had something important, he thought, to communicate. I directed the constable to handcuff Spring and bring him up to my counting house, which was done. Spring's first words on entering the counting house, were, 'We killed him, Mandeville, myself, and Mrs. Snow.' I then proceeded to write down his confession, which he made voluntarily, without any inducement or promise whatsoever. When he had finished, his confession was read over and acknowledged by him. He put his mark to it, in the presence of Mr. Jacob and me."

Pinsent read to the court what he had written on behalf of Arthur Spring who could not read or write:

CONFESSION OF ARTHUR SPRING, BEFORE THE MAGISTRATE AT PORT DE GRAVE ON FRIDAY, SEPTEMBER SIXTH LAST, RELATIVE TO THE MURDER OF JOHN SNOW . . .

". . . that he and Tobias Mandeville, a cooper in the employ of Messrs. Martin and Jacob at Bareneed, and Catherine Snow, the wife of John Snow, his master, are the murderers of the said John Snow, that they planned his murder about a month ago. On this occasion Tobias Mandeville called him out of John Snow's house, and said that it was best to kill John Snow and get him out of the place entirely, and then they would have good times of it afterward. He had often quarrelled with John Snow during the past summer, and he had told Mandeville that he would get his master a beating when his time was out. He thought it was too bad to murder him. It would be better to give him a beating. Mandeville said it was the best plan to murder Snow downright and get him out of the place altogether. After this, he and Mandeville often talked about, and laid out plans for John Snow's murder. About a week after Mandeville spoke to him about murdering John Snow, Catherine Snow told Spring that she wished her husband out of the way; if he was not put out of the way he would have her life. Spring replied, that it was too hard to kill her husband, but she said if it was not done he would kill her, or someone else of the family. Mandeville and Spring planned once or twice to murder John Snow with a hatchet in his stage, but Spring said his heart failed him. On Saturday night last, August thirty-first, John Snow went across the harbour to Bareneed, in a boat by himself, to fetch Mandeville over to his house. Snow had been to Bareneed with his wife during the afternoon of the same day. John Snow left his house about dusk to go over to Bareneed. While John was absent from his house, his wife sent the servant maid and her two daughters to William Hele's wake in Cupids. She told Spring that if they meant to murder her husband, now was the time. She had given him rum after his master had left home. She told him to take the gun, which was always kept loaded by his master on the rack, down with him to the stage, and wait there until his master and Mandeville came over in the boat from Bareneed, and then to shoot her husband. Spring took the gun and went down to the stage, and waited about half an hour expecting the boat across with Snow and Mandeville. When the boat arrived at the stagehead about ten o'clock that night, Mandeville immediately got out of the boat, and came to Spring, leaving Snow in the boat to moor her. When Mandeville came into the stage, he saw Spring with the gun in his hand. He told him to fire it at John Snow just as he got from his boat to the stagehead. Spring lifted the gun to fire but his resolution failed him. His hands trembled so much that he dropped the gun down on the longered floor of the stage. Mandeville said, 'What are you about?' and he replied that he had not courage enough to fire. Mandeville told him to stand out of the way and he took up the gun himself and fired it at Snow, who was at the moment entering the stage door coming in from the stagehead. John Snow immediately fell dead on the stagehead. He never spoke a word after the gun was fired, nor did he give a groan. Spring thought the load went into Snow's breast, as Mandeville was not more than three or four yards from him when he fired. The men then slung Snow's body with a rope under the arms, and a half hitch of the rope round his neck, and lowered him over the stagehead into the water. They then fastened the end of the rope to a grapnel and took the grapnel into the boat and towed the body off into deep water, and sank it with the grapnel fastened to it. The men then returned in the boat to the stage, and there slightly fastened her to one of the strouters. They then went up to John Snow's house and told his wife that they had murdered her husband, and had carried him off into the harbour and sunk his body in deep water. She told them to say nothing about it. She then went from her husband's house to Edward Snow's house and the men went to William Hele's wake at Cupids. They arrived there at eleven o'clock and stayed there until about three o'clock the next morning. They returned to John Snow's house with the Snows' two daughters and servant girls, Catherine White and Mary Connolly. Spring and Mandeville then went back to the wake and stayed there until daylight. Then they returned to John Snow's house. A few minutes after this Catherine Snow came to her own house from Edward Snow's. She told Spring to go down to the flake and take some fish from one of the piles and strew it about the flake to make it appear that robbers had been there in the night. He accordingly did so. Spring believes that Tobias and Catherine intended to be married after John Snow's death, and to sell his property and to go live elsewhere. He has heard it rumoured that they carried on a criminal intercourse for some time past, but he never saw anything of this sort between them. Spring says that his inducement to assist in the murder of his master was that Mandeville promised him his full wages at the end of his time, without any deduction for things taken up by him from his master in account. Then he might quit the country."

Catherine felt bile rise in her throat. Pinsent was trying to get her on adultery. If Arthur said he saw nothing between her and Tobias, how could he think that Tobias would be able to get him his wages – unless he was planning on stealing Jack's money box?

Twenty-Nine

By mid-afternoon, light coming in through the courtroom windows was growing dim. Lanterns that stood in brass sconces on the court walls were lit. Flames flickered and flared. Oil smoke mingled with pipe smoke and then settled.

Catherine had no idea what time it was when Judge Boulton rose and banged his gavel, saying, "The court stands recessed. God save the King." Then he and the other judges took leave of the court. Catherine lifted her pale face to give Mrs. Perchard an urgent look. She beckoned her to her side where she whispered that she needed to go to the latrine. She was led out into a narrow chamber on the outer wall of the court accessed only from the inside.

Catherine staggered as she was taken back inside the court. Mrs. Perchard thrust a flask of water into her hands. She gulped it while her empty stomach rumbled. She tried to settle on the hard seat while she waited for the judges and lawyers to return to the courtroom. She sighed, thinking, *They're likely getting themselves full of salt beef, new cabbage, and fresh taties.* It was a long wait with the child inside her weighing on her hips and back. Catherine felt her weariness grow as dense as night. She wanted to lie down and drift into sleep where she would dream of sunny days on Salmon Point, days full of her children's laughter.

The judges came back from the recess and the court proceedings continued. *Me lawyer has not come anight me to beg ques-*

tions, she thought miserably. *I dare not trespass on the court's procedure for fear 'twill do me ill.*

Pinsent's examination resumed. He told the court that Spring made his confession with his understanding about him, perfectly sober. He said that while Spring was making the confession to him and John Jacob, a report came that Mandeville had fainted. Pinsent said, "After Spring's confession, we dispatched Constable John Bowes to arrest Catherine Snow. Bowes had taken the key of the lock-up house with him so the men were obliged to burst open the door. Mandeville was found stretched on the floor in a faint."

Catherine looked toward her lawyer, thinking he should be making a note to ask if Tobias had been left alone in the locked cell. If so, who brought the report that he had fainted? And why did he faint?

Pinsent said that Bowes and other men went to Catherine Snow's house. They reported on their return that she had absconded and could not be found. He added that, on September eighth, three parties were dispatched in different directions in search of Catherine Snow, but after being absent the whole day, they returned without having found her. Pinsent said he brought Spring and Mandeville across to Portugal Cove on September eighth. They were handcuffed together and lashed down to the thwarts of the boat. Pinsent claimed that, on the passage across, Mandeville volunteered, "I declare to you as it were in the presence of God, and as a man who has no hope of life, and no inducement to tell an untruth, that I did not fire the gun, but that this man (pointing to Spring) fired the gun."

According to Pinsent, Spring replied, "No, I did not; it was you who fired the gun." Mandeville retorted, "How can you tell such a lie – you know it's false?" Mandeville acknowledged he was present at the murder. Pinsent said he asked what they had done with the body, and Mandeville told him they had towed it off and sunk it on the outer edge of the fishing ground, he supposed in a strain between Snow's house on the south side and French's house on the north side. Catherine knew that the French family lived under Dock Mountain, not far from the Martin & Jacob warehouse, and that the area had already been searched.

Pinsent claimed to have asked Mandeville about his relationship with Catherine. Pinsent looked at her as he said, "Mandeville told me he had been criminally connected to Mrs. Snow for some time before."

Pinsent's words went through Catherine like scattered shot from a musket. *Tobias would not have told such a lie!*

Pinsent added that he enquired if Tobias knew where Mrs. Snow was, and he said he did not. Pinsent said that Mandeville asked him if he thought there was any chance for him, and he said he could not tell.

Pinsent was then asked if anyone else had heard the conversation. He said they had not. "William Hampton and John Bowes were in the boat when the conversation took place between Mandeville and me, but they might not have heard it because I told them to keep back."

Catherine let out a sigh of frustration. Surely the court would know that Pinsent was lying. He would not have told Hampton and Bowes to keep back. He would have wanted them as witnesses to a confession.

Pinsent went on. "I was present in Magistrate Broom's office at St. John's when Mandeville and Spring were brought up. Spring's confession made on September sixth at Port de Grave was read to him in my presence. It was signed by Spring."

Signed by Arthur, thought Catherine. *He could only mark X. Anyone could have done that and said it was Arthur's X.*

Pinsent looked at Mr. Broom. "The chief magistrate," he added, "cautioned him not to incriminate himself, unless he did so voluntarily. Mandeville, on that occasion, refused to admit anything he had before stated. He said he had nothing to say. He knew nothing about it."

When Pinsent was asked if there had been a search for John Snow, not seen since August thirty-first last year, Pinsent replied that there had been a partial search for the body on September fifth, and on the tenth. There were fifty men employed, in five boats for several hours, in dragging that part of the bay where they thought the body had been sunk, but without success. On the fourteenth, they had a large sloop engaged for five or six hours in dragging with a fishing trawl, without effect.

Pinsent looked at Catherine as he said, "The body has never been discovered. A number of sharks had been seen near that particular part of the bay, about the time of the search. Sharks are frequently seen there about that season of the year."

A plan of Port de Grave, Bareneed, and area was shown to Pinsent who admitted that the plan exhibited gave a tolerably correct idea of Port de Grave and the places and houses referenced. He said, "The bottom of that bay is very uneven and rugged, falling away in a very short distance from twenty to forty fathoms. It would be very difficult to hook anything on such a bottom. There were high winds with a good deal of sea in Port de Grave Bay in the beginning of September, making the search more difficult."

Catherine expected cross-examinations from lawyers Emerson and Robinson before Pinsent was allowed to leave the witness box. She gave the prisoners a quick glance and felt dismayed at their looks of helplessness when neither lawyer rose to question the witness.

Catherine waited to see what Magistrate Thomas Danson would say as he took the stand. After he was sworn and had identified himself, he stated that Catherine Snow was brought before him on the eighteenth of September last for examination. The clerk handed him a document and asked if this was the prisoner's statement. Danson said it was and that it was made voluntarily, without any inducement or promise of favour. He read the statement he wrote for the court.

"Catherine Snow says she knows nothing relative to the death of her husband, except what has been stated by Tobias Mandeville and Arthur Spring. That on the eleventh instant, Tobias Mandeville, who was apprehended on suspicion of being concerned in her husband's murder, told her that her husband was shot by Arthur Spring, his servant, while standing near the splitting table in the stage – that the said Arthur Spring did on the night of the thirty-first of August last, take a gun from the rack in his master's home. She did not enquire what he was taking it for, as he often took it to shoot the dogs. She told him not to hurt himself, to which Spring replied, 'Never mind, I'm not going to hurt myself with it.' She heard the report of a gun about three quarters of an hour afterward and within half an hour afterward, Arthur Spring and Tobias Mandeville came to her house. Spring then had no gun with him. She asked, 'Where is the master?' Spring replied, 'He will soon be up.' This was about ten o'clock of the same night. After some time she asked what could be keeping her husband – supper being ready – when Mandeville said, 'Cheer up your heart, there is nothing the matter.' Spring and Mandeville did not sit down to supper, and soon after went to a wake at Cupids, where Catherine's two daughters and a servant girl had gone. Being afraid to remain by herself, Catherine put the two children to bed – took the youngest in her arms, and went to her brother-in-law's house, where she went to bed for the night. Sometime before day, her eldest daughter came there. When she asked what her father had done to them for delaying so long, the daughter replied they had not seen their father. Her daughter then went home and Catherine remained until six o'clock. Then she also went home. There she found Spring and Mandeville with the girl, Catherine White, who told her they had just returned from the wake, having gone back there after seeing John's daughters home. She then went upstairs and told her daughters to go and look for their father, which they did. Catherine White had previously told her that, on her return home, she went to the top of the bank in front of the house, and while there she heard people talking and cursing under the bank. Bridget, her eldest daughter, said she heard the sound of oars, but did not hear any voices. Catherine then went with her daughter, and the servant girl, and several neighbours in search of her husband, but obtained no tidings of him. Spring and Mandeville went the same day to William Hele's funeral, and returned to the Snows' house after the funeral.

Mandeville remained there during the night until the following Tuesday, when he returned to Bareneed, to the employ of his masters, Martin and Jacob. Spring remained on the premises until he was taken by the constables on Tuesday. When the constables came to apprehend him, Catherine went out and told him that Mr. Jacob, Mr. Pinsent and the constable were there for him. Then Spring said to her, 'Damn me then. I'll have your life if you say a word of what passed between him and me (meaning himself and his master) during the summer.' She replied, 'My dear soul, I never said a word to anyone about you.' The constables then took Spring, Catherine's second-eldest daughter, Eliza, and the servant, Catherine White, to Bareneed. All of them returned home in the morning. At supper Spring asked Catherine what she would take for his clearance. She told him not to mind his clearance, that when his time was out, he would have his wages. Spring replied that when their own boat came home, as she was going to St. John's, he would put his box on board and go in her. She replied, 'So you can, and go yourself by land when your time is out.' Catherine said that on the sixth instant, she left her own house and remained in some of the neighbours' houses until she gave herself up to Mr. Cozens, and she has nothing more to say." Danson finished with a quick look at Catherine.

She gave him an angry look. She thought it outrageous for a learned man to expect a jury to believe she would state that, on September eleventh, Tobias told her that John was shot by Arthur. The magistrates knew, and the jury had learned, that she could not have seen either of the men after September eighth when they were brought to Portugal Cove. *The two magistrates must have gotten together to write confusing, contradictory statements,* she decided. *It is not my way to use the word tidings, yet both of the men used it in the statements. I wouldn't have told Arthur not to hurt himself. He was used to handling a gun.*

JOHN JACOB, ESQUIRE, was called next and sworn. The merchant told the court that he was a Conservator of the Peace residing at Port de Grave. He appeared awkward and out of place as he testified that he knew John Snow and all the prisoners at the bar. Arthur Spring was a servant of John Snow's, and Tobias Mandeville was a master cooper in his employ under the firm of Martin & Jacob. Mandeville had lived with him for two years as his servant to August last. He knew that John Snow disappeared in August last. John and Catherine Snow were at his Bareneed premises, delivering fish on August thirty-first last year. They left for home together.

"How far would that be from your premises?" he was asked.

"No more than three-quarters of a mile across to John's house," he answered. "They left an hour before sunset."

When he was asked how long Mandeville was absent from his employment, Jacob said he was gone from the evening of the last day of August until the evening of the following Monday. He told the court that he and Pinsent went across to Snow's house on September third to make enquiries respecting the sudden and mysterious disappearance of John Snow.

He was asked, "When did you see blood on the stage?"

"After Spring had made a confession, I examined the stage and saw marks of blood on the shores and longers. Parts had been cut out of the longers, as if to conceal the blood. Down along the shores which supported the stage there were several marks of blood, and along one of them a stream of blood was very perceptible. It appeared to be fresh blood, of perhaps three or four days standing. Spring made a confession a few days after in my presence respecting the part he and others had taken in the murder of John Snow."

When he was asked what Mandeville had said, Jacob replied, "Mandeville made a verbal statement to me in the cell of the lockup house September eighth, which he reduced to writing about an hour after."

Catherine wondered why, if there was a handwritten statement made by Tobias, it wasn't shown in evidence, and why Jacob wasn't questioned that, if he saw blood six days after John disappeared and it was standing for three or four days, it couldn't have been John's.

Jacob was saying, "During Spring's examination a report was brought that Mandeville had fainted. I went to the lock-up house and found him speechless, lying on his back in the cell. After he had recovered he asked what Arthur Spring had been saying. I told him that Spring was making a confession implicating Mrs. Snow and him in the murder of John Snow. Mandeville immediately said, 'Lord, have mercy on me.'"

Jacob was asked what else he had to say.

"On the evening of the sixth, Mandeville communicated some circumstances to me with regard to the murder which he wished me to keep within my own breast. He told me he was not the man who fired the gun, but he assisted in towing the body out into the harbour. On September eighth, I went to the lock-up house, and when Mandeville saw me he said he would be glad if I would go into his cell. He wished to disclose something to me. I manifested some hesitation and Mandeville said he particularly wished me to go in, as he was anxious to make a full confession respecting the murder of John Snow. I cautioned him against doing so, but Mandeville persisted, and said I might make what use of it I thought proper. He said his object in making the confession was that he did not want me to think him that 'perfect monster' he had understood Spring had made him out to be. He said he didn't fire the gun, but he assisted in towing the body out into the harbour."

Catherine drew in a sharp, quivering breath. Who would have told Tobias that Arthur had made him out to be the perfect monster? The men had likely been played against each other, like Downing and Malone – each implicating the other to save himself. She stared at John Jacob as he went on. "Mandeville told me that on October eighth, 1831, he went from Port de Grave to Harbour Grace with Catherine Snow, and that in the woods between the two places a criminal connection took place between them."

Catherine turned her head quickly and took in Tobias's look. His jaw tightened and he dropped his head. *What nonsense!*

Catherine thought. *What chance would Tobias have? He worked six days, and John Jacob never let him out of work until late Saturday evening. And I suppose I'd be folleying about Harbour Grace like some dolly-girl, and the cold wind of October in the air, and little Thomas, born before his time that summer and doing poorly. He wasn't baptized until the second day of October when I was already carrying Johanna. I wouldin be knockin' about with all the work to be done getting summer wrapped up. Quite the sail from Salmon Cove to Harbour Grace and a longer walk ashore. I thought that John Jacob was our friend. What is he up to? And there I am having him down as a defence witness.*

Jacob went on boldly. "Mandeville told me that from that time up to the time of the murder, similar connections had taken place between them whenever an opportunity offered. He said that from the period of the first connection they had determined on murdering John Snow and putting him out of the way, and as soon as the affair was blown over, to get married."

John Jacob continued without looking Catherine's way. "Tobias said that during that period several plans for Snow's murder had been entered into between them, but that he had not sufficient courage to carry them into execution, Snow being the more powerful man of the two. Catherine Snow had often found fault with him for not doing so, saying there was no fear of the affair ever being known as no one was in the secret but themselves. Mandeville said to her in reply, 'The King and the public would take notice of it, and, on enquiry, the matter might be brought to light.'"

Jacob added, "This kind of excitement under which Mandeville laboured continued until four or five weeks before the murder when he, by desire of Mrs. Snow, spoke to Spring to know whether he would assist him in murdering John Snow. Spring consented, and Mandeville stated that from that time up to the period of the murder several plans had been looked into, which they had not had sufficient courage to carry into execution, to all of which Mrs. Snow was party."

Catherine looked stunned as John Jacob continued. "On Saturday, August thirty-first, John Snow and his wife came across the harbour to my premises at Bareneed where Mandeville was living as a cooper. Mandeville told me that while they were there she and Mandeville made arrangements for murdering Snow that night. She said she would send her daughters and servant girl away to the wake at Cupids. This would make a good opportunity for *doing it*, as the neighbours also would be at the wake."

Catherine shook her head, hoping the jury would remember that Ruth was her nearest neighbour. She had children and a visitor who were not going to the wake.

Catherine stared at Jacob as he continued. "As soon as the fish was discharged, Snow and his wife left for home together. After dark, Snow returned to Bareneed for Mandeville, as he was in the habit of doing every Saturday evening to settle his accounts. He accompanied Snow in the boat across to Salmon Cove. On arriving at Snow's stage, Mandeville was the first out of the boat, leaving Snow to moor the vessel for the night. Spring was in the stage at the time with a loaded gun. He had been sent there by Mrs. Snow, as had been agreed on between her and Mandeville when they parted at Bareneed in the evening. When John Snow came out of the boat, and walked toward the stage door, Spring discharged the gun and shot him through the breast. Snow instantly fell dead without uttering a groan. Spring then took Mandeville by the hand, and said, 'Isn't that well done?' Mandeville replied, 'It is.'"

Catherine couldn't visualize Arthur taking Tobias by the hand under any circumstance.

Jacob carried on. "Spring and Mandeville then tied a piece of rope around the body and lowered it into the water. They fastened a grapnel to it. Then they tied the rope to the after part of the boat, and towed it out into the harbour where they sank it. Mandeville further stated that it was not for the sake of Snow's money or lucre, or for any hatred or ill will against him, but wholly for love of the woman that he had taken a part in such a deed."

Catherine moved to loosen her aching back, thinking, *Tobias, with his soft ways, could not take the place of a hearty fisherman. He's for figuring accounts and turning the hoops on barrels, not for turning the soil or hooking fish through stormy waters. He'd not make a fisherman or a planter. And what time would I have with a young gaffer, me with me hands full with all the children and John's demands? What would Tobias want with me? He could set himself up in the place with any young maid. Some of them along the cove likes the look of him and eyes him with blushes and giggles. He may be taken with them. That's not for me to know.*

She took in a deep breath and let it out, relieved to see her lawyer stand to cross-examine the merchant. She waited for him to challenge John Jacob. She thought he might ask why Mandeville had fainted. She recalled how, some years before, James Lundrigan's skin had been stripped as if his flesh were no more than a pig's rind when he wouldn't co-operate with the merchant. Bowes was the magistrate's lackey, quick with the whip. She wondered if he had whipped Mandeville to force a confession. When that hadn't worked, he may have led him to believe Spring was saying unpleasant things about him.

She felt a painful tightening in her breast as her lawyer asked questions he already knew the answers to. "Was Mandeville in the habit of going over to the Snows' every Saturday evening?"

Jacob answered that he went over on Saturday and returned Sunday evening to be ready to go to work on Monday morning.

"Did you ask why he did not return to work on the Monday following Snow's disappearance?"

Jacob answered that he didn't.

Catherine thought, *Tobias stayed to search for Jack, a man he knew well. Besides, the harbour was loppy that morning.* Catherine had hoped that John Jacob would have been kinder. She was learning that the merchants and the magistrates were linking a chain of words against her.

Thirty

CONSTABLE John Bowes was sworn and acknowledged himself as a resident of Port de Grave who knew all the prisoners at the bar. He was asked if he remembered William Hele's wake at Cupids about the time of John Snow's disappearance. He said he did.

He was not asked if he saw Arthur and Tobias there, or if he, himself, attended the wake. He told the court that both Mandeville and Spring had told him circumstances relative to the murder of John Snow. He said that Spring admitted the murder was planned between Mandeville, Mrs. Snow, and himself. Spring had stood in the stage with a loaded gun to shoot Snow, but his courage failed and he could not fire. Bowes claimed that Mandeville told him that he had as much a hand in killing John Snow as Spring, but that he did not fire the gun.

Bowes told the court that he had been to the Snows' on the Monday after John's disappearance. He said he saw Mandeville at John Snow's house and that Mandeville told him he slept with Mrs. Snow on Sunday, the day after the murder.

Catherine's face paled with exasperation as she looked at Bowes, thinking, *Some people don't need a long arm to eat with the Devil. On Sunday, the men had searched for Jack; then they went to the funeral. The children and neighbours were all about and John Wells from Port de Grave stayed over to the house after coming from the funeral. Might they not know then that this made no sense?*

Bowes told the court that when he went to Snow's house he saw Mandeville coming out of the parlour where Mrs. Snow was. Mandeville told him that she was from one faint to another. Bowes added, "When I saw Mrs. Snow immediately after, she did not appear in a very weak or distressed condition. She said she was but little obliged to Mr. Pinsent for meddling himself about the business. I remarked to her that it was his duty to do so."

"When did you next see Mrs. Snow?"

"I saw her at Port de Grave when Mandeville and Spring were in custody."

Catherine knew by now that her lawyer wouldn't ask Bowes anything without already knowing the answer he would give.

Sure enough, Emerson asked Bowes when he saw Mandeville at the Snows'.

"After dinnertime on the Monday. I could not cross before that time in the day, as it was blowing too hard."

"Could you have been mistaken as to Mrs. Snow's observations respecting Mr. Pinsent?" asked Mr. Emerson.

"No," said Bowes.

No, thought Catherine in despair. *He was not mistaken. I did not want Robert Pinsent meddling himself about John's business, asking where his money was. I have a mind to stand up and tell them all where to go. There's too much suffering I've been having and not knowing why, and no evidence of Jack's death, only of hes disappearance.*

JAMES SHELLY WAS next called for the prosecution. He glanced at Catherine and she looked back at him, wondering if he was going to treat her any better than the others had. He said he lived at Bareneed and that he knew that John Snow was the husband of Catherine Snow, the prisoner at the bar. He said he also knew the prisoners Mandeville and Spring. He saw John Snow for the last time on the evening of the day he was murdered. "I saw him," said Shelly, "at Bareneed in Martin & Jacob's kitchen between eight and nine o'clock in the evening. Mandeville was also there, and he left the kitchen with Snow to go across to the latter's house. Snow told Mandeville he was waiting for him and the latter said he was ready to go."

Catherine stared at her lawyer, wanting him to ask what John was wearing when he left Jacob's kitchen. If Shelly said that John was wearing his hat and blue waistcoat, then the court would know that the testimonies entered as Arthur's and Spring's were false. Both belongings were found in the house the next day.

CATHERINE WHITE WAS sworn and identified as being John Snow's servant at the time of his disappearance. She was asked when she last saw John Snow. She drew in a deep breath and answered in a timid voice. "The master and the mistress went in the middle of the day to Bareneed. They got back home before nightfall. A short time later, the master went across to Bareneed by hesself. As soon as he left, I got me soppa with Arthur Spring and the children and went to William Hele's wake."

"What time of the day was it?"

"Not altogether dark. 'Twas on the even' of Saturday, last August thirty-first."

"Why did you go to the wake?"

"My mistress told me to go with Bridget and Eliza. It was dark at the time."

Not altogether dark, she said, and now she says it was dark, thought Catherine. *People get mixed up in their memories.*

She was asked if Spring went to the wake with her and she replied, "No, but me mistress told me to go with the children, Bridget and Eliza."

"Did you wish to go to the wake?"

She shrugged. "I don't know. I s'pose I did when me mistress told me to."

"So it was after John Snow had gone the second time to Bareneed, that you went to the wake."

"Yes, me mistress told me to go to the wake with the children. She didn't want 'em goin' alone. I had a sore foot at the time and I told me mistress I could not put on me own shoe."

"What did your mistress say to that?"

"Nothing. She gave me one of her own shoes."

The jury will think I'm mean, thought Catherine, *sending her to the wake with a sore foot. She had a little swelling from a bee sting. My shoe was of the same make, only a little larger. Her foot wasn't too sore for her to stay at the wake a long time.*

"Who was in the house when you left for the wake?"

"Me mistress and Spring and the t'ree youngsters."

Catherine White said that it was pretty dark at the time, but it would not have taken her half an hour to walk to the wake house. "Me mistress told me not to bide long at the wake. I was thinking I might stay a couple of hours. Then Arthur Spring and Tobias Mandeville come to the wake in the night and brought me and the girls home. When we got home there were only the two young ones in bed. I didn't see the mistress or the master."

"Did John Snow have guns in the house?"

"Yes, he kept 'em up on a rack and one of 'em always loaded."

"Had you ever known your master to fire a gun at night?"

"No, but I knowed Arthur Spring to fire the gun to keep dogs away from the fish. I didn't hear a gun fired that night. There was no fire in the house, so Bridget went to her uncle Edward's for tinder to make a light. She didn't bring back any, so someone struck a light with powder."

"Who did?"

"I don't know – Tobias Mandeville or Arthur Spring. They left ag'in, together, saying they were goin' back to the wake. The mistress come back to the house in the marnin."

"What did she say to you?"

"She asked if the master had come home. I told her that he hadn't. She said he was about the house when she left it."

"Do you know what became of John Snow?"

The maid shook her head. "No, I don't, Your Honour. I saw hes boat early on Sunday marnin, loose near the rocks at the stage."

"Did you see any blood on the stage?"

She shook her head. "No, I didn't."

"What was Tobias Mandeville wearing when he went to the wake?"

"He wore a dark blue jacket and a pair of fustian trousers."

"What was John Snow wearing when he left home in the evening."

"He wore a blue jacket, fustian trousers, and a blue, striped shirt."

Kitty White couldn't know what Tobias was wearin' when he left for the wake, thought Catherine. *She could only say what he had on when he got there. She'd know what Arthur was wearin' before she left; she'd be able to tell if he was wearin' the same thing at the wake. Tobias wouldn't be wearin' Jack's trousers if he shot Jack. The trousers and shirt would be in a fine state. One's got nothing to do with the other. It would make more sense for the court to ask John Jacob what Tobias was wearin' when he left his place, and ask Kitty what he was wearin' when he got to the wake. That's what the prosecution should be asking.*

"Who slept in the house on that Sunday when Mr. Snow was missing?"

"Tobias Mandeville, Arthur Spring, meself, and the children slept in the house."

"What were the sleeping arrangements?"

"There were three bedrooms upstairs. The master and mistress commonly slept in the room over the parlour. Mrs. Snow slept there on the Sunday night, and meself, with two of the children, Johanna and Maria."

"Where did Mandeville sleep?"

"He slept in the room he always slept in."

"Did he sleep alone?"

"I believe a man named Wills slept with him."

"Do you know if Mrs. Snow got up during the night?"

"No."

"Did you hear anyone going into Mrs. Snow's room?"

"No."

"Were a pair of trousers found in the house?"

"I don't know of a pair of trousers being found in the house."

Catherine's head dropped to her hands in frustration at the foolish questioning. *Of course there were trousers in the house. There were three men to wash for! Why don't they ask whatever it is they want to know, and let this be over so I can have food and rest?*

"Do you know of a pair of trousers found in Mrs. Snow's room?"

"I do mind that Mary Connolly found a pair of fustian trousers in the mistress's room."

"When did Mrs. Snow leave the house?"

"It was on the Friday after the master's disappearance."

"Do you know why she left?"

"She said she was going to Brigus to get some papers settled for her children."

"When did you see her again?"

"Not until the Monday afterward, when she was in the custody of Patrick Walsh at Cupids."

The prosecutor looked at his papers and back at his witness. "How long did Tobias Mandeville sleep at John Snow's house?"

"He slept there on Monday night, September second, and left on the following morning to go back to his employers."

Catherine thought, *John Jacob testified that Tobias returned to his place Monday night. I can't be sure, meself, now.*

"Where did Mrs. Snow sleep?"

"In her own room."

"Did anyone wash the stagehead on Sunday morning?"

"Not that I know of."

Catherine's lawyer stood up to cross-examine the servant. "You say you saw Wills and Tobias Mandeville going upstairs together on that Sunday night?"

"Yes."

"How many routes were there to upstairs?"

"There were two flights of stairs – one for the servants, the other from the parlour."

"Did your mistress wash for Mandeville while you lived there?"

"Yes."

"Where did you sleep on Monday night?"

"I went upstairs with me mistress."

Catherine sank back in her seat, her eyelids flittering shut in exasperation. *Why didn't my lawyer point out to the court that if someone has to ask if the stagehead was washed, it means that my accusers have no recollection of seeing fresh blood on the stagehead until later in the week?*

RUTH SNOW CAME to the witness box, her soft, freckled face looking strained. Her greying hair was pulled back into a bun tottering on the back of her head. The tall, thin woman was sworn and asked where she lived.

In a barely audible voice she said she lived on the south side of Port de Grave Bay.

"How are you related to the deceased?"

"I'm the wife of Edward Snow, Jack Snow's brother."

"How far do you live from John Snow's house?"

"My house is about a hundred yards away."

"Do you remember Saturday, the thirty-first of August last?"

"Yes."

"Did you see John Snow?"

"I didn't see him all that day, but I saw him the day before."

"Have you seen him since?"

"No."

"Did you see the prisoner Catherine Snow on that night?"

"Yes. Kit came to my door when I was in bed. I asked her the time and she told me it was between twelve and one o'clock."

"Did you ask her anything else?"

"I asked her what was the matter. She replied, 'Jack's very angry.'

"'What did you say to make him so?' I asked.

"'Nothing,' she said.

"'So much the better,' I replied. 'You had better come in and lie down.'"

"How did Catherine Snow answer you?"

"She said, 'Oh no, I'll sleep up here in the kitchen.'"

"What else did she say?"

"She told me that all the girls had gone to Bill Hele's wake. There was a woman named Patience Boon in the house. When Catherine found that she was there, she said, 'Oh Patience, if I knew it was you, I'd have asked you to come down to sleep with me.' She was taking off her clothes when she made this remark."

Catherine's eyelids quivered from weariness. *I thought John would fall asleep on the bench, likely as loaded as his gun bees, and when he awoke he would not show his anger with Patience in the house.*

Ruth continued. "She asked me to let my daughter, Ann, one of her nieces, speak to her uncle Jack on account of his rough treatment."

"How long did Mrs. Snow stay?"

"All night. Bridget Snow and Mary Connolly came to the house to look for tinder."

"Did you hear a gun anytime during the night?"

"I heard a gun that night while at tea; I thought it was fired near the flakes, as usual."

"Did you ask Mrs. Snow about the gunshot?"

"I did. She told me that Jack had fired a gun."

"How long after the gun was fired before Mrs. Snow came to your house?"

"It was a good while."

Catherine pulled her shawl around her. She hoped Mr. Emerson had taken note that her sister-in-law had said the gun was fired near the flakes, *as usual*, and that when he stood up to cross-examine Ruth, he would bring this up. Instead, he asked a question he already had the answer to. "When did Mrs. Snow come to your house?"

"I was asleep. I don't know the hour. Kit told me it was between twelve and one o'clock."

Thirty-One

MARY Connolly was next to take the stand. She straightened her bonnet and drew her cloak around her as she hurried to the witness box like someone on an important mission. She smiled at Judge Boulton and curtsied as she was sworn.

"Where do you live, Miss Connolly?"

"I live on the south side of Port de Grave."

"Do you know all the prisoners at the bar?"

"Yes. I knew John Snow, I knows his wife, Catherine Snow, the prisoner at the bar. I lives not very far from their house."

"Where were you on Saturday night, the thirty-first of August last?"

"I was at William Hele's wake."

"When did you leave the wake?"

"I walked back from the wake with Bridget and Eliza – John Snow's two daughters – Catherine White, Tobias, and Arthur; 'twas two or three o'clock in the marnin."

"Who was in the house?"

"The two youngsters."

"When did you next see Mrs. Snow?"

"Not till Sunday marnin."

"Where did you see her?"

"She was standing near her own flake."

"Did you see Mrs. Snow on Saturday?"

"Yes, I left her place to go to the wake soon after dark."

"Did you see Tobias Mandeville at the wake?"

"Yes. I asked him if there'd been quarrellin' between John and Catherine. He said, 'A little, but it was almost over when I left the house to come to the wake.'"

Catherine let out a sigh. *The lawyer could have asked Mary why she would think there would be quarrelling. Jack didn't want his daughters walking the path at night, and I always got in a quarrel when I let them out behind his back.*

"When did you last see John Snow?"

"I saw him goin' across to Bareneed on that Saturday evening at nearly nightfall for Tobias."

"Have you seen him since?"

"No."

"Why did you go to the wake?"

"I had no intention of goin' until Mrs. Snow asked me. I had been there the two nights before."

Catherine shook her head. *Mary came down the path from her house looking for the girls. I told her where they had gone and asked if she was goin'.*

"What is your business with Catherine Snow?"

"I often worked on John Snow's fishing room."

"Did the Snows get along?"

Mary looked at Catherine. Then she answered boldly, "Angry words had often occurred between 'em; they had lived a discontented life durin' the summer."

"What else do you know?"

"During a quarrel some days before John Snow's disappearance, I heard Mrs. Snow say to him she'd have hes skull cracked for that, when he little thought of it; he dragged off her cap at the time but he didn't strike her."

Not then, he didn't strike me, Catherine thought. *What woman assaulted by her husband over and over has not breathed murthur and felt it in her heart, only to have it subside when all is well and the man turns a benevolent face to her? He was me bread and butter, and that of our children.*

"What else do you remember?"

"I recollect findin' a pair of fustian trousers belongin' to Tobias Mandeville in Mrs. Snow's room folded up between a barrel and a trunk – spotted with blood concealed with ink. I showed them to Catherine White, who made no remark. I knew they were Tobias's trousers as I had often washed them."

Catherine shook her head in exasperation. *If Jack had been sprayed with shot, tied with rope and dragged over a stagehead there'd be more than blood spots on a pair of trousers, and there'd be blood on Tobias's shirt, and on Arthur's clothes.*

"When were the trousers found?"

"After Mrs. Snow was committed to the Harbour Grace gaol."

Mr. Emerson stood to cross-examine the servant. He asked, "Did you often go in Mrs. Snow's bedroom?"

Mary sounded defensive. "Yes. When I found Tobias's trousers, I was lookin' fer a piece to mend a pair of trousers. I saw other clothes in the room in a heap, but none belongin' to Tobias, except the trousers."

"Did you see anything else?"

"Yes, a pair of trousers belongin' to Arthur Spring. I saw Catherine White folding up Tobias's trousers a few days before, but I didn't know where she put 'em."

"Did you ever see blood on Mandeville's clothes before?"

"No, never."

Not then either, thought Catherine. *Still, the jury must know that it's not unusual for someone who bees in a fishing boat to have blood on his clothes. People lend themselves to ignorance when they pretend not to know why there bees humps and hollows, and blood creases in a splitting table, or cuts in a stagehead.*

THE PROSECUTION RECALLED Catherine White to ask, "Were you in the habit of folding Mandeville's trousers?"

The maid looked at the jury. "I never folded a pair of trousers belonging to Tobias Mandeville, nor did I see them until Mary Connolly brought them downstairs."

Catherine looked toward her lawyer. She could see that he wasn't going to cross-examine Mary.

MARK HENNEBURY WAS sworn and took the stand. He appeared tense as he told the court he lived at Bareneed and that he knew John Snow and all the prisoners at the bar.

"When did you last see Mrs. Snow?"

"I saw her after Mandeville and Spring had been taken; the night after they were taken, she slept in my house at Bareneed."

"What happened then?"

"The next morning Mandeville sent up from Port de Grave to say he wished to speak to her."

"What did she do?"

"She went to Port de Grave with a man named Michael Manning. I met them on the road on their return to Bareneed."

"What happened then?"

"I asked her, 'What is the news from Port de Grave?'"

"What did she say?"

"She answered, 'Bad news.'"

"I asked, 'How's that?'"

"She replied, 'There wouldn't be such a hold on Arthur and Tobias if it wasn't for you.'"

"'How's that?' I asked again."

"What did she say then?"

"'Because,' she said, 'whatever Spring told you to tell me, you didn't tell me, and you told Mr. Pinsent of it.'"

"What was your reply?"

"I replied that I didn't tell Mr. Pinsent, but I told John Bowes, Frederick Kenny, and Thomas Butler, and I'm not sorry for it."

Catherine had often wondered what Arthur told Mark to tell her. He should state it now, instead of talking in riddles.

"What did she say then?"

"She told me that when she goes down to see Arthur, she will not be allowed to see him. She asked me to go down and tell him, in Irish, not to tell anything."

Not to say anything about his fights with Jack, Catherine had reasoned, *in case they tripped him up.*

"When did you next see Mrs. Snow?"

"I did not see Mrs. Snow afterward."

Mark's face relaxed as he left the stand.

PATRICK WALSH WAS sworn and identified himself as knowing John Snow and all the prisoners at the bar. He was asked if he knew that John Snow was unaccounted for on the first of September last.

"Yes," he answered, his lusty red face puffed and bloated above a white collar.

"When did you last see Tobias Mandeville?"

"I saw him at Cupids on that day."

"What was said between you?"

"He said, 'There's the Devil to pay in Salmon Cove. John is missing since last night.'"

"What did you say to that?"

"I said, 'I suppose he's gone off in a fit of jealousy.'"

Catherine thought, *He was jealous, but not of me lately. He wanted the girls close. Jealousy took him like a bad spell.*

"'I don't know,' Tobias said. 'I miss him more – more than anyone else, for if ever I wanted a crown or a pound I could go to his box and get it.'"

Catherine pressed her lips tight. *Did he really say that, and only a few hours after Jack was missing? And Jack not that easy with his money! Maybe Tobias was stealing from the box, he or whoever is the cause of Jack's disappearance. The court should reason that if Tobias and I were having a criminal connection and caused Jack's disappearance, he would have access to the box.*

That's it! she thought. *They're after John's money and the first one to blame is Tobias. John might have give him a crown for his work, but never a pound, hard enough it is to get. What kind of a boast is that for Tobias to make! Maybe he didn't. . . .*

"When did you last see Mrs. Snow?"

"I didn't see her until I apprehended her at Cupids on the ninth of September at the house of Denis Hartery. She was in bed when I went there. I had been in search of Mrs. Snow for some days before."

RICHARD TAYLOR WAS sworn next. He told the court that he lived at Salmon Cove, Port de Grave, and that he had fished on John Snow's room during the last summer.

He was asked, "What do you know of his disappearance?"

The fisherman rubbed a thin, worn hand along his jawline and answered. "In August last, I was a boat master in a western boat. I had landed a grapnel in Snow's stage before I left on August tenth for the westward. When I got back on the fifth of September, it wasn't there."

Catherine tried to catch her lawyer's eye. *A fisherman could have borrowed or stolen it. It had no bearing on why John's boat was yawing back and forth against the stagehead the morning of September first. The boat had its own grapnel. Richard wasn't asked if he had landed any wet, bloodied fish when he came back on the fifth, the same day Tobias and Arthur were arrested. It was the next day that John Jacob noted blood, three or four days old, on the stage.*

JAMES MCCABE WAS sworn and gave his place of abode as Salmon Cove, Port de Grave. He indicated that he knew John and Catherine Snow. He said he was not at home at the time of Snow's disappearance. He came home on Friday, the sixth of September.

"Were you sent by Catherine to Mandeville and Spring to convey any messages from them to her?" he was asked.

"No, I wasn't. I didn't see Tobias or Arthur when they were taken. I saw Kit Snow at Mrs. Britt's; she didn't say what she was doin' there."

Another rumour, thought Catherine.

MARY BRITT WAS sworn and then asked her place of abode.

"I live at Caplin Cove, Port de Grave," she said, giving Catherine a quick glance.

"What do you know of John Snow's disappearance?"

"I knowed he disappeared about the time of William Hele's wake. Kit Snow showed up at my house on the following Friday night and told me she was going to be taken by the constables."

"Did she say why?"

"She said she didn't know why. The constables come to me house the next day in quest of Catherine. They didn't find her. She was in bed at the time. The constables told me how John Snow had been made away with. After the constables left I told Kit she couldin stay in the house with me. She said, 'I'm clear of it,' and she left the house."

CATHERINE BREEN WAS sworn next and asked where she lived. She answered, "I lives at Cupids."

"Did you know John Snow and his wife?"

"Yes."

"Did you know that Snow disappeared?"

"Yes, I knowed it was about the time of William Hele's wake; about a week after that, Catherine come to me house before daylight and said she was afraid of bein' taken by the constables."

"How long was she there?"

"Till the next night, and then she went to Denis Hartery's."

"What did she say about her husband's death?"

"She said she knowed nothing of hes death or how he disappeared."

Catherine's look met the cold, grey eyes of Attorney General Simms as he stood to close the case for the prosecution.

Thirty-Two

JUDGE Boulton looked up from his file and nodded at Catherine's lawyer. "Your first witness, Mr. Emerson."

Catherine drew in a deep breath and let it out slowly as her lawyer looked toward the jury box. She followed his gaze before she was drawn back to the bench by a request for her to take the stand in her own defence. She found it hard to rise. When she did, she walked unsteadily to the stand, weak and hungry, and discomforted by the fullness of her bladder and baby. She stood there facing the crowd's scornful looks, and all she had meant to say left her. The baby turned and she drew in a sharp breath. *The judge won't sentence me to hang – not with a baby inside me, surely!* She steadied herself and looked the jury in the eye, from the first man to the last, and said in a shaky voice, *"Caitríona is ainm dom* – My name is Catherine – " She stopped as she felt a sharp dig under her ribs.

Emerson gave her a firm look. "The court knows your name full well, Catherine Snow. Did you have cause to quarrel with John Snow the night he disappeared?"

Catherine lifted her chin. "I may have spoken in anger against Jack. Many a woman bees wishing her husband gone from her sight in the heat of a quarrel." She turned to the judge. "I did say one time when he was mean to our son that he'd have his skull cracked, Your Honour, with no thought of it happening. My outburst would not give Tobias and Arthur reason to act on my foul words. I don't believe they did. Sure the men and the servant girls heard me vexed with Jack on times. They knows hes temper. He did say more than once that he'd skin me alive – but that's not done – 'tis a saying like others that people use when they gets riled." Catherine turned back to the jury, her eyes watering. "There were times I thought the sea had swallowed Jack. He's spent nights stowed on some beach, or in the lun of cliffs unable to get home, caught in the net of fog, or the wiles of the sea. But he's always answered the sea's spit with a laugh. And there's been times he's been laid up somewhere overnight in the drinks – "

Emerson broke in. "I ask you in earnest, ma'am, did you have mind, hand, or action in the death of your recently deceased husband?"

"If he's deceased I'd like a look at him – to be sure. Perhaps he's been playing in the merchants' pockets too long. I don't know what happened to him." Her voice trembled as she turned back to face Judge Boulton. "Your Lordship, *Níor mharíos m'fhear céile* – I did not kill my husband." Her voice rose. "There's no proof that he's not among the living, but if he is dead, he's alive in our children, alive in me body this instant." Dizziness overcame her and her lawyer rushed to help her back to her place.

CATHERINE HARDLY NOTICED as Emerson recalled Kitty White. He asked her if Spring and Mandeville had their clothes washed at the Snows' house. She told the court that they always had that habit while she was there. She added that, after her mistress was taken to Harbour Grace, she collected all the loose clothes in Mandeville's room and in the other rooms and put them in Mrs. Snow's room.

CATHERINE LET OUT a gasp when Bridget, her daughter, was brought into the courtroom and called to the witness box. Her face looked white and drawn as she was sworn. She turned toward the judge, her lips trembling, as she told the court that her mother was very bad on the day following her father's disappearance. "We didn't expect her to live."

I didn't realize me children were so concerned about me, Catherine thought. *Maybe they were afraid they'd lose me too.*

Bridget was asked why Tobias's clothes were in her mother's room. She replied that, after her mother was taken by the constables, she asked Kitty White to collect all the clothes about the house and put them in her mother's room.

The police could have searched the house and the grounds if they believed there was evidence there, Catherine thought bitterly. *They could have found the trousers referred to, found them with dark spots from where Tobias had splattered ink while doing John's books.*

EMERSON CALLED THREE witnesses to speak to Catherine's character. Catherine listened gratefully as John Connolly, John Doyle, and James McCabe told the court that they had known her for years and had never seen her act unwomanly or dishonestly in her dealings with them and other people.

LAWYER BRYAN ROBINSON stood up and came forward, pulling a cupped hand down over his face as he called Arthur Spring to the stand. When he asked Arthur what he had to say in his defence, the young servant lifted a troubled face, his eyes big and solemn. Then he faced the jury, looking defeated. He shook his head and stated in a quiet voice, "I had nothing to do with the master's disappearance. If he be dead, it's by hes own hand, or someone else's. The statement declared to be mine is false."

Arthur gave John Jacob and Robert Pinsent a defiant look as he sidled back to the dock.

WHEN EMERSON CALLED Tobias to the stand, he dawdled along as if his feet were too heavy to lift. His face looked anguished and his eyes brimmed with tears as he stood before the jury. He claimed he was innocent, but instead of pleading for his life, he turned to look at Catherine. "This woman has done nothing wrong. She always treated me with the respect she showed her children. She washed me clothes and shared the food on her table. If – " He stopped, as if his mouth was full of water. Then he blurted in sobs, "If I said anything as was read in a statement John Jacob claimed to be mine, it may have been at a time when I was unconscious of what I said."

Catherine faced the young fellow, her own eyes smarting with tears. She wondered what happened the day Tobias was found in his cell unconscious. She believed that statements attributed to him and Arthur – if theirs, though there was no proof – were made under a threat or on the promise of a favour. She hoped the jury would come to the same conclusion.

Tobias's eyes filled with fear as he turned sharply to the sound of Robert Pinsent clearing his throat. The young cooper stopped as if silenced. Then, in the quietness of the courtroom, he raised his voice and solemnly declared, "If I said anything to make the missus appear guilty, I withdraw any such expression. I never saw the statement of confession." His voice dropped. "I signed only the statement of innocence."

Tobias left the stand, looking more settled.

EMERSON CALLED PHILIP Bourne and John Walsh to the witness stand to state their knowledge of Tobias's character. Both men agreed that they knew Tobias and had found him to be honest and well-behaved.

THERE WAS A quiet expectancy in the court once testimonies ended. Emerson turned to face the jury. "Catherine Snow declares herself to be a wretched, sinful woman, but as innocent of any participation in the crime for which she is accused as an unborn child. She had not even the most distant presentiment, at any time, that her husband would have fallen under the hand of an assassin."

He then bowed to the jury and took his seat.

Chief Justice Boulton proceeded to charge the jury in a grave voice. "Regarding Arthur Spring and Tobias Mandeville, the evidence appears to be so conclusive, as to leave no doubt of their guilt in my mind. I particularly direct your attention to those parts of the evidence which affected the charge against Catherine Snow. If you do not consider the evidence sufficiently conclusive and satisfactory as regarded her, you are bound to give her the benefit of the doubts you might entertain of her participation in the guilt of the others. In a case like this, you cannot bring in a verdict of manslaughter – you should either convict, or acquit."

Catherine let out a tiny gasp. There was no evidence to convict her. Her heart lifted on a wave of joy. *I'll be freed at last!* She could already see her children running toward her. She could feel their soft bodies in her arms.

After the jury left the courtroom, the sheriff gave Mrs. Perchard permission to take Catherine to a holding cell – a side room with a heavy, locked door – where she got to relieve herself and take some bread and broth that the gaoler's wife offered her. While they waited for the verdict, Catherine lay on a pallet. She closed her eyes and drifted into sleep. A light touch on her arm awoke her. She had been dreaming that she was home with Jack and the children.

"It's been only a half-hour, but the jury is on the way back with a verdict," Mrs. Perchard told her with a sad smile. "It's been a long day and the men'll want to get gone to their families for supper or to a tavern for a tipple. We have to get back to the courtroom."

Catherine was just seated when she heard the quick tread of the jury returning to the court. The room stirred to life with anticipation.

THE JURY WAS ushered into the courtroom, each juror taking his place without casting a glance toward the prisoners. Catherine stared at the faces of the twelve jurors as she and the young men were ordered to rise and face them.

Tobias and Arthur stood up quickly. Catherine rose, faltered, and dropped back, as if staggered by the belief that she was going home. She imagined Johanna running into her arms, her stream of hair tickling Catherine's face as she held her baby close. Maria followed with Martin, Johnny, and Katie catching up. She could see Eliza's and Bridget's faces spread in happy smiles. She gathered her shawl around her and steadied herself to get back on her feet.

The clerk of the court asked, "Gentlemen, have you agreed on a verdict?"

The jury replied in unison, "We have."

"Who shall speak for you?" asked the clerk.

Again the jury spoke in one voice: "Our foreman, the Honourable Mr. Bland."

The clerk then instructed the jury to look at the prisoners, and the prisoners to face the jury.

Catherine's look took in the first juror to the last. She noted their solemn demeanour and she began to tremble.

The clerk asked, "How say you, gentlemen? Are the prisoners at the bar guilty?"

"All guilty," Mr. Bland replied in a husky voice. He cleared his throat and added, "With no recommendation for mercy."

Arthur hung his head and mumbled under his breath, "'Tis a miserable life, always under the fat thumb of another man, and those months imprisoned have added to it. I'd sooner be rid of it."

Tobias's mouth opened in a soundless cry. His hand went to his breast as if the jury's words had stabbed him.

All! Catherine's mind seemed to fall in pieces around her. She felt as if she were floating away on a tiny piece....

A shuddering movement under her heart brought her back; it was as if her unborn child had felt her shock and recoiled. She lifted her hand to her lawyer and he came to her side. "Tell the judge," she whispered, her face white and pinched, "that I'm soon to give birth."

Judge Boulton faced Tobias and asked him what he had to urge that the sentence of death should not be passed upon him. Canvas pants bagged against Tobias's trembling knees as he answered, "I submit to the law." He looked at Catherine and then at the judge. His voice was pitiful as he begged, "May Your Lordship find it in yourself to grant me a long day to prepare for the fate that awaits me. I ask that my body be giv' to me friends for burial."

Arthur said, "I've nothing to say, except to add to Tobias's request. I'll be wantin' the same."

Judge Boulton's bushy brows drew together as he answered, his look penetrating. "It is not in my power to comply with such a request; the law has left me no discretion."

Instead of asking Catherine why the sentence of death should not be passed on her, the judge looked down at the prisoners and ordered, "Prisoners, stand before the box." He paused as the three came forward. Then he raised his voice. "You have been found guilty of murder. For the murder of John Snow I pronounce the sentence of death on you, Tobias Mandeville. You are to be hanged by the neck until dead; your body will be dissected and anatomized. Arthur Spring, the servant, and Catherine Snow, the wife of the deceased, you are declared guilty of petit treason, and accordingly sentenced to be drawn to the place of execution on a hurdle – and your bodies, after death, also to be given to the surgeon for dissection and anatomized. This will be executed on Monday, January thirteenth, 1834. So sayeth the court. The law has been satisfied."

Catherine's insides lurched as if the baby had grabbed hold to steady itself. She let out a sharp cry. "Save my baby!"

Emerson steadied her with his arm as he looked at Judge Boulton and urged him to respite Catherine until after her baby was born.

The chief justice drew his lips tight for a moment. Then he commanded the sheriff to summon a jury of matrons to enquire into the prisoner's situation the next day. It was too late at that hour – half past eleven – to procure such a jury.

"The matrons will say upon their oaths whether the said prisoner be pregnant of a quick child or not," the judge said in a dispassionate voice. "However, I have passed sentence of death on

Catherine Snow. I hereby order the bailiff to remove her from the court."

Amid the clack of the assembly's tongues and feet, the judge banged his gavel and Catherine was grabbed by rough hands. For one moment, as Catherine turned to the noise of the crowd, her eyes caught the intense look of another mother. Eliza Boulton turned away from the condemned woman, disturbed by the unease she felt in looking into the anguished eyes of a mother she knew the court hadn't proven to be guilty of murder.

A sense of the awful sentence that had been imposed on her and the men hit Catherine like a maul and she fell to her knees screaming, *"Ní theastaíonn vaim bás a fháil* – I do not want to die!"

Strong, bruising hands hauled her to her feet. As she was dragged toward the courtroom exit, she turned to face the tormented eyes of Tobias and Arthur for the last time.

CATHERINE WAS HUSTLED back to the holding cell and told she would remain there until she was examined and a decision made regarding her fate. Throughout the night, the door was unlocked and the matron was let in to make sure Catherine was not in labour.

She spent the night shivering on a thin pallet, her eyes open to darkness. Fear surged like the waves of an ocean, beating and pulling at her thoughts. She could hardly breathe, thinking, *Will these matrons admit a pregnant belly?*

Her thoughts got more wretched as night wore on. Doubts that the judge would save her child surged like sea billows. *What if he orders his doctor to force the baby out of me so that it will escape the gallows?* She didn't know that day had come until the door was unlocked and light from a corridor streamed in. The matron offered her a bowl of porridge. She took it without a word and laid it aside as soon as the matron left. She was too full of worry to eat.

Thirty-Three

JURORS George Lewis, William Buckley, and James Tobin offered their wives – Jane Lewis, Mary Buckley, and Elizabeth Tobin – as lady jurors. To complete the list, Chief Justice Boulton sent Sheriff Benjamin Garrett out into the community to summon other women jurors.

The clomping of a horse's hooves outside Margaret Ball's house early Saturday morning awakened her. She jumped in alarm as a knock beat upon her door and a voice called, "Open in the name of the King." She hastened into her robe and down the stairs to answer the heavy hand. Sheriff Garrett handed her a summons to be at the courthouse by ten o'clock. He went to several houses, giving each door a knock and repeating his call. The startled women quickly submitted to the summons – relieved that there was no trouble on them.

After twelve respectable women were chosen, empanelled and given instructions by Judge Boulton, they filed into the small holding cell outside the courtroom where Catherine lay curled on a pallet. Mrs. Perchard held a lamp as the women lined up to take a look at the condemned woman.

Move, baby, move – save your life! Make yourself known so you can live to know the scent of the land, the voice of the sea, and the sense of me love. I want you to live and know that my body was your first home.

"Relieve yourself of the shawl," ordered Margaret Ball, a respected midwife who had been appointed fore-matron.

A cold sweat gripped Catherine as Mrs. Ball drew aside her shawl. The jurors drew close to take in Catherine's midriff under her tight dress. "Bare your belly," the fore-matron requested in a gentler voice. Catherine lifted her worn, wool frock and petticoats to reveal a rounded belly.

"She's bulged and tight," Mrs. Ball said probing Catherine's abdomen with both hands.

Another juror jabbed her and was startled to feel a quick movement under her hand. She jumped back with her mouth open.

Catherine caught the strong smell of spruce beer as another juror poked at her. The woman stood up, chewing a wad of frankum. She challenged the other jurors. "The cord, itself, hangs more than one baby before it catches its breath. Why should pity save this one conceived of a convicted murderer, another Catholic child come into the world? There'll be trouble enough when it's grown. I say let the child go with the mother and get rid of bad blood."

"We don't know if 'tis a baby," said another juror, shaking her head. "I s'pose youse never heard tell of Mary Jane Crowley – lived down in The Battery, she did. The villagers thought she was havin' a bastard. Sure her father tried to beat it out of her – who she'd been with, I mean.

"'No one, Poppa. No one,' she whimpered, as pitiful as you'd ever see.

"Her father said, 'I've never heard tell of a woman getting in child without a man, not since the Virgin Mary who had a heavenly visitor.'

"Nine months passed – then ten. Mary Jane was pooked off in the belly, and slender everywhere else. Her face looked as if something was sucking the blood out of her. She was showing a lump for nigh on eleven months without being relieved. A seed of Satan not able to bear fruit was the rumour after the doctor cut out a monstrous mass of flesh and hair. Upon examination, the doctor told her father that young Mary Jane was as pure as Adam's ale. "'How was we to know? 'Tis best forgotten,' said her father. Mary Jane's trembling hand went to her cheek, bruised by her father's hand more than once. That night Mary Jane died." The juror turned to the other matrons. "We have to be careful. What if she's innocent?"

Catherine's palms and armpits felt cold and clammy. She swallowed hard. "Can't you tell I'm with child?"

Fore-matron Ball looked at the other jurors. "I too heard tell of a young one whose father beat her black and blue, accusing her of having her barrel up. It turned out the girl had something growing inside her that would never come out. It filled her until her middle was gross. It took over her belly, pressing everything out of the way until she got sick and died. But this one's havin' a baby all right, a lively one to be sure."

Another woman turned a snooty nose to Catherine. "'Tis women like you tries to use a babe to clear themselves; it won't do you good then. Sure there's no reason why Dr. Kielly couldn't be ready with the knife to take the child the moment you drops in the noose."

Catherine closed her eyes and tightened her lips to keep from spitting in the juror's face.

One matron suggested, "If Catherine be given a dose of castor oil, the child'll be born before Monday. Then she can be added to the gallows."

Mrs. Ball shook her head and gave the other jurors stern looks. They left the cell, leaving Catherine to draw her mother's shawl protectively around her. *If my baby is born today there will be nothing to keep me alive after Monday.*

A HALF-HOUR LATER, Catherine was summoned to the courtroom to stand before Chief Justice Boulton.

He coughed into his fist, cleared his throat and looked up. The bags under his eyes, like squashed apricots, moved in irritation as he eyed the condemned woman quivering before him. His voice was curt as he asked, "What do you have to allege why you should not be executed?"

She rushed to answer. "Your Lordship, I plead for me very life so that me baby, soon to be born, can live."

The judge nodded toward the sheriff coming into the courtroom with the jurors. He beckoned Mrs. Ball and the other jurors to approach the bench.

Mrs. Ball told the judge, "I beg your Lordship to consider that we are in full agreement that the prisoner, Catherine Snow, is quick with child and in an advanced state."

The judge then looked to the other jurors. Each agreed that the prisoner was indeed pregnant of a quick child.

"There's no sign of it being born, I suppose," the judge said brusquely.

Mrs. Ball gave the judge an intent look. "It's hard to say what the shock of being sentenced to death can bring upon the prisoner."

The chief justice announced, "We must keep this prisoner in health until after the birth of the child. Perchance it is John Snow's own offspring. Still, even if the child is a by-product of a felonious bundling, we have no mind to kill the innocent with the guilty. The prisoner shall be respited until the next session of the Supreme Court." He banged his gavel and ordered that Catherine be returned to a dungeon cell.

Catherine felt faint with relief. *My baby has saved me for now!* Her hand slid to her belly. Her tired eyes lit up as she felt a gentle poke under her palm.

LANTERN LIGHT FOLLOWED Catherine as she was taken down stone steps back to a small cell. The light's glow settled on the earthen floor like a warm sun in a dark night.

"This is where you'll be kept until the next court session," Mrs. Perchard said, not unkindly. "The cell is only small – six feet by five – but you'll be without a cellmate. The only light you'll be getting is a glimmer through the cell bars from the upstairs passage. Candlelight will come with your breakfast and supper. Here." She passed her a pair of vamps and a sheepskin. "Your daughter left these articles for you. She had to catch her passage home."

Mrs. Perchard left with the light and Catherine pulled on the vamps and wrapped herself in the quilt, drawing in the scent of home. She closed her eyes against the darkness – all alone but for the child moving under her skin. The sun would rise, dawn would come, but her days would be lived as if they were nights, with short reprieves. She finally slipped into sleep, only to be rapped awake by the beating of a tin cup against the cell bars. She pushed her cayla and sheepskin back and looked up, shaking her head against the cup of water and bowl of porridge the matron held out. Her hands drew back from the frigid air to the warmth of her body heat. She slid down under the clothes and huddled against her mattress, crying and wishing she could have stayed asleep until after Monday.

Thirty-Four

"THE sea's buckin' under ice out there today," Wallace, a young guard Catherine hadn't seen before, called through the cell bars after Mrs. Perchard had brought her breakfast. He shook his head. "If anyone wants to see the swingswong, they'll have a fine push to get in through the harbour. But the criminals'll be hanged for sure today. People are already gathering, and there's not a foot of bare ground in the courtyard. The roads'll be crowded too."

"They're only young," Catherine whispered. "Tobias is twenty-five and Arthur twenty-eight."

"And frightened to deat'," the guard replied. "Sure I said to the men after the last hanging, 'You'll not want to be like Downing, such a poor mortal, and the people in the place in such a fright at having to look at one of their own hanging for the crows and weather to barbarize.' Sweat peased on Arthur's lips and forehead. Sure he almost knocked me down for telling him what happens to gibbeted men. Tobias broke out screechin'. I told them to hope for the best. Then, when Tobias was convicted and he asked the judge to let his friends have his body for burial, Arthur wasn't long behind him, asking for the same thing. You heard the judge tell them it was not in his power to give in to their request, the law having left him no discretion. 'No discretion!' I said to meself. Sure Downing was sentenced to be hanged and his corpse separated like pieces of butchered meat. How savage is that! Instead, he was gibbeted. Now you and Arthur are sentenced to be drawn on a hurdle. That might be done in England. Here you'll walk to the Sessions Room and out the window to the gallows." The guard's face broke into a wide grin. "You'll be butchered or left hanging like scarecrows. The judge seems to have discretion after all."

When the guard heard footsteps, he clinked his knuckles against the bars and left. Catherine curled herself around her baby, her body trembling as she waited for news of the men. She didn't stir when Mrs. Perchard came back for the candle she'd left with Catherine's breakfast. She lay trying to dismiss thoughts of the man who had the task of springing the trap that tightened the rope around a victim's throat. Still, her mind kept straying to him. Did he eat his breakfast before he did the deed? Had she and he fastened looks at some point? She imagined the hangman walking the Lower Path, looking over the water, feeling its cold spray in the wind on his face as he fingered thirty pounds – fifteen pounds for each man. She wondered if the money made his hand sweat. *It can't be an easy task to take human life. The easy part must be spending the money on hes wife and children. Likely they never knowed how he got it.* The matron said the hangman was a crew member of the colonial yacht *Forte*. Mrs. Perchard had cautioned her that this was merely a rumour, and that Captain David Buchan and the owner, Governor Cochrane, had protested against having the yacht's image blackened.

THE EXECUTION OF Peter Downing on January sixth had been the first hanging in the colony in nearly nineteen years. Downing and his accomplice, Patrick Malone, were convicted of killing three people: Robert Crocker Bray, a schoolmaster, Samuel, his baby, and Ellen Coombs, Bray's female servant. Malone was saved by Royal Proclamation for giving evidence against Downing. Judge Boulton had ordered the men to be hanged, and their bodies dissected and anatomized. Instead, Malone was respited and Downing hanged. His body was taken to Portugal Cove and hanged there on a pole until the packet boat took it to Harbour Grace. Once in Harbour Grace, the body was gibbeted in chains. The inhabitants were outraged. January was a harsh enough month without livyers having to open their doors to the sight of someone they knew hanging like a scarecrow. No one could abide the sight. Come spring, it would be a ghastly display. After weeks of being frozen, snowed on, rained on, and thawed, Downing's flesh would give way in the sight of the hardened, the soft-hearted, and children playing in the path.

Already gibbets were being built on Spectacle Hill for the corpses of Arthur and Tobias. Sparble Hill, as older people called it, was a monstrous cliff that rose high above Cupids. The gruesome spectacle would be seen in plain view of inhabitants as far as Salmon Cove.

Long before sunrise on Monday, January thirteenth, crowded skiffs and punts holding hard against floating ice sailed in from around Conception Bay. Men from Port de Grave and Harbour Grace had come with a purpose. It was not just to push their way through the horde ready to witness the rare double hanging. They had a plan. The men made their way along roads clotted with loaded horses and carts and people on foot marling about. The sun, an icy brightness above new snow, cut like a shining blade across their eyes, stinging them to tears as they stared at the courthouse window for the sight of Tobias and Arthur.

Spectators shivered in the cold air.

One man nodded to another. "Great day for a hanging, what!"

"Great day, indeed," answered the other. "A cruel day to have two young men strangled like rabbits in a snare. Rumour can tie a knot for a man's throat."

"'Tis a most unusual conviction, and unjust that the law absolves murder with murder," a man was heard muttering as he walked toward the courthouse.

THE MATRON CAME into Catherine's cell with supper. She lifted a candle to the sconce. Catherine whispered, "Has it happened? Have Tobias and Arthur been done in?"

The matron sighed, her heavy face sad. "Your friends be gone, hanged to death this very marnin from the west wing of the courthouse. They stepped through the window of the Sessions Room and faced the gallows and the hangman at the new drop. They died with the finest fearlessness you ever sid, goodly dressed in blue jackets, white trousers, and white gloves, as if they be goin' to a banquet. There they hung straight like soldiers. Sure they wouldin 'ave worn better dubs fer Mass. A bit overdressed, some would say."

Catherine lifted her chin, her voice indignant. "Overdressed to meet their maker. I think not. The police force in Carrick dressed in uniforms of those colours."

The matron's face reddened. She went on. "Dr. Fleming, hes own self, spent the melancholy occasion of the past two nights in the cell preparing the prisoners. He giv' them full attention, celebrating Mass on Sunday morning and early today. The young men went to the gallows looking resigned and composed. Messrs. Edward Troy and Patrick Ward walked them to the scaffold in the repose of prayer. While the crowds stood below with raised heads the young men spent a few minutes in prayer. Some people in the paths blessed themselves as a black hood was placed over Arthur's head and another one placed over Tobias's.

"Tobias gave in to the rope and was lifeless in a quick. But Arthur's dying was an awful sight. He was a brawny one with a thick neck and it took awhile for the noose to do its undertaking. Time is long in goin' when a man's heels are kicking in a dance ag'in death. The longest three minutes of his life, I can tell you that. But the courts said he deserved it and it's not for me to say yea nor nay."

Catherine's hands tightened into fists. She pressed them to her aching brows, unable to believe the men were dead. Sobs rose up and burst through her tight lips.

Unheeding her, the matron went on. "For half an hour after the convicts stopped moving, they dangled there. Then their bodies were cut loose and thumped down into a dead cart. There was an awful racket from the crowd in from Port de Grave and

Harbour Grace. Dr. Kielly was unable to do his duty. He nicked the men with a penknife – some people said he cut their throats – and gave the bodies up to be fixed in their coffins. Tobias's friends had come in a fisherman's shallop to take the corpses across the bay. Spectators cleared the way for them to grab the bodies. Their arms and legs lolled about as they were carried off to the boat. Someone in the crowd heard Philip Bourne say that the men would have a grand funeral, a procession with fife and drum."

The matron went on. "Don't suffer yourself none about the men hanged. There are prisoners who have been in gaol for years, manacled at the ankles with sorry-looking bruises and mean lacerations. They'd be better hanged than left there in chains to suffer life more than they would suffer death, sores creeping over their bodies. Sure that's what'll happen to that Fanning fellar for beating his wife and baby to pulp. It should quench your grief to know that Tobias and Arthur got their wish. They can rest in peace – in one piece."

Catherine dropped to the ground, her face screwed in a soundless cry. *They're on for killing me too, and severing me from meself without proof of murder. I'm goin' to be hanged until I am dead! Dead! Dead!* The dreaded word pounded through her head like a fast pulse. *There had been no one to save Arthur and Tobias from the eye of the rope and* – her lips quivered – *I'll be next.*

The matron slipped the candle out of the sconce. As she left, she admonished Catherine with a shake of her finger. "Don't you be nursing sorrow over the men gone to the gallowstree. You'm wit' child and it needs to be born in health."

Catherine crawled to her mattress, her cell pitch-black like her thoughts. She closed her eyes and placed her hands on her belly – her warm white egg holding a precious gift. *I'll think on this for now. If I haves a son I'll call him after me brother, Richard, whose whereabouts lies a mystery.*

Thirty-Five

ONE morning, Mrs. Perchard came to Catherine's cell, speaking kindly. "Sure you be weak as water. Would you be wantin' a coupie egg if I could spare you one? Your babe's nigh on comin' and you in a trembling state. I said to the governor, 'If we're saving the baby for life then we have to save the body 'tis bidin' in.'"

"I'll take the egg and be grateful. Indeed, I will then," Catherine answered, raising herself on an elbow.

The woman was true to her word, and she doubled her offer and brought two eggs. "You'll need strength for the babe and nourishment to bring in your milk. I've stirred the eggs with goat's milk. Drink it on down."

Catherine drank the snotty mixture, trying not to gag. Immediately she felt her strength rise. "'Tis a tonic for sure, and I'll be thankin' you for it," she said, passing back the wooden cup.

"You'll have a midwife to see you in your time," Mrs. Perchard said, casting a swift look at Catherine's belly. "Take heart. Don't give up on your own life. There was another woman in your predicament, five months gone with child, she was. That was back in 1772. Sure in April 1773 she was pardoned by the King's warrant. A petition to King William is what you need."

And who'd be doin' that for me? Catherine wondered. *Neither me lawyer or a priest has come anighst me since the verdict.*

That night, Catherine slept little. Toward morning, she fell asleep. She woke, mumbling, "I wish Jack wouldn't do that!" She came fully awake with a remembrance of how, often when she was too tired for anything but sleep, John had pressed hard against her behind. Sometimes he had pulled up her nightclothes and pushed himself into her. Other times he pressed her nightclothes between her legs and thrust his hardness against her, finally moving away, leaving her soiled.

She sat up shivering. Her clothes were wet. "My water's broke!" she exclaimed. Then she smiled at how funny that sounded.

Hours later, Catherine felt a familiar grip; her body recoiled from its force and she fell against the cold, damp wall before she slumped to her bed. When the pain let go she dragged her body to the cell door and screeched, "Someone – for mercy's sake, help me!" Her energy gone, she slumped back to her bed. She heard a voice: "Stop your screeching. I'll get the governor of the prison to bring his missus. She's a midwife and she'll help get the baby to rights."

Pain took her again and again, bore her on its tides. She didn't hear the matron open the door. "I've got you some mulse. Gulp it down," she coaxed. "It's just boiled wine sweetened wit' honey. It'll ease you some." She stooped and put her arm around Catherine's thin shoulders to hold her steady as she put the drink to her lips.

It seemed a long time before a large-bosomed woman was let into Catherine's cell, one of the women who had felt her belly after her sentencing. She called to the matron, "This is a bloody mess. The prisoner's blood is draining as thin as water. I'll thank you to bring me a basin of warm water for me to wash me hands after 'tis done, and keep the gaolor aclear of women's business."

The midwife had come with a birthing stool. She and the matron tried in vain to lift Catherine to the U-shaped bench. She didn't have the strength for sitting and pushing. Thoughts of her children floated, then drifted away like a bedsheet torn from a clothesline in strong winds. She was falling inside herself, into a dark place. She heard her own mother scream, felt her blood. She surfaced to her own voice: "I took your life, Mamma. It was for me you lost it."

She caught a glimpse of her baby boy creamed with blood and vernix – arms and legs gently unfolding from his tiny body. He was a pitiful, tiny thing, his face scrunched in a weak cry. His arms splayed out as his whole body shuddered.

"'Tis a scrawny little thing," the midwife said.

"Might he live?" Catherine whispered, holding out her arms.

"If God wills it," the midwife said, putting the baby to Catherine's breast. He latched on to a flowering nipple. "Richard." She mouthed the name before she went out like a light.

SHE WAS LYING in damp darkness like a vegetable stored in a root cellar through a long winter, a grainted, gnarled parsnip among musty, soft potatoes, their eyes sprouting like white worms.

"Mamma!" A far-off voice reached Catherine's ears and her eyelashes flittered open. It was a familiar voice, coming as if through water. Bridget's eyes squinched under a heavy hood hiding her dark hair. Her soft hand touched her mother's forehead. "They hardly saved you," she whispered.

Catherine looked up, her face white and drawn, skin tight against the bone. Her eyes looked bruised and tired. "The baby – where's Richard?" she asked.

"He's ben taken to a wet nurse, I've been told, and given into the care of the priests for baptism."

Catherine let out a sigh. "I'll be wantin' him brought to me."

"Yes, Mamma, I'm sure that will be done."

"How did you get here? Such a time of year too."

"By the packet boat. I would have come before if I could have arranged with the governor of the prison for a visit."

"You got money for it? Sure 'tis five shillings. And John Jacob not easy to get money out of for Jack's fish."

"I saw you take money from behind a brick in the chimney. I found some shillings left behind."

"It was money your old gran left. But I'd ben thinkin' you might have got in to St. John's with Richard Taylor."

"That poor man's ben dead these past three weeks."

Catherine shook her head. "The court used him against me, but there was no cause. Did he get his share from the western boat?"

"No one said, but he seemed despondent and in want, though he died in health. No cause that anyone knows of. Anne is left a widow and fussing, I heard, with John Jacob."

Bridget's voice grew intense, her blue eyes heavy as she asked, "Mamma, can I tell you what I know of what happened *that* night?"

Catherine shook her head. "No. Not unless you have the truth in full and the proof of it. There's too much rumour now, and the gaoler's likely listening. Go easy in your mind with anything you know. Nothing is your fault." Catherine wouldn't let herself think of what might have happened after the girls and servants came back from the wake. She scattered her thoughts, unable to bear the possibilities.

"But I made Poppa angry."

Catherine's mouth tightened. "He's been angry before."

The gaoler rapped his knuckles against the bars. "Time's up. Out you go."

"Here, Mamma. I've brought you a new shawl. It's heavy to warm your shoulders and keep your back from drafts." She placed the grey shawl around her mother, drawing it against her neck. Then she bent down and lifted her mother's thin legs wrapped in stockings full of holes. She peeled them off with her vamps. Then she gently pulled woollen stockings over her feet and up over her calves. "I knit these triheens meself, double-stitched." She stood up and slipped a brin bag off her shoulder. "Apples from our tree. I picked them after you were taken and kept these many in the cellar for you. If you're not strong enough to bite them, suck the juice."

"I will," Catherine answered, feeling her daughter's arms

tighten around her. She had missed the touch of someone belonging to her, her own flesh and blood. Now she yearned to be held as if she were a child. But the gaoler was rapping the bars impatiently. Bridget hastened to loosen her hold. "Goodbye," she said softly. "I can come in but a scattered time. That's all's allowed. And the young ones don't want me leavin'. They bees always havin' an eye out for you. Maria and Martin still stir from sleep every morning calling 'Mamma.' They and Johanna bees quite fussy on times. I'll come when I can. I wants to know where they've taken me baby brudder."

Catherine felt her eyes water. She tried to hold her tears until Bridget left, and then she sobbed so pitifully that the matron called, "You be doin' that and there'll be no more company in your cell."

The matron brought Catherine bread and broth for supper. She stood eyeing her, the back of one hand lodged on her hip. "Dr. Kielly, Judge Boulton's own doctor, was here. He did his best to save you for the hanging after the midwife had trouble gettin' you from yer faint. Your insides didn't tighten like it should after a birt'. We let the baby take your beestings to allow him a good start. The sucking helped slow your bleeding, along with tea I made from steeped dried lady's mantle. But you didn't take to it until you'd lost streams of blood. Mrs. Perchard bundled the baby and sent him off to a wet nurse on Father Troy's instruction. 'Tis a vessel of God's grace, every child is, no matter how corrupt the body was that carried the little eervar." Catherine knew an eervar was an animal born after all the rest, like the last of a litter of pigs, small and hard to keep alive.

"I wants me baby here."

"That's no way for a good mother to talk. This place, with rats, bedbugs and other crawlers, is not fit for a new mother, never mind a baby. The dampness alone could kill him. The week you come to the dungeon, the gaoler caught a white rat with red eyes. A strange omen that was. You'm lucky the midwife's hands didn't have to go up inside you to bring the baby down. I've seen women who've ben handled that way die of fever. A cruel end it bees to have a baby hungering after its mother's milk, and she and her breasts cold in some grave. You'm fortunate not to have milk fever from milk gathered in your breasts and gone bad. We had to keep your breasts tight; you know the nipples are open to drafts after a baby's born."

Catherine's hands went to her breasts and the oakum binding them. There were crusts on her bodice from where her breasts had wept her first milk, and yellow stains from the oakum. Her milk had already dried up, so she pulled the oakum – a frayed bundle of what looked like coarse, ash-brown hair – from inside her clothes and dropped it on the floor. She turned from the strong oily smell, longing for the scent of her newborn. She closed her eyes and whimpered, "I'm like a gutted cod."

"You've a visitor, woman," the gaoler called, rapping his knuckles against the cell bars.

Catherine looked up from her bed, her face pale and drawn – and hopeful. "Is it Bishop Fleming, hes oewn self, come to see me?"

"No 'tis not then."

"And here I've been in the gaol these six months and not seen hide nor hair of a priest. I could have been dead and buried."

The sheriff was let into the cell. Catherine could scarcely open her eyes to look at him. Her body weighed her down like a stone. "You've suffered greatly in this place, and you not well," he said awkwardly. "I'm here to advise you that if you can get a priest or Bishop Fleming to petition Governor Cochrane for you, you could get your life."

"And how can I get someone to do that?" she asked weakly. "I don't remember getting a visit from a priest or Bishop Fleming."

"They're not being paid to visit the prison," the sheriff said bluntly. "They visit only under religious obligations."

WEEKS LATER, A husky man, likely over six feet tall, dressed in a black vest and black trousers under an open grey coat, stood ready to see Catherine. The matron left a candle for the sconce and went out, leaving Father Edward Troy. The priest stooped to lower his head under a black ship hat which he lifted off his head as he came close.

Catherine smiled at him, her eyelids, like clouds, lifting away from brightening eyes. *Perhaps he can tell me where me baby is!*

Father Troy spoke gently. "I was here to see you, and to offer you the Holy Sacrament after your baby was born. You were too sick to know it."

She eased herself off her bed and, in an unsteady gait, slipped to the stool. She leaned against the damp wall, shivering under two shawls wrapped around her shoulders and clutched in bony fists.

She realized now that the priest had come to see her after Richard was born for the sole purpose of taking him away. She gave him a hostile stare.

Father Troy responded with a kind look. "The bishop hopes to get to see you at a later time. He asked me to assure you that your child was baptized under the Christian name heard on your lips when you were so ill. Richard, who is being nourished by a wet nurse, will be nurtured in the gospel of the Holy Church. The bishop's sister, Johanna, who has lately married John Kent, will likely mind him until she has children of her own."

"Until such a time as I leave here," she said, lifting her chin in resolve. "Mrs. Perchard told me to hope for freedom."

The priest cleared his throat and said abruptly, "I must ask you to confess whatever truth there is, in order to seek absolution."

"I will, Fardher, I will," she said penitently. "I was a wretched woman, angry at times. I fought with Jack. In me mind I may have done him in a dozen times, but not in deed."

"My dear child, no one is all bad, but there is One who is all good, and He forgives those of us who aren't – if we confess." He raised stiff, grey eyebrows. "Nothing you confess can turn my face red or white. In probing the hearts of sinners I have had bare-buff sins raunching my ears on more than a few occasions."

"I must confess, Fardher, there were times after Jack went missing that I felt free for the first time in years, free like a sailboat on calm waters away from growlers that could sink it. There were other times when I yearned for him with me heart and soul – and body. Maybe he murthured hes oewn self to get back at me for standin' up to him."

After the sacrament, Father Troy stood up to go. He faced Catherine. "I believe all you tell me. No woman who believes in her faith would risk her eternal soul by lying." He laid his hand on Catherine's head and blessed her. "May Mary and her Son guard you, and God in heaven keep His eye on you while St. Bridget spreads her cloak under God's eye."

Catherine pulled on his sleeve as he turned to leave. "You must put in a petition to save me." Her mouth quivered. "I have to be with me children."

The priest nodded. "I'll do what I can, but it will be a struggle."

After he left, Catherine lay curled in a ball, muttering to herself. *"Ní féidir leis an Easpag Pléamonn mé a shbháil* – Bishop Fleming cannot save me." She tightened her mouth in resolve. *"Sabháilfidh mo neamhchiontacht mé* – My innocence will save me."

Mrs. Perchard came inside the cell with deloused and thicker bedding. She lifted the old bedding, stained with bedbugs and other substances and marked by Catherine's thin knees and elbows, and threw it outside. Then she spread the new bedding, glancing at Catherine. "You won't remember Dr. Kielly being here. At the time he showed concern for the sores on your body. This bedding has just now been received." She went out and came back with a parcel. "A concerned mother left you clothes. She was at your trial, but I'm not at liberty to give her name."

Catherine remembered a well-dressed woman in the courtroom who had cast her a painful look, as if she was struck by the wretchedness of a mother sentenced to death.

Mrs. Perchard dropped a red wool dress, a high-brim bonnet,

petticoats, and several undergarments on the mattress. She said quickly, "All washed, every bit of it, and taken in with the needle, for you're but a skiver."

She helped Catherine wash and dress in the underclothes. Afterward, she slipped the voluminous dress over Catherine's head. It fell down around her legs, warm and comforting. She lay back down, her strength gone.

"Someone's trying to save your life," the gaoler's wife promised her. "You'll have to be patient."

Matron Newell came to the cell with Catherine's supper. "All dressed up you bees then, and praying on your beads. But don't be expectin' to see hide nor tail of the bishop." She looked down her nose at Catherine and said sarcastically, "The Irish Franciscan has come up in the world. The Right Reverend Dr. Michael Anthony Fleming has more to worry him than the fate of a poor Catholic mother on death's list. 'Tidin proper for the man of the cloth to try and save a woman convicted of taking a young man's innocence and helping him and a servant kill her husband. Fardher Troy, hes own self, got no tolerance for fornicators. He'd as likely drag you through the streets with your own guts stuffed down your throat as attend to you. Mind you, I'm not meanin' to be blunt."

Catherine looked at her without a word. The matron left and Catherine slumped down on her fresh bedding. *I'm afraid for me life, but that'll do me no good when I've to get well for me children's sakes.* Sometimes as she breathed the dank air of the dungeon cell, feelings came rushing in of times gone like a dream. *Living with Jack was like riding an anchor. Marriage did not improve my lot, give me claim. I was always a servant. "Kit, fetch me tay." Sometimes he slapped me behind hard enough to knock me to one side. There were times when I wouldn't have cared if he had taken off with some floozie. In later years, John was jealous of the girls. They were going a distance beyond his reach....*

She heard Mrs. Perchard's quick step as she came down the

stone steps, the gaoler behind her with a lantern. A beam of light showed the woman's cheery face. "There's fresh flippers on the go," she said, "and the governor of the gaol has ordered that you have some for your soppa. You've been poorly since you borned the babe. Sure you're fadin'. Your body, 'tis wire thin."

"Flippers?" Catherine's eyelids shivered shut. "I never liked swile, but its flippers were the worst."

"A tasty flipper in gravy would do you wonders," coaxed Mrs. Perchard.

"I couldin eat a flipper on a near-empty stomach. Sure if it went down 'twould chase itself back up. 'Tis not a prisoner's fare. Is the governor wanting to waste good food on someone he expects to die?"

"Hush yourself! Don't be talking like that," Mrs. Perchard said. "There's hope to one's last breath." She left the cell and Catherine lay still – hours of dark solitude around her like damp, dead skin.

She fell asleep, and, when she awoke it was morning. The matron had brought her breakfast and a candle and left without waking her. Catherine's hands went to her neck. She held her prayer beads in trembling fingers. Prayers for her children's well-being went into heaven from her dry, cracked lips. *How silent it is inside me now, almost as if my heart has stopped. My baby's heartbeat is gone and mine is weak. I was lucky to carry ten babies, unlucky to have lost two to heaven, and one is gone into the unknown.* She opened her dress to her belly and let her fingers run over the silver rivulets patterning her skin, where her belly had stretched to hold ten children. She cried for her son, the memory of his scent lingering in her mind like a tease. *Will Richard live without my care? Will he have someone who will raise him gently? Please, God, not someone who will step on him!* The fear of the latter imprisoned her more than the walls of the gaol.

Thirty-Six

BRIDGET came from around the bay in May. She got over with a skipper bringing salted salmon to the inport. She brought food and clothes, noting how skivered out her mother looked. *Either way, she's not long for this world*, she thought with a shudder.

She answered questions about the children until her mother was satisfied that they were living as well as possible without her. Then Bridget told her mother that there had been letters from people wanting the children and money to look after them. Magistrate Robert Pinsent was asking the court for guardianship of the plantation and the children. Catherine stared at her daughter and whispered, "I'm going to be done in, and I'm not even dead."

Bridget took in her mother's white, startled face. She dropped down beside her. "I'm sorry, Mamma. I shouldn't have said anything. Maybe it's but a rumour."

Catherine drew her daughter against her, afraid it would be for the last time. "Hush, Macushla. 'Tis not what you said that hurts; it's what Pinsent is trying to do, and me with no means to stop it."

Mother and daughter stayed within the comfort of each other's arms until Bridget was told to leave. Catherine blinked back tears as she reminded Bridget to tell her brothers and sisters that she held them in her heart and hugged them with her thoughts every day. After Bridget left, Catherine sat with one hand over the other, as if to take comfort from her own body.

ONE MORNING, THE governor of the gaol came to speak to her. He leaned down, his dark hair quiffed into a wave above winged eyebrows. "You should eat to get better from the toll of childbirth. You'll be going to court in July."

Catherine asked, "Where is Solicitor Emerson to offer a petition to have the proceedings against me stayed? He showed no resistance to the arguments against me in the January assize. Now he's abandoned me."

"He's back in Governor Cochrane's office following his advice," the governor said.

Catherine mumbled, "I suppose he's holding to the old Irish proverb, as he did in court, 'Whatever you say, say nothing.'"

The governor continued. "If someone would make a petition on your behalf to the court, and if there were many signatures, it would be the duty of the judges to decide its merits. Though, I can't promise you a satisfied outcome. Acting Judge Archibald says that 'Courts of justice are not political agents to be turned aside from their duty by popular clamour.'" The governor shook his head.

Mrs. Perchard brought Catherine's breakfast, and the governor urged, "Eat! No one knows what will be on the morrow."

"Eat!" she murmured. "So I'll be well enough to get a foot in front of the other for me hanging. If I don't have strength to walk, Judge Boulton can always have me drawn to the gallows on a hurdle."

Her lips curved in irony as she turned her back to the governor and faced the damp wall. Water had stained it like rivulets of tears.

Thirty-Seven

ELIZA Boulton sat listening to Bishop Fleming on a Sunday morning in May. In between drifting with her own thoughts, she caught snatches of the reverend's plans for building his new cathedral. He stroked his small chin as he told his congregation that he was soon leaving on a missionary journey around the bays of Newfoundland. *His nose precedes him and his chin and forehead recede him*, Eliza thought. *He looks as if, when he was being born, someone pulled on his nose to get him out, and when they saw the face of him, they pushed on his chin to get him to go back in. He had to be a priest. No woman would have the likes of him.*

The bishop proceeded to preach with blistering fervour as he looked down over his long nose at his congregation. "This place is rife with sin and ungodly fishermen who take Sunday for Monday with no benevolence for the Blessed Son and His Mother, the Holy Virgin!"

Eliza had heard it all before and often since Catherine Snow's trial. Now her mind was drawn away from the sermon to the woman her husband had condemned to death. They had something in common. Both were high-spirited Catholics who had married Protestants and had eight living children. Eliza Boulton and Catherine Snow had another thing in common: their husbands wanted people to fear them. Eliza had mentioned to the judge that she'd like to pay a visit to Catherine Snow. He had forbidden her. "You'll not be sympathetic to that woman. The court has spoken and the people's will is to be done."

"Since when was the people's will done in this colony?" she retorted.

Eliza knew that her husband believed Catherine Snow to be a Mary Magdalene, and that John, her Protestant husband, was ousted by Tobias Mandeville, a young papist. She was grateful for her station in life, but it didn't mean she didn't have an eye for younger men. She knew too that the judge's eye often flickered appreciatively over the face and stature of a comely young woman. She imagined Tobias, not long come from Ireland. When Catherine saw the young Irishman for the first time, it would be like having the scent of home grass and peat fire. There would be a rush of feelings toward him. Her bold, blue eyes would turn away for fear the young Irishman had noticed. He was young – too young for her to think of him in that way. There were older men in the harbour with young women, but not older women with younger men. Never an older married woman with a young man! Still, no one would ever suspect them. He would speak Irish and their looks would meet. She would answer and something would strike them both, each wondering if the other felt it too, a strong, dangerous pull that could only cause trouble – but a pull too strong to resist.

Eliza shifted in her seat. Her mind's eye followed Catherine and her young lover in hot pursuit of each other, not a care but for the moment, gone off berry picking, he coming from one direction, she from another, running over the berry hills, her limbs feeling young and supple, her body strong. They'd meet and she'd drop to reach under cool fen to pick magna berries. Then, with their breaths sweetened with the cool, minty flavour of the tiny berries, they'd spread out on soft moss in the lun of a hill and do the deed. Eliza went further and imagined it was herself and young, handsome Tobias, who at the trial had seemed none the worse for his time in gaol. Before all her children came she had loved to skip off and go berry picking on a warm, breezy day. She drew in the memory of tasty magna berries, wild, black heather berries, and tiny, red lassy berries sliding down her throat. Once, she had let down her hair, rolled down her stockings and skittered about, chanting, "White as milk, but that it's not, green as grass, but that it's not, red as a rose, but that it's not, black as squid squirt, but that it's not. It's a blackberry! That it is! Ripe for the bread pudding." Peachy pearl cloudberries were most to her liking for tarts; red and black plumboys were treasures not easy to find. Now she imagined picking berries on the hills when Tobias came over a knob. She'd watch him outlined against the sky. Warm, baffling winds would tease the hair on her neck and she'd let it down and wait for the young man to pin her against velvet cushions of moss, a sprig of reindeer moss scraping her bare leg like a pricked conscience as she let him lick berry juice off her lips. She'd lift her skirts, the sun's caresses in the wind like kisses, the strings of her bodice loosened. His brigs would slide down over his young body over his pulsing upstart.

When a man, like the judge, makes a practice of ploughing into his wife's soft flesh, priming her, then leaving her rising to answer just as he falls on her spent – a dead weight – her imaginations can take her anywhere, Eliza thought. *Still, I suppose I should wipe my sins off on the ears of the priests.* She smiled. *And that I won't then!* She had challenged holy water and Easter water and she hadn't had her children baptized Catholics. Her confessions were haphazard efforts. She didn't know why her prayers had to go into a priest's ears and get to God's ears secondhand, and a little worse for wearing on the priest's ear.

She rolled her eyes and thought, *A priest's body might be pure, but his mind must be a cesspool from parishioners dumping confessions of deeds hardly thought possible to imagine, much less doing. So-called respectable people use his ears as honey wagons to dump their weekly garbage. Housemaids wear the skin off their knuckles cleaning the priest's garments spotless. Under the vestment there is only a human frame bearing up a head that claims to be full of God's Word.* Eliza turned back to the sermon. *Fleming is like my husband – full of his own power.* The bishop wasn't with the in-crowd; he had sat for a sumptuous dinner at Government House with Governor Cochrane only twice. His invitations were as scarce as those sent to most women. Only females, whose station would admit them, dined at the governor's home, along with others who were of a superior station. Eliza Boulton and other highly placed women were expected to converse within their own circle and not interfere in the religious and political talk of the men. Eliza enjoyed eavesdropping on the men's conversations while socializing and talking about the fancy ball coming in the fall. She could do all the dances, despite her ample figure fortified with stays she'd made and laced herself. There were quadrilles, waltzes, country dances, and reels. She had enjoyed the last masquerading party with all the upper class. The Honourable John B. Garland was there as a French soldier. Merchant John Bayly Bland, foreman for Catherine Snow's trial, came as an Albanian chief, and his wife, Johanna, as a gypsy. Bryan Robinson came as Shylock. Judge Boulton was in court dress. Eliza had suggested to her husband that at the next ball she would dress in a scarlet dress with her head in the eye of a rope. "You dare not!" her husband had snapped.

"Someone needs fisticuffs in the face," Eliza had retorted to her husband after she had accompanied him to Government House one July evening. Soldiers and other uniformed men, shop and fish merchants, with oiled, curled beards, gathered at the taproom to hold tankards of ale. Guests wandered off to other rooms to play billiards, chess, poker, and cards, candlelight wavering under their breaths as they let out boorish guffaws. As the evening wore on, people began to make bets on whether or not Catherine Snow would die in a quick drop or kick about like Arthur Spring. His three-minute struggle had spectators holding their breaths in shock.

"A mother's life is in jeopardy and her children are about to be orphaned. Yet men make bets on her degree of suffering," Eliza had complained to her husband when she got home. "Catherine may have wished her husband dead, though there's no evidence of that. Maybe she did after a beating. Maybe she didn't. Words are not bullets. She might have been free with words, not thinking they could be strung into a rope for her neck. Half the women in this place have wished their men gone when they've been struck in the mouth or taken still raw after the birth of a new baby. A woman's words can kill her, it seems – if they slip into the wrong ears, and down on tongues of people out to use anything against her. You have often said you'd knock my head off or skin me alive when you've been vexed with me. Words without action are used in the colony time and again."

Boulton was pulling off his tie. He stopped, as if he'd just noticed Eliza. "Stop your pacing and get out of your dress and stays, or you'll be in a swoon from your hurried speech. I pay no mind to your rambling." He glanced at her large bosom. "There's a rent in your dress. You'll need to get a darning needle."

She stopped suddenly, took in a long breath and felt for the place in her bodice broken away from its stitching. "Well then, I'll have the servant girl work it. To set about darning one's own clothes is to premeditate poverty." She intended to hold to her station as long as she could.

Eliza turned back to ask, "Henry, have you no feelings for a mother who bore ten children? Even if she took a life, she gave ten. Is there no redemption in that?"

The judge arched his brows, his face hard and as mottled as a brown, speckled rock. "If you dared to do me in, my dear, I'd want a rope at your throat and your eyes popping under the strain. Catherine Snow's base nature got the best of her and now she must pay for her crime, made an example of as a female threat to men, and a lesson to women who have murder in their hearts."

Eliza tried again. "Think of the newborn – and the other children. Look for the truth! The evidence was given only in words, and they mischievous and wanting in gist."

"It is the jury who convicted her."

"It was you who sentenced her to death in the absence of demonstrative evidence that a crime was committed," she retorted, "and if I had the power to present a petition to save the woman, I would."

Boulton gave his wife a derisive look. "I would mind the barking of a little cur in the street as much as I would care for the rabble and their petitions. This colony is upholding laws that Mother England has gone wishy-washy over. Women are no longer dissected and anatomized there."

"Holy Mother of God!" she cried. "You're not thinking of doing that to Catherine Snow, pushing your authority beyond her death! That's never been done to a woman in this colony – and you know it's been abandoned in England since 1816! I thought this was just a show of words as 'drawn to the place of execution on a hurdle' must be."

"It's the law with the sentence and she's not the Holy Mother of God. Her husband's death was occasioned by his wife's infidelity."

"Maybe the young cooper showed her what it was to be a woman loved and not just used for a man to spend his lust." Her eyes blazed. "Men in power who make unwise decisions can be recalled, but their life and death deeds can't be undone."

Boulton tightened his lips, his eyes as stormy as a sea caught in an easterly gale. Then he turned to Eliza, his voice terse. "Go to bed then. Give yourself the chance to sleep on that wild tongue of yours before it strays too far." He lifted his long, black coat and tall hat from the stand and hastened from the room. *Off to take ale with his cronies at the London Tavern*, Eliza thought with disdain.

She raised her eyes to the looking glass above the mantel and spoke softly to her own image. "My husband will commit an atrocious and barbarous crime if he executes the hanging of Catherine Snow. He will, therefore, be an accessory before the fact."

Thirty-Eight

CATHERINE wasn't sure where she had heard the name Dr. William Carson before. But here he was, looking down at her, his bald head putting her in mind of a large white egg. She looked up and asked, "Have you come to appeal to the governor for me life?"

Carson shook his head. "That would not be effective. In a letter to the Secretary of State in March, Governor Cochrane wrote that, in some respect, the murder of your husband was more atrocious in its character than the murder of the three people by Downing and Malone. The Governor said this with the knowledge that a man, whose foot had often rocked Samuel Bray's cradle, would be convicted of murdering him, his father, and a servant girl." Dr. Carson smiled ruefully. "The Governor has an ass where his face ought to be if he thinks that the murder of one man – yet to be proved – could be worse than the taking of three lives, one of whom had his whole lifetime ahead."

Catherine liked the man's boldness. Her words rushed out in a torrent. "Tobias's confession was on the hearsay of men of the law – friends of each other. Arthur's confession was on the say of Magistrate Pinsent and his friend John Jacob, and confirmed by a relative, John Broom, Chief Magistrate, St. John's. Arthur and Tobias could have been pitted against each other, each told that he was being accused by the other. Arthur couldn't read, write or sign his name. In court, the men were not asked to identify the confessions as theirs under oath." She stopped with a quick indrawn breath.

Dr. Carson leaned against the door. "As a member of the House of Assembly, I called the attention of the legislature to the monstrous fact that the sheriff was carrying out duties he was not authorized by law to do. He has empanelled juries and used them to try charges of capital offences. The dread sentence of the law pronounced upon Downing, Spring, Mandeville, and yourself was put in execution by the same officer. Still nothing is being done."

"I can't talk on the law," said Catherine. "I'll be thankful if someone will petition the judge on my behalf."

"It's an imponderable situation, this is, but I'll speak to the priests," Carson promised. He left with an uncertain look.

Catherine knew then she would be going back to the court without a petition.

THE STONE-FACED SHERIFF came for Catherine one July morning. He nodded at her but said nothing. She shivered from worry as she gathered strength to walk up the steps to the courthouse. She could hardly face it, for fear she would again hear the sentence of death. She resolved to tell the judge how wrong the judgment was.

When the door to the courtroom was opened, Catherine lurched and drew back. It took her a moment to adjust to the brilliant sunlight splashing the floor from the window. A hand steadied her and she was taken to the prisoner's box, gripping her beads, her lips moving in silent prayer that she would be reprieved.

She glanced at other prisoners, all with despondent faces. When Judge Boulton, Judge Brenton, and Acting Judge Archibald sat in their places they cast scant looks toward Catherine and the other prisoners.

Before the rising of the court, Judge Boulton announced that there was nothing to urge why the sentence passed upon the prisoner Catherine Snow in the January assize should not be carried into execution.

Catherine stood up bewildered. She pleaded, "A petition, Your Honour, was to have been entered on my behalf."

Judge Boulton scarcely regarded her as he directed the sheriff to carry the said sentence into execution on Monday the twenty-first instant. Then he nodded at the court clerk who immediately dipped his pen into an inkwell, lifted it and began to write the judgment.

The brutal pronouncement fell on Catherine like a blow from a maul and her mind seemed to break away from her body, rise in madness, pieces of it slipping off her tongue in moans and cries against the judge's ears. She slipped to the floor and lay cringing, as if the judge's boots were on her knuckles. When her arms were grabbed by strong hands and she was lifted to her feet, she cried, "*La gra dé ní dein me é!* – For the love of God I did not do it!"

She hardly breathed as she was dragged back down the steps to the dungeon cell, its damp air eating at her shocked body. She drew back, sniffles stogging her nose, and swallowed hard. *My fate is sealed under the judge's gavel. The next time I walk in the outside air, my neck will be placed in the eye of the rope.*

Thirty-Nine

"THERE'S going to be a petition, Catherine, on the belief that you were improperly convicted. We are having it circulated for signatures. Then it will be presented to Judge Boulton." Father Troy's voice was a whisper in her ear. She hadn't heard his step or seen him let into her cell. She turned, a frail, ghostly figure blinking against the light held in the priest's hand.

She lifted dark eyes to the priest. "It's a late hour, but I'm grateful." She settled herself, thinking, *God and the priests will save me from the Devil's oewn sentence so I can look after me children – and keep Jack's business from the merchants' grasp.*

After the priest left her cell, Catherine took the jug of water left on the floor from the day before and a dish of broth and loaf. She drank and ate heartily. *Hope! I have hope!* The word swung through her mind as if it were a lead ball against her death sentence. Again she envisioned going home. She imagined John back from wherever he had gone. She'd try to be a better wife and not let her Irish dander be a match for his English temper and arrogance. She smiled at memories of sunrise awakening the place, spilling brilliant light over the land, and how the evening shadows were like a blanket drawn over the day as a loving mother would draw a blanket over a child settling for the night. She closed her eyes, and it seemed that the light of God's very eye was shining into darkness, finding her, warming her body, kindling her spirit.

That night, she dreamed she was at home sitting outside in a wattle chair. In the summer sky, birds sang as they flittered from tree to tree; leaves stirred in soft breezes. The children skipped about the yard and off in the meadow. John threw a hemp rope over a birch tree, tied a knot and dropped some slack for the seat. He lifted the end and tied it to another birch tree a short distance from the first. He made a spraddleboard and notched it. Then he called for Catherine to come and have a swing.

She slid on the wooden seat, grabbed the ropes and swung high into the air, her fists so tight her knuckles were white.

"I want to double up with you, Mamma!" Katie called as she ran toward her. Catherine stopped pumping the air with her legs. Her hands slackened on the rope and the swing began to fall straight. Katie climbed into her mother's lap and Catherine lifted her burlap apron over her daughter's head and let her look through the bib collar while she tied the strings around the little girl and herself. She smelled the rope, felt it rub against her hands as she swung herself and Katie into the heavens. The blue sky spread into endlessness and she felt herself drifting. . . . Her dream changed. Now there was an empty space between the two birch trees. *The rope is wrapped around Jack . . . around Jack . . . around my neck.*

She awoke with a start, swallowing breaths of dense air. She turned from her bed and sat up just as the matron called, "Father Thomas Waldron is come to see you."

Candlelight flickered against the darkness as the matron opened the cell door, and a pleasant-faced priest she had never seen came inside. Her heart seemed to stand still as she put her hand to her breast and clasped the rosary. "Where's Fardher Troy?"

The priest shook his head. "Father Troy has been busy writing letters. He also sent a memorial to Judge Boulton and the two other judges on the fourteenth of July. It was signed, but not by more than three hundred people."

Father Waldron turned aside in discomfort. "The Protestant newspapers are to blame as much as anything for the refusal of many people to sign the petition. Published excerpts from your trial were not in your favour." He shook his head sadly. "There are about ten thousand Catholics in St. John's. That includes women and children, but many people can't read and write. The women would not have the right to sign, even if they were literate, and there are men afraid to go against men of money and power."

Catherine's hands flew up in exasperation. "I've been told by Mrs. Perchard that as soon as the flag is lifted on the flagpole signifying the beginning of a church service, parishioners flock to the chapel. Any petition put out by the Cartlic church is expected to be signed by parishioners attending Mass. If the St. John's population be three-fourths Cartlic a petition should have received many signatures – if it had been presented. It *was* exhibited on the table at the door of the chapel – was it not, Fardher?"

"I'm afraid not," he said heavily. "Bishop Fleming was not here to approve it."

"Does he approve of me hanging then?" she asked spitefully. "'Tis a good thing I didn't pin me hopes to his sleeve. What did the memorial say?"

"It petitioned the court, asking that your case be laid before the British Government for review. It pointed out that you have eight living children, and that you have already suffered a close imprisonment for nearly a year – and with harrowing feelings. It asked for a less severe sentence on the grounds that you had been improperly convicted. The document also called into question the verdict of the jury who convicted you. The petition complains that no evidence was brought forward to prove John Snow's death, and that the jury convicted you even though Judge Boulton had forbidden them to regard the so-called confessions of Arthur Spring and Tobias Mandeville. Otherwise, it could not offer any substantial evidence that the jury's verdict was an improper one."

"It could not!" She stared, her face ashen.

"Sadly, you had a lawyer who did not speak for you. You had representation without defence."

Catherine's eyes, glistening in tears, loomed large in her shrunken face as she searched the priest's countenance, her frail voice wavering with the weight of her question. "Why didn't someone try to save me before now?"

The priest skirted her question. "I wasn't at your trial but the *Public Ledger*, a Protestant newspaper, gave an account – though, from all respects, it was inaccurate by omission as well as in submission. There was no direct word of defence given by you or the men."

Catherine's voice came low and tight. "But there was, Fardher. I told the court that there can't be proof of me committing a crime when I didn't. Now I'm deprived of me children, deprived of me home and property, and John's savings. Am I to be deprived of me very life?"

The priest touched her shoulder. "Judge Boulton has replied in a letter that the court will meet on the eighteenth of July to hear legal arguments in your favour."

Catherine drew her head up in relief. "So, I'm not done in yet then." Her longing for good times with the children filled her like a terrible hunger. She remembered her girls in their muslin frocks playing in the grass, or pulling ripe carrots from the kitchen garden and crunching them between their white teeth. She smiled, remembering Johnny dipping his mouth and tongue in the boiler of milk put out in the porch to cool. He had denied doing so even while cream skimmed his lips. She could see her boys running through the clear dimpling water of the little pool in the dip of the hill up from her house. She imagined the children stopping whatever they were doing to run toward her, their laughter filling the air at their sight of their mother coming home. . . .

FATHER TROY CAME on Friday to tell Catherine that he and Fathers Waldron and Ward had sent a further memorial to Governor Cochrane, assuring him that there was very slight evidence against her. "We have asked for a referral to London."

Catherine's voice lifted a little. She let out a sigh. "Thank you, Fardher."

Father Troy was back on Saturday, his face grim. Catherine lifted her face from her mattress and whispered, "Is it for saving me you've come then, or is it to mourn me fate?"

The priest hesitated; then he shook his head. "No answer has been received from the court. It is a late hour, and I urge you to prepare your soul to our merciful God." He added, "If there is anything I can do, you poor woman. . . ."

"There is, Fardher."

"Yes?" He leaned forward, looking grave.

She lifted trembling lips. "If I am to die, I want to see me children – all of them."

The priest turned kind eyes to look at her. He assured her in a grave voice, "I'll see what I can do. We will write up our arguments over week's end and seek to see Judge Boulton early Monday morning to ask him to stay your sentence until there is an appeal, and a lawyer with the backbone to state your case in earnest. The other hangings were at eleven. There should be time. Though I cannot promise a stay of proceedings. Bishop Fleming and Chief Justice Boulton don't see eye to eye. The bishop has made unsavoury remarks about the judge for his belief that Irish Roman Catholics belong to the lower order and Protestants are of the higher order. Then there's the bishop's will to have the support of fishermen who are counting on him to help them get rid of the truck system, which keeps them at the mercy of merchants whose accounting practices take advantage of fishermen who can't read or write. If the bishop incites the anger of the merchants, they will not deduct a tithe of fishermen's earnings for the building of the cathedral. The bishop has to depend on the favour of Newfoundland merchants."

Catherine found the strength to lash back. "Does he not care about a penniless Irish woman who has spent her body giving children to the church?"

"It would be jeopardizing Bishop Fleming's status to go out on a limb to save you."

"Climbing trees is he then?" she said sarcastically, her eyes flashing.

"Such a temporary life this is for all of us," the priest said solemnly. "To be saved for eternal life, a span that has no measure, is a good Catholic's goal. You have lived out your child-bearing years. To go with God is no burden for someone with hope."

"This is the only life I knows. My children needs me."

"They will be cared for. Magistrate Pinsent requested guardianship this past spring."

Catherine's eyes widened. They grew fierce with venom. "That man put me here. Now he wants to run our plantation. It all fits now."

"It fits?"

"He and John Jacob likely wanted me out of the way so they could keep John's accounts unpaid. Likely they got Jack's money box."

The priest gave her a look of reproof. "Do not accuse someone without evidence, when you are so near to meeting God."

Catherine smarted under his gaze. "These men accused me without proof. Because of them I have suffered life and I will suffer death. If I am to meet God I will ask Him why He created men who would destroy an innocent mother's life."

Father Troy cleared his throat self-consciously. He raised a tight fist against his mouth, as if to keep in anything he might say that would lead to another outburst from a woman under such strain. He blessed himself and uttered, *"Absit omen!"* as he started to leave the cell.

"Is it Latin you're using, Fardher?"

He nodded, and she asked, "What is it then?"

He answered gravely, "May what is threatened not become fact."

The priest bent down and placed his hand on Catherine's arm. "The bishop believes in your innocence and his prayers are with you."

Catherine asked, "Will Bishop Fleming be coming to see me? I'm in hopes that he will be here to offer prayers if I must die. He was with Tobias and Arthur for two nights before the Monday morning they were hanged."

The priest was apologetic. "The bishop is on a missionary

journey and suffering much in his hardships to bring the gospel to wayward parishioners and to heathens. He will be back in St. John's by August. If you are still in gaol. . . ." His voice fell silent.

"By then I'll likely be saved from this hell," she said, resigned.

The priest moved uncomfortably. His collar shifted, pushing up his second chin as he paraphrased a Bible verse. "Don't fear those who can destroy your body, but not your soul; fear Him who can cast both your body and soul into hell."

Catherine gave him a tense look. "I am in hell in this dungeon where melancholy, darkness, and dampness bees one thing, biting through me skin, me heart, and me mind. If I can't go home to me children, I resign myself to seek eternal life."

After the priest left, Catherine sank on her bed. She lay shivering, her lips moving silently and frantically. She tried to hold her mind against the knocking of hammers as workmen removed the sashes from the courthouse window and built the scaffold and gallows. She pulled thoughts of her children around her, as if they were a cayla she'd once quilted with pieces of cloth from her children's worn and outgrown clothes. She now had to turn and face the dread that had been gnawing at her like a rat, accept its bite and let it be over.

CATHERINE DID NOT stir to the sounds of the key in the door or open her eyes to the light in Mrs. Perchard's hand. She lay silent and unresponsive to the woman's urge to eat. *For what,* she thought. *I will soon step out a window and twirl above the straining necks and eyes of a mob below. There'll be murderers there, for sure, some who will never be convicted by the law or their conscience, while I die innocent.*

The next morning, she looked up as the matron pulled the shutters and rapped on the bars of her cell, a light in her hand. "You'll soon be with the gallows lads, be sure of it," she called. "The bishop's had six months since the hanging of your friends to get serious about savin' yerself. You'm an Orange Cartlic sure, marrying that Protestant and gittin' yerself in the way of murder.

You and the judge's wife, Eliza, is a pair then, not the kind of Cartlic the bishop favours."

The matron went out. She closed the shutters, letting her taunting words fall into the darkness inside Catherine's cell – inside her mind. Catherine drew in an exhausted breath. *Come Monday, I'll be in the eye of the rope and strangled like Arthur and Tobias.*

Forty

FATHER Waldron told Catherine she would lose only her physical self by dying. That was not such a bad loss. Her body had become a weak, shrinking vessel she sometimes felt detached from. She hadn't seen her face in a long time. When she was a little girl, she'd pass a looking glass hung in the linhay and smile at her healthy face. Other times she'd catch the sight of her whole body above a pool of calm water reflecting the sky and it was as if she were standing in the clouds. She felt amazed that she could find her likeness imprinted in a pool of water – even more amazed that her reflection moved with her like a second self. There had been times during her years with John when life seemed all physical. She had little time to dwell on her feelings. Only with the loss of her children had she let herself be pulled inside herself to the pain it brought. In this dungeon, thinking was the essence of who she had become. It took her away from a body whose only use was to bring her pain and discomfort. The priest told her that soon her untainted, spiritual self would rise above her earthly body and be free. While he was speaking these words, she believed them. After he left, though, she descended inside herself, longing for a body that was whole and free and able to hold her children close.

    She had seen ripples on ponds, ironed away by the dropping of the wind until there was a deep calm. Now she tried to pull herself into a calm pool by thinking that death could not be worse than life spent separated from her children in this box as dark as the grave once the door and shutters closed. But like a sharp wind, reality pulled across the surface of that calmness. Her will was to live and fight her way out of the dungeon.

The tiny flame of hope that had brightened each dismal day was douted when a tall stranger was let into her cell. He gave her a grim, bald-eyed look. "I've come to measure your length."

Her voice wavered as she asked, "For me dead box?"

"No, not for your box. You won't need a long box after they've finished with you. It's the hangman's consideration for the length of the rope. If the rope is too long and if you drop too far you can lose your head. If the rope is too short you will suffer longer. Quick is the best way."

The shock of what was going to happen shook her frail body. Her mouth trembled with her words. "I didn't know what it really meant to lose hope until now. Through days past, hope dropped inside me almost too far to be reached, but then it rallied."

Father Waldron had followed the graveyard man, and now he told Catherine bluntly, "My good ma'am, it is my duty to entreat you to lay aside any hope. It is in heaven your hopes are to rest."

She grabbed her beads and whispered, "God, Hes oewn self, has forsaken me."

The graveyard man's face tightened as he took Catherine's length. "Don't blaspheme when you're so near to seeing God face to face."

The governor of the gaol came to offer Catherine delicacies from the gaol kitchen. He bent down and said in a kind voice, "Mrs. Perchard told me that these past two days you've hardly touched a morsel." He urged her to take a little. She turned her face from the food, murmuring, "Nourishment is nothing to me. God wants me to suffer death, and there's no way to get out of it. If I'm to die such a terrible death I may as well add to it. Heaven will right me."

In the gaol kitchen, the cook heated spiced wine, blending the fragrances of orange, cinnamon, ruby port, and brandy. Mrs.

Perchard brought a flagon to Catherine and the priest urged her to drink. "Christ too took wine before His cruel death," Father Waldron said softly.

Catherine lifted her lips to the jug. She took a sip and closed her eyes, remembering the scent of berries on the hills and the warm aroma of the cinnamon John had brought home from St. John's for her cakes. She huddled down inside herself, fearful of the Monday morning soon to come.

The flickering light of a thick candle, left to burn through the night, could not penetrate the darkness under her lids. She lay with her back to it, her body curled into itself. She must have drifted into twilight sleep. The turning of a key in the door startled her. It was 3:00 a.m. and Fathers Waldron and Troy had returned to enjoin Catherine to look to God for her comfort. "You must give yourself to God in the assurance that life is more than the physical trinity of blood, flesh, and water," Father Troy said.

Catherine's bleary eyes looked at him. She mustered the strength to ask, "What of the trinity of love, hope, and justice? I will be separated from all three by the hangman's noose."

AT FIVE O'CLOCK the priests left the cell, leaving Catherine to her private prayers and ablution. Fearful of the day to come, she lay curled like a wrinkle in its shell, feeling as if her life was shrinking, being gathered to a tiny core inside her, soon to be extinguished.

Mrs. Perchard came inside the cell holding the hooded death garment, made from a ream of brown cloth by women at the workhouse. She held a sharp knife in her hand. At Catherine's startled look she responded, "You'll be needing a quick hanging. Your hair will only prolong it." She grabbed Catherine's long, thick braid and cut through it with a sharp knife. Catherine let out a harsh cry as her hair was pulled and loose strands caught against the knife. Her hair dropped to the bed and her long, thin hands reached up to touch her bare poll. She drew back quickly at the thought that a rope would soon follow the knife. The matron came behind Mrs.

Perchard with a basin of warm water and a rag. The two women helped Catherine sit up. Then they stripped off her tatty clothes, leaving her shrunken body shivering. Catherine fell back to her mattress, a weakness spreading through her as if she was paralyzed. Mrs. Perchard gently washed her face and body. Then the matron slipped the death garment over Catherine's head. She lay unable to lift a limb, as if every part of her was weighed down with the gravity of the fate awaiting her.

Mrs. Perchard put her arms across Catherine's back and helped her to her feet. Catherine glanced at the looking glass the matron had hung beside the candle. The skin on her face had sunk against the bone, and, for a moment, her eyes looked back at her from a face she didn't know. She let out a shriek once she realized it was her own face – a face she hadn't seen for almost a year. Her body, no more than a rasher of wind, fell in a huddle at Mrs. Perchard's feet. In kindness she turned the looking glass away. Then she helped Catherine back to her mattress, where she folded her trembling body into a ball. She pressed her fingers against her swollen eyes, smarting from hot tears. "I was hoping for a visit from me children."

Mrs. Perchard said kindly, "There is still time."

FATHER WARD HAD joined the other two priests. Now they entered the cell with their scapulars about them to offer the Holy Sacrifice of the Mass. Father Waldron said gently, "Catherine, there is a place that is our home where we've never been, a place where we shall live forever."

"Will I see my angel children?" she asked in a bivering voice.

Father Troy answered promptly. "By getting in with John Snow, you endangered your soul and theirs. God is your judge in the hereafter."

"They were baptized by Cartlic priests," she answered. She closed her eyes and whispered, "Thomas! Emilia!" Now one thought comforted her. *If there is life after this one, then I will see them. I will be with them forever.*

Forty-One

SUNDAY was over, another holy day gone. Monday's early darkness had scattered, and the sun rose up on the lip of the sea and pressed through fog coming in over the harbour and wrapping the place in its damp skin. Eliza Boulton awakened with a lurch, her own voice in her ears: "I'm glad I'm not Catherine Snow!" It was better to have the foul breath of the man beside her, the smell of his sweaty body on her, than to have the fear of the hangman's noose. Catherine's head would drop forward as she fell away from her own life into a crack of pain and blackness. Eliza knew that other women would rise from their beds and go stare at a woman they didn't know twirling like a marionette.

Eliza leaned on her elbow and looked down on her husband. Then she slid out of bed away from the Honourable Henry J. Boulton, who took his pleasure from being the most powerful and the most hated man in the colony. This was a man believed by many to be a cold-blooded murderer, a man who planned the death of a mother without evidence of a crime. Eliza's hand went to her belly. For this man she was delicate with another child.

ACROSS TOWN, DR. Edward Kielly felt the weight of his onerous task. The forty-four-year-old St. John's native, a former surgeon in the Royal Navy, was a Catholic with prominent

Protestant friends. He was Judge Boulton's friend and doctor. His office was under government control.

On the night of July twentieth, Kielly's maid had been instructed to leave the doctor alone so he could get a full eight hours' sleep and be rested for the task at hand. If Dr. Kennedy down the hill could not be fetched, pity then any wretch who got in trouble with sickness.

When Dr. Kielly woke, he wasn't sure if his mind held dreams as truth or if there had been sounds in the night, fists thumping on the front door and the voice of a woman calling for him to save the life of her child. The dreariness of the morning pressed in on him as he drew the bedroom's heavy red drapes apart. It was day, but fog was as thick as night, its ghostly, grey self pressed against the windowpanes. The day got greyer as he remembered his task. He looked at his long, strong hands, used for healing the sick, his fingers always ready to make music. Didn't he love to play his fiddle at parties and gatherings on dreary winter nights? There had even been a ditty published about him. He smiled as it played through his mind. "Oh! Did you see Dr. Kielly, oh! His boots are all polished so highly, oh! With his three-cocked hat and his double bow knot, and his fiddle to coax the ladies, oh!" Aware of the gruesome task he was called upon to perform, the fiddler tried to shut off the lines as frivolous.

Shaking his head, he eyed himself in the looking glass with one raised eyebrow. His dark hair ran back from his white, raised forehead, his sideburns like patches under his cheeks. He turned abruptly to reach for his clothes lying across a chair from the night before. He hurried into them, trying not to think, for as he had told himself a thousand times, thinking causes insanity. Minds are to be used for getting things done, not for debating whether or not they should be executed. His undertaking was at hand. It was the law, laid down and enforced by Judge Boulton. He buttoned his white shirt, his hands unsteady. Having to carry out, to the letter, the law of a powerful judge could unnerve the best surgeon. He thought of how Judge Boulton had eyed him, unflinching in his words. "She is to be quartered."

The colour had drained from Kielly's face. "I'm not a coroner, that I should have to cut into the dead. And for what reason? England has dispensed with such cruelty."

Boulton was blunt. "It is not of your will to do or not do. It is an order. I am not aware of ever having done a public act which I did not believe would redound to the public good."

The doctor had turned away, aware that the threefold character of Judge Boulton was that of judge, jury, and executioner.

Solly, Kielly's young servant girl, interrupted his thoughts with a knock on the door. He called for her to enter and she hurried in with his breakfast. His feet felt heavy as he dropped into the armchair by his table. He buttered a brown bread roll and ate it, as well as a bowl of porridge fortified with rum-soaked raisins. His hand shook. *If I was not Judge Boulton's doctor and his friend, I would remove myself from this revolting deed. Perchance there will be an intervention as there was after the Spring and Mandeville hangings.*

He looked toward the harbour just as the sun sliced through rolling fog, burning it off the water. It would be a hot, sunny day. He took a deep breath and settled his conscience with the thought, *It is not my place to determine the woman's guilt, but to carry out the sentence of the court on her body.* He made himself ready.

"WE MUST ESCORT you to the window now, though it's not yet nine o'clock," Father Troy said with a nod at Catherine. She fixed her gaze on him so intently that he looked away and got to one side to help her face the death walk. Fathers Ward and Waldron joined him in helping her from the cell. She made small steps; a time or two she backtracked with grief. When she reached the window, she drew in a long breath and stopped.

"It's a short plank you have to walk, Catherine, a few feet."

The voice seemed far away – beyond the frantic heartbeats sounding in her head – as she tried to lift her feet. The walk to the rope took all her effort as each step brought her closer to the heavy coil of manila rope that would hold her neck, snap it. She tried to think past this day, past death – that unfamiliar territory where

Emilia and Thomas had gone. Past it to. . . . Her mind was having trouble. Her thoughts had gathered inside her head and settled into a hard knot.

Her hands were tied behind her back with her grandmother's old shawl, and she was helped up the plank by the priests and out the window to the platform. There was a quick, pleasant rush of fresh air against her face as she was released from the staleness of the prison.

Spectators below followed the faltering figure moving like a shadow, the hood on her head shading her face. She caught sight of the thick rope hanging from the gallows and her executioner standing beside it. A wig of black sheep's wool covered his head and his shoulders, and a black mask hid his face above his long black cloak.

The knot of fear inside her head loosened, and she cried out in a bold voice, "I was a wretched woman, but as innocent of any part in the crime of murder as a child not born. I had not even the most distant omen that Jack would disappear." She turned to search for familiar faces – strained in vain to find her children among the crowd: gentle Bridget, lively Eliza, spunky Katie, mischievous Johnny, quiet Martin, spirited Maria, sweet Johanna – and Richard. She pulled them together inside her mind. She closed her eyes to hold them against the murmuring voices of the priests in prayer and the hangman's voice: "Your walking's done, ma'am." The masked hangman stepped behind her and stooped to tie her legs. The wind got wily and restless and Catherine's hood fell back. The hangman reached to lift it off her thin shoulders and straighten it over her head and down over her face, shutting out all light. She felt his hand as he slipped the eye of the rope over her head and around her neck and adjusted the noose. He turned to the crowd and bowed.

There was silence and then the cry of a baby. Catherine's head turned sharply just as the sheriff gave the signal. Her mind opened to Emilia and Martin, her little lost boys in flowing white gowns, reaching their arms to her.

Forty-Two

DR. Kielly had refrained from viewing the hanging. He knew that after the drop the woman would be unconscious. Death could take eight to fifteen minutes to set in and paralyze the heart. He waited through the longest minutes of his life, and then he gave the nod for the dead woman to be taken down. Spectators gathered close to see if Dr. Kielly would carry out the last sentence on Catherine Snow's body. They were silent now, stunned as they had been at the hangings of Mandeville and Spring. Then, as soon as he had shown his knife, they had turned on him. He had given the bodies a quick cut to make sure the men were dead, before giving up the bodies to save his own life. He dared not handle this mother with his knife in view of the public. Besides, there'd be a swarm of flies once the body was cut into. Catherine's limp body, her face covered, was quickly placed on a barrow and carried inside.

Kielly hesitated. Then he drew back Catherine's hood. Bruising had formed around her neck and on the whites of her staring eyes. He pulled her lids down, and her dark lashes fringed white skin. He set her tongue back inside her mouth. Here was a mother whose children likely would be scattered like snow before an easterly wind, children who would always search for their mother's arms and voice. Her face was settled now that her tormented life had ended, and the heart that had beaten inside her like a trapped animal was now in quietus. Kielly looked on the white, beautiful visage that had attracted John Snow so many years before. It would be left untouched by his knife. He drew back, reluctant to cut into the white Irish skin. He slit open the brown gown and gasped at how thin her body was. Mrs. Perchard had said she hadn't recovered after the birth of her baby, and she had not eaten well after little Richard was taken from her. Kielly thought, *I'm forced to do a deed I have never done before, and God willing I will never have to do again.* He opened Catherine's bruised skin with the blade of his knife and began the macabre laying out of the body, letting what Boulton may have seen as bad blood. Kielly thought of the biblical admonition, "What therefore God hath joined together, let not man put asunder." *And hadn't God joined a woman to herself, and to her children, as much as she could be joined to any man?*

Hereafter, every time Dr. Kielly washed his hands, and every time he played his fiddle he remembered his hands using an instrument to part the body of Catherine Snow.

Forty-Three

MAGISTRATE Robert John Pinsent sat reading the Tuesday, July twenty-second, 1834, edition of the *Public Ledger* run by the Protestant, anti-Catholic Henry Winton.

"The prisoner, Catherine Snow, who was convicted in the January term of the Supreme Court, of aiding and assisting in the murder of her husband John Snow, suffered the extreme penalty of the law yesterday at the western extremity of the courthouse. From the time of her conviction down to a very late period, she had exhibited a great deal of hardihood and recklessness and when brought before the court last week and informed of the time her execution would take place, she manifested anything but symptoms of contrition and persisted in her innocence of the crime of which she had been found guilty.

Latterly, however, a subdued tone of feeling took the place of her former obduracy, and some sense of the awful situation in which she stood appears to have been thrust upon her. She proceeded to the gallows yesterday with a firm step, and with a demeanour which indicated a resignation to her awful fate. She was conducted to the platform, attended by the priests, shortly before the hour of nine o'clock, and the usual preliminaries having been arranged, the unhappy woman, after a few brief struggles, passed into another world. Her remains were interred last evening in the Catholic burial ground.

A petition was got up last week for the commutation of the sentence upon the ground, we believe, that the woman had been improperly convicted. It was handed around the town by the Catholic clergy, and received several signatures. If we are rightly informed, however, the document was by no means calculated to produce the effect contemplated by it. It arraigned the verdict of the jury who convicted the prisoner, without offering any substantial evidence that their verdict was an improper one, and it was therefore clear that if the petition had been subscribed by five thousand individuals, it would have equally failed in its effects. Had the promoters of it pursued a different course, or ground, their appeal open to the single attribute of mercy toward the weaker sex, added to some slender considerations in extenuation of the prisoner's guilt, if any there were, they would more than probably have had a very numerous accession to their list of signatures, and the petitioners might, perhaps, have been induced to cherish some ray of hope, but this we apprehend would have been all. The sentence of the law would have been carried into execution, nevertheless, unless some legal ground could have been shown to justify a departure from the sentence. . . ."

Pinsent folded the newspaper and laid it aside. He cradled his wife's belly. In a few days, he would be holding a new baby. He imagined having a son who would grow up to be *Sir* Robert Pinsent. Thoughts of the late Catherine Snow and the whereabouts of her infant son drifted far from his mind.

BACK FROM HIS missionary journey, Bishop Fleming sat reading newspapers saved for his perusal. A report had come to him that Robert Pinsent, the Protestant magistrate, had petitioned the court for guardianship of Catherine Snow's children and John Snow's estate, and that he had already received a letter of recommendation from E. M. Archibald, Chief Clerk and Acting Judge of the Supreme Court. Archibald had been one of the judges involved in Catherine Snow's trial.

Fleming drew his eyebrows together and set his mouth in a firm line. It was a curious thing that there was no money for the children's upkeep, though John Snow had been a prosperous planter. *Pinsent is only interested in the estate. I shall make time to write England and ask for funds to provide for Catherine Snow's children. I will have them removed from the Salmon Cove home and taken to St. John's. The boys shall be placed under the care of the brethren. The girls will be put with good Catholic families and with training will make fine servants.*

Bishop Fleming closed his newspaper. His mind went back to thinking, *I am engaged in the structure of a cathedral on a scale of unusual elegance. No one in this place has ever witnessed such magnificence.* He linked his hands, fingers laced against his palms. "Here's the cathedral." He lifted his thumbs together. "Here's the steeple. Open the door." He opened his hands. "See all the people." He smiled.

Epilogue

—*July Twenty-First, 1846*—

Anastasia Mandeville spoke to Maria Snow as they stood at the door to the small house of a former gaol matron. "I'll tell you as much of your mother's story before she left Salmon Cove, whatever stirs in my mind about it, after we talk to Mrs. Newell. People around this area have gone mute to what they know about your mother. I was young at the time and on for marrying a man who, after we wed, died of the pleurisy, leaving me in a disheartened frame of mind. Then I married a widower, Richard Mandeville, a relative of Aunt Kit's. He knows only that your mother was thwarted in her efforts to reach him when the law was after her. But I'll say no more until we see this woman."

Anastasia knocked on the door and, after some time, a doughy-faced woman in a mobcap unlatched it. She smoothed a stray strand of grey hair behind an ear and looked uncertainly from Anastasia to Maria.

Anastasia was blunt. "We've not come for any bad reason, but for fact. Mrs. Perchard is discreet and keeps prison secrets. But I hear that your tongue is on the loose, and hardly ever kept to itself. A reward you'll get for telling the truth – as God is my witness."

Mrs. Newell ignored her tone. "I got your letter about poor

Catherine Snow. I will tell the truth as I know it." She hesitated, then added boldly, "Once you crown me palm."

Anastasia widened the drawstring of her purse and lifted out two coins, speaking bluntly. "Tell the girl what she needs to know for her own peace. Otherwise, she'll never rest."

The woman looked down. "Sovereigns they are then. Mind I wouldn't take them if they couldn't be spared. But by the looks of you, you'll not soon be in the poorhouse." She stared at the fine wool coat Anastasia was wearing and the matching hat on the crown of rich brown hair.

Maria moved out from behind Anastasia, and Mrs. Newell swung her head to one side. "Sweet Jesus! She's the face and eyes of her, except for the light hair. Come in and sit. Fair glad I'll be to spare the time o' day."

Anastasia and Maria followed the bulky woman into a small room. They sat on a high-back bench while the matron took a chair facing them. "It was hardly a chance anyone had, caught between the power of merchants and constables as close to each other as the Devil's skin is to his own bones. 'Twas a bad time to be accused of murder, an easy time to be sentenced to death by Chief Justice Boulton, the hanging judge."

Maria's eyes widened at the mention of that name. The woman didn't seem to notice as she continued. "There was no charity from the English Protestants for the Irish soul – "

Anastasia interrupted her. "Never mind the politics. Tell her what she needs to know to satisfy herself."

"I will," Mrs. Newell promised. She began by telling her about her mother's time in gaol and why she was there. She finished with the day she was hanged.

Maria's face went pale and screwed into a cry, her lips trembling. "You're saying my mother was hanged." Then her eyes flashed. "I knew the courthouse housed evil! Its western window is in line with my bedroom window like a square black eye."

"I gave Father Troy her rosary of garnets with its heavy Celtic cross," the matron said.

"Her rosary!" Maria's head tilted back. She closed her eyes. "I have it!" She felt faint with the realization.

Mrs. Newell leaned to place her hand on Maria's shoulder. "Your mudder worried about her children, especially the little ones. That would have been you, and the toddler, Johanna, and her baby born in gaol. His name was – is – Richard, baptized the twenty-second day of March, the year of 1834. If I know right, the priest took the baby to grow into a helper in the church. If 'tid ben a girl, she could have been taken into a family's home to be raised as a maid. A girl could be well-bought with a merchant's money. Some of it would go into the church coffers to help other orphans."

Maria interrupted her with a sour look. "Well-bought, perhaps, but not well looked to. I was taken from my brothers and sisters by Bishop Fleming and given to a family who wanted no love from me, else they would have shown me kindness. They squeezed me for work and if a task wasn't done in jig time, I was whipped, and if not whipped, bruised. I still carry the markings of a family's ill will. A kind woman took me when I was old enough to earn my keep."

Mrs. Newell shook her head. "For sure she's her mother's daughter. God save us! Catherine might have lived had she been more submissive to the will of those in authority over her. She cried often, wondering if her children would be looking to the sea for the sight of a boat bringing her home."

"That was so," Anastasia said. "The girls hung Aunt Kit's lantern on the pole of the stage and lit it at dusk all that fall, as they waited for their mother to come home. The lantern could be seen swinging in the wind, its glow flaring across the waters."

Mrs. Newell smiled. "Anastasia can tell you about the other children in your family."

"They were scattered," Anastasia said. "By spring, Robert Pinsent was about the Snow property, taking charge of everything, hiring his own people for the western boat and to till the ground. By summer, Kitty and Mary, the servant girls, had gone to the employ of others and the children had been taken to places unknown. Still, you may be able to track down Eliza. I heard that your mother's brother, Richard, got clear of the fighting in Ireland and came over to Harbour Grace the year she went to gaol. Though he wanted nothing to do with your mamma for marrying an English Protestant, he was willing to give Eliza a place to live if she'd help with work."

Maria's voice was no more than a whisper as she asked, "What happened to my mother's body?"

Anastasia cast Mrs. Newell a quick look and turned back to Maria. "I can tell you about that. You'll be grateful that her body was interred in sacred ground in a Catholic cemetery, at the bottom of Long's Hill by the courthouse where her trial was held. The clergy believed her to be innocent, and so it let her lie with its dead."

Anastasia didn't tell her that she, Michael Manning, James McCabe, and Catherine Breen had come together in boat to bring the body home in a coffin they had brought. They had waited well into the afternoon to see if they could have the body, to be buried alongside Arthur and Tobias. A man came out a door facing the Lower Path and told them to lay aside the coffin. "You won't be needing a long box here."

The men were handed a box a little longer than its width, not the size for a full-length person. There were no priests to offer the Sacrament of Burial. No one had the will to speak as James lifted a shovel and tore away the earth. He dug deep to make way for the box that held Catherine's remains. The men then covered the box and filled in the earth over it.

Anastasia swallowed hard and smiled at Maria as she told her, "The night of the day your mother died, a light was seen bobbing across the waters between Salmon Cove and Bareneed, steady at times; other times it fractured on the waves. Every July twenty-first, it's the same thing. It's known as Kit's light. There was talk of having a priest bless the light to lay your mother's spirit to rest."

She nodded to Maria. "Come along then. Take everything you

have heard, and everything you will hear, and ponder it at will – God's truth and the Devil's tale entwined like the strands of a rope. One thing is sure: Your mother loved her children."

Maria's lips trembled and her eyes welled with tears as Anastasia tightened her arm around her shoulder. "Your mother's at rest, now, girl. She's no longer suffering in a dungeon. You can hold her in your heart where no one can take her."

MARIA TRUDGED UP the rutted path of a steep hill. Alongside, a stream gurgled over small round and jagged stones. She turned to look down the high path to Cupids where her mother had arrived after her hurried flight from Salmon Cove on her way to Brigus. Maria looked down the road. Her gaze took in the tiny house of Denis Hartery, the last house her mother had set foot in.

She glanced back toward Spectacle Hill. High on the bluff a couple of blackened wooden posts stood askant: the remains of gibbets livyers said had been meant for Tobias Mandeville and Arthur Spring. They remained as a reminder, not of what the men had done, but as a reminder of what the law could do to humans.

She followed a swampy path, passing an outhouse and several houses at Rip Raps. The community lay sheltered in a valley under high cliffs. Now several goats stood outlined against the sky on rugged high cliffs up from Goats' Cove. Maria stumbled over lumpy sods covered in grass and came across to pasture land and grazing cows. She did not go down to Caplin Cove where her mother had stopped at Mary Britt's on the Friday night of the week following her father's disappearance. Instead, she crossed the meadow and walked down to Salmon Cove. She passed sheds and barns and small houses whose residents seemed to be biding indoors, though there were flutters of curtains at the windows as she passed. Her trek took her down a valley past high cliffs she'd been told had crevasses deep enough for a person to fall into – never to be seen again. She came out on a steep stretch of ground that went out to a rugged point of land. She passed a house – her uncle Edward's, she supposed –

and went on down to the rundown Snow plantation. It skirted the large, empty Snow house. Maria stopped, not sure she would have the courage to go inside – not yet.

Instead, she took the narrow path down to a rugged fishing stage. It looked like an empty skull, the stagehead its skeletal body. Long, grey-boned legs still held steady in boulders sticking up from the sea. She buckled her knees and dropped to the stagehead, letting her legs dangle over the rails. She swung back a mane of blonde hair, closed her eyes and took a deep breath. *This is where I lived with my family – and I don't remember anything!* There came soft gulps of water against rippled rocks under the stage, and the effervescence of the sea against a large red, ridged rock. It was rumoured that her father's blood had stained the rock, though residents knew that it and other rocks around the point had always been ochre red.

Maria stayed on the stagehead while night fell and enclosed her like a heavy blanket. The moon slipped out from behind clouds and shone across the water. She straightened her back and tightened her fingers on her mother's rosary. Then she looked up at the house – dark, except for moonlight reflected off the water in the window facing the bay. Its square eye seemed to stare out over the ocean, as if holding the secret of a long-ago night.

I can almost see St. John's from here, half of it burned by a cruel fire. I imagine fog rolling in over the blackened socket of the window in the brick courthouse where they hanged my mother. I like to imagine I burned it – burned everything but the brick walls. It could have been a spirited wind blowing in through the Narrows that brought the flames to other buildings, though there's been other stories.

She let out a long sigh. *My nightmares have gone now that I know how strong my mamma was to have endured a gaol cell for so long, and she holding a child inside her. She would have gone mad had she not held hope like the promise of day in the darkest night. She left her strength in me, giving me courage to seek out my family, and the baby brother who came into the world in a dungeon. I sit here hoping that my father and his money box will be found, and whoever is responsible for the beginning of our trouble will meet with justice.*

She looked across the waters to where John Jacob and Robert Pinsent lived, and promised, "I have learned to write now, and I will search out my mother's story – truer than what has been told on oath. I will find my brothers and sisters and bring them home."

A cloud, like a dark thumbprint, covered the moon and darkened the night, leaving the stage in shadows. A soft wind whispered against Maria's ear and blended with the gentle voice of water lapping at the stage. She fancied she heard her mother's strong, Irish voice: *"A iníon mo chroí –* daughter of my heart."

A white light bobbed across the harbour waters and came to the stagehead. It hovered over it for ten blinks of an eye. Then it went out. Kit's light had roamed the harbour – as usual on the anniversary of Catherine Snow's hanging.

Author's Note and Acknowledgements

This novel is based on real people and events. On the tenth of January, 1834, Catherine Mandeville Snow was found guilty – without demonstrative evidence – as an accessory in the murder of John Snow, her husband.

The trial of Catherine Snow – along with Tobias Mandeville and Arthur Spring, who were convicted as Catherine's accomplices and hanged – is based on newspaper reports and actual court documents.

The case of a mother sentenced to hang became a *cause célèbre*. A petition containing nearly three hundred signatures protesting Snow's death sentence appears to have gone missing. After Snow was hanged, her body was brutalized by the knife of Dr. Edward Kielly before it was laid to rest. Snow was the last woman hanged and the first and last woman dissected and anatomized in Britain's oldest colony.

What happened to John Snow and his money box remains a mystery. Researchers' attempts to trace the Snow/Mandeville lineage may have been partially successful. To add to the confusion, there were several John Snows living in the Conception Bay area at the time.

Kit's light was, apparently, put to rest by a priest and his prayer in the 1950s. Catherine's ghost may still roam the streets of St. John's near the place where she was caught in the eye of the rope.

It is always a challenge to be true to places and people. For this reason, I am indebted to the following contributors and resources: the Waterford Library, Ireland (There, by a strange coincidence, I met a John Snow who gave me information on the Mandeville genealogy.); Seán Ó Loingsigh and other Irelanders were helpful with the Irish language; also Michael Boyle.

I thank the Sirius Arts Centre, especially Séan Ó Huigin and Peggy Sue Amison for inviting me as a writer-in-residence.

I would like to thank people who contributed information: enthusiast Maud Pinsent, Mona Petten, the late Newton Morgan, Olive Slaney (the Supreme Court Registry), Joyce Skanes and Father F. J. Aylward (Harbour Grace Roman Catholic Parish Records), the Grand Falls Roman Catholic Parish, *Monitor* editor Larry Dohey (the Roman Catholic Basilica Archives), researcher Edward Chafe, genealogist Deborah L. Jeans, Joan Ritcey (the Centre for Newfoundland Studies), and Harbour Grace Museum employees Terri-Lynn Crocker, Adrianne Haire, and Kimberly Keeping.

Other sources: Criminal Records of the Supreme Court, the *Newfoundland Patriot*, the *Public Ledger*, the *Newfoundlander*, the *Newfoundland Vindicator*, and the *Royal Gazette and Newfoundland Advertiser*, Provincial Archives of Newfoundland and Labrador (Colonial Building and The Rooms), Registry of Crown Lands, A.C. Hunter Library, Port de Grave Anglican Burials 1829–1869.

Helpful books were Gerald W. Andrews's *Heritage of a Newfoundland Outport: The Story of Port de Grave*; Brother J. B. Darcy's *Fire upon the Earth: The Life and Times of Bishop Michael Anthony Fleming, O.S.F.*; John P. Greene's *Between Damnation and Starvation: Priests and Merchants in Newfoundland Politics, 1745–1855*; Gordon W. Hancock's *So longe as there comes noe women*; Patrick O Flaherty's *Old*

Newfoundland: A History to 1843; and Dr. Patrick C. Power's *Carrick-on-Suir and Its People*.

Other insightful materials include: documents showing Magistrate Robert John Pinsent's appearance in the Supreme Court regarding his guardianship of the minor Snow children, and his efforts to control the estate of John Snow; Governor Thomas Cochrane's letters to Sir E. G. Stanley, Secretary of State for Colonial Affairs; Bishop Michael Fleming's letter to D. O'Connell; Eliza Boulton's letter to Bishop Fleming; and a letter by the judges of the Supreme Court to Governor Prescott.

I am grateful to the Canadian Embassy in Ireland, and Marie Stamp, then Canada's Senior Trade Commissioner to Ireland, for inviting me to read from my work in progress. Also, I would like to thank the Newfoundland Arts Council for awarding me a 2003 travel grant, and the Canada Council for awarding me a 2004 travel grant. Both aided in my Ireland research. I appreciate Jean Young and Page One's organization of several truly wonderful and successful book launches.

My thanks to Ed Kavanagh for his editing skills. As always, my appreciation to the Flanker Press team for its diligent efforts to promote my work. In particular, I would like to thank Jerry Cranford for his editing contribution and Margo Cranford for marketing.

Recommendations for Book Club Discussions

1. Discuss dangers that early immigrants like Catherine Snow faced on ships crossing the Atlantic Ocean.

2. Why do you think Catherine asked Ruth Snow to let her daughter, Ann, speak to her uncle Jack about his rough treatment of her?

3. Ruth Snow told the court that she had heard a gunshot earlier in the evening while she was having tea. She thought it was fired near the flakes – *as usual*. Discuss.

4. Discuss why Bridget might not have been surprised to find her mother at Ruth Snow's on the night of her father's disappearance.

5. Mary Connolly testified that she found a pair of trousers spotted with blood concealed with ink folded up between a barrel and a trunk. She was not questioned regarding the colour of the trousers and how she knew blood was concealed under ink. If Tobias had helped drag a bleeding body, his trousers and shirt would have been *smeared* with blood. Arthur's trousers and shirt would have also been smeared with blood. Why do you think Mary's statement was not challenged?

6. The court asked Catherine White if anyone had washed the fishing stage on the Sunday morning after John disappeared. Clearly there was no show of blood at the time. Discuss.

7. Eliza Snow, Catherine White, and Arthur Spring were taken to Bareneed for questioning, and kept all night. Why do you suppose there were no statements submitted to the court from this time?

8. Can you suggest why two contradictory statements attributed to Catherine Snow were submitted to the court? Take note of Robert John Pinsent's words: "She made a voluntary statement *nearly* as follows."

9. Chief Justice Henry J. Boulton said, in his charge to the jury, ". . . nothing said by either of the prisoners, Spring and Mandeville, upon their examination, can be admitted to implicate her (Catherine Snow) in the act." Would you agree?

10. Do you find it puzzling that Magistrate Pinsent would testify that while Mandeville and Spring were being brought to St. John's in boat, William Hampton and John Bowes might not have heard a confession Mandeville made because he told them to keep back? If there had been a confession, wouldn't Pinsent have wanted as many witnesses as possible?

11. Do you see it as "telling" that a man supposedly planted under the table in the jailhouse holding Spring and Mandeville was not called as a witness for the prosecution? He was not even identified by the prosecutors.

12. Why do you suppose the court showed no interest in identifying a man named Wills?

13. Why do you think there were no witnesses in court to confirm or deny that Spring and Mandeville were at the wake a second

time and why no one was asked what they were wearing each time?

14. According to Magistrate Danson, Catherine told him that her maid had, on her return home from the wake, gone to the top of the bank in front of the house, and while there she heard people talking and cursing under the bank. Bridget also heard the sound of oars, but did not hear any voices. Do you think it odd that the daughter and maid were not questioned about what they heard, if anything?

15. Discuss how Catherine's and Arthur's illiteracy may have resulted in inaccurate statements attributed to them. Do you think Catherine was at a disadvantage from the first? She was not asked to verify statements attributed to her and read out in court.

16. Do you think that religious prejudice played a part in the conviction of Catherine Snow, Arthur Spring, and Tobias Mandeville?

17. According to a statement attributed to Mandeville, he felt that Spring had made him out to be "the perfect monster." Do you think the men were pitted against each other? Does it seem possible that the men were beaten into confessing? Tobias fainted while in the jailhouse at Port de Grave. If he was so prone to fainting, one would suppose that he would certainly faint when he was sentenced to death.

18. Discuss the possibility that Catherine suspected her older daughters of knowing more about their father's disappearance than they were willing to say.

19. Do you believe Catherine may have known more about John's disappearance than she was willing to say?

20. In court, Magistrate Pinsent was shown a statement and asked to identify it as Arthur Spring's confession. Why do you think the statement was not read to Spring in front of the court and jury so that he

could confirm or deny it was his? When Mandeville was taken to the St. John's magistrate, he denied a statement attributed to him.

21. Do you feel that the trial may have taken a different direction if John's money box and account books had been entered into evidence? Discuss people who might have had something to gain by Snow's disappearance.

22. Do you think that Bridget, now eighteen, should have been allowed to make decisions about the care of her siblings and the family estate?

23. John Snow, though illiterate, had successfully handled his plantation. Why do you think his brothers were dismissed as unsuited to run his business?

24. Bishop Fleming did little to save Catherine's temporal and spiritual life. What does this say about his regard for this Catholic mother?

25. What do you see as Judge Henry Boulton's reason for his cruel sentence on Catherine Snow's body?

26. Kit's light was reported roaming the harbour well into the 1950s. What might be another explanation for Kit's light?

27. What impression do you get of George H. Emerson and Bryan Robinson as defence lawyers? Discuss the possibility that the prisoners' lawyers wanted to please Judge Boulton as much as the judge wanted a conviction. Note that in the early 1800s lawyers were known as "pleasers." Who do you suppose they pleased?

28. In this twenty-first century, people often complain that we don't have a justice system: we have a legal system. How would you compare it to the legal system in 1834?

29. Tobias Mandeville begged Judge Boulton to grant him a long day to prepare for the fate that awaited him, and to allow his body to be given up to his friends for interment. Arthur Spring joined in Mandeville's request. Judge Boulton replied that it was not in his power to comply with their request, saying that the law left him no discretion. He then pronounced the sentence of death on Mandeville and Spring to be carried into execution on Monday. Discuss this response in light of the fact that Boulton's sentence was not executed as instructed.

30. *The Wordsworth Word Finder* by Marc McCutcheon defines "accessory before the fact" as "a person who plans a crime, gives advice about a crime, or commands others to commit a crime, but who does not actively commit the crime." What do you think is the irony in Eliza Boulton calling her husband an "accessory before the fact"?

31. What part would you say the newspapers of the day played in the public's perception of Catherine's innocence or guilt?

32. How different might the author's approach to this novel have been had she not attempted to follow the available historical version of the events following John Snow's disappearance?

33. Though this book is fictional, its story is built around real people and events. Catherine lost much in her lifetime: two young children prematurely, her other children, her husband, and her home. Yet she maintained a measure of hope until the end. Does this novel and the questions it poses change the historical perception of Catherine Snow?

About the Author

NELLIE P. STROWBRIDGE is one of Newfoundland and Labrador's most beloved and prolific authors. She is the winner of provincial and national awards and has been published nationally and internationally. Her work is capsuled in the National Archives as Newfoundland's winner in Canada's Stamp of Approval Award for a letter written to Canada 2117.

Strowbridge, a former columnist and editorial writer, is also an essayist and an award-winning poet. She has been Writer in the Library, a mentor to young writers, and an adjudicator in the Provincial Arts and Letters Awards. She has held school workshops in Canada and Ireland, and also hosted a Seminar/Gabfest for International Women's Day in Cobh, Ireland, where she was writer-in-residence.

The author is a member of the Writers' Alliance of Newfoundland and Labrador, the Writers' Union of Canada, the League of Canadian Poets (Newfoundland and Labrador/Nova Scotia Representative), Page One, and the Newspaper Institute of America.

Previous books: *Widdershins: Stories of a Fisherman's Daughter*; *Doors Held Ajar* (tri-author with Isobel Brown & Peggy Krachun); *Shadows of the Heart*; *Dancing on Ochre Sands* (shortlisted for the Newfoundland and Labrador E.J. Pratt Book Award, 2005); *Far From Home: Dr Grenfell's Little Orphan* (a bestseller, shortlisted for the Newfoundland and Labrador Historic and History Award 2006); *The Gift of Christmas* (reviewed by the *Aurora* as "A Newfoundland and Labrador Christmas Classic"; and *The Newfoundland Tongue* (a bestseller).

also by
NELLIE P. STROWBRIDGE

"[*Far From Home*] is involving, informative and refreshingly unsentimental regarding children who are often cruel to each other and certainly always merciless towards starfish and sculpins." THE TELEGRAM

"[*Far From Home*] is studded with wonderful, fresh, rich words and phrases that stimulate, enrich and enlighten your understanding of life in the 1920s on this island." THE NORTHEAST AVALON TIMES

"The vitality of the narrative will make *The Newfoundland Tongue* a delightful work to dip into or pore over for tourist and 'livyer' alike." ATLANTIC BOOKS TODAY

"Mixing reminiscences with long lists [in *The Newfoundland Tongue*], Strowbridge shows a wry, self-deprecating wit and covers a great deal of ground, from customs and superstitions to weather and medicine." CANADIAN GEOGRAPHIC